Family Thang

James Henderson

BROKE-TOOTH DOG PUBLISHING
MORRILTON, ARKANSAS,72110

Chapter 1

Reverend Stanley Lucious Walker stood inside his church, Greater Paradise, admiring the magnificent interior, *his* magnificent interior. Filigreed cornices, hand-painted moldings, polychrome stained glass windows, ornate wainscotings, mahogany pews with handcrafted ends and blue velvet seat cushions.

He enjoyed telling people he built this church with his bare hands. Actually, he glimpsed the floor plan and once, only once, picked up a hammer and banged a few nails. God had inspired him that day.

Yet today he felt he had defiled his church and himself. He considered genuflecting before the gold cross inlaid in the black marble pulpit and asking for forgiveness. Instead he closed his eyes and prayed silently.

"Who knew?"

A poor excuse, he thought, if today's event took a bad turn. *A very poor excuse!*

Two days ago, Ida Harris, a friend of an infrequent parishioner, visited his office and requested the use of his church for her husband's funeral. Of course he'd declined. She and her husband were not church members.

Ida Harris retrieved an envelope from her purse and slid it across his desk. It bulged with currency.

Reverend Walker then lost sight of his divine purpose, for he cleared his throat and changed his mind.

"Mrs. Harris, at some point your husband intended to join Greater Paradise, did he not?"

"No."

"He ever listened to one of my taped sermons?"

"No."

"Drive by the premises?"

"I don't think he did."

"Ever mention the church or my name?"

Mrs. Harris looked uncomfortable. "In a good light or bad?"

"Either."

"Then, yes, quite often."

"Amen. Your husband is welcome here."

"Reverend Walker, my husband suffered a rather horrible death. Are you aware what happened to him?"

"No, I'm not. My main concern--"

"The ride in the ambulance he professed his love for Jesus."

"Bless his soul. Mrs. Harris, the Good Lord doesn't care when you jump on the bus. He cares you don't miss it. Scheduling is not as important as showing up."

After he tucked the envelope inside his gray three-piece pinstripe suit, Mrs. Harris requested an eulogy for her late husband's pet, a Pekingese, Kenny G, a name the reverend would never forget.

Honestly, he hadn't taken her request seriously; no one proffered a dog an obsequy. Mrs. Harris was distraught, and once she'd given the matter a little thought, she'd realize how outrageous the request. Or, one of her family members would inform her the idea was preposterous.

And that, he'd thought, would be the end of that.

Then, last night, the director at Owen's Funeral Home called him to confirm that two caskets, standard size and a mini, in which rested a small dog, were to be delivered to Greater Paradise the following day.

"A damn dog! Inside my church! Are you crazy?"

"Well, the lady, a Mrs. Harris, said you were in full accord with the arrangements. I wanted to confirm this with you because it's quite unusual. For the record, Reverend Walker, we did not prepare the dog. Moe's Taxidermy provided that service."

Reverend Walker remembered, groaned and almost choked. He'd had to sit down. Not only had he forgotten the agreement he'd disseminated (he preferred *disseminated* to *spent*) the entire two thousand dollars Mrs. Harris had stuffed in the envelope.

What could he do? Nothing except follow through with his promise; after all, he was a man of God. He looked up at the ceiling, copper-plated tiles from one end to the next, and massaged his nape.

An inspiration came to him: he would keep the mutt's casket closed and he wouldn't mention a word about it, not even to his staff. Yes, there would be speculation, a lot of speculation--*so what?*

"Reverend Walker," a voice behind him.

He turned to see Reverend Jones walking up the aisle.

"Yes."

Reverend Jones stepped beside him before saying, "Sir, there's a major misunderstanding in today's service."

"What misunderstanding?"

"The grapevine has it we're burying a dog today."

"Reverend Jones, you're not castigating a deceased man for his sins, are you? We've all fallen short of the glory of God."

"No, no, no! Not a man, a dog…a pooch…a canine…a mongrel. You know nothing of this?"

Reverend Walker stared at the self-assured but uninitiated gleam in the young man's brown irises. *Herman Cain affixing names to a blank globe.*

He'd taken Reverend Jones in as an associate pastor as a favor to his father, Brother Bobby Jones, an erstwhile deacon who'd served twenty years of faithful service at Greater Paradise.

A big mistake!

Reverend Jones, attired in a diamond-white Brooks Brothers suit, was Reverend Walker's polar opposite: young, single, handsome, well-educated, a full head of black curly hair and an idol to every lonely woman in the congregation.

Yes, Reverend Walker thought, he's fit to be a legit hit. *And he preaches like a dyslexic reading a French dictionary.*

"Reverend Jones, let me handle today's service. Need I remind you rumors tear down walls, not build them up."

"Yes, sir. However, I was told--"

"Reverend Jones, look toward the front. What do you see? Obsidian, top to bottom. Why? So the Good Lord and everyone else, saints and sinners, can see the good works performed here."

"Yes, though I was told--"

"Reverend Jones, listen closely." Louder: "I got this!"

Two hours later the mourners started to pour in. Reverend Walker assumed his seat directly behind the pulpit in a hand-carved Bishop chair between two similar but smaller chairs. Reverend Jones sat to his right.

Blessedly, Reverend Tim Moore, the other associate pastor, was absent. Tim had a disconcerting habit of fainting during funerals. *Reverend Moore on the floor. Again!*

7

The choir director, Paul Williams, a thin, dark-skinned man, entered the sanctuary through a side door and sauntered up the dais in a yellow three-piece suit and yellow silver-tipped shoes.

"Reverend Walker," he said into a yellow handkerchief. "Reverend Walker, we have a problem."

Reverend Walker wanted to ask him the name of the clothing store what sold him a suit that contrasted so violently with his complexion.

"Yes," noticing the man also wore a yellow polka-dotted shirt.

The choir director knelt before Reverend Jones. "There are two coffins outside. Two," holding up two fingers. "Two!"

"And?" Reverend Walker said.

"Two! One contains a dog."

Reverend Jones shook his head.

"And?" Reverend Walker repeated, detecting a fruity smell about the man. *Boone's Farm Peach Wine?*

"Are you sanctioning this? If you are I refuse to conduct services for a dog. It's…" He paused, left eye twitching, glancing at Reverend Jones. "It's…it's not right!"

"Mr. Williams, need I remind you I'm the pastor here, not you. If you entered through the front entrance you saw my name on the billboard out front, my name engraved in the sidewalk." A whisper: "Therefore, if I say we conduct services for a cat, a horse, a cow, a yellow-bellied sapsucker, then it shall be done."

The choir director's right eye started twitching.

Reverend Jones crossed his arms, started whistling.

"Now," Reverend Walker continued, brushing imaginary lint from his pants, "let the service begin."

Just then, as if on cue, the glass doors opened and two silver caskets were wheeled in.

"Mr. Williams, usually a musical number starts about now, does it not?"

The choir director's mouth opened and closed, both eyes twitching, then he backed away, staring at Reverend Walker. He stumbled on a floor speaker on his way to his stand in front of the choir.

He motioned the choir, a group of thirty or more, all but three draped in gold robes. They stood uniformly and started singing *God Is Keeping Me*.

The family entered behind the caskets, walking in tandem, in step to the music. First Ida Harris and Robert Earl, then Ruth Ann and Lester, and bringing up the rear were Shirley and Shane. An usher directed them to the front pew and they stood solemnly until the music ended.

A long moment of silence occasionally interrupted by coughing, throat clearing and an infant crying.

Reverend Walker stepped to the pulpit, adjusted the mike to his height, cleared his throat and said, "Amen."

He looked over the congregation, a small group, mostly funeral regulars, those who relished every opportunity to ogle a cadaver.

Three people sat in the balcony despite the ample seating on the ground floor.

"Amen," the congregation responded and sat down.

"Amen," Reverend Walker said. He made the signal for the head usher to open the casket, scratching the left side of his neck.

Sister Bea Hammonds, a rather plump woman, crossed directly to the smaller casket.

Reverend Walker cleared his throat and waved his hand. Sister Hammonds looked confused. He shook his head.

She got the message and moved to the larger casket and raised the lid.

"Amen," and realized he hadn't prepared any notes. He'd been so concerned about the dog he'd forgotten to do so.

I'll wing it.

"We're gathered today to pay homage to Brother..." *What's the man's name?* "Amen...praise God..."

"Rick Perry," Reverend Jones whispered.

Reverend Walker turned and gave him a withering look: *You know damn well that isn't his name!*

"Larry Harris."

"Amen. Larry Harris. Yes, amen. Larry Harris, our beloved brother, has transcended this world to my Father's house. Brother Harris waited till the last minute to hop on the bus en route to glory, yet he made it in the nick of time. A minute more and Brother Harris would've been left behind. Amen. One minute--sixty seconds between paradise and eternal damnation.

"Often the bus driver sees you running late and he keeps going. He doesn't have to stop. No, he doesn't. If he keeps on going, you can't blame *him*. No, you can't blame him at all. He's only the driver of the bus, not the vehicle which determines where you'll spend eternity.

"A number of you will not be as fortunate as Brother Harris. You'll wait till the last minute to go to the bus stop and get caught up…in something unanticipated, something unexpected…something unforeseen…Amen!…A traffic jam, an accident, bad directions, your watch was too slow or too fast. Doesn't matter what caused your delay, you still missed the bus and got left behind. Don't blame the driver! 'He could've waited for me!' No, don't blame him. He's doing his job, facilitating transport."

He paused, took a sip from the glass of ice water an usher had set before him and stared into the faces of the congregation. Most looked as if they were at a bus stop, bored and ready to move on.

Reverend Walker accelerated: "Don't wait until the last minute, amen, to catch the bus. Now is the time to catch the bus to glory. Don't you want to get on the bus? Do you want your ticket now? Do you?"

Stretching out his right arm: "Don't take the risk…Get on the bus…while the opportunity is now. Don't wait until you're sick, laid off your job, downsized, broke, on your back in the hospital…The doors are open. Step up on the bus. Why don't you try Jesus? Try Jesus! Please, try Jesus!"

He shook his left leg, the signal for the choir director to instruct the choir.

"Why don't you try Jesus? He has your ticket. He's waiting on you."

No rustling sound of the choir standing. Reverend Walker cut an eye toward Paul Williams, sitting on the duet bench with the organist, head resting on the keyboard, eyes closed.

By God, he's asleep! Already!

"Wake up!" Reverend Walker shouted into the microphone. "Wake up to Jesus!"

The choir director sat up, eyes bloodshot red, and stared at Reverend Walker shaking his leg as if something had crawled up his pants. Remaining seated, he motioned the choir and they stood up and started singing *Amazing Grace*.

Reverend Walker sighed in relief. All good, he thought. If this pace continued, he would arrive home in time for the second set of the tennis match between Venus and Serena. He took his seat and closed his eyes. *Thank Jesus.*

An anguished, baleful scream rose above the choir voices. "Noooo!"

Reverend Walker hummed the song and patted his black patent leather Stacy Adams shoes to the beat. He didn't need to look to know that one of the family members was now being assisted by the ushers. He'd witnessed the scene a thousand times. Now the tortured outbursts irritated him more than anything else.

"Noooo!"

On the way home he would pick up a gallon of ice cream and a liter of root beer…watch the match and make a root beer float. Maybe some chocolate chip cookies.

"Not Kenny G! Nooooo!"

Reverend Walker's eyes snapped open. He hadn't heard what he thought he heard, had he? Hesitantly, he stood up and peered over the pulpit.

One of the family members, a young man, was struggling against two ushers, trying to get at the smaller casket.

To Reverend Walker's horror, the young man broke free and ran to the casket and opened it. Gasps from the front row.

There, in a small burgundy-colored three-piece suit, complete with bow tie, a handkerchief in the front pocket and a miniature godfather hat, lay Kenny G.

"Oh my God!" someone yelled.

The young man leaned over the casket and started stroking the dog's head; then he lifted it out of the casket, the hat hitting the floor, rolling down the aisle.

Now the entire congregation could see the Pekingese, and could see the suit was a partial, no backing whatsoever.

13

Reverend Walker felt a burning sensation in the pit of his stomach and regretted the Deluxe Breakfast he'd picked up at McDonalds.

More than half of the congregation started for the exits, and several of the choir members were leaning over the rail trying to get a look at what was causing the commotion.

I'm ruined, Reverend Walker thought. *Ruined!* He would have to get a job. A job requiring sweat. At his age, seventy-two, he couldn't afford to sweat. Not able to stomach the sight any longer, Reverend Walker resumed his seat, put his head between his knees and prayed he wouldn't be sick.

* * * * * *

Ruth Ann watched, stupefied, as her seventeen-year-old son, Shane, broke free and ran to Kenny G's casket. She closed her eyes, knowing what would happen next. She prayed she was dreaming. *Please, God, let me wake up in my own bed.* She heard the casket open. *Please, God!* She opened her eyes and she was still in church, still sitting in the front pew, a few feet from where her son was caressing a dead dog.

Shirley, sitting to her right, nudged her. "Ruth Ann, shouldn't you be doing something about this?"

"What you suggest I do?"

"Tell Shane put Kenny G back into the casket."

"Momma and Daddy raised him--he won't listen to a word I tell him."

Robert Earl, sitting on Shirley's right, leaned forward and whispered to Ruth Ann, "Get your boy. He's embarrassing the family."

"You go get him!"

"He's your son."

"He's your nephew. You go get him. If I go up there I'll knock the daylights outta him."

Robert Earl frowned at her. Ruth Ann ignored him. "Forget this!" he said, getting to his feet.

"What's he fixin' to do?" Shirley asked. "Tell me he's not fixin' to do what I think he's fixin' to do." Robert Earl advanced toward Shane. "Ruth Ann, he's fixin' to make a scene at Daddy's funeral."

A scene, hello? "Where's Leonard?" Ruth Ann said, looking away, focusing on a stained glass window depicting a nativity scene.

"Probably with his friend," Shirley said, not taking her eyes off Shane and Robert Earl. "I told him it wasn't a good idea for him to come."

"Boy," Robert Earl said, approaching Shane, the dog draped over his shoulder. "Put the dog back inside the casket. Now!"

"No!" Shane said. "He's not going in a hole. He can't breathe in a hole. I won't allow it! I won't allow it! No! I won't allow it!"

15

"Boy, the dog can't breathe now! It's dead. Stop acting a dang fool and put it back in the casket. Don't you see everybody watching you?" Robert Earl lunged for the dog, almost catching hold of its rear leg.

"No!" pulling the animal out of reach. "No, no, no, no!" Then he ran.

"Catch him!" Robert Earl shouted, and gave chase. Shane ran down the aisle along the right wall, with Kenny G bouncing on his shoulder, to the rear of the church.

"Stop him!" shouted Robert Earl, only a few feet behind. "Trip him!…Dang it, boy!"

Shane ran up the center aisle and jumped up onto the dais with the ease of a gazelle. Robert Earl tried to do the same, but his right foot caught in the silver latticework and he fell backward and landed with a splat on his back. A moment he lay there groaning. Then he jumped to his feet.

"Give me the dog, boy, or I'm coming up!"

"No, no, no, no!"

With both hands, Robert Earl placed his right Oxford shoe onto the dais. His brown corduroy pants, obviously two sizes too small, ripped, revealing to all who cared to look, an ashy brown fanny.

A woman screamed.

Up on the dais, Robert Earl moved toward Shane. "Give me the dog, boy!"

Backing away, Shane stumbled and tossed Kenny G into the air. Reverend Walker, finally shaking the urge to hurl, sat up just in time for Kenny G to land in his lap.

Reverend Walker shrieked and threw the dog to the floor. Shane got to his feet, snatched up Kenny G, jumped down, ran down the center aisle and out the glass doors. Robert Earl jumped down and gave chase, one hand covering the rip in his pants. Halfway to the doors he stopped. "I'll never catch him."

A pregnant woman jumped up, shouted, "This is insane!" and ran the way Shane had fled.

"You'll never catch him," Robert Earl called after her.

"Look, Ruth Ann," Shirley said. "Reverend Walker just lost his lunch."

"I'm not looking," Ruth Ann said, eyes closed. "I paid Emma Stewart to videotape the service. I can watch it later."

Shirley poked Ruth Ann until she opened her eyes. "Look," pointing. In front of the adjacent row of pews, Emma Stewart lay supine on the floor, a video camcorder beside her. Two ushers fanned her with paper fans.

"Ruth Ann, you lost money on that deal."

Robert Earl returned to his seat. "I tried."

"Can we have order?" A new voice on the microphone: Reverend Jones. "Please! Can we have--"

A loud shriek from the rear of the church and then a woman dressed head to toe in white ran up front, arms flailing as though she were in the throes of electric shock.

"Is that Estafay?" Shirley asked Ruth Ann, who had closed her eyes again.

"I don't know! And I don't want to know!"

When Estafay hopped onto the dais, Reverend Jones, horrified, immediately stepped away from the pulpit. Estafay snatched the microphone out of his hand.

Reverend Walker, on all fours, gagging, looked up and saw Estafay, her face contorted, said, "Dear God!" and threw up again.

"Jeeeeeessssuusss!" Estafay screamed into the microphone, her head tilted back, thick tendons in her neck. "Jeeeeeeeeessssuusss!" she screamed again and stomped her feet, whirled in circles, wrapping the microphone cord around herself, and started bouncing on her toes.

"Robert Earl," Shirley said, "isn't she with you?"

"No, she isn't. I rode in the family car with you, remember?"

"She's your wife, remember?"

"Don't you think I know that!"

"God has looked down on this church," Estafay told the handful of people who had remained in their seats, "and He has wrought vengeance on an evil and hypocritical congregation. Hallelujah! He told me to tell y'all the time is near. Rebuke your abominable, wicked ways and join the Holy Professors of Truth…my church, the church where God lives and breathes."

"Is that here in Dawson, Arkansas?" Shirley asked.

"Yes," Ruth Ann said. "It's on Highway Six. You can easily spot it by the nuts writhing in the front lawn."

"Gummba…yabbaaa….akkkkkaaaa…" Estafay shouted.

"What's wrong with her?" Shirley asked.

"She's speaking in tongues," Ruth Ann said.

"For Pete's sake, Robert Earl," Shirley said. "Go up there and get your wife. She's making a spectacle of Daddy's funeral. Think about Momma."

They looked at their mother sitting at the far end of the pew. She wore a black blouse and black skirt and black-and-white hat with a white veil on the brim. She looked catatonic, her eyes fixed on her deceased husband.

"Look," Ruth Ann said. "She's upsetting Momma."

On the dais, Reverend Walker had regained his composure and was trying to wrest the microphone away from Estafay.

"Get away from me, you heathen!" Estafay screeched.

Reverend Walker had one hand around her neck and the other on the microphone. "Give it to me!"

"Now you see why I don't attend this church," Shirley said.

Ruth Ann shook her head. "Shirley, after this I'll be too embarrassed to watch TBN."

"Let it go!" Reverend Walker shouted. Estafay held on. They struggled, one moment Reverend Walker taking the advantage, Estafay the next.

Reverend Walker grabbed Estafay in a headlock and she squealed.

"Ruth Ann, that's what I call speaking in tongues."

"Don't talk about my wife!" Robert Earl said. "She's a sanctified woman."

Ruth Ann said, "Go up there and get your sanctified woman, Robert Earl! Please do! This is ridiculous!"

Estafay lifted Reverend Walker, who still held her in a headlock, up like a baby and carried him to the edge.

"This fixn' to get ugly," Shirley said.

"I hope she's not going to do what I think she's going to do."

"Robert Earl," Shirley whispered, "is she this spry around the house?"

Robert Earl sprung to his feet. Estafay dropped Reverend Walker and, praise the Lord, Robert Earl caught him.

Chapter 2

Sheriff Ennis Bledsoe shifted uncomfortably in the swivel chair. He didn't like delivering bad news.

"Your father was poisoned."

"Poisoned!" Ruth Ann said. "Daddy was poisoned. That can't be!"

"I'm afraid so, Ruth Ann. I'm sorry."

"No...uh-uh...Who would--are you sure?"

"I'm sure. The coroner's report came in two days ago. I decided to wait after the funeral to break the news. A toxicology screen revealed a large amount of arsenic in your father's system. Your father's dog suffered the same fate."

The state lab in Little Rock had pinpointed the arsenic to a specific pesticide; info he thought best withheld.

"Kenny G! My goodness! Kenny G was poisoned, too?"

"The dog's name?"

"Yes. Daddy named him, said he barked like a white boy. He loved Kenny G."

"If not for the dog's death I would not have suspected foul play."

"Why? Why would someone poison him? Why?"

Sheriff Bledsoe stared at her. "Your father?"

"Of course. I couldn't care less about the dog."

"Well, that's what I intend to find out. It appears your father and his dog came into contact with the poison at or about the same time. Neck bones, barbecued neck bones to be exact, were found in both their stomachs." Ruth Ann grimaced. "I'm sorry, Ruth Ann. I know this is difficult for you." He cleared his throat. "Who cooked the neck bones?"

Ruth Ann buried her face in her hands, sighed and then ran her fingers through her long black hair. "I don't remember. We were having a barbecue. Daddy likes barbecued neck bones. No one else would touch them."

Sheriff Bledsoe picked up a pen. "Who all were at the barbecue?"

"Let's see…Robert Earl and his wife, Shirley and her son, Momma, a few neighbors and their kids…and…I'm sorry, I can't remember who else."

"What about your other brother, the one from Chicago?"

"Sheriff, if you know Leonard was there, you know about the barbecue. Why play twenty questions with me?"

Sheriff Bledsoe interlaced his fingers, rested them on his expansive paunch and leaned back in his chair.

"Ruth Ann, this is my job. Don't take this personally. I know a bit of what happened, not enough to form a complete picture."

"Yes, Leonard was there. He came late and he didn't stay long."

"Didn't he and your father exchange words? An altercation of some sort?"

"I wouldn't call it an altercation. Daddy and Leonard had a minor disagreement. Leonard left and the fun continued until Daddy took sick."

"A minor disagreement?"

Ruth Ann squinted at Sheriff Bledsoe. "Hello? Leonard didn't poison Daddy, Sheriff. I know what you're inferring. Leonard didn't do it!"

"I didn't say he did. Ruth Ann, don't get defensive. I understand this is your family we're discussing, but we are also talking murder. Everyone at the barbecue is a suspect." Pause. "Including you."

Ruth Ann snorted. "You can wipe my name off your list. I didn't poison my daddy, and I don't do neck bones." She opened her purse and retrieved a handkerchief.

Dabbing the corners of her eyes, she said, "Daddy and I were close, real close. In fact, to be honest with you, I was his favorite child."

"Ruth Ann, what exactly was said between your father and Leonard?"

"It wasn't much of anything. Daddy called Leonard a name and told him never set foot in his house again."

"A name?"

"He insulted Leonard's manhood."

"Uh…uh…your brother is--"

"Gay. He's not a flamboyant fairy. You wouldn't even know he's gay unless someone told you."

"Your father didn't know he was gay until the barbecue?"

"He knew. *Everybody* knew. One of those family thangs no one talks about, you know what I mean?" Sheriff Bledsoe nodded. "I guess Leonard couldn't breathe without it being official. He brought this white boy with him, as if he needed tangible proof of his being gay. You can't blame Daddy. His son standing up in front of everybody and proclaiming, 'I'm gay.' Don't get me wrong, I'm not homophobic. I just think there's a right time and place for everything."

"Didn't you say there were children present at the barbecue?"

"Yes, they were. Leonard and Shirley ushered all the kids inside the house before Leonard made his announcement. Shirley, bless her misguided soul, cosigned Leonard's foolish idea to out at a family get-together. If he'd asked me I would have told him to pick another date. April Fool's Day would have been perfect."

"His friend, the white boy, what's his name?"

"I don't remember. He's not hard to spot. Pale, baldheaded, chubby, a weak wrist."

"How long after Leonard's departure before your father took sick?"

"Leonard came back."

"He came back?"

"He left something--keys, wallet, something."

"Another exchange?"

"No. Leonard did all the talking."

"What did he say?"

"Nothing, really. He told Daddy to go to hell with his eyes open."

"Your father didn't respond?"

"He didn't get a chance. Shirley blocked Daddy from Leonard, and she was yelling at Leonard to leave."

"Shirley, she's your younger sister?"

"Yes. Robert Earl is the oldest. Then me, Shirley and Leonard."

"At any point whatsoever did you see Leonard come into contact with the neck bones?"

"No. The food was cooking on the grill when Leonard and his friend arrived. When Leonard came back the second time everyone was eating."

"Tell me if I'm wrong here. Leonard angrily tells your father, 'Go to hell with your eyes open,' and then your father takes sick?"

"A bizarre coincidence. Daddy started coughing, choking, and fell out of his seat clutching his throat. I thought he'd choked on a piece of meat."

Shaking her head: "It was horrible…horrible!…Momma started screaming and her screaming started other people overreacting. Shirley whopped Daddy on the back really hard, sounded like a door slamming. This guy, Harold, I believe his name. Claims he's our cousin--I doubt it, just an excuse for free food.

"He pushed Shirley aside, picked Daddy up and started shaking and squeezing him…Daddy's flapping and flopping and his face all tore up, eyes bucked, tongue hanging out, and Harold steady shaking him. Daddy made this god-awful gurgling noise and threw up…just exploded."

"Projectile vomiting," Sheriff Bledsoe said. "A symptom of arsenic poisoning."

"The idiot kept shaking and squeezing Daddy and whirling him this way and that, and Daddy started spraying people and they started hollering and knocking things over trying to get out of the way, as if being puked on by a dying man was the worst thing in the world to have happen to you."

"What Leonard doing during all of this?"

"I don't remember. Such a commotion going on. People panicking and running down the street. Shirley fainted and fell on her face. Momma running in circles calling Jesus. Kenny G howling like a coyote, and this nut whirling Daddy around like a human water hose. I was just worried about my daddy, that's all, nobody else. I couldn't tell you what someone else was…"

She stopped abruptly, buried her face in her hands and started crying.

Sheriff Bledsoe took this moment to appraise his small jail. The gray paint on the walls was peeling, large flakes exposing white paint underneath. Cold air blew from the air conditioner, though it rattled noisily and had to be turned on with pliers.

Duct tape held the cushion together in his chair. The other chairs were in poorer condition. Rust coated every bar on the one-man jail cell. Solve this case, he thought, and maybe, just maybe, the mayor would allocate the funds to refurbish.

"I want to know!" Ruth Ann snapped. "I want to know who did this to my daddy, Sheriff Bledsoe. My daddy had his faults--he didn't deserve this. He didn't!"

Sheriff Bledsoe nodded. "I'm going to nail whoever poisoned your father." He puffed up his chest: "I guarantee you!"

Later, a very short time later, he would regret making this statement, and regret even more the first time he laid eyes on Ruth Ann Hawkins and her family.

Chapter 3

Leonard stood in front of the mirror adjusting his tie. "Are you sure you don't want to come?"

Victor, in bed with the sheet around his waist, shook his head. "No, I'd rather not."

Leonard stepped back from the mirror and pirouetted. "How do I look?"

"Great. Just great, Leonard. You…" He stopped short.

Leonard sat on the edge of the bed. "What?" Victor looked away. "What?"

"You blame me for what happened? If you do I understand."

"No, Victor." Leonard stroked his face. "I don't blame you one bit. I blame myself for thinking my family, especially my father, would understand."

"I thought one of your sisters, Shirley, understood what you were going through."

"On a certain level she does. My other sister and brother--forget it!"

"How can the police think you...you know?"

"I killed my father? You know I didn't do that." Pause. "I can't believe he's dead. He was too mean to die easily." Shaking his head: "I should have gone to the funeral. They say you'll never have closure if you don't attend the funeral."

"Leonard, this is so bizarre...so strange."

"I told you events might not go as expected."

"You didn't mention neck bone poisoning and a murder investigation, nor a motel room with cockroaches the size of crabs."

Leonard gave Victor's knee a playful squeeze. "I'll settle this today. When I get back you and I will check out of this flea-bitten room and go back to our wonderful apartment and enjoy our wonderful life."

"Is it really wonderful, Leonard?"

Leonard leaned in and kissed him on the chin. "Yes, it most certainly is. You sound as if you're having second thoughts."

Victor shook his head and smiled.

Leonard stood up. "I better go now and get this over."

Victor, wearing only a pair of red Hanes, rose from the bed and embraced Leonard. "I love you!"

"I love you, too," staring into the dirty mirror above the dresser.

Leonard, thin, dark-skinned, early thirties, mini afro; Victor, portly, pale white, late forties, bald.

"Victor, I should go before I get excited. Imagine the Sheriff's reaction if I appeared with an erection."

Victor followed Leonard to the door. Stepping outside felt like stepping into a furnace. Leonard waved at Victor, hoping he would close the door and go back inside the room. Victor blew a kiss.

Leonard surveyed the parking lot. No one in sight. Thank God. He would remind Victor where they were, Dawson, Arkansas, not Chicago, Illinois. Here, public displays of affection by same-sex couples could result in an arrest or a busted head or both.

Inside the rental, a gray Chevrolet Lumina, Leonard looked into the rearview and saw Victor stepping out onto the balcony. A man and woman stepped out of the room next door and the man stared long and hard at Victor. Leonard started the car and drove away. He needed to hurry. The sooner he got Victor back to Chicago, the better.

Arriving at the Dawson County jail twenty minutes later, Leonard composed himself before going in. *Stay calm and don't reveal any unsolicited information.*

Just as he neared the door a cruiser pulled up and Sheriff Bledsoe got out carrying a box of Shipley Do-Nuts with two large Styrofoam cups balanced on top.

Leonard held the door open and followed him inside.

"Leonard Harris, I presume?"

"Yes."

Sheriff Bledsoe put the box down on a desk and extended a hand. "Sheriff Bledsoe, nice to meet you."

Leonard shook his hand. "Same here."

"Have a seat. You'll have to overlook the mess."

Leonard noticed every chair looked an accident waiting to happen. A large air conditioner, held in a window by cut-off bars, clanged noisily. A familiar scent of cologne hovered in the air. Old Spice, he thought at first. *No, too cloy.*

"Yes, they're rickety," Sheriff Bledsoe said, "but they're sturdy. Have a seat."

Leonard considered sitting atop one of the desks. *Not the time for practical jokes.* Now was the time to tell this adipose hayseed the skinny, exonerate himself, and get Victor and himself the hell out of Dawson, never to return again.

He sat down in a chair with a sawed-off baseball bat for a leg.

Sheriff Bledsoe busied himself about the room, transferring paper from one cluttered desk to another, and then disappeared inside a bathroom.

He's acting rather nervous, Leonard thought. He heard running water. The noise continued…and continued. Either Sheriff Bledsoe was taking a shower or washing his hands. The noise wasn't loud enough for a shower faucet.

He's washing his hands bloody because he knows I'm gay and he touched my hand.

You're being paranoid.

Presently, Sheriff Bledsoe came out, drying his hands thoroughly with a paper towel. He nodded at the doughnuts and coffee. "Help yourself. The coffee machine is on the blink, I picked up an extra cup."

"Thanks," getting up and retrieving a glazed doughnut. "I've already tried the coffee, not my particular brand." He bit into the doughnut and looked up.

Sheriff Bledsoe was frowning, staring at the two cups. "You took a sip?"

"Yes, I sure did." Leonard could tell by the Sheriff's expression he was dying to ask which one.

"So you're from Chicago," Sheriff Bledsoe said, sitting behind a desk.

"No. Originally I'm from here, Dawson. I moved out of my father's house when I was in high school. I moved to Chicago eleven years ago, right after I graduated college."

"Which college?"

"University of Arkansas at Monticello."

"Is that right? I went there myself. Business administration. Didn't graduate. I lack a few credits. One day I'll go--"

"Sir, I didn't poison my father." He then recognized the cologne that seemed to breeze in through the air conditioner.

"I didn't say you did."

"Why I'm here, isn't it?" Hai Karate, the cheap cologne his father used to slather on. *Where in hell can you purchase Hai Karate today?*

"Okay, Mr. Harris, you want to cut to the chase. As you know, your father was poisoned with arsenic, along with his pet, which I think was poisoned incidentally. And, according to eyewitnesses, you and your father got into a heated argument shortly before his death."

"Yes, we had a few words. If your eyewitnesses were completely honest with you, sir, they would have told you my partner and I were late arrivals to the barbecue. My partner can attest to that. He accompanied me from Chicago."

"I see. What's his name?"

"Fields. Victor Fields."

Sheriff Bledsoe nodded, but didn't write the name.

"Sir, I'm sure your eyewitnesses have informed you I'm gay, and Victor is my mate of five years."

Sheriff Bledsoe loosened the collar on his beige shirt. "Kinda hot in here, isn't it?" Leonard shook his head. "So…uh…" He cleared his throat. "So at no time did you come in contact with the neck bones prepared exclusively for your father?"

"No. Not once."

"If someone said they saw you--"

"They're telling a damn lie! I don't poison people's food, Mr. Bledsoe. My father and I had an argument, which I truly regret and will regret till the day I die. I did not poison him!"

Sheriff Bledsoe interlaced his fingers and nibbled on both thumbnails.

Leonard held his gaze for a moment, then looked away. He noticed the jail cell, the thin mattress covered with what looked to him a piss-stained sheet, and the aluminum commode. *I'll die before I go in there.*

He returned his attention to Sheriff Bledsoe. *What the hell!...*The man was still staring at him. Leonard stared back.

The man wore his afro in a shag that went out of style fifty years ago. And that goatee, another joke: the peach fuzz under his broad nose didn't droop far enough to connect with the fuzz that formed a crude U under his chin. *Big boys should never try anything more than a moustache anyway.*

"Well?" Leonard signaled by raising an eyebrow.

"You have any idea why anyone would want to harm your father?" Leonard shook his head. "Let me rephrase that. Who do you think poisoned your father?"

Leonard let out a nervous laugh. *Who's the detective here?* "You're asking me? I don't have a clue." Then he remembered: "The damn money!" he said to himself.

Sheriff Bledsoe sat up straight. "Excuse me? I didn't catch that."

"The money."

"What money?" Sheriff Bledsoe picked up one of the coffee cups, flipped the lid with a thumb, put the cup to his mouth, stopped and put the cup down. "What money?"

"Daddy worked at Hillard Catfish Farm forty-three years, started when Robert Earl was a baby. He invested his money in the company's stock, accruing a rather hefty sum, most of which he put in his will. Daddy was parsimonious, extremely stingy. When we were kids Daddy didn't give us money, he *loaned* us money and we had to pay--"

"How much?"

"--him back with interest. Thirty percent. He charged a penalty if--"

"How much?"

"--we didn't pay him back on time. Why I was shocked when I heard Daddy had willed his money to his family."

"How much?"

A thin smile played on Leonard's lips. "One-point-three million dollars."

Sheriff Bledsoe whistled. "Everyone in your family knows about this?"

"I'm afraid so. Mother told Robert Earl, the mouth of the south, about the money. Mother telling him was her way of ensuring all her children got the news. He called me at three in the morning and told me."

"Has the family received this money yet?"

"Not yet. I'm not sure how it works. I guess the money won't be doled out until we find out who murdered Daddy."

Sheriff Bledsoe shook his head. "You're thinking insurance money. As long as your father was of sound mind when he made out his will and had three witnesses, he determines the whenever and to whomever his estate is to be issued. Who's the executor of your father's will?"

"I don't know."

"The name of the beneficiaries?"

"Mother, Ruth Ann, Shirley, Robert Earl and me."

"Have you seen the will?"

"No, I haven't."

"Hmmm. Do you often fly home for family barbecues?"

"No. The barbecue was planned as an early celebration of my parent's golden wedding anniversary. Shirley and Ruth Ann scheduled it to accommodate my vacation week."

"I see. Anyone you know, friend or family member, who held a grudge against your father?"

Leonard stared at the floor, concentrating. "Daddy aggravated people. Snide comments, name-calling, insults. He'd raise holy hell if you didn't pay his money back. If he borrowed from you, he got amnesia, then got testy if you insisted reciprocation. One time Daddy took a rather nasty whooping over an unpaid debt."

"From who?"

"Joe Hill. A long time ago, and after Joe whooped Daddy, Mother paid him. I doubt Joe still holding a grudge."

"You sure it was Joe? I know Joe, he's not the fighting type."

"Borrow thirty dollars from Joe and don't pay him back, then tell me what he won't do. I was there when he ran to the house, smoke blowing out his nostrils."

"Joe Hill whooped your daddy at your daddy's house?"

"Not inside the house. When I yelled, 'Joe's coming,' Daddy ran out the back door. Joe caught him in the backyard."

"Anyone else whom your father disagreed over money."

"There was a tiff between Daddy and Robert Earl, but Daddy didn't owe Robert Earl money."

"A tiff? A disagreement or a fight?"

"I wasn't there. Shirley told me about it. According to her, Robert Earl went to Daddy and asked for an advance on his share of the money, fifty thousand dollars, if I'm not mistaken. Daddy, as usual, feigned amnesia, told Robert Earl he'd lost his one and only marble. Robert Earl called Daddy a tightwad. They pushed and shoved each other, but it didn't get dirty."

"Sounds to me Robert Earl needs money in a bad way. He's having financial problems?"

"No more than anyone else. You see, Robert Earl dreams of opening a combination snake farm and gas station."

Sheriff Bledsoe arched an eyebrow. "Snakes?"

"I'm afraid so," wondering if Sheriff Bledsoe thought his entire family was insane.

"Here in Dawson?"

"Yes." Leonard sighed. "Right here. Robert Earl stopped at a gas station displaying snakes when he was in Arizona. It definitely made an impression on him; he's been talking about it for years."

"Has Robert Earl--"

Leonard cut him short. "Robert Earl is not a murderer. He's a snake lover, a blowhard, a coward, a nut--he's *not* a murderer. He's also a homophobe, though I'm sure you wouldn't hold that against him."

Sheriff Bledsoe ignored the slight. "I didn't say he was a murderer. Money brings out the worst in people, good and bad people." He paused and looked Leonard straight in the eye. "I have to ask you this. Did you murder your father?"

"I said it once and I'll say it again. I did not murder my father."

"You willing to take a polygraph?"

"Yes," Leonard snapped. "Day or night."

"When were you planning to return to Chicago?"

"Today, just as soon as I leave here."

Sheriff Bledsoe shook his head. "Uh-uh. I prefer you didn't, not until we clear this up."

"I can't stay!" Leonard said, raising his voice. "I have a job, a life, in Chicago."

"Your father was murdered during a family gathering. And not only were you there, you threatened him."

"I didn't threaten him. Who said I threatened him? Who?" He waited...Sheriff Bledsoe didn't respond. "No way can you construe what I told my father as a threat. Please! I just told you we, Victor and myself, arrived late. Everybody knows that. This is a waste of time!"

"I've got plenty of time, Mr. Harris." Leonard stood abruptly. "If you leave town prematurely, Mr. Harris, I will issue a warrant for your arrest."

Leonard stared at him. He wanted to say high cholesterol makes rational thinking difficult, doesn't it? Instead: "This is ridiculous!"

"Maybe so. Here in the country we treat murder seriously."

"How long will it take you to complete your investigation?"

Three creases appeared on Sheriff Bledsoe's forehead. "Not too long," he said, and Leonard detected a tinge of doubt.

"I heard a murder investigation runs cold if the perpetrator isn't caught within the first forty-eight hours. My father's murder is, what, four-days-old? You're not sure how long this investigation will take, are you?"

Sheriff Bledsoe didn't respond.

Leonard crossed his arms and scrunched up his nose. "I'll stick around for as long as it takes. I'm not the litigious sort, but if I lose my job before you realize I did not murder my father…well, as the old saying goes--"

"I will see you in court," Sheriff Bledsoe finished for him. "You're free to go, Mr. Harris."

Leonard walked to the door, opened it and then stopped. "Have you ever lost a family member to murder?" he asked. He didn't wait for a response. "Words can't describe it. Numb, anguish, pain--don't even come close. Then to be suspected--"

A black truck drove by, a rebel flag in the back window. Leonard lost his train of thought. "Have a good day, Sheriff," and stepped out into the afternoon's heat.

Chapter 4

Along Highway 10, two miles east of Dawson's city limits, a mile or so short of a vacant lot where Robert Earl planned to build a gas station and exotic snake farm, stood the Blinky Motel. The only building before a ten-mile stretch to the next town, Hamburg, it lit up the sky for miles around.

A full moon hovered above. A large neon sign in front flashed INKY, missing the first two letters. Along the edge of the roof, red Christmas lights blinked intermittently from one end to the other.

Nine rooms comprised the single-level building, one inhabited by the manager, an Iranian who boasted American citizenship; thus the sign American Owned and Operated in the office window.

Three cars were parked in front on the gravel lot. In back, a late-model Chevrolet S10 truck hid among a copse of pine trees. Its owner, Eric Barnes, sat on a bed in room number seven, watching a video, *Deep Throat*.

Mesmerized by Linda Lovelace's oral resuscitations, Eric didn't hear the soft knock at the door.

"Eric?" a woman whispered, followed by a tap on the window. "Eric!" This time he heard and hastily took out the video and changed the channel, *The Cartoon Network*.

"Who is it?"

"It's me."

Eric opened the door and Ruth Ann, wrapped in a trench coat, stepped in.

"I've been out there a long time," she said, looking around the room. "What you doing you didn't hear the door?"

"I musta dozed off." Ruth Ann brushed past him and sat on the bed. He wondered why she wore a coat in the middle of July. "Something wrong?"

She stared at the television; a petite woman slammed Johnny Bravo on his head. "The funeral, my father, everything, really…" She shook her head.

He sat beside her and ran his hand through her hair. "What you talking about, baby?" She pushed his hand away. "What's the matter? Don't you still love me?"

"Eric, my daddy was murdered. Somebody poisoned him. His funeral was just yesterday."

"He was murdered! Damn! Ain't that a bitch! Take your clothes off, let's get busy."

Ruth Ann shot him a cold look. "For your information, Daddy and I were real close. You wouldn't understand." She covered her eyes and started crying. "I miss him so much!"

"I miss him, too," tugging on the trench coat. Good girl, he thought as he slid the coat down her shoulders.

To his surprise, Ruth Ann sported a blue skin-tight jumpsuit underneath the coat; crying loudly now, her sobs drowning out Johnny Bravo begging for a date. Even in her distress, he wanted her.

Ruth Ann was an attractive woman. Coal-black hair fell loosely to her shoulders. Brown eyes below pencil-thin eyebrows slanted upward, giving her a slightly Asian appearance. Her complexion resembled liquid caramel, creamy smooth. Figure curved in all the right places, especially in the rear.

What mostly fascinated Eric was her mouth. Lips full and sensuous, almost always sporting a sparkling cherry sheen. When she talked her lips barely moved, concealing her teeth, straight and snow white.

He hugged her. "It's going to be all right, baby. I'm here." He palmed her breast and she pushed his hand away.

She stopped crying and said, "I've been doing some thinking, some serious thinking."

"Is that right?"

"Yes, I have. Daddy's death triggered my conscience. I've allowed my moral compass to shift to depravity and self-gratification."

"Yeah," Eric said, not having a clue what the hell she was talking about. "Me, too."

"Really? You feel the same way?"

"Yeah, hell yeah! I feel the same way you do. Now let's get naked." He pulled her to him and started kissing her neck, then tried to push her onto the bed.

"Stop!" Ruth Ann shouted, pulling free.

"What's the matter, baby? We don't have much time. I took two Levitras and rented this room for an hour."

"Didn't you just say you felt the same as I do, guilty and ashamed? Morally depleted?"

"I did?" *When did I say all that?* "No, I didn't!"

Ruth Ann got up and went into the bathroom. Eric kicked off his sandals, hopped out of his baggy short pants and snatched off his V-neck T-shirt. He lay on the bed stark naked, his erection pointing north.

Ruth Ann stepped out, drying her face with a washcloth. She glanced at Eric, then sat down in the chair next to the bed.

"C'mon, baby," Eric said, patting the bed. "I'll make you feel better, all tingly inside."

"Eric, you're not listening. I can't do this anymore. My sister, your son's mother--I can't do this anymore, not in good conscience. It's wrong. It was wrong from the start. This should not have happened. I can't do this anymore."

Eric sat up. "Okay. I'll start using a damn rubber."

"No. Listen to what I'm saying. I cannot do this anymore. You hear me? I cannot do this anymore! Shirley's my sister and technically she's your wife. We can still be friends, but the hanky-panky is over. We were lucky no one got hurt. No longer we have to worry about Shirley or Lester finding out about us. You see what I'm saying? No more guilt feelings. We can live a moral life. You see what I'm saying?"

Eric wasn't listening, watching his erection shrink slowly but surely.

He stood up directly in front of her. "One for the road, okay? Just once more, and then we'll start being friends." He was on the rise again. "Come on, baby."

Ruth Ann shook her head.

"C'mon, Ruth Ann, one more time. Look, he's all excited." Ruth Ann closed her eyes. *Damn...double damn!* She was so close. "Ruth Ann, look at me."

Shaking her head emphatically: "No, Eric!"

He moved closer and brushed himself against the side of her face.

"No, Eric!" and pushed him. He fell onto the bed. "It's over, Eric." Starting for the door: "It's best you understand that."

Eric jumped to his feet, ran to the door and pressed his back against it. "Hold on, Ruth Ann, just hold on. Let's talk, okay? Don't leave me like this!"

Pulling on the doorknob: "I've got to go, Eric. I told Lester I'd be back in thirty minutes. I've been gone an hour."

"Fuck Lester!"

"Let me out, please!"

"Ruth Ann, wait a minute. You can't leave me like this. I…" He swallowed. "I-I love you, Ruth Ann. I really do!" That was hard, incredibly hard. His father had warned him never to tell a woman those three words unless he planned to marry and take care of her. Until now he'd obeyed the edict. "Honest, Ruth Ann. Cross my heart. I swear!"

Ruth Ann paused, stared him straight in the eye for a beat. *Is she giving in?* He could only hope. So he told her those three awful words again and again.

"Ruth Ann, I love you more than…" *Than what?* This was shaky ground; if he named something he treasured, she might want him to fork it over.

"I love you more than anything in the whole wide world." That seemed safe. "Don't end our love like this. Please, baby, not like this." He hugged her and she didn't resist. "I love you so much." Kissed her ear, eye, nose, neck. "Too much, really." Urged her toward the bed. "I love you, Ruth Ann."

She stopped at the bed. "Do you have a prophylactic?"

"A what?"

"A rubber."

"Oh, yeah. I got one right here." He picked up his pants, fished inside the pocket and pulled out a small red package. "Here it is."

Ruth Ann took it. "Lie down. I'll do it."

Eric practically dove onto the bed.

"Close your eyes," she told him.

This was new, yet he was more than willing to play along. He heard the package open--*she's using her mouth?* She was so skilled with her mouth. And then he felt her hands on him.

"Say arrivederci," Ruth Ann said.

"Arrivederci."

He waited, anxiously, eyes squinched tight. He started to tell her to go 'head and do it when he heard the door opening.

"Get back here!"

Ruth Ann closed the door behind her. Eric gave chase. She was walking casually down the walkway toward the end of the motel when he ran out.

She looked back, saw him running toward her, shrieked and started sprinting. Eric caught her just as she turned the corner.

"Ruth Ann, come back inside." He pulled her by her wrist.

"Let me go, Eric. Let me go! Stop it now!"

"We have to talk…inside the motel room…like normal people. C'mon, stop acting silly."

"No, Eric! I said stop. If you don't stop I'll scream."

"C'mon, Ruth Ann. You gonna make people think I'm doing something to you." He said this calmly, rationally, as if they were on a stroll in a public park instead of him stark naked and her resisting being pulled by the wrist.

Ruth Ann screamed and collapsed into a ball on the pavement. The door directly behind them, room number two, opened and a tall white man wearing only boxers and alligator-skinned boots stepped out.

"Pardon me, young fellow," he said just as Eric was attempting to lift Ruth Ann into a fireman's carry. Louder: "Pardon me!"

Eric turned and looked up. The blinking red lights made it impossible to discern the man's face.

"There's a western showing on the tube, cowboy. This here ain't your business." He returned his attention to Ruth Ann and tried to lift her, but couldn't get a good hold. "C'mon, Ruth Ann. Stop this nonsense!"

All he had to do was pick her up and carry her the short distance to the motel room. Yeah, he thought as he kneeled to get a better grip, get her back inside, talk to her, bang her real good, and everyone would be happy.

Ruth Ann, arms wrapped around her legs, fingers interlocked, head tucked between her knees, screamed.

"Excuse me young fellow," the man said again.

"Didn't I tell you get some business, Roy Rogers?"

"Ma'am, is this fellow bothering you?"

"Yes, he is!"

"Step away from the lady, young fellow. Now!"

"Make me!" He moved to lift Ruth Ann in a jerk-and-roll maneuver when he heard a metallic clip-clap. He froze.

"I'm mighty tired of repeating myself. Step away from the lady, boy!"

Eric swallowed. He knew what he would see before turning--the transition from *young fellow* to *boy* was too quick for the man not to have a gun--and when he did, sure enough the cowboy was aiming a weapon at him. Not a gun, uh-uh; not an old rusty revolver, what you would've expected from a galoot like him, but a shotgun.

Eric felt his heart in his throat. He raised both hands as he stood up. Where on earth had the man concealed the damn thing?

"You're moving too slow to my liking, boy," gesturing with the shotgun.

Eric, moving his head left and right, not liking at all the shotgun shadowing him, said, "Sir, is there a problem?"

"Shut your pie hole, boy. Hey, Ebb, get out here."

Another cowboy, this one shorter, rounder in the middle, in a pink bathrobe, stepped out of the motel room. "Yes, Harold," he said.

"Ebb, help the lady to her feet."

Ebb moved to assist Ruth Ann, but she stood on her own. "I'll guess I'll be going now," she said.

"I called the police," Ebb said.

"Police!" Eric shouted. "Ruth Ann, tell these cowpokes what's really going on. We do this all the time, don't we? Tell em! Tell em, Ruth Ann, before the police come."

Ruth Ann walked away. "Yes, we do this all the time. I love being dragged to a motel room by a naked man. It's exciting. See you on the news, Eric. Ta-ta."

"No, Ruth Ann. Tell em the truth. Ruth Ann!" She'd turned the corner, flipping Eric a finger before disappearing.

Eric smiled nervously. "You guys mind I go to my room, put my clothes on? I'll come back. Give me a few minutes, I'll be right back."

"Mosey along, young fellow." He lowered the shotgun. "The lady's gone. But let me share this with you, partner. I don't saddle up with a man who forces himself on a woman. That kind of thing chafes my hide."

Eric shook his head. "Sir, believe me, even at gunpoint, I wouldn't chafe your hide."

The man spat a wad of tobacco a few inches short of Eric's feet. "Next time I see you forcing a woman, any woman, to do anything, it won't go so easy. You see what horse I'm riding, boy?"

Back to *boy* again. Eric nodded and backed up toward his room, not giving a damn if Silver was hitched around the corner.

Inside the room he closed the door, locked it and threw on his clothes. A siren warbled in the distance. *Shit!* He ran to the bathroom, pried open the small window and shimmied out. Thank goodness he'd registered under an alias.

He hurried to his truck and hopped in. It whined but didn't start. The siren sounded closer. "Damn!" No other choice, he got out and ran through the woods.

Chapter 5

Albert, an albino boa constrictor, slid across the lawn. Its owner shouted, "Albert, you get back here! You know those people don't like you."

Albert kept going, not realizing he was slithering perilously close to the yard next door where his owner's neighbor had posted a sign on his unfenced property that read All Snakes Will Be Shot.

"Albert, you hear me! I said get over here!" Robert Earl crossed his arms and stomped his feet. "Stupid snake," and walked over and picked up Albert.

Disoriented midair, Albert wriggled fitfully.

"Bad snake! Bad snake!" Robert Earl tapped the six-foot, orange-and-white snake on its bulbous head. "When I tell you come here, I mean come here!" He tapped it again, to ensure it got the message.

Albert almost wriggled free...Robert Earl grabbed its midsection and held it up eye to eye. "Do you hear me?" Onyx eyes stared defiantly at him, so Robert Earl shook it. "You hear me?"

Albert flitted its black forked tongue.

"Okay, then. Stop acting like you don't know come here from sic em."

"Robert," Estafay called from inside the back porch.

"Yeah." He couldn't see her through the wire mesh screen. "Yeah, honey."

Estafay stuck her head out the door, her eyes never leaving Albert. "Telephone."

"Who is it?"

"Someone from the mill."

"Dang! What they want? Okay."

When Robert Earl, holding Albert, crossed to the house, Estafay quickly retreated. He dropped Albert into the snake house, three plywood boards abutted to the skirting panel. Two days ago Albert had companions, two rattlesnakes, Killer and Diller, who escaped after a storm blew the boards down.

Robert Earl went inside and picked up the phone in the kitchen. "Hello."

"Robert?"

"This him."

"Robert, Dale Brown. Over at the paper mill. We were wondering when you were planning to come back to work."

"Y'all was?" Robert Earl replied, sitting at the kitchen table, stretching the phone cord to its limit.

"Yes, we sure were. When are you coming back?"

"You know I just buried my daddy yesterday. The mound on his grave hasn't leveled. If there is a mound. Sometimes they don't cover the hole till days later, you know. Why it's a good idea to check on em."

"I didn't know that, Robert. If you could give us a rough date to when you're coming back. We need to mark something on the calendar."

"Uh...I really don't know when I'm coming back. When a man's daddy is murdered it takes time adjusting, even though I couldn't stand the sorry rascal. If it wasn't for him I wouldn't be here."

"I understand. I just need a--"

"Do you really? Or are you just talking? Your daddy probably still alive while mine is six feet under. Worm food. Smelling like--"

"Robert, I hate to cut you off. I just need a date. Take all the time you need, just give me a date when you think you'll be able to return to work."

Drumming his fingers against the table: "I'm not coming back."

"Are you quitting?"

"Yeah," and hung up the phone.

Forget him! Go back, go back for what? So Dale and his buddies could continue laughing behind his back, calling him the snake man and handing him the majority of the work load. *Forget him, forget em all!* He noticed his fingers were shaking.

Might've been a bad idea, he thought, remembering the long line he'd seen at the unemployment office. He started to call Dale back.

"No!"

He had money coming, and once he got his hands on it he would go down to the mill and tell Dale and his buddies to kiss his rusty, black butt. And once he got his money he could finally catch up on all his bills, start his own business.

Estafay entered the kitchen wearing a red terrycloth bathrobe. "Bad news?" she asked, taking a pot from the cabinet.

"Dale wanted to know when I was coming back to work."

Estafay filled the pot with water from the tap and set it on the stove. "What you tell him?"

"Told him I'd come back when I feel like it, not a second earlier. Told him not to call me no more. Dale ain't nothing but a devil. Smile in my face then talk about me behind my back."

"Rent due next week," Estafay reminded him. "And a payment due on those teeth in your mouth."

Robert Earl took out his dentures and set them on the table. "When we get that money I'm buying me some real teeth, the kind don't hurt my mouth. Won't have to work at no smelly mill, either."

Estafay scooted around Robert Earl and opened the refrigerator. "Not on the kitchen table, Robert. How many times must I tell you? That's nasty!"

He put the dentures in the front pocket of his gray flannel shirt.

"Robert, that's not where your teeth go. And the next time I find them inside the refrigerator, they're going in the trash."

"Freezing em makes em softer on my gums."

"Put them in ice water, not my refrigerator."

Robert Earl hung his head, his chin resting on his chest. *My refrigerator?* He was the one who bought it. Shoot, he'd bought everything in their one-bedroom house. Estafay sat at the table opposite him.

"Robert, do you really think a snake hole can make money here, in a small town in the sticks?"

Robert Earl jerked his head up. "Not a snake hole, Estafay. A combination gas station and exotic snake farm. There's not one here or anywhere near here, possibly not in the entire state. Honey, it can't go wrong. You'll see."

"We're living in a shack. Look in the front door you can see through the entire house. The commode in the bathroom has been leaking for years. It'll fall through the floor sooner or later. The refrigerator doesn't freeze properly, only one eye on the stove works, the little furniture we have is worn out, and on top of all that we have a snake pit in the backyard."

"A snake house. It's a snake house."

"Whatever. We need a new house, new appliances, furniture. I need a new car and…" She drifted off and looked away. Softly: "And some work."

"A job!"

"Noooo!" Estafay said, frowning. "Woman's work. Surgery."

"Oh," looking confused and disappointed. "You know I've been planning a gas station and exotic snake farm for a long time. It's my dream. When we start making money from our business we can buy all the stuff you talking about."

"Let's not argue, sweetheart." She took his hands in hers. "I'll fast and pray on it. When the Lord tells me what to do, we'll do what He says. He'll tell me the right thing to do. All we need to do is obey His word. Now who do you think did it?"

He didn't hear the question, fretting over doing what the Lord told *her* to do. Every time she'd sought the Lord's guidance in a disagreement between them, the Lord's response always favored Estafay's argument. *Always!*

"Who do you think did it?" Estafay repeated.

"Did what?" wondering if he should just cut her loose and pursue his dream.

"Killed your daddy?"

"No doubt in my mind, the fag did it."

"Leonard?"

"The only fag in my family, and he told the old man to catch the next bus to hell. Then--plop!--the old man buys the farm."

57

"Are you upset?" releasing his hands.

"No."

"You sound upset."

"I'm not upset."

"Robert, I'm your wife, and as your wife I will follow your lead. But the Lord is the head of this household. A divided house cannot stand--you know that!"

"Yes, you're right," fearing she would embark on a long sermon.

"Have you talked to Sheriff Bledsoe?"

"Not yet. I will, though. He's calling everybody in for an interview. I'll tell him what I know when it's my turn."

Estafay interlocked her fingers, closed her eyes and shook her head. Oh-oh, Robert Earl thought, here comes the sermon.

Estafay opened her eyes and said, "Maybe you shouldn't wait till he calls you. Maybe you should call him. Maybe you can help him, keep him from going in the wrong direction. The sooner he solves this case, the sooner we get our money."

Robert Earl nodded. She was making sense. "I guess I could."

Estafay got up, retrieved the phone and handed it to him. "You know the number, don't you?"

As he dialed he looked at Estafay. Her short hair parted in the middle, brushed down the sides. *What kind of style is that?* She stared back at him and he looked away.

Sheriff Bledsoe picked up on the first ring. "Sheriff's office. Sheriff Bledsoe speaking."

"Ennis, this Robert Earl. How you doing? Hey, Ennis, we need to talk about my daddy's murder, the sooner the better."

"Yes, Robert Earl, we sure do. In fact, I was about to call you."

"Is that so?"

"Yes. I was reaching for the phone when it rang. Your mother, Ida, she's here in my office."

"Momma?" He heard someone crying in the background.

"Yes. She's here. Uh...she just confessed to murdering your father."

Chapter 6

The smoke alarm whistled. Shirley, lying on the couch in the living room, didn't hear it. Dreaming: Eric and she were standing in a chapel before Reverend Walker.

Eric dressed in a baby-blue tuxedo. She wore an off-white gown with a train trailing down the aisle. Wedding bells rang in the background. Smoke filled her nostrils. The pews filled to capacity. She sniffed…sneezed.

Smoke?

"Ain't something burning?" Eric yelled from the bedroom.

She jumped to her feet and ran into the kitchen. White smoke billowed from the skillet. What once were two sausage patties and three eggs was now a black lump dancing and sizzling in the skillet as if it were alive. Shirley turned the burner off and pushed the skillet off the red-hot coil with a spatula.

"Ain't something burning?" Eric yelled again.

Shirley tiptoed and removed the smoke alarm from a nail in the wall.

"Yes!" she shouted. "Your breakfast!"

She heard him cursing. The gall of that man. He'd come home late last night, after midnight, sweating, his pants unzipped, talking about the truck had broken down, he'd had to walk.

He'd justified everything, but one thought dominated her mind: *he's cheating.* Again. Yet she didn't confront him.

She stepped out onto the back porch and placed the smoke alarm on the window ledge. In the backyard a large raccoon pilfered through trash scattered around an upended trashcan.

It stood on its hind legs and bared its teeth. "Git!" Shirley shouted, feigning to throw something at it.

It grabbed whatever it was eating and disappeared into the pine trees lining the back of the mobile home park. *Confronting Eric a waste of time; he'll only lie.*

Maybe she was jumping the gun. He could have taken a leak and forgot to zip up. If he'd been cheating, surely he had enough sense to tidy up before coming home.

No, Eric wouldn't cheat on her the day after her father's funeral. She heard the doorbell ringing inside the house.

Eric was tiptoeing to the front door in his underwear when she stepped into the living room. "You expecting company?" he asked. He looked into the peephole. "Darlene. Blabbermouth Darlene."

"Come in," Shirley said, and Darlene--tall, thin, two diamond studs in one nostril, braided hair extensions brushing her butt-- pushed the door open.

"Get out of here with no clothes on!" Shirley told Eric.

Eric just stood there, eyeballing Darlene. "You need to gain some weight," he said. "A strong wind might carry your narrow ass away. I don't appreciate you coming over here filling Shirley's head with bullshit about me. Why you ain't got no man, huh?"

"Don't disrespect my friends," Shirley said. "I don't disrespect your friends."

"I don't have no friends."

"Wonder why," Darlene said under her breath.

"Say what?" Eric said, moving toward her. "Say it so I can hear it."

Shirley cut him off at the path. "Go put on some clothes. She didn't come here to see you."

"She came here to talk about me. She had a man she wouldn't be over here all the time dropping salt on me." Shirley pushed him toward the bedroom and he circled back. "A buncha men round here and she can't snag *one*!"

"Let's go outside and talk, Darlene," Shirley said, frowning at Eric. He started to say more, but Shirley walked out behind Darlene and slammed the door in his face.

Cumulus clouds blocked the sun, granting a brief respite from the stifling heat.

Darlene stopped at the foot of the stairs, started to speak, then gestured toward the house.

Shirley turned and saw Eric looking out the window. "Forget him," she said. Several houses down, her nine-year-old son, Paul, was playing tag with one of his friends.

"Shirley," Darlene whispered, "you know I'm not one to dip in people's business, but it's something I feel I should tell you."

"What?" Shirley said, knowing this was something she didn't want to hear.

"Shereka called me--you know her, don't you? Donnie Ray Hall's wife?" Shirley nodded. "She called me from the Blinky Motel. She and Lucky Davis were there--that's another story. Anyway, she said she saw Eric there." Darlene paused and glanced over Shirley's shoulder. Shirley looked too; Eric was no longer in the window. "In the parking lot. Girl, he was flat-foot, *bucky* naked!"

"Darlene, please!"

"Ain't the worst of it. Shereka said he was pulling on a woman, trying to rape her or something."

Shirley's face warmed. If her right leg started shaking, she would go into the house, or else Darlene would be at risk for serious injury. "Is that it?"

"Ain't it enough? Shirley, don't denigrate 'cause I'm telling you what Shereka told me. Eric was trying to assault a woman, and if this white man hadn't stepped in, Lord knows what Eric would've done."

"Darlene, we're girlfriends, been girlfriends for a long time, right?"

"Right. Shirley, I'm telling you--"

"No, listen. I don't talk about your man"--*if she ever got one*-- "and I don't appreciate you talking about mine. Besides, that's the craziest shit I've ever heard. If what you say is true, why isn't Sheriff Bledsoe over here kicking the door down? Eric's not a ugly man--he doesn't have to take it! Please!"

"Hmmph!" Darlene snorted. "He might be handsome, I'll give him that. He's still a dog, Shirley. He's a dog other dogs don't mess with. Remember what happened with him and Linda Riley? Not for me you wouldna known what was going on."

Shirley inhaled and held it for a beat, not wanting to recall the episode when Darlene paged her at Wal-Mart and told her to rush home, which she did, and discovered Eric and Linda Riley in bed.

"Darlene, that was a long time ago."

"Nine months ain't a long time ago."

"To me it is!"

Darlene frowned, her small features squeezing to the center of her face. "You hating me with all you got, ain't you? He's handsome, but he ain't good for shit!"

Shirley felt a slight tremor in her right leg. "I've got to cook breakfast, Darlene. See you later." She started up the steps.

"Where's the truck?"

Shirley stopped. "What?"

"The truck? Sheriff Bledsoe searched a black S-Ten pickup parked in the back of the motel. Who you know drive a truck like that?"

Shirley's temples started throbbing. *Bastard!* "See you, Darlene. I'll talk to you later."

Eric was not in the living room, the kitchen, nor the bathroom. She found him in the bedroom, and the sight of him lying in bed fully clothed, eyes closed, snoring, as if he'd not been at the window a moment ago but asleep all the while, made her blood boil. She stared at him a long time.

In the kitchen she took a pot from the cabinet, filled it with water, set it atop the stove and…Her fingers were on the knob. *This isn't right!* It also wasn't right for him to cheat on her again and again.

The arrow moved from OFF to HI. This would be the last time he humiliated her.

Twenty minutes later she stood at the foot of the bed, holding the pot with a large bath towel. "Eric," she said softly. He groaned and rolled from his side onto his stomach.

"Eric, sweetie, we need to talk."

"Woman, I'm trying to sleep."

"Where were you last night, baby?"

"I told you I was checking this guy about a job." He grabbed a pillow and covered his head. "Don't believe everything Darlene tells you. She wants us to breakup so you can be in the same boat with her. Lonely. Depressed. With a stinky two-way dildo."

"Last night you said the truck broke down, you had to walk."

"Yeah, right. After I checked with the guy about the job, I was on my way home and the truck broke down."

"Look me in the eye, honey, and tell me you weren't at the motel last night with some woman."

He snatched the pillow away and quickly sat up. "What the hell are you--" The words caught in his throat. His Adam's apple yo-yoed and somehow he managed to cast one eye on the pot and the other on Shirley's face. "B-b-b-baby..."

"Tell me to my face you weren't with some woman at the Blinky Motel last night. Tell me. Don't lie! Your truck was there, you were there! Don't lie to me, Eric."

Eric scooted toward the headboard, pulling his limbs close. "B-b-baby, I promise I wasn't! I swear on my daddy's stones I wasn't!

66

The truck broke down, me and another guy pushed it off the road. Baby, put the pot down. Please!"

"Why were your pants unzipped when you came home?"

He raised both hands. "Please, baby, put the pot down! I took a piss, forgot to zip up. Please, baby, for the love of Jesus, put the pot down!"

Shirley started crying. "All I ever asked was you to love me. If you don't want me, tell me and I'll leave you alone. We don't have to go through all this." She lowered the pot…then brought it up again. "Tell me the truth, dammit!" she shouted. "Or I'm going to dash you!"

Sweat blotching his face, Eric said, "It wasn't me, baby! I swear 'fore God and three Jehovah Witnesses it wasn't!"

Eric screamed as the water flew at him.

He continued screaming after realizing the water was lukewarm. Then he jumped up and hurried to Shirley and smothered her with kisses. "I love you, baby! I love you, baby! I love you so much! I do, I do, I do, I do…"

Shirley allowed him to move her onto the wet bed. "Don't hurt me, Eric. My daddy is dead, I can't take no more hurt." She held him tight. "I can't take no more hurt, Eric."

Eric, remaining perfectly still in her arms, mumbled, "I won't hurt you, baby." The doorbell rang. "Don't get it, baby. Let's just sit here, you and me."

"It might be Paul."

"He can wait."

The doorbell rang several more times…and then there was a knock at the bedroom window.

"Shirley?" Darlene said. "Shirley, Robert Earl just called. Your mother is in jail. She confessed to murdering your father."

Chapter 7

Sheriff Bledsoe downed three aspirins and two Pepsid AC tablets with a cup of hot coffee. His stomach simply couldn't keep up with all the disappointments in the last twenty-four hours.

Yesterday, nausea set in shortly after he'd talked to Bud Wilson, the owner of BW Feed Store. Juggernaut Gopher Bait, the high-level arsenic pesticide which ended Larry and his dog's days of playing fetch, was a restricted use product: illegal to purchase without first obtaining a license from the Arkansas State Plant Board.

Bumbling Bud Wilson didn't keep proper records, a felony; thus anybody could have purchased the pesticide.

I should have arrested his lazy butt.

With each passing hour, the prospect of solving the case, his first homicide investigation, was dissolving like an Alka Seltzer tablet in a swimming pool.

Usually, Pepto Bismol did the trick, a couple or three spoonfuls and pain ceased. But last night, after arriving at the Blinky Motel and missing the victim and the assailant of a purported assault, he downed half a bottle of Pepto Bismol and instead of instant relief, the sharp, burning pain scorched up his stomach to his chest.

A moment he thought he was experiencing the big one. *How can you tell the difference, heart attack or gastric indigestion?* They both hurt like the dickens.

He wondered who were the players involved in the shenanigans at the motel. Several eyewitnesses reported a naked man assaulting a woman wearing a trench coat was thwarted by a cowboy in underwear toting a shotgun.

Unimaginable!

He had Eric Barnes' truck towed to an impound lot, yet couldn't imagine Eric, a petty ne'er-do-well, gallivanting naked in a parking lot. He'd called Eric's brother, Duane, who said Eric lived with Shirley Harris in the mobile home park north of town but they didn't have a phone. Duane gave him a neighbor's number, a Darlene Pryor.

He was dialing her number when Ida Harris waltzed into the station. The look on her face he could tell she had bad news. She took a chair in front of his desk. The phone to his ear, he gestured a hello. Darlene's phone rang and rang.

Mrs. Harris still had on her funeral attire, black skirt and blouse and a black-and-white hat she wore tilted to the side. He hung up the phone.

Smiling: "Hello, Mrs. Harris, how are you--"

Before he could finish she burst into tears. Her small chest inflated and deflated with each sob and a grayish mixture of tears and mascara gushed down her face. Sheriff Bledsoe sat quietly. He offered her a Kleenex, which she declined.

Ruth Ann, he thought, would one day look exactly like her mother. Even now, save for the gray streaks of hair and crow's feet around the eyes and the marked loss of muscle tone underneath the neck, Ruth Ann was the spitting image of her mother. Both shared the same caramel-colored skin tone, the small, hawkish nose, the thin mouth and the same Asian eyes.

"I kilt him," she said. "I did it. I kilt him. Lock me up and throw away the key."

Sheriff Bledsoe struggled to stave off elation. "Ma'am, Mrs. Harris, what are you telling me?"

Her eyes narrowed. She snatched a Kleenex out the box and blew her nose. "Are you deaf? I said I kilt my husband, lock me up."

"Ma'am, why don't you tell me all about it. Take your time. Would you like a cup of coffee?"

71

Ida shook her head, tears still flowing down her face. "I just want you to lock me up. I confessed." She blew her nose again. "It's all my fault. Lock me up."

"Before we go any further, Mrs. Harris, I need to read you your Miranda rights. You have the right to--"

"I know it already. Just lock me up so I can get it over with."

"It's not so simple. Where did you get the arsenic?"

Ida stared at him. "The who?"

"The arsenic. The poison. Where did you get it?"

Her lips quivered and she dissolved into another round of body-racking sobs. Sheriff Bledsoe realized then she was not the killer, as obvious as the varicose veins in the back of her small hands.

Why she confessing to murder? Protecting someone? Her children! She's sacrificing herself for one of her children.

"Mrs. Harris, you and I know you didn't murder your husband. I think you *know* who did."

"What you talking about?" Ida snapped. "I said I did it. I used rat poison. I don't know anything about arsenic. I know Raid, D-Con and Black Flag. I said I did it, all you need to know."

"I see," Sheriff Bledsoe said. "Tell me why you did it?"

"What?"

"You said you did it, tell me why."

She licked her lips and glared at him.

"Why? Why after fifty years of marriage you decide to murder your husband?"

72

"Because I felt like it!"

"Oh, I see. You *felt* like it. We're cooking with hot grease now. Where did you purchase the poison?"

"Piggly Wiggly."

Sheriff Bledsoe scooted his chair near her and took her hand in his. "If you know who murdered your husband, it's best you tell me. It's illegal to withhold that kinda information. I understand you want to protect your family...This isn't the way to do it."

Ida snatched her hand free. "Are you a pissy fool? I told you I did it. What more I have to do? Hitchhike a ride to the penitentiary?"

He picked up the phone. "Why don't I call your children? Let's see--"

"No, no, no, no!"

"--what they think about all this."

Ida stood up. "What kind of sheriff are you? Why you want to stir up a bunch of confusion? My children don't even know I'm here--ain't no need calling them!"

He put the phone down. "Who killed your husband, Mrs. Harris? Leonard? Ruth Ann? Shirley? What's your other son's name?"

"Robert Earl."

"Did he do it?"

"Oh, my sweet Jesus!" and dropped into the chair and started sobbing much louder than before. She sat there, head on her knees, crying…and crying…

Sheriff Bledsoe waited patiently; he wanted to ask her about her husband's will. Who's the executor? Did she have a copy?

She never gave him the opportunity, her sobbing increased several decibels. Ten minutes later the noise irritated him, greatly. He was reaching for the phone when it rang. Robert Earl. *Thank goodness!* He would be right over.

Her sobs equaled hogs squealing and long nails scratching a blackboard, grating on his last nerve, and each time she paused for a few seconds to catch her breath, he thought it was finally over and then she'd start up again.

The burning sensation returned to the pit of his stomach. He stared at the door, hoping Robert Earl, or any one of her children, would come in and take her away.

He was rolling up bits of Kleenex, for earplugs, when the front door flung open and caromed off the wall. Shirley barged in, followed by Leonard, Ruth Ann and Robert Earl.

"Where's my momma?" Shirley shouted.

Sheriff Bledsoe pointed at Ida. "There's your mother, and if you don't mind, lower your voice?"

Leonard, Ruth Ann and Shirley ran over to Ida. "Momma," Ruth Ann said, "what's the matter? What's the matter, Momma?"

Ida sobbed even louder, which Sheriff Bledsoe had thought was a physical impossibility.

"What the hell did you do to her?" Shirley demanded.

"What's going on, Sheriff?" Leonard asked.

"Frankly," Sheriff Bledsoe said, "I don't have a clue."

They started shouting at him. He gleaned: "Why you harassing my momma?…What did she do?…She's an old woman!…You oughta be ashamed of yourself." And, though he wasn't quite sure: "You need yo fat ass whooped!"

"Hold on!" he shouted over the din. "Everybody just hold on!" The cacophony ceased. "Everybody calm down. This is a police station." He stood up and the pain in his stomach jumped a circuit and sent a jolt to his kidney. "Your mother came here on her own accord and I haven't harassed her. Ask her."

"Did he hit you with a phone book, Momma?" Shirley asked.

Before Ida could respond, Shirley turned to Sheriff Bledsoe. "You fat asshole!" She moved toward him, her face tight with rage. Reflexively he reached for his holster. Shirley kept advancing. "You better get your gun," she said, "'cause I'm fixin' to kick a clot in yo fat ass!"

"Shirley!" Ruth Ann shouted.

"You need to calm her down," Sheriff Bledsoe said. "She's bucking pretty close to a night in jail."

Leonard laid a hand on Shirley's shoulder. "Why don't we let Sheriff Bledsoe tell us what's going on. Sheriff, please tell us what's going on here?"

Shirley pushed Leonard's hand away. "Why don't we all kick his fat ass! He beat our momma with a phone book."

"No, I didn't! And I'm not going to be one more fat ass."

"Tell us what's going on, Sheriff?" Ruth Ann said.

"What's going on is…" He paused and pinched his right side; the pain didn't stop. "What's going on is your mother confessed to killing your father."

They all stared at Sheriff Bledsoe, mouths agape. In perfect unison, they slowly turned their attention to Ida, who stopped crying, raised her head and nodded.

"Ohhhhh!" Shirley yelled and fainted into Leonard's arms.

"Help…me!" Leonard gasped, struggling to keep Shirley upright. "She's too…heavy. Help me!"

Ruth Ann and Leonard took hold of an arm and Sheriff Bledsoe and Robert Earl grabbed a leg.

"Over there," Sheriff Bledsoe said, indicating the cot inside the cell. They carried Shirley, her blue dress dragging across the floor, into the cell and dropped her on the cot.

"I can't believe this," Ruth Ann said. "This is a nightmare." She rushed to her mother and knelt on one knee. "Momma, tell me the truth. Did you hurt Daddy?"

Ida sat up straight and stared at the floor. "I did it. I kilt him. It's all my fault. Fat ass over there don't believe me."

"No, Momma. Don't say that--you didn't do it."

"Dammit!" Ida shouted. "I did it! How many times I gotta tell it! Y'all want me to write it on the wall. Damn!"

"Jesus!" Leonard exclaimed, arms covering his head. "Help us all, Jesus!"

Robert Earl stepped back from Leonard and said, "You fall I'm not catching you."

"Will everybody just relax," Sheriff Bledsoe said. "Now it's obvious to me your mother hasn't killed anyone." He let them chew on that for a moment. "It's obvious to me she's protecting someone else. Perhaps one of her children?"

He stared at Ruth Ann, who stared back. At Leonard, who looked away.

Finally at Robert Earl, who said, "What you looking at me for? I didn't do it. Momma said she did it, I can take her word for it."

"You bastard!" Leonard said. "You know Mother didn't do it."

"Who did, little brother?" Robert Earl shot back. "Who you think killed Daddy, little brother? Huh? Who? Let me tell you what I *know*. I *know* a certain gay, college-educated family member told Daddy to take the scenic route to hell. Daddy started choking and puking, chunking his guts on everybody. Next thing I *know*, Daddy deader than a doorknob."

Leonard lunged at Robert Earl and seized him by the throat, sending them both crashing to the floor. "I'll kill you!" Leonard shouted. "I'll kill you! I'll kill you!"

Sheriff Bledsoe grabbed Leonard around the waist and pulled...Leonard held on. Large veins appeared on Robert Earl's forehead and his eyes rolled back. "Heh...heh...heh...heh...help!"

"Let him go!" Sheriff Bledsoe shouted. "I said let him go!" Ruth Ann came over and tried to push Leonard off but couldn't. Robert Earl started gagging, saliva bubbling out of his mouth. "You heard me, I said let him go!" He released Leonard, pulled out his .357 Magnum, pointed it toward the ceiling and fired. Plaster rained down. "Let him go, or the next one will be in you!"

Leonard immediately let go and stood up, looking rather embarrassed.

The gunfire awoke Shirley. She rose up, looked over at Sheriff Bledsoe, gun in hand, standing over a prostrate Robert Earl, and lay back down.

The pain in Sheriff Bledsoe's right side returned to the center of his stomach; it felt like a vice compressing his innards. "I want all y'all the hell outta here!" he shouted. "Now!"

Robert Earl, massaging his neck, staggered standing up. "He tried to kill me!"

"Out!" Sheriff Bledsoe shouted.

"What about our momma?" Ruth Ann asked.

"Everybody out! Take the one inside the cell with you!"

Ruth Ann took Ida by the hand and pulled her to her feet. "Come on, Momma, let's go." To Leonard: "Get Shirley! Tell her to come over to momma's."

Leonard helped Shirley, looking dazed, to her feet and hurried her out the door.

In the parking lot, Ruth Ann and Ida got into Ruth Ann's Ford Expedition. Leonard got into the Lumina; Shirley into Darlene's Pinto.

Robert Earl stumbled up to the Expedition. "Momma," rubbing his neck, "Leonard choked me. He tried to kill me, Momma."

"Save it for later, Robert Earl," Ruth Ann said. "We're all going over to momma's. We'll talk about it there."

"Will Leonard be there?"

"Yes, Robert Earl. Now go get in your truck and let's go."

Sheriff Bledsoe watched from the doorway, kneading his stomach. "Fat ass," he said to himself. Shirley was no lightweight by any standard and she had the nerve to call him fat ass. *Ha!*

He watched the two cars and one truck pull away and then fade in the distance down Main Street. He went inside, found a phone book and flipped the pages to gastroenterology.

Chapter 8

"I want my car," Ida said. They were a mile away from the jail.

"We'll get it later," Ruth Ann said. "Right now we're going home to sort this thing out."

"There's nothing to sort out. Don't talk to me like I'm your child. Better yet, don't say anything to me at all!" She crossed her arms and stared out the window, giving Ruth Ann her back.

Ruth Ann sighed, knowing it was futile talking to her mother in a foul mood. Yet she desperately wanted to ask did she murder Daddy. And if so, why? The money?

She cut an eye toward Ida. She looked more fragile, smaller, since Daddy's death.

No, her mother would not have killed her husband for money. The whole thing just didn't make any sense.

"Momma, I hate to ask you this. I need to--"

"Then don't!" Ida snapped.

"Are you upset with me, Momma? I'm only trying to help. I know he was your husband, he was also my daddy. Did you do it, Momma? Tell me--I won't tell anyone. Promise. I just need to know."

Ida turned and looked at her for a beat. She snorted and returned her attention to the window. "You know," she said, addressing the passing trees, "you can raise a child the best you know how, live in a respectable manner, teach right and wrong, go to church every now and again…" She shook her head. "Then you realize you've raised a monster. A monster."

"What do you mean? Are you talking about anyone in particular? Me?"

"Did I mention anyone by name?"

"No, you didn't, Momma. Only you and I are here, I'm inclined to believe you're talking about me."

"Ruth Ann, you're inclined to believe whatever the hell you wanna believe."

Ruth Ann almost said something mean. *Take her home and be done with her.* Next time her mother needed something, anything, then she'd better not call her. *Call one of her children who isn't a monster.* Let one of them take her shopping, let one of them drive her to Little Rock when she needed to see the doctor, let one of them loan her money.

She made a quick right onto her mother's street and sped up. After whipping into the driveway and coming to a body-lurching stop, she said, "Here ya go. Home sweet home." As Ida fumbled with the door handle, Ruth Ann put the stick into reverse.

"Can you at least wait till I get out the damn car!"

Gun it, Ruth Ann thought. *Gun it and watch Granny break dance on the concrete.*

She was easing her foot off the brake pedal when she heard a door slam behind her, and then Leonard appeared at Ida's side, helping her out the car.

"Come on, Mother," he said. "I'm here. I'll take care of you."

Now Ida found it extremely difficult moving a foot. "My dear Leonard," she said, "I could always depend on you."

Ruth Ann wanted to scream. "Any damn day," she mumbled.

"What was that, Ruth Ann?" Leonard asked. She didn't respond. "Aren't you coming in?"

"No, Leonard. Wal-Mart is having a sale on monster food, hate to miss it."

Shirley walked up to the car. "How's Momma doing? Is she all right?"

"She's going to be fine," Leonard said.

"You think we should call a doctor?" Shirley asked.

"Doctor Frankenstein," Ruth Ann said.

Leonard and Ida, arms around each other, walked toward the house. "Leonard," Ida said when they were at the door, "I know you had nothing to do with it."

"Yes, Mother."

Ruth Ann and Shirley exchanged puzzled glances. "Shirley," Ruth Ann said, "could you back up and let me out."

"Aren't you coming in?"

"No. Momma's in a I-only-care-for-my-son mood."

"Come on, Ruth Ann. She's having a hard time. We need to show her our support. She's so upset she's confessing to a murder she didn't commit. You know she didn't kill Daddy."

"Where's Robert Earl?"

"He kept going. Come on."

Ruth Ann reluctantly stepped out and followed Shirley to the one-story, four-bedroom, red brick house. The black barrel her daddy had converted to a barbecue grill lay on its side in the front yard, a heap of ash spilling out from it.

Ruth Ann wondered why no one had picked it up and put it in the shed. Her daddy's late-model Ford truck was parked in the open bay garage. It was dusty. If her daddy were alive, you would not have found a speck of dust on it.

Ruth Ann struggled with the grill. "Shirley, help me with this." Shirley joined her and they uprighted the grill. "Where's Shane?" Ruth Ann said, rolling the grill to the side of the house. "He should be seeing to things around here." She slapped the dust off her hands.

Shirley held the front door open. "Come on, Ruth Ann. Don't worry about that now."

Inside, Leonard was sitting in her daddy's favorite chair, reading a newspaper, feet propped up on the table, as if he'd assumed the role of man of the house.

"Where's Momma?" Ruth Ann asked him.

"In the kitchen."

"In the kitchen? Doing what?"

"Cooking."

"Cooking!" Ruth Ann and Shirley exclaimed. Shirley started for the kitchen.

Leonard put the paper down. "Leave her be, Shirley. Mother is under a lot of stress right now. If cooking takes her mind off her troubles, then let her cook."

"Maybe you're right," Shirley said. "What's she cooking?"

"I don't know. Whatever it is I'm going to eat it." He motioned Shirley to come closer. Whispering: "You, too, Ruth Ann."

He grabbed the remote and clicked up the volume on the television. "Don't you see what's happening?" he asked, looking from Shirley to Ruth Ann. They shook their heads. "Mother thinks one of us killed Daddy, and she's blaming herself. Imagine the anguish she's experiencing now."

"She told you this?" Ruth Ann asked.

"No, she did not. It's the only thing makes sense. We know she didn't do it."

"You really think she believes one of us did it?" Shirley said.

"Correction," Ruth Ann said. "She thinks one of us among you, Robert Earl and me did it. She exonerated Leonard outside, remember?"

"Well, yes," Leonard said. "Mother knows I didn't arrive in time to plot and execute a murder. Whoever did it was already here."

"You can tell her to scratch my name off her list," Ruth Ann said. "I didn't do it."

Leonard said, "She doesn't know exactly who did it, but she suspects one of her children. You can't blame her for thinking that. Who else other than a family member stood to gain from Daddy's death? Mother is suffering now."

Ruth Ann snorted. "Hello! She's not the only one suffering. I'm suffering, too, but I'm not pointing a finger at anyone."

"Leonard," Ida called from the kitchen.

"Yes, Mother," Leonard replied in a tone that rubbed Ruth Ann's nerves.

"Would you like an apple pie?"

"Oh, Mother, apple pie would be delightful."

"This is outrageous," Ruth Ann said. "She's totally forgotten she has three other children. What's she going to do when you go back to Chicago, Leonard? By the way, when are you going back?"

Leonard crossed his arms and leaned back in the chair. "Ruth Ann, am I detecting a tinge of jealousy?"

"Yes!"

"If she gives me a slice of pie, I'm fine," Shirley said.

"For your information, Ruth Ann," Leonard said, "I've decided to stay here until Mother comes to terms with what happened."

"That might take years," Ruth Ann said.

"I doubt it. I'm in for the duration. It's the least I can do."

"What about your job?" Ruth Ann said. "And whatshisface?"

"His name is Victor Fields, and our relationship and my job are secure."

"Leonard, the possibility the money will be split four ways instead of five if one of the family committed the murder didn't weigh on your hasty decision to stay, did it?"

"Please! My mother's welfare is my only concern."

"We're her children, too," Ruth Ann said. "Believe it or not, Leonard, we love her just as much as you do. We--Shirley, Robert Earl and I--stayed here when you ran off to Chicago. It's not fair she exclude us."

"Exclude you from what, Ruth Ann? Other than the barbecue, when was the last time you visited Mother?" He waited for a reply. None came. "Mother needs a little down time. Why don't you and Shirley come back later, after she has rested?"

"Negro, please!" Ruth Ann said, fed up with this conversation. Leonard said something, but she ignored him and walked into the kitchen.

Ida stood next to the sink, beating batter in a bowl with a wooden spoon. A boiling pot covered every eye on the stove. The smell of baked fish drifted from the oven. Sarah Vaughn's voice emanated from a transistor radio on the refrigerator.

"Momma, can I give you a hand?"

Ida did an about face, giving Ruth Ann her back again. The rhythmic thump thump thump thump from the bowl grew louder.

"Momma, if you need something, or if you need me to do anything, then call me. You know my number, don't you?" Of course she knew the number…thump thump thump thump thump…"I guess I'll be going now, Momma. Call me."…thump thump thump thump thump…

Ruth Ann turned on her high heels and headed for the front door. "I'm outta here," she said. "Shirley, please move your car!" The screen door slammed before Shirley could respond.

"Ruth Ann, hold up," Shirley said, catching up with her. "What's the matter?"

Ruth Ann turned, started to speak…couldn't.

Shirley embraced her. "It'll pass, honey," holding her tight, rubbing her back. "It'll pass. She's upset. We're all upset. I miss Daddy, and I know you do, too."

Ruth Ann had wanted to rid herself of her family, to get as far away from them as possible…Shirley had caught her off guard. She buried her face between Shirley's large breasts.

"She ignored me!" Ruth Ann blurted, and started crying. "Sh-sh-she acted like I wasn't even there."

87

Shirley kissed her forehead. "It's okay, Ruth Ann. It's okay." Shirley wiped away Ruth Ann's tears with her hand, and brought her face close to hers. Looking her straight in the eye, she said, "Ruth Ann, remember this. Whatever happens, no matter what, we're family." Bringing her face even closer, their noses almost touching: "I'll always love you, Ruth Ann. Always."

Ruth Ann looked away, unable to maintain eye contact. "Thanks, Shirley." She stepped back. "I better go. Lester is probably hungry."

"He can't cook for himself?"

Ruth Ann laughed. "Lester has trouble dialing Dominos. Men, what are they good for?"

"You got that right. I can't begin to tell you the trouble Eric and I are having."

Ruth Ann's shoulder jerked, as if someone had sneaked up and grabbed her. *What have I done?*

Eric, his name throbbed in her head like a toothache. Why had she betrayed her baby sister? Her only sister. Shirley, sweet Shirley. Fat, loveable, sensitive, puppy-dog eyes, give-you-the-shirt-off-her-back Shirley.

What have I done?

"What?" Shirley said. "Why are you looking at me like that?"

"I love you, Shirley, I really do. I might not act like I do, but I do. It might not seem like I do...I do! Really. Cross my heart, hope to die. Honest!" Aware she was groveling, but couldn't stop. "I really do. Always! Till I die. No matter what happens, or what somebody says, remember I love you. No man could come between…I mean, even if a man did come between us, it wouldn't mean anything. Wouldn't mean a damn thing!"

"Ruth Ann, relax. I know. Trust me, I know."

"Huh?" Ruth Ann gasped, heart skipping beats. "You know?"

"Yes, I do."

Ruth Ann started to kneel, but they were standing on concrete and she was wearing a dress. "Please forgive me, Shirley. I didn't mean for it to go as far as it did. You gotta believe me!"

Shirley gave her an odd look. "What the hell are you talking about?"

Ruth Ann backed up to the Expedition and leaned on it for support. Woozy and nauseous. She'd almost stepped out on a greased limb. "Lester! I was talking about Lester, Shirley. I let our relationship go too far."

"Ruth Ann, you're married to the man."

"Yes, you're right. I better get back to him." She hopped into the Expedition and started looking for the keys.

"In the ignition," Shirley said.

"Oh, yeah. See ya, Shirley. I love you!" She started the engine.

"Wait a minute! Let me move Darlene's car out the…" Before she could finish, Ruth Ann drove across the lawn and then sped off down the street, in the wrong direction from her house.

Chapter 9

Robert Earl lay on the couch, a damp towel wrapped around his neck. He'd come home an hour ago, hurting, his ego more bruised than his neck. His weirdo baby brother had actually gotten the better of him, an ex Marine, a real man.

A minute there, on the floor with Leonard's thumbs pressing his goiter deeper than it was designed to go, he thought it was over. A few seconds more and he would have lost consciousness. *Choked to death by a fag!* The thought made his neck hurt even more.

Leonard couldn't confront him man-to-man. No, he had to dive in the air, catch him off guard. If he'd been expecting the move, he would have caught Leonard midair, whirled him around a couple of times, lifted him overhead and body-slammed him.

He adjusted the towel around his neck, a wicked smile under his bushy moustache, the imagined sound of Leonard's body bouncing on the jail floor echoing in his head.

And where's Estafay? When he needed her she was nowhere to be found. His neck needed a massage.

As his daddy used to say, "A woman ain't good..." He couldn't complete the thought. His daddy never liked Estafay, and hadn't mind saying so, even to Robert Earl's face. No one had a better reason than he to kill the rotten, tightwad so-and-so. His daddy had never given Estafay a chance, not once.

An ugly memory played in his mind. He shook his head, trying to recall something more pleasant, but the memory continued...

Honorably discharged from the Marine Corps, he'd returned home with his bride of two weeks, Estafay. His family was sitting on the front porch when he and she got out of the cab.

He strutted up to the porch in his dress blues, Estafay a couple of steps behind, his chest puffed up, head held high, arms swinging six inches to the front and three to the rear, as they'd taught him in boot camp.

He could not have asked for a better day, early April, a light breeze, the afternoon sun hitting his bronze buttons and patent leather shoes just right.

He stopped a few feet short of the porch and said, "Momma, Daddy, Shirley, Ruth Ann, Leonard, I'd like y'all to meet my wife, Estafay. She's from Oceanside, California."

Estafay nodded hello.

A long, awkward minute they all stared at Estafay, looking her up and down. And then...his head ached just thinking about it...his daddy shook his head, looked down at the floor and shook his head some more.

"Boy," his daddy said, "all those beautiful women in California--millions of em! On a beach you can throw a stick in a crowd, knock two centerfolds upside the head. And you come back here with a goddamn orangutan!"

They--Ruth Ann, Shirley, Leonard--burst out laughing; not hee hee and haw haw, but full blown gut-holding laughter. Ruth Ann dropped to all fours, laughing so hard she started coughing and crying.

Robert Earl clutched his fist, unconsciously, as he had done that day, years ago, when his family had laughed in his and Estafay's face.

He'd wanted to kill his daddy, put his hands around his scrawny throat and choke the life out of him. If Estafay hadn't whispered in his ear, "Let's go somewhere else, honey," he might have done just that.

Estafay practically had to carry him back to the motel, three miles away, holding him up by the arm, urging him onward each step. Tears clouded his vision and he stumbled forward as if he were drunk.

Estafay walked in carrying grocery sacks in each arm, overlooking her ailing husband. He watched her put the sacks on the table and stock groceries.

Yes, Estafay was a tad on the frumpy side, more weight on the bottom than atop. The left side of her face was darker than the right, a color line zigzagging down the middle. Her large brown eyes were askew, the right a bit higher than the left, which conveyed a curious scowl.

Large nose, open-faced nostrils. Bad teeth, the uppers in exceptionally poor condition, two of which protruded out of her mouth even when closed.

She noticed him. "What happened?" she said, coming near.

Her forehead rather expansive, the hairline bordering the top of her head. He wondered how she would look in braid extensions instead of the unflattering style she favored, her short, auburn-colored hair, a tint of orange at the roots, parted in the middle and brushed down.

"What happened?" she asked again.

"The fag choked me!"

Estafay sat beside him, gently removed the towel and tenderly rubbed his neck.

She ain't Halle Berry. Or Rihanna. But she ain't a dang orangutan!

"Does it hurt?"

He grimaced. "Only when I exhale."

"Why did he choke you?"

"Momma confessed to killing Daddy. I said something, can't remember what. Next thing I know the fag snuck up behind me and started choking me."

"Your mother confessed?"

"Sure did."

"She didn't do it."

"She said she did. Why would she say she did if she didn't?"

Estafay rewrapped the towel around his neck. "It's just bruised. Should feel better in the morning. If not, we'll go to Doctor Springer. You want a couple of aspirins?"

"I've already taken two."

"Did Sheriff Bledsoe arrest your mother?"

"No. After Leonard and me got into it he ran us all out. A good thing 'cause I was fixin' to wax Leonard's ass real shiny."

"There's no reason to be profane."

"I'm sorry."

"We need to pray. Ask the Lord for strength, help us through this crisis."

"Crisis?"

She gave him a stern look, eyes squinting, almost lining up evenly. "Yes, this is a crisis. Get on your knees."

"Honey, my neck."

"At least close your eyes."

He did, though reluctantly. He didn't like Estafay's impromptu sanctimonious exultations, and he certainly didn't enjoy joining in. He'd gone along with all of it--eight or nine different religious conversions--had even accompanied her to several revivals, not liking one bit all the chanting and shaking and shouting going on.

He opened his eyes.

Estafay knelt on the floor a few feet before him, rocking back and forth, hands clamped together, eyes clenched shut. She didn't have a clue how gruesome she looked when she prayed.

"Ohhhhh Lord!" she shouted, and Robert Earl jumped. She held her hands overhead, as if waiting her chance to wave at a football game. He knew what was coming next, had seen it a thousand times, so he closed his eyes again. Estafay was convulsing, shaking harder than an overloaded washing machine. He heard a thud and forced himself to take a peek. She rolled on the floor, ankle-length white dress bunched up around her waist, revealing white cotton panties.

Rolled away from the coffee table…and then back again. Another thud. *Can't she feel her head hitting the table?* Apparently not. He closed his eyes again, tighter.

Several thuds later she stopped. Robert Earl waited for her to say amen, and then he mumbled amen and opened his eyes.

"Did the Lord speak to you?" she asked, rubbing a spot on her head.

God, he hated when she asked him that. He nodded.

"He spoke to me, too," Estafay said. "What did He tell you?"

"Uh…He told me to pray more often."

Estafay stared at him for a beat. "Give Him the glory! You definitely should pray more than you do. He told me your mother didn't kill your father."

"Really?" Estafay shot him an icy look. He knew not to question her spiritual insights. If the Lord told her something, she'd explained a million times, then the least he could do was listen. "Uh…" searching for the right words, "…uh…did He happen to mention who did?"

Estafay stood up and brushed off her dress. "Yes, He did."

Robert Earl waited.

Estafay said nothing, sat down in the wicker chair and picked up her Bible from an end table.

Ninety-nine times out of a hundred, Robert Earl very well knew but rarely voiced, Estafay's spiritual messages were dead wrong. Once she'd been directed by divinity to invest all their meager savings in a venture called CowPatty.com, which attempted to sell manure via the Internet. *What a stink!*

"Well," he said, "who do you think did it?"

"I don't think, Robert, I know! The Lord told me."

"Okay. Who did the Lord say did it?"

"Ruth Ann," barely audible.

"Excuse me, I didn't hear you."

"Ruth Ann," almost a shout.

Robert Earl shook his head. "Uh-uh. She's too scary. A spider will send her into a conniption. Ruth Ann--are you sure?"

Estafay opened her Bible. "The Lord has spoken," she said and began to read.

Chapter 10

Eric took off his wet clothes and hung them on the shower rod. Though Shirley had doused him an hour ago, his legs wouldn't stop shaking. Stark naked he sat on the rim of the tub. He grabbed his right leg with both hands and tried to still the shaking.

Tap water! I just knew it was hot grease!

If Shirley had had an inkling the woman in question was Ruth Ann, then it would have been hot acid. His legs started shaking more than before, thighs jiggling like Jell-O.

He imagined himself in the hospital, burned head to toe, his skin shiny with butter or whatever the hell doctors applied to burn victims.

The doorbell rang. He got up and tiptoed to the front door and looked in the peephole. Darlene. He opened the door wide. Darlene gasped and stepped back. "Come on in, Darlene," he invited, smiling.

Darlene looked stricken, not knowing where to rest her eyes. "I-I-I…." She quickly turned and skipped down the four steps, dismissively flipping her hand. "You should be ashamed," she said. "Ashamed!"

Eric scoped the neighborhood. No one in sight except Mr. Joyner sitting on his porch.

He stepped outside. "What you come over here for? You know Shirley gone."

She stopped, turned, flipped her braids back with a long fingernail and said, "For your bee's wax, I came to give you a message." Not once did she look at him, choosing to stare up at the sun, blazing hot and bright. "I'm going to tell Shirley what you doing."

"Tell it, smell it, go downtown and sell it! What message?"

"Duane called and told me to tell you Sheriff Bledsoe is looking for you."

"Looking for me. For what?"

Darlene turned on her heels, braids fanning out behind her, and started toward her mobile home, only a few yards away.

In her doorway she stopped and looked him straight in the eye, a big smile on her face. "What rhymes with attempted rape?" she said, and slammed the door.

Eric went inside mumbling to himself, "Tempted fate...jail bait...suicide date...What the hell she talking about?"

Ruth Ann!

Sheriff Bledsoe thought he'd attempted to...He couldn't finish the thought; the words were too ridiculous to associate with his name.

Eric Barnes and attempted rape in the same sentence--Ha! Women attacked him, not the other way around. Everyone knew that. Everyone except Sheriff Bledsoe, or he wouldn't be looking for him.

In the bedroom he put on khaki shorts and a blue shirt. He checked his billfold. Two dollars. No better time than now to go to Little Rock and visit Uncle June. Stay a week or two.

What if Shirley got her share of the money while he was piddling around in Little Rock? She might put her ass in a bag, claim he deserted her and not give him a dime. With women you really needed to be there during the pivotal period, the interval between check deposited and check cleared.

Another disastrous possibility came to mind: Shirley finding out about him and Ruth Ann. He gulped. *Shit!* If that happened, not only would he lose a chance at the big money, he would have to change his name to Eric Burns.

A long while he sat on the bed, chewing his thumb. Finally the answer struck him. "Yeah!" He would call Ruth Ann and demand she set the record straight. If she refused, he would threaten to tell

Lester and Shirley everything--the cheap motels, the fantastic oral sex, the little trick she did with ice cubes.

Everythang!

He slid his feet into sandals and hurried next door to Darlene's to use the phone.

"Hell no!" Darlene said, shaking her head. "You must think I'm a lollipop, a reusable sucker. I politely came over and delivered you a message, something I didn't have to do, and you opened the door naked. Before that I needed to gain some weight. 'Narrow-ass, don't come back to my house no more.' Go use somebody else's phone."

"Aw girl, you know I was just joking with you. Go get the phone and stop playing." He showed her his best smile. "If you don't I'll tell Shirley how I really feel about you."

She slammed the door in his face. He was taking the steps when the door opened again.

"Here," Darlene said, putting the phone on the porch. "Use it out here. Don't make a long distance call on my phone."

"Is Jamaica long distance?" She slammed the door again.

Ruth Ann's phone rang and rang. He wondered if she had also gone to the jail.

He started to hang up when someone answered. "Hello." A man's voice.

In falsetto voice, Eric said, "Is Mrs. Ruth Ann there? Can she come to the phone?"

"Who is this?"

101

Before Eric could respond, Paul rode up on his bike. "Daddy, can I ride my bike to the store?"

Eric covered the mouthpiece: "I don't give a damn!" Resuming falsetto voice: "Linda."

"She's not here. Would you like to leave a--wait a minute, that's probably her coming in now. Hold on for a sec, I'll go see."

Lester, Eric thought, what a wimp. "Hey, Lester, what gives good head and has a mole on her tail? Got you stumped, Hot Lips? Here's another clue, the answer rhymes with *your wife*." He laughed.

"Hello," Ruth Ann said.

"It's me, Eric."

"Oh, Linda. What a surprise. How you doing?"

"You need to call Sheriff Bledsoe and set him straight. Today. Right now!"

"Girl, you don't know how surprised I am to hear from you. It's a shock, I tell you, a real shock. I don't know what to say."

"What? Is Lester nearby?"

"You got that right. How's your mother--"

"Tell Lester to move his ass!"

"--doing? Good. I'm glad to hear she's doing fine."

"I need to see you so we can straighten this--"

"No thanks."

"Tell Lester go outside and play with hisself."

"Girl, I couldn't do that." Eric heard a door shut in the background, then Ruth Ann said, "Why the fuck you calling my house?"

"Sheriff Bledsoe's looking for me. He thinks I tried to rape you."

"Not my problem," and hung up. Eric called right back and she picked up on the first ring. "What is your problem? What is your problem? It's over! Why can't you understand that? It's over. O-V-E-R! Understand? Stop calling my house!"

"Uh-huh. Guess I'll tell Shirley and Lester about our little four-year fling. Wonder how Lester will react when I describe the birthmark on your yingying. You don't think he might try to off hisself again, do you?" He paused to let that sink in.

Adopting Alex Trebek's voice, he said, "Sorry, Lester, though you gave the correct answer to Who Gives The Best Head West of the Mississippi, you should've put the answer in the form of a question. *Who* Is Ruth Ann, my wife?"

"I will kill you, you sick sonofabitch!" Ruth Ann hissed. "I swear I will!"

"Yeah, I know you will. Let's not forget Shirley. You remember her, don't you? You have any idea how much she looks up to you? Always talking Ruth Ann did this, Ruth Ann did that. She wants to lose weight and be just like you one day. Skinny and scandalous. It'll break her heart when I tell her the skills dear Ruthie has with a string of beads."

Ruth Ann laughed. "You're so full of shit...so full of shit! You had me going with the threat to tell Lester. You and I both know you're not telling Shirley a damn thing. You do and she'll stomp your ass a hole in the ground."

This wasn't going as he expected. Yes, she was right, no way in this lifetime would he tell Shirley a word of him and another woman. He tried to think of a snotty rejoinder. "Uh…"

"Listen, Eric. You leave me alone, I'll leave you alone. This is not necessary."

"Are you going to call Sheriff Bledsoe and clear my name?"

"I'll call him. But don't ever call here again! Is that understood?"

"No problem. Just one more thing…meet me at the motel one last time. Please! Meet me one last time."

"Are you crazy? Seriously, are you crazy? I said it was over and you can't comprehend the fact. It's over, Eric. Get it through your thick head!"

Just then Shirley drove Darlene's car into the yard. "Gotta go," he said, and hung up.

"Who were you talking to?" Shirley asked.

"I was trying to get hold of Sheriff Bledsoe. What happened with your mother?"

Darlene stepped outside. "Shirley, is everything all right?"

Shirley walked up the steps and handed her the keys. "Thanks, Darlene. Let's go inside and I'll tell you about it."

"Tell me about it," Eric said. "Tell me about it now. Is she charged with murder? Not that I want her to be--you know we need the money."

Shirley and Darlene both gave him a look. They stepped inside and once again Darlene slammed the door in his face.

Chapter 11

Leonard and his mother sat opposite each other at the kitchen table, a half-eaten apple pie between them.

"It's for the best," Leonard said, wiping his mouth with a napkin. "They'll only serve as a painful reminder. I also think we should sell the truck."

Ida groaned. "Your daddy loved his truck. Each morning he got up at five o'clock and washed it, even when it was raining." She sighed. "His clothes, I don't think he could stand someone wearing them."

"Mother…Daddy is…" *What's the right word here?* "He's at rest. He wouldn't want you keeping his stuff when doing so caused you more sorrow. Trust me, okay? I'll handle everything."

Ida looked at him through puffy, red eyes. "I…" she started, couldn't finish.

Leonard crossed to her and hugged her. "This will pass, Mother. It'll pass in time." He held her for a while. "Come on, let's go into the living room and watch something funny." He helped her to her feet. "There's a comedy show on BET I know you'll like."

"Is it on satellite?"

"No. Not in Chicago, it isn't."

"We don't have satellite. Your daddy said cable is cheaper." She sat on the couch and Leonard couldn't tell if she or it sighed.

"Anything in particular you'd like to watch?"

Ida didn't respond, just sat there staring blankly. He channel-surfed and stopped at an *Everybody Hates Chris* rerun. "This is funny. Have you seen it?"

She shook her head. "Turn to *The Discovery Channel*. Your daddy loved to watch it."

On *The Discovery Channel*, three lions chased a boar into a hole. "You sure you want to watch this?"

"Yes." Leonard started to leave the room when she said, "I thought you were going to watch with me."

"Yes, sure, Mother."

The lions took turns inspecting the hole into which the boar escaped. Then, squealing for dear life, the boar shot out, only to be instantly pounced upon and seized by the throat by one of the lions. The feast began.

Leonard thought he might be sick.

"Leonard, you know he loved you."

"Who?" Leonard said, unable to pry his eyes away from the television.

"Your daddy. He loved you. He just couldn't say it. Men like your daddy have a hard time saying I love you. He loved all his children."

"Who did he love the--" He caught himself.

"He loved you all. He and Ruth Ann were extremely close. Ruth Ann has a way with men. Always has, even when she was a little girl. You can't blame your father."

"I'm not blaming him, Mother. I was just curious. Speaking of curious..." Venturing into uncharted territory: his mother and he had never discussed his sexual orientation, and now seemed a good time as any to broach the subject.

"Mother..." The words were too hard.

She looked him straight in the eye. "How did he feel about your being gay?"

She couldn't have put it more bluntly than that. "I know how he felt, Mother. I was curious how you felt."

She seemed to stiffen right before him. Perspiration slid down his back.

She returned her attention to the lions, dozing, while hyenas and buzzards squabbled over the boar's remains.

She's going to leave me hanging? He regretted initiating the subject.

A commercial for Viagra came on and she said, "I'd rather you married, had children." His face flushed with heat. "What I don't understand I don't judge, fret over. All I know is you're my son, I love you and I'll love you if you grew an extra head."

Tears rained down her face to her black dress, doubtless the same dress she'd worn to the funeral. Guilt cascaded over him in waves; he wanted to go to her, tell her he loved her, tell her he's normal *and* gay, but he didn't. He just sat there, with each wave of guilt almost drowning him.

How could he possibly say Mother, it's not your fault, it's not Daddy's fault; hell, it's not anyone's fault. He was who he was because he was who he was. *It's that simple.* And nothing in the world could change that.

He stood up, his stiff knees popping. "Mother, if you'll excuse me, I better start packing Daddy's stuff away."

He started to leave when she said, "Leonard?"

Please, no more. Please! "Yes, Mother." *Why does being gay demand explanation?*

"When you're finished, would you go get Shane?"

"Shane? Isn't he with Ruth Ann?"

"I don't think so. Ruth Ann would have brought him back by now."

"Sure, Mother. I'll go get him as soon as I finish packing."

"Thank you, Leonard. He's at the Boy Scout camp."

"Shane's a scout? I didn't know that."

"He's not a scout."

Something told Leonard to exit the room now, but he didn't. "Mother, if he's not a scout, what's he doing at a Boy Scout camp?"

"When the scouts are not having campouts, he goes up there and hangs around."

Hangs around? "Mother, when he's hanging around up there, what does he eat?"

"Whatever he hunts." After a pause: "He eats berries, too. He knows which are poisonous."

This was sounding more bizarre by the minute. Go, a voice told him. "Uh…Mother, what does he hunt with?" *Please don't say his hands.*

"A bow. A crossbow."

"Who gave him that?"

"His daddy."

"Lester? You allowed him to keep it?"

"Shane has more sense than people give him credit. He's slow in some areas, a whiz in others. He can name every player who ever played for the Dallas Cowboys. He also knows all the players on the Arkansas Razorback football and basketball teams."

Great, Leonard thought. *Invaluable knowledge in the job market.*

"Call his name when you go get him. Otherwise he might mistake you for a…" She drifted off, the carnivores on the television suddenly more interesting than their conversation.

He waited, hoping she would tell him what he might be mistaken for, but she didn't speak.

He crossed to the front door and looked outside. Pitch dark, save for streetlights and lights in neighbors' homes. He imagined himself in the woods, in complete darkness, stumbling around and calling Shane, then--swoosh!--an arrow in his chest.

"You know, Mother, I haven't seen Shane in what, ten, eleven years? I wouldn't know him if I bumped into him. Nor would he know me."

"Why you call his name when you go up there. Tell him it's all right, he can come home and tell him he can bring Kenny G with him."

"Kenny G? He has--I thought Kenny G was buried alongside Daddy."

Ida shook her head. Leonard sensed her annoyance with the conversation.

"Shane," she said, "grabbed Kenny G and ran away. Robert Earl tried to catch him. Shane's ten times faster than Robert Earl." She said this with a mixture of pride and admiration. Her emotionally challenged grandson could outrun her mentally challenged son. Any matriarch would be proud.

"Mother, when did all this happen?"

111

"I'm tired, son. I'll rest better with Shane here. He's out there all alone and he hasn't a friend in the world. When he was just a baby, Ruth Ann brought him here and dropped him off. Just left him. That was wrong. Wrong! Your daddy understood him, and he loved your daddy. He's hurting, out there alone, all by himself."

He has Kenny G and a crossbow. What more does a boy need?

"Get some rest, Mother. I'll go get him first thing in the morning. Promise. You just concentrate on getting some rest."

She rested her head on the back of the couch, eyes open, staring at the ceiling.

Entering his mother's bedroom, Leonard wondered how she would react when he lied Shane couldn't be found. Of course she would be upset.

Yet he'd be even more upset traipsing in the woods in search of a mentally challenged boy with a crossbow. Two funerals in one week, the last his, in a special designed coffin to accommodate the arrow sticking out of his chest.

The bedroom hadn't changed since the last time he'd seen it, a decade ago. Same queen-size bed, covered with a purple quilt and two pink pillows. Same faded picture of Martin Luther King Jr. above the headboard. Same rust-colored shag rug on the floor, the only room in the house with carpet.

Same small black-and-white television sitting atop a rustic black trunk at the foot of the bed. Same oak chiffonier near the door that blocked the light switch. He squeezed his hand between it and the wall and flipped on the light.

So many memories here and most of them unpleasant. The large dent in the far wall occurred when Shirley, seventeen-years-old, threw an iron at him, twelve-years-old, and missed. The black file cabinet next to the bed contained his father's extensive porno magazine collection.

Leonard remembered the day his father called him, at the tender age of nine, to this very room.

"Close the door, boy!" his father had said. Leonard had hesitated, not liking the look on his father's face, the stench of Bacardi Rum in the air. "I wanna show you something."

His father had frightened him, had always frightened him, with his deep voice and piercing stares; and there Leonard stood in his father's bedroom, his father attired only in boxer shorts, his skin oily with rum. Everyone else had gone to the movies.

"Sit down, boy! You act like you scared of me. You scared of me?"

"No, sir."

"Yes, you are. Look at ya, trembling like a pecker in the projects. Ain't no reason to be scared--I ain't gonna hurt you. You my son...*my son!* No son of mine should be hanging with women folk all the time." He moved to the file cabinet and took out a magazine. "Look at this here, boy, and tell me what you see."

Leonard had seen nude women in magazines before; pornography wasn't what rendered him speechless, made his underarms itch. What caused apoplexy was the way his father, the man who had never once called him by name, never called him to his room, was acting, as if his life depended on his son's ability to identify a vagina in a magazine.

He pressed the magazine into Leonard's face. "What you see, boy? Huh? Ain't it the prettiest thing you've ever seen?"

Leonard started crying. Tears dripped down his face and one landed on the magazine, a wet spot on the woman's breast.

His father turned angry. "Look at ya, you…you sissy!" He rolled up the magazine and whacked Leonard over the head with it. "Get out of here! Get the fuck outta here!"

Leonard shook his head, remembering he had tried to flee his father but couldn't get the door open fast enough, and his father had kicked him and whacked him over the head with the magazine several times.

Leonard sat on the bed, packing his father's belongings now a laborious task he lacked the strength.

Another contradiction, he thought, I hate him and I love him. He stared at the faded poster of Marcus Garvey in full regalia on the closet door. His father had admired Marcus Mosiah Garvey Jr., one of the few men he regarded favorably, and the only man whose full name he remembered.

He wouldn't call me by my first name if you paid him.

114

The closet door was halfway open. Leonard saw his father's well-worn Stacy Adams shoes in the shadows. Next to those was what looked to him a yellow cereal box.

Doesn't make sense. Cereal in the closet?

He got up, turned on the closet light…and stopped. The word Poison embossed in bold, black letters atop the box, next to a skull and crossbones. Leonard, fingers trembling, picked it up and read the front label.

Juggernaut Gopher Bait.

Chapter 12

Out the bedroom window Ruth Ann could see her Ford Expedition in the driveway. The note on that big boy was over five hundred dollars a month; she didn't know the exact amount because she didn't pay it. Lester did.

He also paid the mortgage, thirteen hundred plus a month. And the utility bills, and the grocery bill and her weekly allowance, ninety-five dollars, the one expenditure she knew the exact amount.

If Eric told Lester about their affair, Lester might walk. She could live alone, she thought as she lay in bed, but couldn't live with Lester taking anything away from her house, not even a single piece of furniture.

The thought of losing this house, *her* house, a two-story Spanish Colonial, was too painful to contemplate.

Regardless what Lester might claim in divorce court, she was the one who searched day and night for this plot of land, she who assisted the architect with the design, she who picked out the furniture, selecting only the best, and she who kept every room clean and orderly.

Even if the judge granted me everything, Lester would have to continue paying the bills.

She grabbed Teddy, a white teddy bear with blue eyes, and curled up in a fetal position. She imagined Lester taking the witness stand, the corners of his mouth turned down...and that would be all she wrote. One look at Lester's mouth and the judge would grant him the whole shebang.

"This is terrible," she whispered to Teddy. "Terrible!"

The bedroom door opened and Lester entered, wearing his work clothes, tan cotton shirt and pants.

At a distance Lester was a handsome man. Trim. Dark chocolate-colored skin. A small afro kept neatly trimmed. Up close...well, by no means could Lester be considered ugly, especially if the focus centered on his nose and eyes.

Who can do that? Ruth Ann wondered. *Who can look in a person's face and not look at the mouth?*

"Ruthie, honey," Lester said, "is everything okay?"

Ruth Ann studied his mouth as he spoke. Perfect in size and shape, but a pinkish-white circle covered it. *At least he has the sense to forego a moustache.*

She looked away. "I'm fine," though feeling the urge to cry.

He came closer and she could smell the Polo cologne he favored. "I'm here for you, Ruthie. I'll always be here for you." He sat on the bed. She hugged Teddy tighter. He leaned over and buried his face in her hair. "Forever."

This made her want to cry even more. "I know you will."

"I love you, Ruthie," the words tickling her neck.

She knew she should say I love you, too, but couldn't force herself to utter the words. In fact, she hadn't told him those words in a long time, though Lester said them daily.

Lester released her and reared back, feigning astonishment. "Baby, you're s'posed to say I love you, too, Lester."

Ruth Ann closed her eyes. "You know I do."

"It would be nice to hear you say it every now and again, you know. I hate to whine, but it would really be nice to hear you say it."

Ruth Ann opened her eyes and studied the window curtains. Priscillas, gray trim. She remembered the day she bought them and hung them up.

"Watch my lips," Lester said.

Has he lost his mind? His lips were the last thing in the world she wanted to look at.

Lester touched his lips, actually put a finger on the mark, the mark that couldn't be washed off, a permanent reminder of his idiocy, his stupidity, his infidelity. "Come on, honey, watch my lips."

Yes, he's lost his mind!

"I…love…you…Lester," he said.

Completely!

"You and I together. I…love…you."

Ruth Ann mouthed the words.

"A little louder," Lester insisted. "I…love…you."

"I love you," she said, a whisper.

"Was that so hard?"

Yes!

"Give me a kiss, honey," Lester said, puckering his lips.

Will this madness never end? she wondered, staring at his mouth, which now looked like an atrophied cow teat. She sat up and gave him a quick peck on the cheek. "I'm sorry, Lester, I haven't brushed my teeth. Give me a minute."

Inside the bathroom she locked the door, sat fully clothed on the commode, covered her mouth with both hands and sobbed, not certain for whom she was crying. Her daddy? Shane? Lester?

There was a knock on the door. "Ruthie?" Lester said.

She grunted in response.

"You okay?"

"Uh-huh."

She didn't love Lester. He was a good man, she couldn't deny that. He loved her, truly loved her, and practically bent over backward attempting to make her happy. Still, she did not love him. Yet she needed him.

What made the situation so unfair, so damn frustrating: she needed him. Holding my breath in an out-house, she thought, desperately needing oxygen but can't stomach the smell.

If not for that damn mark, she thought as she dabbed her eyes with tissue, I possibly could love him. She stood up and flushed the toilet, and then a thought hit her: once she got her share of the money she wouldn't need Lester. She wouldn't need him at all; she would be able to take care of herself, and even if she lost her house, she would have enough money to buy another one.

The first time that day she smiled, thinking everything might work out. Lester, after a fashion, would find someone else, forget all about her. And she--her smile turned into a grin--would be free to find a man whom she could love, a man who wouldn't foolishly burn his mouth.

She opened the door, and Lester stood there in the hallway.

"You okay?"

She nodded, avoiding his eyes.

"Come on," taking her hand. "You need some rest."

He led her to the bedroom and she lay down.

"Where's Teddy?" she asked him.

Lester retrieved Teddy from the floor. "Here he is. Get some rest, Ruthie." He sat on the edge of the bed looking at her.

What's he waiting on?

As if reading her mind, Lester said, "Ruthie, before I go, may I have a hug?"

"Yes, Lester," and didn't move. Lester sat there, no doubt waiting for her to reach up and hug him.

Not in this lifetime!

Lester leaned down and hugged her. Ruth Ann held her breath. He continued hugging her as her arms lay to her sides. She groaned softly, to cue him enough was enough.

"I love you," Lester whispered.

Another groan, much louder, and Lester started kissing her neck. Ruth Ann squirmed...and groaned again. Lester's heartbeat thumped against her chest.

"I love you, Ruthie," kissing her clavicle...chest...She groaned again. Lester pushed her shirt lapel away with his chin and started kissing her breast.

She heard his breathing turn into a pant and realized Lester was mistaking her groans for pleasure.

"Lester!" attempting to push him off.

He ignored her and started sucking her breast so hard it hurt.

"Lester! Lester!" His hand sought entrance inside her pants. "Lester!" Again she tried to push him off, but he was too heavy. "Lester!"

Lester stopped to unzip his pants, and Ruth Ann rolled onto her stomach. He hopped onto her and started humping so enthusiastically she heard one of the slats snap.

"Lester!" clawing her way to the edge of the bed…and they both fell to the floor.

Ruth Ann jumped to her feet and watched Lester hump the floor, his eyes closed, completely unaware he had no partner.

"Lester! What the hell are you doing?"

Mid-hump, Lester turned to her, an astonished look on his face, wondering how she'd gotten away from him.

"Hello! What the hell are you doing?"

Lester got to his feet. "I-I'm sorry, Ruthie, I got carried away."

Shaking her head in disgust at his exposed erection: "Damn right you did!"

"I'm sorry, Ruthie." He tucked away his organ and zipped up. "Honey, it has been a long time. Seven weeks and five days, to be exact. That's a long time, a very long time."

"What! What!" Ruth Ann shouted. "So we're counting days now? Is that what we're doing, Lester? Keeping track of our sex life?"

"No, honey, I'm not keeping track. I just, you know, noticed on the calendar."

"I can't believe you! How many hours has it been? You've calculated the number of weeks and days, tell me the number of hours. I can't believe you! My father was murdered, hasn't been in the ground three days and you have the gall to throw sex in my face now. *Now*, Lester! I can't believe it. I just can't believe it." She looked at the bulge in Lester's pants and shook her head again. "I just cannot believe it!"

Lester scratched his forehead. "I'm sorry. I don't know what come over me. Forgive me, Ruthie." He reached to take her hand and she snatched it away.

"Don't start that shit again!"

"I'm going outside, sit on the porch for a spell. If you need something, just call me."

Ruth Ann cut him a look. "Yes, why don't you do that!"

Lester closed the bedroom door behind him, and Ruth Ann wondered had it really been that long since she and Lester had had sex. *Seven weeks?* No, seven weeks and five days. She tried to remember the last time…couldn't. Even if she could, what was there to remember, Lester hopping on and hopping off? *Hello!* Still, seven weeks and five days was far too long: a sex-starved Lester might get suspicious; even worse, if Eric blabbed his mouth, a sex-starved Lester might click.

A few hours later she awoke with a scream, "Noooo!" Looking about the room she realized she was safe in her bed. Shirley wasn't chasing her down an alleyway, swinging an ax at her head.

A nightmare.

It had seemed so real. She put her hand to her chest and felt her heart beating arrhythmically. A silly nightmare, she told herself, because no way in hell would Eric tell Shirley; he'd be putting his own life at risk.

What if Shirley found out anyway?

Shirley would click, go absolutely ass-kicking berserk. She remembered when Shirley and she were waiting in the ER with six-year-old Paul, who'd broken his arm in a fall out of a tree, sitting on Shirley's lap, whimpering.

As a nurse periodically called other patients to a room, people who looked in far better shape than Paul, Ruth Ann tried to make small talk, sensing Shirley was getting hotter by the minute. After the nurse called a man exhibiting no visible ailment whatsoever, Shirley stood up, gently put Paul in the adjoining seat...and exploded!

"You sumbitches!" she shouted. "My boy has been out here in pain for more than an hour!"

That said, the television was snatched off a stanchion and hurled across the room, landing with a thunderous crash near the entrance. A metal chair flew into the receptionist's cubicle--the woman had fled before the television landed. The three people, a man and two women who were also waiting, ran out through a side exit...and Ruth Ann ran behind them.

In the parking lot she heard another thunderous crash and sprinted faster to her car. Three days later she saw Shirley and Paul, his arm in a cast, at Wal-Mart. Of course, she wanted to know what had transpired at the hospital, but didn't think it wise to ask someone who'd clicked, and who in all likelihood would click again, "What happened?"

Ruth Ann sat up in bed. "Lord, what have I done? What have I done?"

There was a knock at the door. "Ruthie?" Lester said.

"Yes."

"Someone here to see you."

"Who?"

"Sheriff Bledsoe."

Chapter 13

A special report interrupted the soap opera. Shirley lowered the volume by remote control. A short, fossil-looking man dressed in an ill-fitting suit, thick glasses, and thin silver hair above a wide forehead, flanked by a stone-faced Air Force general, talked for a few minutes.

The general pointed to a black-and-white video screen depicting a bomb destroying a row of buildings.

"Turn it up," Eric said. "I want to hear it."

"Eric, there were people in those buildings. People, human beings. All they give a damn is the bomb hit the target. The people don't mean nothing. Go in the bedroom and watch."

Her very voice pissed him off, something in the timbre that irritated him. The special report ended and the soap opera resumed. Shirley increased the volume and stared raptly at the television.

"I'm hungry," Eric said.

"Hush!" Shirley snapped. "I'm trying to hear this."

"I'm hungry."

"Go to work and buy something to eat."

"The truck broke. Can't work till I get it fixed. You want me to push the lawnmower house to house like a bum?"

Shirley nodded.

"Why don't you put some clothes on?"

"Why don't you get the air conditioner fixed?"

"You still intend to buy that rich redneck woman a car?"

"Mrs. Avery, her name. She's not rich anymore, and yes I do."

"Woman fired you and you wanna buy her a car?"

"She didn't fire me. She couldn't afford to keep me on."

"Same difference. Tell her buy her own damn car!"

"She has to walk to work."

"I do, too! Give her some orthopedic shoes. Why you gotta be the one buy her a car?"

Shirley didn't answer.

He stared at her sitting on the couch, chunky legs propped up on the coffee table, attired only in a large pair of pink panties.

She reminded him of the cartoon who pitched tires on the TV commercial. Tires for a belly, chest and legs. *Yeah, she looks just like him. Only he doesn't have stretch marks.*

"Shirley, what if the boy comes in? You want him to see you naked, do you?"

"The door is locked," not taking her eyes off the soap opera.

Not able to stomach the sight of her any longer, he got up, crossed into the kitchen and looked into the fridge. Nothing but diet food.

Damn! She's getting bigger and I'm starving to death.

He slammed the door shut and picked up a box of Corn Flakes and a box of low-fat powdered milk. He rinsed out a bowl and spoon, shook out a cupful of powder, added water from the tap, and then, without stirring the lumpy concoction, poured in the flakes. He sighed and sat down at the table.

"Look, Eric! Come here, hurry up!" Shirley said. "Come quick, Count Monie just gave Lila a diamond ring."

Eric remained in his seat. "I sure hate to miss that."

"C'mon, hurry up!"

"Naw. My gourmet dinner might get cold."

"Count Monie sure knows how to treat a woman. You could learn a thing or two watching him, Eric." She paused, and then asked the question Eric knew was coming next: "How come you never romance me?"

Eric, a spoonful a few inches from his mouth, froze. Slowly he turned and gave her a hard, long look, starting first at her feet, talon-like toenails, to her linebacker-size calves, to her stomach, a series of rolls and folds. Above a double chin were thin lips, a small nose, brown marble-size eyes. Her short light-brown hair sprouted in different directions, a style Eric secretly dubbed Electric Buckwheat.

"Why you looking at me like that?" Shirley asked. He put the spoonful in his mouth and returned his attention to the bowl. "When are we getting married, Eric? When?"

He swallowed a lump of powdered milk. "Whenever you want."

"I'm serious."

"I'm serious, too," and forced down another spoonful.

She stepped into the kitchen and stood behind him. He focused intently on the bowl. "Eric, why won't you marry me?"

"Good grief, woman, I'm trying to eat here! I said I would." She caressed his neck. "Shirley, please, you're disturbing my digestion!"

"I need stability in my life. Daddy's death, you know what I'm saying? I'm almost thirty-six-years old." She kissed the top of his head. "Paul will be ten next year. He knows we're not married."

"When we get the money we'll get married. Then we can have a decent wedding and honeymoon."

Shirley pulled out a chair and sat beside him. In his periphery he could see her large breasts spilling onto the table like two water balloons.

"I've been doing some thinking," she said. "If we wait till we get the money to get married, my family will think you only married me for the money. They'll say you're using me for the money. They'll say you wouldna married me if not for the money. You see what I'm saying?"

"I don't care what your family thinks. They don't pay our bills-- who cares what they think?"

"I do! I care a lot. We've been together the last thirteen years, then--Pow!--when I get some money we're walking down the aisle. You see how that looks?"

"When *I* get some money? I thought we were in this together."

"When *we* get some money. It doesn't matter, it'll still look the same. It'll look like you married me for the money."

Eric put on his tough face and looked her in the eye. "Why you always worried what your family think? Huh? Who the hell are they? One's a punk, one's a hoe and one's a nut."

Shirley winced, lips pursing into a thin line. "Who's the hoe?"

"Huh?"

"Who in my family you calling a hoe?"

"Robert Earl."

She stared at him so intensely he looked away. "You know, there's a lot of stuff you've done I've overlooked. A lot of stuff made me question my own self-esteem. You know--and you definitely should know by now!--I don't take kindly to anyone talking down my family, especially my sister."

130

Eric considered an apology, but feared another word out of his mouth would tip the stick on her broad shoulders. So he sat there staring at soggy flakes floating in lumpy low-fat powdered milk.

"And," Shirley said, "now with my daddy gone…you know I'm not putting up with your bullshit!"

He noted the sharp emphasis on *your bullshit*. This wasn't good. He could hear Shirley breathing, tense and raspy. He well knew not to say anything about her stupid family.

If he had known Shirley was the type of woman who would wig out, go spastic, fight and continue fighting long after her adversary had lost interest and energy, he would not have gotten involved with her. The air inside turned stifling hot. His armpits were dripping sweat.

Shirley said, "I know you were talking about Ruth Ann. Yes, she's had a few boyfriends--she's not a hoe." He could see the shadow of her head on the table, rocking side to side. "She's not a hoe! With your history you should never fix your lips to call anyone a hoe. Never!"

He wished she wasn't sitting so close. A roundhouse to the side of his head, and lights out. He stood up. "I'm going outside, check on Paul."

Shirley stood with him. "A damn good idea, 'cause I'm itching to play double jeopardy with your ass!"

She moved past him, and an impulse suggested he sucker punch the back of her head. *Do it!*

Hell no!

If he hit her and didn't knock her out, there would be hell to pay. She resumed her seat on the couch as he crossed to the front door. The air outside, though baking hot, felt cooler than inside.

"Shirley, I apologize. I don't know anything about Ruth Ann. She ain't a hoe--she just loves sucking dicks."

He quickly stepped out onto the porch, slamming the door behind him...but it didn't slam, didn't go Blam!

He hurried down the steps, looking over his shoulder, thinking she wouldn't come after him...Wrong!...She was right behind him...He yelped and cranked up to run...Too late!...A forearm wrapped under his chin and he was pulled up the steps.

She's outside naked!

He couldn't believe it.

He hooked his right foot into the balustrade. Now his body was suspended. "Cut it out, woman!" he said through clenched teeth. "Stop it, Shirley, fo' the neighbors see us! Cut it out!" She pulled harder and his foot fell free. She almost had him inside the house when he grabbed either side of the doorframe.

"Stop it, Shirley! The neighbors watchin'! You hurtin' my neck!" Hurt hell, if she kept pulling she'd break it.

Darlene appeared at the foot of the steps. "Shirley, is something wrong?"

"No shit!" Eric grunted.

"Help me…get him…inside," Shirley said, panting. "Pry…his…fingers loose."

If you do, Eric thought, I'll burn your damned house down. Then, save his soul, he felt his legs being pulled in the opposite direction.

"Let him go!" Shirley demanded.

"No, Momma!" A child's voice. Paul, his beloved son, here to rescue his father. *Pull, boy, pull!*

Shirley said, "Oh my God!" and let him go. He fell flat on his back with Paul still holding his legs.

"Let me go, boy!" Eric shouted, thinking he wasn't out of danger just yet. Paul released his legs and he felt a jolt when his heels hit the porch.

"Daddy," Paul said, "why you and Momma fighting?"

Eric looked over his shoulder. Shirley was nowhere in sight, the door closed.

"Why you fighting Momma, Daddy?"

He got to his feet. "Stop asking stupid questions, boy. Your momma wigged out again. I didn't want to hurt her."

"Hmmph!" Darlene snorted. "Looked to me you were about to get your ass whooped."

"Go home, Darlene!" Eric said. "This family business. You can get hurt sticking your nose in family business."

Darlene snorted again and walked up the steps. Shirley's loud sobs drifted out when she opened the door.

"You hurt Momma!" Paul said.

"No, I didn't. You saw her choking the shit outta me." Paul poked out his mouth and balled up his fist. "You want some of me too, boy? Huh, do you?"

Paul moved around him, keeping close to the green aluminum siding to avoid coming within a few feet of his father, and then ran inside the house and slammed the door.

Eric walked down the sidewalk. Mr. Joyner, shirtless, sagging chest covered with gray hairs, was sitting on his porch. Eric waved at him. Mr. Joyner shook his head, didn't wave back.

Thirty minutes later, Eric made his third pass in front of Ruth Ann's house.

Two choices: either work up the courage to signal Ruth Ann or go home and deal with Shirley and that wayward boy. He walked to the end of the block, then turned and walked back.

Fuck this, before someone gets suspicious and calls the police.

But he had to see Ruth Ann, just had to.

Knock on the door and ask Hot Lips to go get Ruth Ann.

Lester wouldn't think much of him visiting Ruth Ann, would he? Maybe, maybe not.

If Lester took offense, he might want to fight. Could he take Lester? Lester was taller and more muscular than he, yet Eric doubted Lester was quicker with his jabs.

What if he was bumping Lester's head and Ruth Ann stepped in and helped her husband. *Then what?* And what if their psychotic son, Shane, decided to throw in a couple licks?

On his fourth pass in front of the house, the front door opened and Lester stepped out and sat on the porch swing. Eric lowered his head and picked up his pace. At the end of the block he wasn't quite sure what to do.

Wait! Rewind the tape!

If Lester was outside trying to get a sunburn to match the skin around his lips, then Ruth Ann was inside, alone. All he had to do was sneak round back and signal her. Bold, but doable. He turned the corner.

He'd expected an asphalt alley; instead discovered a rancid creek streaming parallel to fenced and unfenced back yards. A large polka-dotted dog, untethered in an open yard, barked at him. He hoped it wouldn't give chase.

A white woman came out and yelled at the dog to shut up, and her presence incited the dog to react more viciously. The woman gave him a wary look. He waved at her and kept walking. *Will she call the police?* He hoped not. At the back of Ruth Ann's house he casually walked up the steps to the deck and tapped on the patio door.

"Ruth Ann?" attempting to whisper loudly. "Ruth Ann?" Something stank. Did they have a dog? "Ruth Ann?" He raised his right leg and inspected the bottom of his sandal. Nothing. He then noticed bones scattered on the deck. *Neck bones!* Why would they throw them here? Why not in the yard? A box lay near the neck bones. He picked it up. Juggernaut Gopher Bait.

What's wrong with this picture?

"Freeze!" a man shouted.

Eric raised both hands and froze.

"Eric?"

The voice was familiar, though it wasn't Lester's. He turned and focused on the .357 Magnum the man beamed at his head.

Chapter 14

Reverend Rob Dollar preached on the television. Dressed in an Italian suit, gold cuff links, a Rolex on his wrist, diamond studded earrings in both lobes, he was holding a revival somewhere in Africa.

Each time he paused in his sermon titled Jesus is Lord Over Your Finances, the crowd of Africans, most wearing rags too big for their thin, emaciated bodies, took to their feet and cheered raucously.

Someone's holding up a cue card off camera, Leonard thought, signaling them to applaud. *I'd bet not a one speaks English.*

"I'm sorry," Victor said. "I can't go. Honestly, Leonard, you shouldn't go, either."

"You can just wait in the car."

Victor, naked, extracted himself from Leonard's embrace and moved to the window.

"Someone will see you," Leonard said, "and we'll get kicked out of this motel. This isn't Chicago. You need to remember that."

"You mean I'll get kicked out, don't you? I've been here alone all night. I don't know where you've been."

"You know I've been with my family."

Victor drew the curtains open wider. Sunlight flooded the room. Leonard covered himself with a sheet.

"Victor, would you please close the curtain? Come back to bed. Please! If someone sees you, you might get arrested."

"If only I'd be so lucky."

"What's that supposed to mean?"

"Guess! You asked--no, you begged me to come here and meet your family. Now I'm here you keep me hidden in this room while you're off doing…whatever it is you're doing."

"Don't be silly. If you're insinuating I'm cheating, you're wrong, dead wrong. There's been a tragedy in my family. My mother needs me right now."

"I need you, too."

Victor could be such a…a bitch at times. "Right now my mother *really* needs me. It's not fair you ask me to choose between you and my family during a crisis."

"It's fair you ask me to go track a psycho in the jungle?"

Leonard got up, hurried to the window and snatched the curtains closed. "He's not a psycho, he just has emotional problems. I asked you because I thought you might want to get out for a minute."

"Gosh, I'm so sorry. I misunderstood. All these years I didn't know searching the jungle for a psycho was a source of entertainment. Pardon my ignorance."

"The sarcasm not helping here. Southeastern Arkansas is not a jungle."

Victor turned, face red. "I'm not someone you picked up off the street. Why didn't you ask before we got into bed?"

"Please! Just forget it. I regret I asked you."

Victor grabbed his pants from the floor and put them on, forgetting his underwear. "Maybe I should go back to Chicago." He pulled the zipper so hard Leonard was surprised it didn't rip off. "Back to my mother."

"Don't you think you're overreacting? Okay, to be honest, I asked you to go because I'm afraid to go alone. I can see how you think I was using you. Wasn't my intention. Honest." Victor ignored him, put on a white Oxford shirt and buttoned it up. "If I'd known you'd throw a hissy fit, I most definitely would not have asked you."

Victor stopped and stared at him. "It's the money, isn't it?"

139

"What money?"

"You know what money."

"Don't be childish."

"Childish! I'm childish? The five years we've been together you've rarely mentioned the boondocks and your family. Now, suddenly, your family can't continue life without you."

Leonard tried to embrace him, but Victor pulled away. "My not calling you last night, isn't that the real issue here? I apologize."

"Why haven't we discussed the money?"

"Excuse me?"

"You heard me. The money, Leonard! The money you're inheriting from your father. Why haven't we talked about it?"

Leonard sat down in the chair. "What's there to talk about?"

"How much we're going to invest, how much we're going to spend?"

Leonard stared at a cockroach navigating its way through the green shag carpet, then looked him in the eye.

"Victor…" He cleared his throat. "Victor, my dear, you've mistaken the possessive pronoun here. *My* father! *My* father, not your father, worked to get this money. If I choose to give you some of it, well, you know, that's on me. You can't speak in terms of *we* because we don't share the same father. For you to think otherwise is demonstrably…" He searched in vain for a strong adjective. "…childish!"

Victor stared at him a long moment, mouth agape. Without a word he stepped into his loafers…and walked out.

An hour later, Leonard parked his car in Count Pulaski State Park. He studied the map his mother had drawn for him and wondered if she'd been out here herself.

Three trails led into the woods dense with oak, pine, poplar, spruce and dogwood trees. Leonard got out of the car and entered through Maumelle Trail, as his mother had instructed.

A canopy of branches blocked direct sunlight on the four-foot wide rocky rut someone foolishly labeled a trail. A slight breeze tingled the leaves, though did very little to reduce the humidity. Two squirrels chased each other from tree to tree. A turtle labored in the opposite direction.

Leonard didn't notice any of this; his thoughts were on Victor. *Is he gone forever?*

He wished he'd phrased his words differently. Certainly he intended to share the money with Victor, but he didn't need Victor or anyone else telling him what to do with his money. The trail inclined, and Leonard stopped to catch his breath. A crow cawed and he remembered his purpose for coming here.

To deliver a message to a psycho with a crossbow.

He pushed onward. At the end of the trail he came to a clearing. The temperature a tad cooler here. Amber knee-high grass bowed to the wind.

Two identical cabins constructed of hewed logs stood side by side in the middle of the clearing. A felled oak tree, obviously struck by lightning, split one of the cabins in half. Several buzzards circled below a clear blue sky.

"Shane!" Leonard shouted. His mother had said the boy wouldn't shoot a relative, but Leonard wasn't convinced. "Shane? It's me, your uncle, a blood relative!" No response. "Kinfolk!"

Leonard stepped toward the intact cabin, wondering if the boy had him sighted in crosshairs, waiting for the perfect moment.

Wekeeeeee! Wekeeeeee!

Leonard whirled, looking for the origin of the sound. "What the hell was that? Shane?"

What the hell am I doing out here?

Well, one, sweating profusely, despite the cooler temperature. And two, needing only another strange noise to prompt a mad dash back to his car.

"Shane?"

He'd give it a few more minutes and then go home and tell his mother the boy couldn't be found--and he wouldn't come back.

"Shane?"

Nearing the cabin door, three boards nailed in a Z to eight two-by-fours, he caught whiff of an atrocious odor. Rotten meat? Or something dying? What if the boy lay inside hurt, moments from death? Would explain the buzzards hovering above. He knocked lightly on the door.

"Shane?" He pushed the door open. "Shane?" Silence.

He stuck his head inside. There was a wooden bed frame absent a mattress at the far wall, a worn-out orange-colored couch near the door, and a large stone fireplace to the left. A fey odor tickled his nostrils. No windows, no back door.

What a waste of time. He should've gone to the nearest bus stop and intercepted Victor, and told him he was sorry, told him--

Wekeeeeee! Wekeeeeeee!

The noise sounded directly behind him. He spun around and saw the arrow. Nothing but the arrow. Aimed at his chest. "Sh-sh-sh-shane!"

"What you want?" Shane asked.

Leonard stared into the boy's dirty freckled face, slowly raised both hands and wondered why Shane was squinting, for they were standing in the shade of the cabin.

"I want you to stop aiming that thing at me. I'm your uncle, remember? Uncle Leonard? Your mother's brother?"

Shane in desperate need of a haircut: light-brown hair extremely long, a super afro, speckled with green bits, grass or leaves. Besides that and the dirt on his face, he was handsome. A young Harry Belafonte: sculpted features, freckles, bushy eyebrows above hazel-colored eyes.

"Yeah," the boy said, tilting his head.

"Shane, remember when you were little and I took you and Paul to the fair in Little Rock? You remember?" The boy shook his head.

"You gotta remember. You and I rode the Ferris wheel, it stopped while we were at top, I threw up. It doesn't matter. Shane, it's not polite to point an arrow at your uncle."

The boy responded by raising the crossbow, aiming it at Leonard's head.

Shielding his face with his hands: "Hey! Hey! Hey! Stop it! You might put my eye out!"

"It'll do more than that."

"Stop playing, Shane! Stop it! Dammit, I'm your uncle!"

"Why you kill my dog?"

"What! I didn't kill your dog!"

Shane shook his head to rid a fly from his face. "Yeah, you did. You killed him and you killed pa-pa."

I'm dead, Leonard thought. He's going to kill me with a crossbow...I'll be left out here to rot...Flies...Buzzards...

"Shane, I didn't. I swear I didn't do it! I didn't arrive in time. What makes you think I did it?"

"'Cause you're unnatural."

"What?"

"You like bootie instead of women."

"What! Who told you that?"

"Pa-pa."

"He shouldn't have told you that. Not a nice thing to say."

"Is it true?"

Leonard's mind raced. If he admitted being gay, Shane might misconstrue it as an admission of guilt and shoot him.

"No, it's not true."

"Liar!" Shane snapped.

In his entire life, thirty-three years, Leonard had never heard an African American use the word liar. Not important now, he thought, closing his eyes. Only two things were significant now: pain and decomposition.

"Open your eyes!" Shane demanded.

"Huh?" Leonard said, opening one eye…There wasn't an arrow protruding from his forehead.

"Look," pointing the arrow at Leonard's leg. "You peed yourself."

Leonard looked…his blue jeans sported a wet spot down to his shoes.

Shane laughed, a high-pitch giggle. "You scared, ain't ya?"

"No! No, I'm not. This is usually the time of day I wet myself. An arrow aimed at my head has nothing to do with it."

Shane laughed again, as though the funniest thing he'd ever heard. Leonard feigned a chuckle, noticing Shane was shirtless, shoeless, wearing only black dress slacks.

Maybe, Leonard thought, just maybe. "Knock, knock?"

Shane frowned. "I'm not no damn kid! I'm seventeen-years-old. Be eighteen in two months. Don't talk to me like I'm a kid."

"I didn't mean anything by it, Shane. Just a joke. You like jokes, don't you?"

"No, I don't. I want to know…you know what I'm talking about?"

"No, I'm sorry, I don't."

"You know? What's it like to be with a…you know?"

"Shane, listen to me, I didn't kill your dog." He dropped his hands. "If you want to shoot your uncle, then shoot your uncle. I'm not going to discuss my personal life with a minor." He stepped off the porch. "I came out here because my mother, your grandmother, told me to give you a message." He started walking and fought the urge to look back. "She's worried about you and wants you to know you can come home and bring the dog with you."

Nearing the entrance to the trail: "She's really concerned about you being out here by your--"

Twaanng!…the sound of a rubber band snapping, only louder…Shiiiiiiip!…something whipped past his right ear…Thud!…an arrow struck a tree only a few feet ahead of him.

"Why you stupid, simple-minded bastard!" Leonard said. He turned and charged…He would kick his ass…he would beat the shit out of him, teach him not to shoot arrows at his uncle…He stopped in his tracks…The boy had another arrow already locked and loaded in the crossbow…

That's not a toy!

The tip of the arrow pointed at him looked like three rectangular razor blades melded to a needlepoint. The shaft made of some kind of metal, aluminum or steel.

A wire looped through two small wheels on either side of the crossbow and crisscrossed to an X in the middle. All rested on a green camouflaged rifle stock. No, this was not a toy.

"Call me stupid again," Shane said. "Say it again, I dare you."

Leonard gulped.

"Always," Shane said. "Always come down to me stupid, crazy, simple. 'Cause I'm not too smart makes you better than me?"

Leonard didn't respond.

"Why I live out here. Nobody calls me stupid out here." Pause. "Until you came."

Leonard swallowed, and then found his voice. "Damn, Shane, you shot an arrow at me! Scared the shit out of me. I didn't mean what I said--you scared me."

Shane lowered the crossbow and let it slip from his fingers. It fell to the porch floor with a soft thud.

Another lump formed in Leonard's throat, this one coated with guilt. "Hey...look...I didn't mean...I'm sorry, okay? Okay, Shane?"

Shane started crying, tears leaving dirty streaks down his face.

"Shane, I apologize. You know, when I was your age people called me bad names, made me cry."

"Yeah," Shane sniffed. "Names like what?"

"Sissy, homo, weirdo--silly stuff."

Shane stopped crying. "What you do?"

Leonard stepped closer. "Nothing, really. Mostly cried a lot and tried to avoid them. Shane, some people fear anything they know may very well exist in them. So they call people bad names."

"Then what's your excuse?"

Leonard almost laughed. "I don't have one. I, of all people, should know better."

"Did Pa-pa call you names?"

"He was the main one."

"He called me names, too."

"He did?" Leonard was shocked. He'd thought his father had gotten past that nonsense.

"Yup, he sure did. Ignoramus. Nut case. Airhead. Schizzy was his favorite. I looked for it in the dictionary, couldn't find it. When he really got mad at me, he'd say, 'Shane,'" raising his voice, sounding remarkably similar to Leonard's father, "if brains were tissue, you wouldn't have enough to wipe a mosquito's ass.'"

"Mother, your grandmother, treated you nice, didn't she?"

"Oh, she's the best. She treats me better than my real mother."

"She's worried about you, Shane. She doesn't like the idea of you out here alone."

Shane shrugged. "I'm all right."

"Let's head back home. I had some hot food Mother cooked for you. I left it at the motel. Come on, we'll get her to scrape up a good home-cooked meal. Mmmm-uh, I can smell her cooking now." He started walking away.

"I'm not going back."

"Shane, what happens when the scouts come back? They'll run you off, call the police."

Shane gestured at the damaged cabin. "The scouts don't come up here no more since the tree fell. I'm not going back."

"Shane, surely you'd like a good meal and a hot...a hot cup of coffee." He'd almost slipped and said hot bath.

Shane shook his head.

Leonard looked up and saw more buzzards circling above. "Shane...Shane, you can't stay here. Come home with me."

"I'm not going. I'm waiting for Kenny G to become one with nature. For some reason it's taking a lot longer than usual."

Leonard had a bad feeling what that entailed. "Are you sure you don't want to come home with me?"

Shane answered by picking up the crossbow.

"Guess you are," backing up. "Before I go back to Chicago, I'll try to get back up here and see you." *By plane.* "You take care of yourself. See ya."

"Tell Grandma I..." He stopped...and waved.

"Sure," backing his way to the trail. "I'll tell her. I sure will."

Chapter 15

Sheriff Bledsoe popped four Pepsid AC tablets into his mouth and washed them down with a swig of Pepto Bismol.

"Ah!" smacking his lips. "Hits the spot."

The phone rang. "Sheriff Bledsoe."

A woman's voice: "Ruth Ann did it."

"Did what?"

"Poisoned her daddy. Check her back."

"Her what? Who is this?"

"Not important."

"Okay. What kind of poison was in the chili?"

Silence on the other end. Then: "You wanna play games, go buy yourself a PlayStation. You wanna solve a murder, go arrest Ruth Ann."

"Ma'am, what's your name? I'll keep it anonymous." The voice sounded familiar, but he couldn't quite place it. "Who is this?"

"A concerned citizen," and the line went dead.

"Darn it!" He took another swig of Pepto Bismol.

This case had his stomach twisted in knots. At first he thought Leonard was the culprit, but his alibi checked clean--unless he brought a box of Juggernaut Gopher Bait on the plane with him. Highly unlikely. Or he had someone in town buy it for him. Possible, but also highly unlikely.

Next grandma waltzed in and confessed, rekindling the fantasy the case might be solved soon; yet she didn't offer a single shred of evidence to corroborate her story.

And now this!

Maybe, if he were lucky, he thought as he holstered his .357 Magnum, Ruth Ann would confess and then he could return to the business of serving the good people of Dawson, all five thousand of them, by taking long, uninterrupted naps, which saved the city a tremendous amount of revenue.

Murder was a rare bird to land in Dawson. He couldn't remember a single one occurring here. Now he was mired in a murder investigation straight out of a made-for-television mystery. Arsenic, money and enough suspects to organize a softball team.

If this case went unsolved, he would not win the next election. Any yahoo with a loud mouth could run against him and win by reminding the good people of Dawson of the one murder in decades that, thanks to Sheriff Bledsoe, did not get solved.

He got into his cruiser…and then jogged back inside and retrieved the Pepto Bismol. *Just in case.*

Upon turning down Whisperwood Drive, Sheriff Bledsoe spotted a man walking down the sidewalk. The blue shirt, khaki shorts and sandals the man wore made him conspicuous in this modest neighborhood. *Like a large bag of pork rinds in a Black Muslim Mosque.*

At the end of the block the man hesitated before turning the corner. Sheriff Bledsoe drove past the Hawkins' residence, where Lester Hawkins was sitting on a porch swing. Lester waved.

Sheriff Bledsoe kept going, not noticing. He was in pursuit. Not a whiz solving murder cases, but he could do burglars and peeping Toms. Easily. He turned the corner…and, as he expected, the man was nowhere in sight. He parked and got out, trusty Magnum held to his side.

He moved stealthily, his two-hundred-fifty-pound frame low to the ground, eyes scanning the area like a surveillance camera. *What's that smell? The perp?* Was he getting so good he could track perps by smell?…*Yes!*…God, he loved his job. He spotted the man standing on the Hawkins' patio deck, and crept up on his quarry.

"Freeze!" The man jumped and jerked both hands up, a box in one hand. "Eric?"

Staring at the gun, buck-eyed: "Hey, Sheriff."

Sheriff Bledsoe holstered the Magnum. "What you doing back here?"

"I was...I came to see Ruth Ann."

"Why didn't you go to the front door? I saw you walk right past the house. What you got there?"

Eric stared at the box as if noticing it for the first time. "This? This is nothing."

Sheriff Bledsoe took it from him and glanced at the back of the box. "What you doing with this?"

"It was here when I got here, Sheriff. Honest. You didn't see me carrying nothing, did ya?"

"You could've hidden it under your shirt. What's that I'm smelling?"

"Neck bones."

"You know what I think, Eric? I think you're up to no good back here." He turned the box and read the front label. "Either you were peeking--" He stopped, eyes blinking, going from Eric to the box, to the neck bones, then back to Eric.

"What's the matter, Sheriff? Why you looking at me like that? What I do?"

"Turn around," Sheriff Bledsoe commanded. "Do it!"

"What's the matter, Sheriff?"

Sheriff Bledsoe held him by the collar with one hand, frisked him with the other, and then snapped handcuffs onto his wrists.

"Sheriff, what's up with the cuffs?"

Sheriff Bledsoe didn't answer. He led Eric by the arm down the steps, around the side of the house to the front door. Lester was no longer sitting on the porch.

He started to ring the doorbell when Eric said, "Hold up for a minute, Sheriff. Let me explain, okay? Ruth Ann and I, we're messing around. I wasn't peeking on nobody. I was just trying to get her attention. Honest."

"What's this?" shaking the box.

"Sheriff, I told you it was already there. I just picked it up."

"Uh-huh. You know how Larry Harris was killed, don't you?"

"Yeah. Somebody poisoned--now hold on, Sheriff! You got this thang asshole backward. I swear 'fore living God the stuff was already there when I got there."

Sheriff Bledsoe rang the doorbell. "We'll see."

"Awww, Sheriff! Ruth Ann's not admitting the truth with Lester standing by. Why can't you take my word on it?"

Lester opened the door. "Hey, Sheriff," he greeted cheerfully. He eyeballed Eric and frowned. "Hey, Eric."

"Is your wife in?" Sheriff Bledsoe asked.

"She sure is. Eric isn't under arrest, is he?"

No, he just has his hands behind his back. "Lester, could I speak to her?"

154

"Yes, sure. Come in."

"I-I'll rather stay outside," Eric said.

"We'll wait here," Sheriff Bledsoe said.

When Lester disappeared, Eric said, "Shit, Sheriff! You're not going to tell him, are you? I got these cuffs on, too! What if he goes nuts?"

"I'll tell him if I have to. We're going to get to the bottom of what's going on here."

"I already told you, Sheriff! You gonna get me killed."

Ruth Ann appeared at the door, smiling. When she saw Eric, her mouth formed a perfect circle.

"Sheriff Bledsoe," and stepped out onto the porch, closing the door behind her. "What brings you two gentleman by this late in the evening?"

"Mrs. Hawkins, I caught Eric here behind your house." He held up the box. "With this." Ruth Ann didn't even look at it. "Eric says he was paying you a visit. He says the box was already on your back porch when he arrived, along with a half pound of neck bones."

Ruth Ann nervously fingered the collar to her black satin robe. "I see."

"Does this belong to you?" Sheriff Bledsoe said.

Ruth Ann gave Eric an icy look. "What are you talking about, Sheriff?"

"Don't lie!" Eric said.

"Shut up!" Sheriff Bledsoe said. "Mrs. Hawkins, does this box of Juggernaut Gopher Bait belong to you?"

Ruth Ann looked over her shoulder at the front door. "No. No, it doesn't."

"You're full of shit, Ruth Ann!" Eric said.

"Shut up! I'm not going to tell you again. Mrs. Hawkins, is it possible your husband--"

"No! I purchase all household supplies. We don't have gophers." She rolled her eyes at Eric. "Or rats!"

"What about affairs?" Eric said. "Do you have those?"

Sheriff Bledsoe jerked his arm. "Didn't I tell you to shut your trap!" To Ruth Ann: "Well?"

"Well what?"

"Are you and Eric having an affair?"

"Let's talk away from the house," Ruth Ann said, and walked away. She stopped short of the street. "Where's your patrol car, Sheriff?" she asked, looking back at the house.

Sheriff Bledsoe looked back too and saw Lester peering out the front window. "Maybe we should all go down to the station and sort this thing out."

"No!" Ruth Ann said. "Okay, Sheriff, we had a brief fling, but it's over. I told Eric it was over--he can't get it through his thick head."

"Brief!" Eric said. "A buncha years ain't brief."

"Son, do I need to handcuff your mouth?"

"Sheriff, ask her how long it's been over."

"Son, you open your mouth one more time I'm going to shut it permanently. I'm doing all the questioning here, not you. Do you understand?" Eric nodded. "Mrs. Hawkins, how long has this affair been over?"

"A couple days ago," she whispered.

"Excuse me, I didn't--"

"Two days ago!"

"Thank God," Eric said. "You can take these cuffs off now, Sheriff."

"Not so fast, son. So it were you two acting up at Blinky the other night?"

Ruth Ann stared back at the house. Lester was still watching. "Yes."

"Mrs. Hawkins, do you want to press charges?"

"No. I want to go back inside my house. My husband probably curious what's this all about."

"I wonder why," Eric said.

Sheriff Bledsoe said, "How 'bout I go tell Lester about you. Then mosey round the corner and get the car, take my time getting back while he keeps an eye on you."

"No, Sheriff," Ruth Ann said. "Please don't!"

"Sheriff, I'll shut up. One question. Why am I still handcuffed?"

"May I go now?" Ruth Ann asked. "All my neighbors are watching."

Several of the neighbors were outside, some blatantly gawking; most feigning work in their yards, discreetly gawking.

"Yes, you can go. I need you and Lester at the station within the hour."

Ruth Ann stared at him. "Lester?" Lips trembling: "What on earth do you need Lester for? He doesn't know anything about this. You don't need him. I can answer all your questions."

Sheriff Bledsoe rattled the box. "This may be linked to a murder, and there's neck bones on your back porch, Mrs. Hawkins. Chatterbox claims he didn't put them there and you say you didn't, either. Somebody did, and I aim to find out who. Tell Lester what you need to tell him and y'all meet me at the station."

"You sorry bastard!" Ruth Ann hissed at Eric. "Sheriff, you see what he's trying to pull, don't you? I dumped his sorry ass and he's trying to break up my home. That's all this is, Sheriff."

"Ha!" Eric said. "Your home was tore up long before I came along. Ask anybody, Sheriff. She's serviced more men than an army recruiter."

"Hold on, son. There's no need for talk like that."

"It's true!"

"It's true you murdered my father!" Ruth Ann said.

"Hell naw! You know damn well I didn't!"

"You showed up at my house with poison and neck bones."

"Woman, please! I didn't bring no damn neck bones to your house!"

"Yes, you did!"

"No, I didn't!"

"Yes, you did!"

Sheriff Bledsoe knew he should step in and squash this silly bickering, yet was curious what would happen next.

Ruth Ann got within inches of Eric's face and shouted, "Yes, you damn sure did! And now I think about it, you were the one who insisted on serving Daddy. Remember?" Baritone voice: "Let me fix your plate, Mr. Harris. You need more napkins, Mr. Harris? May I wipe your ass, Mr. Harris?"

"You a lying hoe!"

"Sheriff Bledsoe, is there a problem?"

They all turned to see Lester standing on the front porch.

"Lester," Ruth Ann said, tone cordial. "Lester, everything is fine. We were…we were just having a friendly conversation. Go back in the house, Lester. I'll be there in a minute."

"Is that right, Sheriff?" Lester asked. "Looks to me y'all arguing out here."

Sheriff Bledsoe looked from Eric to Ruth Ann. Eventually Lester would have to be told, though he wasn't sure he should do the telling. *And why hadn't he come out a long time ago?*

"It's all right, Lester," Sheriff Bledsoe said. He grabbed Eric by the arm. "Let's go." To Ruth Ann in a low voice: "An hour, you and Lester at the station."

159

Then he started down the sidewalk with Eric in tow, tipping his Smokey to all the good people on Whisperwood Drive.

Chapter 16

"Rhino-who?" Robert Earl said.

"Rhinoplasty," Estafay said. "Also called a nose job."

They were riding in Estafay's Ford Festiva, Robert Earl driving, Estafay in the backseat fanning herself with a newspaper.

No air conditioning, all the windows rolled down, a steady stream of heat and the stench of cow manure whipping their faces.

"What you need a nose job for?"

"I've always wanted one. Since we can finally afford it, I might as well get it done."

Robert Earl sneaked a look at her in the rearview mirror. Yes, her nose could use some work: nostrils looked like the entrance to two dark tunnels.

"Estafay, what makes you think we can afford a nose job now? I don't have a problem with it, I just don't think we can afford it now."

"Yes, we can afford it now."

"How?"

"Don't worry about it. I've been told to do it, and I will."

"Who? Who told you to do it?" He sensed himself getting angry. If some man told her to get a nose job, or simply hinted at it, he would whip the car around and head straight back to Dawson.

"God," Estafay said.

Robert Earl grimaced; he'd forgotten about Him. "God told you to get a nose job?"

"Yes, He sure did. Remember Friday morning, when I was talking with the Lord?"

"Yeah," Robert Earl lied. She and the Lord conversed so frequently, no way could he remember a specific conversation.

"That's when He told me."

He drove a mile or so before mustering the nerve to say, "So the Lord said, 'Estafay, go get a nose job even though your husband just quit his job and he doesn't have diddly-poo in the bank.'"

"Get thee behind me, Satan!" Estafay shouted. Robert Earl jumped and momentarily lost control of the wheel. "Blasphemy! That kind of talk is nothing but blasphemy. If you don't understand the Lord's work, it's best you keep your mouth shut. Ask the Lord for forgiveness, Robert--right now, before He strikes you dead!"

He steered the car across the centerline to miss a flattened skunk in his lane. The odor lingered for two miles.

Estafay slapped the back of his seat. "Ask Him for forgiveness!"

"Forgive me, Lord."

"You're not asking for a loan, you're asking for forgiveness. Say it with conviction, like you mean it."

"Forgive me, Lord," with less enthusiasm than before.

"It's bad enough we're unevenly yoked, spiritually unbalanced, saved and unsaved, and for you to question the very faith what sustains you, to look righteousness in the eye and mock it-- blasphemy! Adulterous blasphemy! Robert, you know…"

He stopped listening; he'd heard this particular sermon a thousand times. He daydreamed of the day he opened Robert Earl's Gas Station and Exotic Snake Farm. All day, he thought as Estafay ranted on and on, all day and night. No matter what--flood, earthquake, a death in the family--he would keep his station open all day and night.

Heck, he might even live there: a cot and a hot plate were all he needed to live on. Come by anytime, we never close.

Estafay slapped his seat again. "Are you listening to me?"

"Yes, Estafay."

"What did I just say?"

"A divided house cannot stand."

"It sure can't. Amen. He who doesn't know the Lord, he who is ignorant of His works, should keep his fat mouth shut." Robert Earl arched an eyebrow and gave her a look in the rearview mirror; he hadn't heard that one before.

"Whatever the Lord tells me, Estafay Bernice Harris, one of His chosen children, to do, let no man, especially my so-called husband, rend asunder. Do you hear me?"

Robert Earl slowed the car down for a pickup truck going thirty miles below the speed limit. Two events that never failed to occur during one of their rare road trips: Estafay preaching and his driving up behind a geezer in a pickup truck snailing along just when it was impossible to pass because of a curvy stretch of road or steady oncoming traffic.

Either was an agony worthy of pulling his hair out and committing himself to the state hospital. But to endure both simultaneously.

Lord, have mercy!

"Do you hear me, Robert?"

He steered the car onto the shoulder and sped past the truck. A large cloud of dust rose up, preventing him from shooting a nasty look at the driver. Gravel pinged against the undercarriage.

"Yes, I hear you," steering the car back onto the road.

Estafay coughed and said, "If the Lord tells me to get rhinoplasty, liposuction, mammaplasty and…and whatever else, you should have the sense to be quiet and thankful."

"Yes, Estafay. Hey, wait a minute! How much is all this stuff gonna cost?"

"I don't know yet."

"Where's the money coming from?"

Estafay sighed. "What did I just tell you? You haven't heard a word I said. Faith, Robert Earl Harris. The money your father left you will pay for everything."

"The money hasn't come yet and we don't know when it will."

"It'll be coming real soon."

"How do you know?"

"Don't start again! I just spelled it out for you. Have some faith for once in your life. The Lord will provide, just put your faith in Him."

They rode a few miles in silence, then Robert Earl said, "Estafay, aren't you forgetting something?"

"Your teeth? Don't worry, we should have enough to get you a brand-new set."

"No. My dream. Robert Earl's gas station and exotic snake farm. Remember?"

"I pray one day you'll drop such foolishness."

He turned and stared at her. "How can you say that?" A car horn blew and he returned his attention to driving. "How can you say that, Estafay? You know I've been planning this for years. What you think I trained snakes for? What if we can't afford to start my business and get you all the stuff you talking about?"

"No problem, we drop the snake cage."

"What! It ain't a snake cage, Estafay. It's a gas station and exotic snake farm. How many times I gotta tell you?"

"Did the Lord tell you to open a gas station…with snakes…and serpents?"

"No, He didn't."

"What I thought. Don't worry about it. We should have enough money to do both. Faith, Robert, faith."

They rode in silence, through small towns distinguishable only by the name on a water tower.

Lake Village. Masonville. Winchester. Pickens. Dumas. Mitchellvile. Gould. Grady, the home of the infamous Cummins prison farm. Moscow. Pine Bluff, where the two-lane road finally ended and Interstate 640 began.

Arriving in Little Rock, Estafay directed Robert Earl to a three-story medical building. He waited in the car while she, wearing a blue-and-white ankle-length pinafore, walked up the steps to the entrance, holding her beloved Bible to her chest.

Yes, she definitely could use some fixin' up, he thought when she disappeared inside. But dag gummit, why should he give up his dream? The way his luck was going when Estafay paid for all the plastic stuff she wanted, he wouldn't have enough to buy a gallon of gas, let alone open a gas station and exotic snake farm.

The Lord didn't tell him to open a gas station and exotic snake farm. So what? He didn't tell him not to, either.

"Leave her!" whispered a voice. The demon, rearing its ugly head again, tempting him to do something evil.

Shut up! he told it. He wouldn't listen, couldn't listen. The last time he'd listened he'd hurt someone, hurt someone real bad...He pressed his hands against his ears. Shut up! Shut up!

The voice in his head grew louder: *"Leave her, Robert Earl."*

And throw twenty-five years of marriage away? No way, Jose!

"What if the operation goes badly?"

She'll still be my wife--through sickness and death.

"Tara Reid."

Robert Earl thought hard and couldn't recall a Tara Reid.

"Tara Reid!"

He remembered: she was the little white girl whose titty popped out during a photo shoot. A deformed titty, scarred and mutilated thanks to a surgeon's scalpel.

Estafay's operation could go wrong, just like Tara's.

Jeepers! If that happened to Estafay...He squeezed his head harder, hoping to rid the image of Estafay and him sitting at a table in the Waffle House, his teeth slipping out and Estafay's deformed titties popping loose...*Lord in heaven!*

"What's wrong with you?" Estafay asked.

"Huh?"

Estafay got into the backseat. "What's wrong with your head? Looks like you fighting a demon."

"No, just a little headache." He took a quick peek at her chest and a chill ran through his gums. "That didn't take long."

"The doctor said I should take a few days to think about it. It's a medical procedure, you know, so there's a slim possibility of complications."

Robert Earl swallowed. "What kind of complications?"

"Pain. Infection. Scars. The operation doesn't take with everyone. I'm sure I won't have any problems. Unlike most people, I have faith in the Lord above."

He wanted to tell her about Tara Reid, but didn't have the heart. "Uh, did the doctor say how much the procedure is going to cost?"

Estafay fanned herself with the paper. "Let's go. It's a hundred degrees out here. Thirteen thousand dollars. It's hot enough to bake a cake in the shade. Turn the radio on. I don't feel up for much talking. It's too hot."

Robert Earl started the car and pushed the button on the radio. Paul Simon sang about fifty ways to leave your lover.

"Turn to gospel. You know I don't listen to the devil's music."

He let the song play. Paul suggested make a little plan…and set yourself free. If it came down to losing his dream and helping Estafay paste on falsies, he would take Paul's advice.

Estafay tapped him on the shoulder. "Didn't you hear me? Turn to gospel music."

He looked her in the face in the rearview mirror, smiled without a tooth in his mouth and said, "Yes, dear."

Chapter 17

Lysol burning her hand, Ruth Ann scrubbed the tub. It didn't need cleaning. She needed an activity to occupy her mind. The yellow sponge disintegrated into bits and pieces and she kept scrubbing. The bits and pieces rubbed away to nothing and she had to stop.

Ceasing activity for only a minute allowed a horrific thought to take center stage: Lester flipping his lid when Sheriff Bledsoe informed him of her affair with Eric. She sat on the commode and chewed on a thumbnail.

Would Lester kill me?

She bit a nice piece of skin off the tip of her thumb and spit it on the floor. *Yes, he just might.*

When she'd stepped inside, Lester asked, "What did Sheriff Bledsoe want?" She'd shrugged and said, "Nothing."

She couldn't tell him the truth; it sounded so crazy: Eric and I had an affair, I broke it off and Eric got mad and tried to frame me with Daddy's murder by planting poison and neck bones on our back porch, and now Sheriff Bledsoe wants you and me at the station because he's not sure we didn't have anything to do with the poison and neck bones.

There was a knock at the door. "Ruthie, you okay?"

"I'm fine."

"You sure?"

Tell him?

She picked up a tube of Crest toothpaste and tossed it in the air...Tails, she would tell him a modified version of the truth...Heads, she wouldn't tell him shit...The tube landed on the floor, the backside showing...*Shit!*

She got up and opened the door. Lester stood in the hallway, brow furrowed.

"I'm fine," she said. "I was just cleaning the bathroom." *Uh-uh!* He would have to hear it from someone else, and still she would deny it.

"Something's wrong, Ruthie. I can feel it. Talk to me. It's that no-good Eric Barnes, isn't it? He's done something to Shirley, hasn't he?"

Ruth Ann nodded. In a circuitous way he was right. "Yes, Lester, I guess you can say that."

"What has he done now?"

She wondered if he could tell she was shaking like a cheap vibrator. "I'm not quite sure, honey. I better get over to Shirley's and see if she's all right." She started past him and almost screamed when she felt his hand on her shoulder.

"What did you just call me?" Lester asked.

Had she called him Eric? Lord, she hoped not.

"You called me honey," Lester said.

"I-I did? I didn't mean to. I've been under a lot of pressure lately."

Lester embraced her and kissed her nose. "Ruthie, honey, there's no need to apologize. You don't know how long I've wished you call me something affectionate. I love you, Ruthie." He hugged her tighter and kissed her again. "I love you so much."

"I know you do." She cleared her throat and added, "Honey."

"Oh Ruthie, oh Ruthie!" smothering her with kisses.

"Lester," attempting to pull free. "Lester...honey...I've got to go. I'll be back as soon as I check on Shirley."

Lester released her. As she started out the door she took a look over her shoulder...*What the hell leaking down his face? Water? Oh, my goodness!* Lester was crying. She hurried to her car.

So caught up in her thoughts she drove right past the jail.

Tears! Lester was actually crying!

One of two tragedies might happen, she thought as she drove past the city limits: Lester would kill her or Lester would hurt himself again in another foolhardy suicide attempt. Either way she would lose. Another self-inflicted injury and that damn burn mark Lester would have even Judge Hatchett eating out of his hand.

Another potential problem troubled her concentration, jangled her nerves. A problem far more terrifying than anything Lester might do. A problem twice as destructive and life-threatening as Irene and Katrina combined.

Shirley!

"Damn!" she shouted, realizing she'd driven past the jail and almost into the next county. She made a U-turn. All four Michelins squealed and the speedometer zipped from thirty- to sixty- to ninety-miles-per-hour.

The clock on the dash read eight-thirty. Twenty minutes late. Right now Sheriff Bledsoe could be talking to Lester on the phone. At a hundred and twenty-miles-per-hour the Expedition began to rattle.

About two miles before the Dawson city limits, she saw something up ahead, standing in the middle of the road. The descending sun, a gigantic fireball spilling across the horizon, distorted her view.

What the hell is it? A cow? No, too tall for a cow. Whatever it was it stood on two legs. *Bigfoot?* Had to be. Just her damn luck, the day her life hung in the balance Bigfoot crossed her path. She maintained her speed. Bigfoot or Littlefoot, it was no match for the Expedition. Thirty feet from impact she floored the brakes.

The Expedition went into a rubber-burning fishtail, almost tilting over, then spun around two times before stopping short of a two-foot ditch.

Ruth Ann sat there, dazed, clutching the steering wheel. She wasn't sure, but the thing she initially thought Bigfoot was her baby sister, Shirley.

The passenger door opened and Shirley stuck her head inside. "Ruth Ann, you all right? What were you trying to do, run me over?"

Ruth Ann simply stared at her.

Shirley got in and closed the door. "Where's the fire? Why you driving so fast? Didn't you see me when you first flew by?"

"Why…were…you…" She paused and took a deep breath. "Why were you standing in the middle of the road?"

"I'm on my way to the jail. Eric's in trouble again. Where you going like a bat out of hell?"

Ruth Ann started to speak, then started choking. Shirley rapped her on the back with a flat hand. "You okay?" Whap! "You okay?" Whap! "Huh?"

"Shirley...stop...Shit! I'm okay. Thanks."

"You're welcome. You in a hurry? Could you drop me off at the jail?"

Ruth Ann ignored her and steered the car back onto the road and drove much slower.

"Pep it up, girl," Shirley said. "You're going fifteen-miles-per-hour. Somebody's going to come along and knock your rear off. Can you drop me off?"

"Hello, you wanna drive?"

"What's with the attitude? What's the matter?"

"Nothing, Shirley. Man trouble, you know?"

"Same here. No telling what trouble Eric has gotten himself into now. I think he got caught up in some mess with some woman at the Blinky Motel. Ruth Ann, I swear, sometimes I curse the day I met him. Sometimes I could just..." She raised her hands and pantomimed squeezing. "I could just choke him, choke the shit out of him. I guess...well, *I know* I love him."

"What did Eric say when he called you?"

"You know I don't have a phone. Darlene, my neighbor, saw Sheriff Bledsoe escorting Eric in handcuffs and she came over and told me. I would've asked her to give me a ride, but she can't stand Eric."

"Where? Where did she see Sheriff Bledsoe and Eric?"

"Where do you think? At the jail. By the time we get there, Eric will be released for time served. Ruth Ann, we didn't go this slow at Daddy's funeral--speed it up."

Ruth Ann accelerated to seventeen-miles-per-hour. Thirty minutes later, just as a full moon was rising, Ruth Ann parked to the left of Sheriff Bledsoe's cruiser.

Shirley opened the door to get out and Ruth Ann put a hand on her shoulder. "Shirley, you remember what I said? I love you. I'll always love you no matter what. It may come a time you think I didn't mean it, that I was bullshitting. I truly meant it...every word...with all my heart. You gotta believe me, Shirley!"

"Yeah. Sure," eager to go inside. A moth flew in and fluttered against the interior light.

"I double-double meant it. No matter what happens in the future, Shirley, I meant it. Even if you beat me down to a bloody pulp and gouge my eyes out and kick me in the stomach, I'll still love you, Shirley. It's important to me you know that. Though I wish you wouldn't kick me in the stomach 'cause you know my stomach is super sensitive. You remember the time I got hit in the stomach with a volleyball and--"

"Ruth Ann, what in the hell are you talking about? Did you hit your head back there?"

"I'm sorry, Shirley, all I'm trying to say. I really am."

"Is Lester fooling around? You can tell me. Is he?"

There was a tap on the window, and Ruth Ann almost jumped out of her seat.

Sheriff Bledsoe said, "Didn't mean to give you a start. Y'all can join us anytime."

"I don't want to go," Ruth Ann muttered when Sheriff Bledsoe went back inside.

"Stay here," Shirley said. "Eric's not your problem." She stepped out. "Unfortunately he's mine."

Ruth Ann sat there for a while, wondering what degree of physical injury she would suffer before Sheriff Bledsoe pulled Shirley off her. She got out, shuffled to the door, stopped and prayed.

Lord, help me out here and I promise I'll start doing the right thing. I'll go to church regularly. I'll tithe. Be faithful in my marriage...until I file for divorce. I'll even bring Shane home to stay with me. Amen.

She took a deep breath and opened the door.

Chapter 18

"Think about it, Sheriff," Eric said from the backseat of the cruiser. "Only a fool would sneak up to somebody's house with neck bones."

"Only a fool?" looking at him in the rearview mirror.

"Yeah, hell yeah!" Eric pressed his face to the metal grate. "I didn't do it, Sheriff. The shit was there when I got there."

Sheriff Bledsoe patted his front pocket for the Pepsid AC package. He needed something to soothe the pain in his chest in a bad way. Not finding it, he remembered the Pepto Bismol bottle, unscrewed it with one hand and took a long drink.

Eric rattled on, emphatically claiming his innocence. Though Sheriff Bledsoe tuned him out, he realized Eric's denial had a ring of truth to it. Eric's brain was in his shorts, but he wasn't dumb enough to run around with neck bones and poison underneath his shirt.

It didn't make sense.

If Eric didn't plant the stuff, who did? Lester? Ruth Ann?

Sheriff Bledsoe burped and felt a burning sensation rise from his chest to his throat to his nasal cavities. *Geez, that hurt.* Eric rattled on.

He wondered if DNA testing could determine if the neck bones on the porch were from the same batch in Larry's stomach.

"Sheriff?" Eric shouted.

He couldn't charge Chatterbox with such flimsy evidence. Nor could he charge Ruth Ann or Lester because he'd caught Chatterbox with the box in hand. The pain in his chest moved to his lower back. He leaned forward, but it didn't lessen the agony.

Eric pounded on the grate with his head. "Sheriff! Sheriff, are you listening to me?"

Sheriff Bledsoe parked the cruiser and killed the engine. "Yes, Eric, I hear you."

"You know what I'm saying is true, don't you?"

He got out, opened Eric's door and helped him out. "What is true, Eric?"

"I'm being framed. Big time! You know I'm not a killer. I'm a lover. I might steal a woman's heart--I'm no killer!"

He led Eric inside the jail and directed him to a chair. "Why would someone want to frame you?"

Eric shook his head. "I don't know. I really don't know. A lotta people don't like me, especially Shirley's people."

"Why don't they like you?"

"'Cause I mind my own business and I don't stick my nose where it don't belong."

Sheriff Bledsoe considered telling him adultery was a capital case of sticking a nose where it didn't belong.

Instead: "Okay, Eric, let's say you were framed. Somebody says, 'Hey, why not frame Eric Barnes with Larry Harris' murder? Gee, great idea. How? Easy. Put poison and neck bones on the Hawkins' patio. When Eric sneaks over to rendezvous with Ruth Ann, Sheriff Bledsoe will catch him red-handed with the goods.'"

"Naw, Sheriff. I don't think it happened quite like that. But I now know who's trying to frame me."

"Who?"

"You don't wanna know."

"Yes, I do. Enlighten me further of the conspiracy to frame Eric Barnes."

Ignoring the sarcasm: "Lester. He did it, or he had one of his friends do it for him."

"Why? Why would Lester frame you?"

"He's jealous."

"I was under the impression Lester didn't know about you and Ruth Ann."

"I was, too. He wanted us to think he didn't know. You see, then he could do his dirt and nobody would suspect him."

Sheriff Bledsoe sighed. "Lester framed you by throwing gopher bait and neck bones on his patio?"

"He sure did. You know he's crazy, Sheriff. You know what he did to himself when his first wife left him? He drank poison or something and scorched his mouth. Only a crazy person would try to kill hisself, you know what I'm saying?"

"That was a long time ago, and I don't see how his burning himself years ago is related to current events."

"Related! Hell, the two are fucking. Don't you see the connection?"

"No, I don't. And watch your mouth." Why was he even entertaining Eric's cockamamie suppositions?

"It's simple, Sheriff. Lester has firsthand experience with poison, or first-mouth experience, if you wanna be specific. After he burned hisself--you know the man ain't stupid--he read up on the subject so he wouldn't burn up something else. Then he concocted his grand scheme to frame me and kill Shirley's daddy."

"You think he poisoned Larry Harris?"

"Hell yeah! I know damn well he did."

"A gaping hole in your theory, Eric. Lester was not present at the barbecue. You were. And, according to Ruth Ann, you were bending over backward catering to Larry."

"Aw hell. I admit greasing the old man's ego. I was just sucking up. You know I don't know poison and chemical stuff. If I were going to kill somebody, I'd do it face-to-face, man-to-man. I ain't no punk!"

Headlights beamed through the venetian blinds. "Should be Lester and Ruth Ann," Sheriff Bledsoe said.

"Watch him, Sheriff," Eric warned. "Don't let the burn mark fool you. How he tricks people--the sympathy play, you know?"

"Thanks for the advice, Eric."

A few minutes ticked away.

"Your truck is still in the impound lot," Sheriff Bledsoe said. "When are you going to get it?"

"Aw, Sheriff! I didn't know you impound it. Otis charges fifteen dollars a day, not to mention the tow charge. I can't afford all that."

Sheriff Bledsoe didn't respond, and a few more minutes ticked away.

Eric said, "They sure taking a long time to come in. You don't think they're polishing up their alibi, do you?"

Sheriff Bledsoe went to check.

Ruth Ann and Shirley were talking inside the SUV. He assumed Lester was in the backseat, obscured by the tinted back windows.

He tapped on the window and Ruth Ann jumped. "I didn't mean to give you a start. Y'all can join us anytime." He went back inside.

"What are they doing out there?" Eric asked. "Getting their lies together, I bet you."

"Ruth Ann and Shirley are talking. They'll be in soon."

"Who?"

"Ruth Ann, Shirley and Lester."

"My Shirley?"

"Yes."

Eric jumped to his feet and turned his back to Sheriff Bledsoe. "Take these cuffs off, Sheriff! Take em off!"

"What's the matter with you?"

"If Shirley catch me with these cuffs on I'm sawdust. C'mon now, take em off so I can at least have a running chance."

"There's not going to be any theatrics here. This'll be conducted in a civil manner."

"You don't know her, Sheriff. When she gets mad she turns into a Transylvania devil."

"You mean Tasmanian devil, don't you?"

"Whatever, Sheriff, just take these damn cuffs off. Please! Take em off!"

Sheriff Bledsoe took the key from his pocket. Eric's wrists were wet with sweat.

When the cuffs clicked free, Eric said, "Maybe you should lock me up, too. You know, just to be on the safe side."

Just then Shirley barged in, pushing the door open wider than necessary to accommodate her large frame. "What the hell is going on now?"

"Oh-oh!" Eric said, and moved behind Sheriff Bledsoe.

"Calm down, Miss Harris," Sheriff Bledsoe said. "Don't forget you're at a police station."

"I know where I am, Sheriff. Eric, what the hell have you done now?"

"I-I-I…"

"I-I-I--my ass! What have you done?"

The door opened again and Ruth Ann poked her head in and back out and in again, then, slowly, one limb at a time, she entered.

Sheriff Bledsoe couldn't decide who looked the most terrified, Eric or Ruth Ann.

"Where's Lester?" he asked Ruth Ann.

"He," a squeaky whisper, "couldn't make it."

Sheriff Bledsoe pointed to the phone on his desk. "Call him and tell him to get over here."

Ruth Ann shook her head. "He's gone."

"Where?"

"I don't know. He left, said something about missionary work in Zimbabwe."

Shirley laughed. "Ruth Ann, what are you talking about? You know Lester ain't in Zimbabwe."

"We have a time-share in Zimbabwe. I never talk about it because I don't want people to think we think we're all that."

"Oh, yeah?" Shirley said. "Why don't you sit for a spell? I'll drive you home. You might have a concussion."

Ruth Ann, a few feet away from the door, rubbing her hands together, didn't look as if she could sit if she wanted to.

"Mrs. Hawkins," Sheriff Bledsoe said, "I want you to call your husband and tell him to get down here. If you don't I will."

Ruth Ann grimaced. "I can't. I just can't, Sheriff."

"Goodness, Ruth Ann," Shirley said. "No need to get all upset. Sheriff Bledsoe, why you need Lester? What's going on?"

"You might want to lock me up now, Sheriff," Eric said. "Please!"

"Everybody just relax, okay!" Sheriff Bledsoe said. "Why don't we all sit down and sort this thing out." He pulled up two chairs. "I'm sure we can figure this out without a buncha hysterics. Come on, everybody take a seat."

Ruth Ann took a step backward.

"Fine with me," Eric said. "I prefer to sit in a locked cell. You know what I mean, Sheriff?"

Shirley said, "You keep asking to be locked up. Why? The hell wrong with you?"

"Temporary confinement calms my nerves."

Shirley took a seat. "Will someone tell me what the hell is going on here?"

184

"Miss Harris," Sheriff Bledsoe said, "Eric and..." Should he tell her? Eric was staring at him, shaking his head. "I shouldn't be the one telling you...If your sister and your boyfriend won't, I will." He looked over at Ruth Ann; she'd moved closer to the door. "Don't leave!"

Eric went into the cell and tried to pull the bars closed. "How do you lock this thing, Sheriff?"

"Miss Harris," Sheriff Bledsoe said, "today, two hours ago, I observed your boyfriend, Eric Barnes, at--"

"Ohhhhhhhh!" Ruth Ann cried, clutching her chest. "Ohhhh!" She swooned side to side. "My heart! Ohhhh!" She swayed forward, almost falling to the floor. "Ohhhhh!" and stumbled across the room holding her chest and fell backward onto a desk.

No such luck in the world, Sheriff Bledsoe thought.

"Oh my God!" Shirley shouted, running over to Ruth Ann. "Ruth Ann's having a heart attack!"

"No, she is not," Sheriff Bledsoe said.

Shirley leaned over and put an ear to Ruth Ann's chest, listened for a second, rose up and--Whop!--both hands clutched together, down on Ruth Ann's sternum. She listened again, got up and-- Whop! Another quick listen...another Whop!

Shirley found her rhythm: Whop! Whop! Whop! Whop! Whop!

"Hey!" Sheriff Bledsoe shouted. "Don't do that!"

Again Shirley hammered Ruth Ann. Whop! This time Ruth Ann grunted, "Uhhhh!"

Whop! "Uhhhh!" Whop! "Uhhhh!" Whop! "Uhhhh!" Whop! "Uhhhh!"

Shirley stopped and laid her head on Ruth Ann's chest. "I hear it," she declared. "It's pumping too fast now. Gotta slow it down." Whop! Whop! Whop!

"Sheriff!…Sheriff!" Eric grunted, his body suspended perpendicular against the bars, each limb pushing or pulling. "Would you please lock this damn cell! Please!"

"Call an ambulance," Shirley said, and whopped Ruth Ann again.

"Stop before you seriously hurt her," Sheriff Bledsoe said. "She's not having a heart attack."

"Call a goddamn ambulance!" Shirley shouted with such intensity and authority that Sheriff Bledsoe quickly reached for the phone.

Chapter 19

"Shane didn't want to come back with me," Leonard told his mother. "He said he wanted to stay up there a little while longer."

"How did he look?"

"He looked great. Just great."

"He wasn't hungry, was he?"

"No, Mother."

"Maybe you should take him more food. A growing boy needs to keep his weight up. I'll cook something that'll keep for a long time. You can take it to him." She let him digest that before adding: "If you don't mind?"

"No, Mother, I don't mind at all." He hoped she wouldn't go through too much trouble because whatever she cooked was going into the first trash can he saw. He was not going in the woods again.

"Your dinner is in the microwave. A pumpkin pie in the refrigerator."

"Pumpkin pie," already tasting it. "Mother, you shouldn't have."

"Save a piece for Shane, okay?" Ida said, leaving the kitchen.

Leonard washed his hands in the sink, took a paper towel-wrapped plate out of the microwave and put it on the table. This was his reward for fearlessly confronting jungle boy. And in the process, he thought, I've lost the love of my life.

He'd gone to the Greyhound bus stop in town, the regional airport in Lake Village, and then back to the motel. No sign of Victor. *He's gone forever!* He shook the thought.

After blessing the food, he removed the paper towel and froze, staring at green beans, mashed potatoes, two dinner rolls and a steaming heap of boiled neck bones. Leonard swallowed hard.

Had he angered his mother? If he did he couldn't remember doing so. Even if he'd done something to upset her, it couldn't have been egregious enough for her to spike the neck bones. *Could it?* He picked up a neck bone with a fork. This is silly, he chided himself. His mother wouldn't poison him.

He sniffed the neck bone. Arsenic, he remembered reading, didn't have a smell or taste. If Kenny G were afoot, he would have him…He remembered Kenny G whining and howling as his owner was wheeled into the ambulance. He'd thought the poor dog was expressing grief, but then Kenny G threw up and keeled over, his little legs sticking straight up.

The phone on the wall rang. Leonard ignored it, got up, dumped the food and the plate into the trash can and covered it with newspaper. He was headed for the pumpkin pie when he heard a scream. He ran and almost collided with Ida, also running, in the hallway.

"What's the matter, Mother?"

"Come on, Leonard, we gotta go! Ruth Ann had a heart attack!"

* * * * *

Shirley, Lester, Eric, and Robert Earl and Estafay were all sitting in the emergency waiting room when Leonard and Ida arrived at the hospital.

"How is she?" Ida asked no one in particular.

"We don't know yet," Shirley said. "The doctor hasn't come out and told us anything. I'm going to give them a few minutes, then I'm going back there to see what's going on."

Robert Earl and his wife, her face hidden behind a large Bible, were sitting apart from everyone else. Robert Earl, wearing his usual blue jean overalls, slumped in his chair, clamped hands resting on his large stomach, one finger tapping a knuckle, as if he were waiting for his car in the shop.

One look at Eric and Leonard thought he might be high on drugs. His legs were shaking and he didn't seem to know where to put his hands as he swiveled his head back and forth from Shirley to the double doors leading into the emergency room. Shirley appeared on the verge of a nervous breakdown, red eyes, uncombed hair poking up like weeds.

Lester, sitting to Shirley's left, rested his head between his knees.

"What happened, Lester?" Leonard asked.

Lester raised his head a bit. "I'm not sure…I think she had a heart attack."

Leonard patted his back. "She'll be all right, Lester. Ruth Ann's a fighter."

Shirley said, "Ruth Ann, Eric and me, we're at the police station and Ruth Ann just standing there, looking the picture of health. All a sudden--Kabookie!" Clapped her hands. "Ruth Ann let out a hoot and holler, and I looked up and she was lying on a desk. I swear, it scared the living daylights out of me. I checked her heart, didn't hear anything, so I started emergency CPR. Almost lost her right then and there."

"Why were y'all at the police station?"

Shirley rolled her eyes at Eric. "Somebody got arrested."

"Why was Ruth Ann there?"

Eric abruptly stood up. "Where's the john around here?"

Robert Earl pointed to an exit. "Through there and to the left. You better get your own tissue--they out." Eric hurried out the door.

"Butthead got himself arrested again," Shirley said. "Ruth Ann gave me a ride."

"Mercy!" Ida exclaimed and plopped down in the chair beside Lester. "This is all my fault, all my fault!"

"It's not your fault, Mother," Leonard said. "Ruth Ann's going to be all right."

"Lester," Robert Earl shouted across the room, "you and Ruth Ann have insurance, don't you?"

Lester gave Robert Earl a bewildered look.

"Robert Earl," Shirley said, "that's a helluva thing to ask at a time like this. Who called you, anyway?"

"Nobody. I heard it on my police scanner. I know things before the police do. Lester, I sure hope you have burial insurance. Burials are pretty expensive nowadays. Ruth Ann might make it, she might not. Either way you gotta be prepared. Estafay and I are strapped right now so we won't be able to contribute to nothing. Speaking of strapped, Momma, what's going on with the money? You oughta see if the man will give us a little bit."

Ida covered her face with a hand and shook her head.

"Shut the hell up, Robert Earl!" Shirley said.

"We've got insurance," Lester said. "I just...want my wife back...alive." He buried his head between his knees and bawled.

"Contain yourself, man," Robert Earl said. "Ain't nobody said she dead yet. She might make it. I hope she didn't go too long without getting oxygen to her head. If she did she'll be a veggie. I wouldn't blame you not wanting a veggie rotting up the house, attracting a bunch of flies with them big diapers."

Lester's sobs increased in pitch and volume.

Leonard said, "Somebody oughta cut the oxygen off to your head."

"A good idea," Shirley said. "He keeps talking crazy, Leonard, you and I take him outside, see how long he can hold his breath."

"Momma," Robert Earl said, "you hear em, don't you? They talking about choking me again."

"Shut up, already!" Shirley shouted at him.

Sheriff Bledsoe and an Asian man wearing surgery scrubs came through the double doors.

"How is she?" Shirley and Lester asked at once.

"She's fine, just fine," the man said. "Too much stress. Stress not good, causes anxiety attacks. Tomorrow she go home, back to old self, live happily ever after."

"Could you explain it in English?" Robert Earl said.

The man laughed. "You comedienne in the family? You very funny. Very funny, indeed." He left the room.

Eric came back.

"She's all right," Sheriff Bledsoe said. "A case of nerves, I suspect."

"Thank you, Jesus!" Ida said.

"Can I go see her?" Lester said.

"I guess," Sheriff Bledsoe said. Lester started for the doors. "Say, Lester…"

Lester stopped. "What?"

"Never mind. It can wait."

"What about me, Sheriff?" Eric asked.

"What about you?"

"Can I go now?"

Shirley said, "C'mon, Sheriff. This family has suffered enough. Let him go home tonight. It's Friday. You'll have to spend the weekend at the jail watching him. Let him go and I promise you he'll be there bright and early Monday morning."

Sheriff Bledsoe inhaled loudly through his nose. "Okay, Eric, you can go. Now everybody listen up. Here's what I'm gonna do."

He paused and gave them each a hard look. "Since this investigation has turned into a circus, I'm requesting each and every one of you come in this weekend, Saturday or Sunday, and submit a polygraph test. If you don't I'll come looking for you. One of you tell Lester and Ruth Ann when she starts feeling better, which should be in a few minutes." He scanned their faces. "Does everybody understand?"

"Can I go first?" Robert Earl asked.

"It doesn't matter who's first. Just show up."

"I'll be there," Shirley said.

"Me, too," Leonard said.

"I'll go after Shirley goes," Eric said.

"I already told you I did it," Ida said.

"Yes, you did," Sheriff Bledsoe said, and walked away.

"What's eating him?" Leonard asked.

"He's either hungry or he's gassy," Robert Earl said. "Didn't you hear his stomach? Sound like a diesel engine low on oil. He better put something in or let something out before he blows a rod."

"Robert Earl," Shirley said, "where's your teeth?"

Robert Earl covered his mouth with both hands.

"They're in the shop," Estafay said from behind the Bible.

"The pawnshop," Shirley said, laughing. Eric laughed, too.

"Leave my son alone," Ida said, a chuckle in her voice.

Leonard didn't crack a smile, staring at Estafay, head to toe dressed in white. White scarf wrapped tightly around her head. White short-sleeve dress, frayed at the edges. White stockings, a long run along her right calf. White nurse's shoes, the rubber instep missing on the left. Her long, pallid fingers held the Bible in a death grip.

She wasn't reading, she was hiding. Perhaps she was uncomfortably shy amongst her husband's family; they were prone to crude jokes. Or she...Estafay hadn't uttered a word when Sheriff Bledsoe requested everyone come in for a polygraph test.

The Bible slid down and Estafay's eyes met his. She'd sensed him staring at her. Leonard shuddered. Something…something cold… in her eyes, which looked out of alignment, one higher than the other. She held his stare for a moment more and then slid the Bible back up. Leonard exhaled, not aware he'd been holding his breath.

Chapter 20

Ruth Ann lay in her own bed with her favorite bed partner at her side, Teddy. Despite looking into the eyes of death not fifteen hours ago, she'd never felt better. Now she knew how Lazarus must have felt after awakening and not finding himself hosting earthworms: exhilarated.

Not only was she alive and kicking, she didn't have a bruise on her body. Not even a scratch. No small miracle, considering the possibilities.

She remembered her promise to The Man Upstairs.

It can wait.

After all, she didn't say when she would start living a righteous life; she'd said she would, which, of course, meant sometime in the near distant future.

Lester entered the room carrying an antique silver breakfast tray. Toast, sausage, scrambled eggs and orange juice.

"Are you hungry?" Lester asked. She nodded and Lester placed the tray on the bed. "Good. I've cooked a little something to build up your strength." She reached for the fork and Lester playfully slapped her hand. "No, I'll feed you."

What on earth, Ruth Ann wondered, made me think I could live without this man? So what the skin around his mouth looked like the onset of vitiligo. The man loved her. She could search the world and never again find a man who truly loved her as Lester did.

Lester fed her small bits of runny eggs, half-cooked sausage and burnt toast and waited patiently as she chewed.

"I need to get out of this bed," Ruth Ann said between bites. "I need to get up and clean this house."

"No way, honey. The doctor said you need your rest." He leaned over and kissed her forehead. "Let me take care of you."

"Lester, you have to go to work."

"I've got it covered. Valerie is coming over when I go to work this evening. She promised me she'll keep an eye on you when I'm gone."

"What!" Ruth Ann shouted, bits of eggs flying out of her mouth. "Valerie! Lester, you know how your sister feels about me. I don't want her in my house! You know I don't!"

"Honey, she's not moving in. She'll look on you while I'm at work."

"Hmmph! She'll come in here and press a pillow over my head. You tell her keep her malnourished, crack-smoking ass away from me."

"We'll see," and stuck a spoonful of eggs in her mouth before she could respond.

Ruth Ann chewed quickly and said, "I don't want her in my house, Lester. I'm sick. I shouldn't be forced to deal with someone I can't stand. Around you she pretends she likes me--you and I both know she does not. I don't want her in my house, Lester. I mean it!"

"I'll call her and tell her not to come." He picked up the tray and started out. "I guess you don't want my mother here, either. She's on her way right now."

"What! Bebe? In my house?" *Maybe I should have died.* She absolutely loathed Bebe.

"Yes," Lester said.

"The same Bebe who stood up in church and called me a whore on Easter Sunday? You're telling me she's coming to my house! You forgot what happened the last time she was here? She and I got into a fight, the state police came out and we paid a plumber five hundred dollars to unclog her cheap wig out of the septic tank. Hello? Yo momma psychodrama escaped your memory?"

"Ruthie, honey, she's concerned, willing to lend a hand."

"Ha! Please! She thinks I'm suffering, wants to hear me wailing."

"A mean thing to say, Ruthie. I need someone to watch you while I step out for a few minutes."

"I can look after myself. I don't need a gap-toothed buzzard gawking at me, hoping I croak. Where are you trying to run off while I'm here dying?"

"Sheriff Bledsoe requested I come in for a lie-detector test." Ruth Ann's jaw dropped. "Momma said she'd be glad to watch you while I'm gone. What happened between you and her was three years ago. She's not thinking about that. You oughta give her a chance, Ruthie. Let bygones be bygones."

"You...you talked to Sheriff Bledsoe? You and he talked? About what? What did he say?"

"I didn't talk to him. Shirley told me he requested everyone at the hospital come in this weekend and take a lie-detector test. I figured to go get it over with so I can come back and look after you."

"Lester, you weren't there...at the barbecue. You weren't in any way connected to what happened."

"I know that and you know that. Sheriff Bledsoe, apparently, does not. I guess he's trying to cover all the bases."

"Don't go! I mean, call him and tell him you can't make it."

"It's not a problem. I don't go he'll think I have something to hide."

Ruth Ann threw the sheet back and hopped out of bed. "I'm going with you. We'll both go."

"No, honey. Lie down. The doctor said you need to rest a few days. What are you doing?"

Ruth Ann ignored him and stepped to the closet. "Fuck that! I'm going!" She angrily slid several dresses back and forth on the rod. "I'm not sitting in bed wondering what's going on. I need to be there."

"Why? Why do you need to be there?"

A good question, to which she didn't have a good answer.

"B-be-because I'm your wife. It's not fair. It's not fair at all, Lester. You weren't at the barbecue…and…and you had nothing whatsoever to do with my father's death…and I don't appreciate Sheriff Bledsoe calling you in and grilling you over something you know nothing about. I don't appreciate it one bit. It ain't fair, Lester."

She snatched an orange pullover sweater from a hanger--the one Bebe had given her last Christmas, the one she'd never worn--and flung it to the floor. "It's not fair, Lester!" she cried, stomping on it. "It's not fair!"

Lester crossed to her and hugged her. "Relax. It's all right. If it'll make you feel better, I'll call Sheriff Bledsoe and tell him I can't make it till you're fully recuperated."

"May I call him for you?"

"Sure, why not?"

Ruth Ann smiled and allowed Lester to guide her back to the bed.

"Honey," Lester said, "you need to relax." He spread the sheet over her. "Really. You can't go getting yourself worked up." The doorbell rang. "That's probably Momma."

"I'm not up for company."

"I'll handle it. You just get some rest."

When he was halfway out the door, Ruth Ann said, "One more thing, Lester, before you go."

"Yes."

"Come closer." He moved to the bed. "Closer." Ruth Ann rose up and kissed him, long and hard.

"Momma?" Lester said.

Ruth Ann wrapped her arms around his neck and kissed him again. "She can wait...can't she?"

"But..." kissing her neck, "she knows...we're home." He climbed into the bed beside her.

"Wait, Lester. You're on top of Teddy."

Lester got up and put the bear on the table next to the bed.

"Make sure his back is turned," Ruth Ann said. The doorbell rang again…and again.

"I better answer that."

"Hold me for a second, Lester."

He got back into bed and immediately resumed kissing her neck.

"Ruthie…Ruthie…Oh, honey…I love you so much." He kissed her chin…her nose…her eyes, tightly closed. "Oh baby! Ruthie…oh Ruthie…oh baby!"

His facial skin was coarse, scraping her face, the foul-smelling scent of Magic Shave abused her nostrils.

Again the doorbell rang, and Ruth Ann wondered when the old girl would give up and go home. Lester nibbled on her breast through her Bugs Bunny pajama top.

"I love you so much, Ruthie," Lester said. "Baby, I want you so bad."

He unbuttoned the top button and started biting her breast. She could feel his erection pressing against her kneecap. She opened her eyes…Lester's afro came into view first, and then he turned his head and she saw his mouth clamped onto her breast.

"Oh God," she groaned and closed her eyes again.

"Ruthie…Ruthie!"

She couldn't stop him now; she'd let him go too far. A hand squeezed her buttocks, moved along her waist and palmed her pubic.

"Ruthie!"

She let her thoughts drift…and drift…till they settled on that glorious day when she and her father were riding in his '65 Pontiac, the wind blowing her hair as she sat on the armrest next to him, a half-eaten cotton candy cone in her hand.

They'd just returned from the fair, just she and her father, and he'd allowed her to ride every ride she wanted, had even joined her in a bumper car.

"Remember, Ruth Ann, don't tell nobody where we went, not even your mother," her father had said when they returned home.

Lester lifted himself off her, and she returned to the present.

It's over? Please let it be over.

"Baby," Lester said, "I know you're sick…I can't help it, I want you so bad."

His mouth sought her breast again. *No, it isn't over.* With both hands he tried to pull down her pajama bottoms. She knew she would have to rise up if they were to come off, but she let him tug and pull.

Just when she decided to accommodate him, Lester ripped her pajama bottoms off with one violent yank.

"There!" he said victoriously.

She couldn't help but open one eye now. Lester was butt naked, except for his socks and shoes.

How did he take his pants off without removing his shoes? How?

Not to mention when? *And what's foaming out of his mouth?*
Rabies? No, drool. He caught her looking and she quickly clenched
her eyes shut.

"Oh God!"

Lester started kissing her kneecaps, then clumsily worked his
way up. At her inner thigh, a few inches from her pubic, he stopped
and sneezed.

No, he didn't! No, he didn't just come near me and sneeze!

Oh, yes, he most certainly did.

Lester parted her legs…and suddenly he was inside her,
bucking and thrashing as if he were riding a mechanical bull.

"Whoa!" Lester whooped, and collapsed on top of her.

Lightning, Ruth Ann thought. *Only lightning flares up and
disappears faster than Lester.*

Lester stopped gasping to say, "I love you so much, Ruthie!"

Ruth Ann whispered, "I love me, too."

The doorbell finally stopped ringing.

Chapter 21

"It's broke!" Sheriff Bledsoe said into the phone. "What you mean it's broke?"

"Inoperable, damaged, malfunctioned, in need of repair," Deputy Sheriff Jim Barr said. "Broke is broke."

"Fantastic, just fantastic! I have a murder case here with twice the suspects in an Agatha Christie novel, and the only polygraph machine in southeastern Arkansas is broke?"

"I'm sorry, Ennis, it's been down six months. Sheriff Greene said he was going to send it to the shop up there in Little Rock. It might take two years before he gets around to doing anything about it."

"Which may be the same time I solve this case." He sat down and added ruefully, "If ever."

"Take your suspects to Little Rock and use their machine. Sheriff Hughes, over in Chicot county, took a guy up there last week. Those Little Rock boys are obliging enough. You ask them real nice they'll even conduct the interview."

"Bad idea. Each time I get two or more of my suspects in one room, all kinds of commotion break loose. Piling em up in a van on a two-hour trip to Little Rock would get more chaotic than throwing a hornet's nest into a senior citizen home."

"Oh, well. You know there's the old-fashioned way."

"What's that?"

"Make your own polygraph machine."

"Excuse me?" Sheriff Bledsoe said, not sure if he'd heard correctly.

"Make your own machine."

"Jim, are you crazy?"

"My ex certainly thinks so. Listen, all you have to do is rig something together and call it a polygraph machine. When you suspect your perp is lying, make your machine react. Even with a legitimate machine the results are dictated by the person administering the test."

"Are you crazy?"

"A couple of years ago, right before we got the real machine, we hooked up a strobe light to a rape suspect and each time he opened his mouth the light came on. He confessed everything he did back to daycare."

"You are crazy, aren't you? What happens when a defense lawyer discovers his or her client confessed to a homemade polygraph machine? How you explain that?"

"I wouldn't try. Who would believe it? Look, Ennis, I'm only offering a suggestion. You called me, remember?"

"Yes, I'm sorry I did. Bye."

"If you try it, call me back and let me know how it worked out."

"Are you crazy?" and hung up the phone. He popped six Pepsid AC tablets into his mouth and chased them down with a gulp of Mylanta. A fake polygraph machine--Ha!--with a strobe light. *Preposterous!*

The next day, Sheriff Bledsoe directed a disheveled Robert Earl to a seat in front of a pine box the size of a microwave oven, stained and lacquered to a mirror finish. Atop the box were two light bulbs, one red, the other black. Three extension cords snaked out from under it, one leading to a wall socket, unplugged, one hanging down the front of the desk and disappearing underneath to a foot pedal, the last looped in a large circle, crudely covered with Velcro.

Sheriff Bledsoe picked up the Velcro-covered cord and said, "Robert Earl, we'll wrap this around your chest." Robert Earl nodded and allowed Sheriff Bledsoe to rope the cord around him. "The main thing here," Sheriff Bledsoe explained, "is to be completely honest."

"Is it going to hurt?"

"No, no. It won't hurt at all. It's perfectly…" *Or is it?*

Robert Earl was a big old boy, two-fifty plus some, but if enough electricity coursed through his body it could not only hurt him, it might kill him. *I should have tested it at home.*

He needed to check and make sure the wires weren't touching. He stood between Robert Earl and the desk and lifted the box; the wires, wrapped individually with electrical tape, weren't touching.

Still he had doubts. He could already hear the news anchor: "Sheriff electrocutes man with cracker-rigged polygraph machine. Hear the details Live-At-Five."

Maybe this isn't a good idea.

"Sheriff, what was you about to say?"

"Oh, nothing. Just it's perfectly safe."

"You gotta plug it up first, don't you?"

"Yes, right." He plugged the cord into the socket.

"Wait!" Robert Earl shouted.

Sheriff Bledsoe snatched the cord out of the socket; electricity zapped his hand. "Did it hurt?"

"No."

"Man, you scared the mess out of me! What you shouting for? Don't shout, okay?" He wiped sweat from his forehead and noticed his hand was shaking. "No need to shout."

"I'm sorry, Sheriff. I hate to tell you this…"

Oh-oh, Sheriff Bledsoe thought. *Busted.* "What?"

Robert Earl shook his square-shaped head and stared at his large hands. "I've had dreams about killing him."

"Killing who?"

"Daddy."

Fiddlesticks! He'd gotten so caught up with the box he forgot why he built the thing.

"Will it…you know…make me look guilty?" Robert Earl said.

"It depends. Why don't you tell me about the dreams?"

Robert Earl scratched the top of his balding head with both hands. Dandruff sprang up and landed on his red flannel shirt and overalls. "I didn't kill him, let's get that understood upfront."

"Okay, Robert Earl."

"Like I said, I had a few dreams about killing him. Well, shoot, a lot of dreams. He treated me like dirt, I'm telling you, Sheriff. Like I was something stinky on the bottom of his shoe. I've seen people treat dogs better…mangy dogs…one-eyed dogs…and I was his son, his first child."

"In the dreams, how did you do it?"

"How did I kill him?"

"Yes."

"Sheriff, don't forget I'm talking dreams."

Sheriff Bledsoe dropped the cord to the floor. This was far too complicated for a fake polygraph machine. "Tell me how you killed your father in your dreams."

A smile appeared under Robert Earl's bushy moustache.

"One time I chopped his body in little bitty pieces with a hatchet and fed it to some hogs. Another time I booby-trapped the commode with dynamite, like in the movie. You know, the one with Danny Glover and Mel Gibson. In my dream, Daddy blew up and landed outside on the ground."

"You ever put something in his food?"

"In my dreams, right?"

"Yes."

The unctuous smile reappeared and he said, "In this one dream he and I were riding in my truck and he said something snotty about my wife, Estafay, so I slipped him something. Don't remember what it was. Put it in his buttermilk. He started choking and begging me to help him. I sat there watching him turn purple, thinking he shouldna said what he said about Estafay."

"You don't remember what you gave him?"

"No, I sure don't. Bet you just as soon as I leave here it'll come to me."

"Think it mighta been a pesticide?"

"Could have been. I really don't remember. Dreams are hazy like that. Wait a minute, wait one darn minute! I had dreams about doing it and I even thought once or twice about doing it, but I *didn't* do it. Like the preacher said, 'Thinking about it and doing it are two different things.' You can hook me up to the lie-detector if you don't believe me."

"Not necessary. I heard you were experiencing financial difficulties and you confronted your father for an advance on your share of the money, and you and he got into a shoving match. True?"

"Yes, sorta true. He shoved me--I didn't shove him."

"You're experiencing financial difficulties?"

"Yes. Me and everyone else. Estafay, my wife, she wants...You know how women are. Want this, need that."

Sheriff Bledsoe studied him for a moment.

Robert Earl shifted uncomfortably under his gaze. "Why you looking at me, Sheriff? I'm telling the truth. You think I'm lying, hook me up to the lie-detector."

Sheriff Bledsoe thought about it for a second. *Why not?*

Again he plugged the cord into the socket. "Okay, Robert Earl, let's do it. If there's any doubt of your veracity, the red light will light up." Actually, both lights came on whenever he stepped on the pedal. "If you tell a flat-foot, bald-faced lie, both the red and black light will light up. So, Robert Earl, speak only the truth."

"Okay."

"What's your full name?"

"Sheriff, you know my full name."

"Yes, I do. We need to establish a rapport with the machine to see if it's working properly. Your full name?"

"Mitt Romney. Just kidding. Robert Earl Harris."

Sheriff Bledsoe stepped on the pedal and specks of light sparkled through cracks of paint in both bulbs.

"Dang! It can detect flip-flops?"

"Yes, Robert Earl. Let's move on. Do you like snakes?"

"Yes," staring intently at the bulbs; they didn't light up.

"Have you ever flunked an IQ test?"

"Yes."

"Have you ever killed anything?"

Robert Earl jerked his attention from the bulbs to Sheriff Bledsoe. "No!"

Sheriff Bledsoe stepped on the pedal and both bulbs lighted.

"Dang! Do animals count?"

"Yes, they do."

"Yes." The lights went off.

"Have you ever physically injured a human being?"

Robert Earl nodded.

"The machine can't register nods. It requires a verbal response."

Robert Earl pinched the bridge of his nose. "Uh-huh."

"Yes or no?"

"Yes," and pounded the arm of the chair with a closed fist.

Sheriff Bledsoe noticed sweat beading on Robert Earl's nose and forehead. *This thing just might work.* "Robert Earl, have you ever killed a human being?"

"No!" Instantly both bulbs lighted. "Aw, shoots! Yes--I mean no. Maybe. I don't know!" He squeezed his head with both hands.

"What?"

Robert Earl pounded the top of his head. "I didn't mean to do it, Sheriff! I swear I didn't mean to do it! The demon got hold of me."

"Relax, Robert Earl. I'll help you any way I can. Tell me--"

"I knew this would happen! I knew it, I knew it, I knew it!" He kicked the desk. "I knew I shouldna come here. I should've waited till you came and got me. Noooooo! I had to go first." He pounded his head again. "I knew it, I knew it, I knew it!"

Sheriff Bledsoe surreptitiously patted himself for his weapon. It wasn't strapped to his waist. He scanned the room…There it was, a good ten feet away, in a holster hanging on a hat rack.

"Calm down, Robert Earl. I'm going to do everything I can to help you."

Robert Earl jumped to his feet, snatched the cord off his chest and threw it to the floor. He held his fists in a boxing stance. "Are you going to arrest me?"

Sheriff Bledsoe pushed his chair away from the desk, for maneuvering room, and suddenly felt that all too familiar pain in his gut. "I'm afraid so, Robert Earl. You murdered a man."

"What man?"

"Your father."

"I didn't murder him!"

"You just said you did."

"I wasn't talking about him. I was talking about somebody else."

Sheriff Bledsoe stared at him for a long moment. "Excuse me?"

Robert Earl collapsed into the chair. "It was a long time ago, Sheriff."

Sheriff Bledsoe scratched the top of his head, also starting to bald. "I'm not a man who easily resorts to profanity. I'd sure like to know what the hell you're talking about?"

"When I was in the Marines, over in Okinawa, this girl, you know, a bad girl--see what I'm saying?"

"A prostitute?"

Robert Earl nodded. "It was a long time ago, Sheriff. I wasn't married at the time. I..."

Sheriff Bledsoe waited for him to continue. He didn't. "Keep talking."

"I'd been drinking, too. I..." Another pause. Sheriff Bledsoe nodded for him to continue. "I'd drunk six or seven beers and a couple of Mai Tais. You ever drink a Mai Tai, Sheriff?"

Sheriff Bledsoe shook his head.

Robert Earl started to speak, but didn't.

Irritated, Sheriff Bledsoe said, "At this rate, Social Security will dry up. Robert Earl, why don't you get to the heart of the matter, okay?"

"We made a deal and I gave her the money upfront. Before she made good on her end she snuck off with my pants and wallet. I couldn't get back on base without my ID card."

"So you caught up with her?"

"Yeah, though it wasn't as easy as it sounds."

"And you killed her?"

Robert Earl started coughing and patted his own back. "I'm not sure I did or didn't. I was drunk and very whizzed off. I mighta punched her a couple times. Her eyes weren't open, but that don't mean nothing. She mighta been faking."

"Was there blood?"

Robert Earl nodded.

"You can't fake blood, Robert Earl. The Marines never said anything to you about this?"

"Uh-uh. I got an Honorable Discharge, too."

"I can't believe you did something like that," Sheriff Bledsoe said, for lack of anything else to say. "I'm shocked. I just can't believe you did something like that."

Robert Earl crossed his arms and rested his chin on his chest. Talking to the floor: "You think I'll get the electric chair?"

Sheriff Bledsoe studied the top of Robert Earl's head, in search of a lobotomy scar. Nothing except a receding hairline and a bald spot in the middle. Robert Earl didn't have enough lights on in his head to plot and execute his father's murder.

"Robert Earl, I'm going to do something I shouldn't do. I'm going to give you a pass on this one. If I ever hear your name in trouble again, a misdemeanor or anything, you're going to pay for old and new. Do you understand?"

A tear dropped from Robert Earl's face and landed in the top pocket of his overalls. "Yes, sir."

Chapter 22

For the first time in months, perhaps years, Shirley felt light on her feet. A good thing, too, because the walk from her house to the jail was almost three miles. The sun, a white orb against a blue-and-white canvas, magnified heat on the back of her neck.

A swarm of gnats hovered a few feet above her head, one occasionally breaking off to perform reconnaissance missions on her face and neck. Shirley waved them away and maintained her brisk pace, her open-toe sandals click-clocking on the hot asphalt.

Cars and eighteen-wheelers zipped by in both directions; several drivers tapped their horn, but no one stopped and offered her a ride. The sandals were a bad choice for a stroll to town.

Shirley didn't mind, her thoughts were elsewhere. She was in love, and the man whom she loved had gotten on his knees and asked her to marry him. She smiled to herself as she veered around an offal, a possum or a coon, buzzing with flies.

Yes, Mr. Eric Barnes had asked her, Miss Shirley Harris, to marry him.

She swatted a gnat on her neck and picked up her pace. Her life was moving forward. *Finally, thank God.* And if Sheriff Bledsoe would get off his butt and find out who murdered her father, she could start scratching off items on her wish list with the inheritance money.

Eric and she would have a grand wedding, a spectacular wedding, with a band. She would buy Eric a new truck, maybe one that could be switched to a SUV. She would buy Paul a computer and new clothes. A new car for Mrs. Avery and an anonymous deposit in her savings account.

She would treat her mother and Ruth Ann to a mall trip in Little Rock, buy them each new shoes and purses, or whatever they desired, then take them to the Loony Bin, a comedy club.

Up ahead, a van was parked on the shoulder. A prison crew, eight men wearing striped orange-and-white jumpsuits, sat on the ground in the van's shade. Shirley crossed over to the opposite side of the street.

Passing the van she saw the officer sitting in the front seat, all the windows rolled up. She then realized that her navy blue culottes, decorated with red and white daisies, were drenched with sweat. She kept walking, her thoughts traveling to Red Lobster. She hadn't been there in years.

She'd order a Caesar salad with all the trimmings: American cheese, cottage cheese, cucumbers, tomato slices, bacon bits, fresh peaches, raisins, all under a pool of Ranch dressing.

The town proper came into view. Three blocks of non-descript, flat roof brick buildings, circa Civil War, a few vacant, all in need of major restoration. Most were clothing and antique stores struggling to see financial daylight inside the far-reaching shadow of the Wal-Mart Super Center on the other side of town.

Recent additions were a Subway restaurant, a Quik-Print and not one but three pay-day loan businesses.

After the salad she would have a platter of shrimp scampi and a Maine lobster. For dessert she would have a cherry cheesecake. Man, did she love cherry cheesecake. Of course she wouldn't eat the entire cheesecake in public, just half of it. The other half she'd take home for later.

Nearing the jail she saw Robert Earl getting into his truck. She waved at him. "Hey, Robert Earl."

He responded by wriggling two fingers.

"Robert Earl," walking closer, "is something wrong?"

Robert Earl shook his head and backed out of the parking space.

"See ya," Shirley said. "I guess it's my turn for the third degree."

Robert Earl stopped the truck in the middle of the road and drove back into the parking space. "Shirley…"

"Yes."

"Don't try to fool it, Shirley."

"Fool what?"

"The lie-detector machine. The best thing to do, start off with the truth and stick to it. If you don't you'll regret it." He backed up and squealed off.

Shirley was confused when she stepped inside the jail, but the cool air quickly erased her thoughts.

Sheriff Bledsoe was sitting behind a desk. He wasn't what Shirley called handsome, though he wasn't nauseous to look at. Though well past the overweight mark, he kept his afro, moustache, and beard neat and trimmed, his uniform clean and starched.

"Kinda hot out there, ain't it?" Sheriff Bledsoe said. "You can stand in front of the air conditioner if you like."

Shirley felt a pang of guilt for threatening him the other day. "No, thank you, Sheriff. I'd prefer to get this over as soon as possible."

"Well, let's get started, Miss Harris." He indicated a chair in front of his desk. Shirley sat down and peered around a funny-looking box at him. "Miss Harris, have you ever taken a polygraph test before?"

"No, I sure haven't."

"No problem. Let me explain how this works. The machine detects abnormalities in a person's body when he or she responds falsely to a question. In laymen terms, it can detect when someone is telling a lie. Any questions?"

"Where's the machine?" Shirley said, looking around the room.

Sheriff Bledsoe got up and tapped on the funny-looking box. "Right here. Now if you'd allow me to wrap this cord around your chest." He picked up a Velcro-covered cord and approached her.

She pushed his hands away. "What the hell is this?"

"A polygraph machine...the old model."

"Like hell it is! This looks like something you made in your garage. What you trying to pull here, Ennis?"

Sheriff Bledsoe opened his mouth and quickly closed it.

Shirley squinted at him. "You hooked Robert Earl up to this crap, didn't you?"

"Well, uh, I, uh..."

"The reason he left in such a huff. You hooked him up to this junk and he spilled his guts, didn't he? Did he confess to a crime?"

"Yes, he did."

"He's not in jail, so it was something he did a long time ago. Right?"

Sheriff Bledsoe nodded.

"You know what anusitis is, Ennis?"

He shook his head.

"It's a thought disorder, delusions of intellectual superiority. Non-athletic white men with beer bellies are most susceptible to it. They can have a GED and still believe they're ten times smarter than Obama." Staring at the box: "How often you listen to Rush?"

"I played football in high school. Offensive end."

"Practice. You're talking about practice? Not once I saw you in a game."

Sheriff Bledsoe put a fist to his mouth and burped.

Shirley lifted the box and looked underneath. "I don't believe this shit here," and let it drop to the desk with a resounding thud. "This is the wildest shit I've ever seen in my life."

Sheriff Bledsoe patted his chest.

"Ennis, you think my family are a bunch of imbeciles, don't you? Does the mayor know you made this?"

Sheriff Bledsoe flinched, but didn't speak.

"Maybe I should go talk to him. Is he in his office? Maybe I should go talk to those civil rights people over in Greenville. Or maybe I should tell my family to stop cooperating with you and hire a lawyer. I wonder what a lawyer would say about this."

"Shirley...Miss Harris, I apologize."

"Wow, golly gee whiz! How big of you!"

"Look, I made a mistake. I apologize. The polygraph machine I needed to use is broke, so I tried this. I see now it was a terrible and silly mistake on my part. I wasn't trying to outsmart anyone."

"Uh-huh," Shirley snorted.

"Honest. This is a heckuva case, Shirley, a heckuva case. To be honest with you, I'm getting nowhere with it."

"Who's your main suspect?"

"I can't tell you."

"Do you even have a main suspect?"

"Yes, I do. In fact, I have more than one. The problem in a nutshell--too many main suspects."

"You can eliminate Momma and me." He gave her a wary look. "Don't look upside my head--I didn't do it. The sooner you find out who did, the sooner I can collect my share of the money and get married. I've got a good idea who did it. I'd like to know who you think did it. Maybe you and I are on the same page."

"Who? Who do you think did it?"

"First tell me who you think did it."

"C'mon, Shirley, this isn't a game. This is a police investigation. I've said too much already. This is totally against police procedure."

Shirley pointed at the box. "Is this against police procedure?"

Sheriff Bledsoe frowned, held her gaze for a moment, then blurted, "Eric Barnes."

"What about him?"

Sheriff Bledsoe gave her a look.

Shirley gasped. "What! Hell no! Why…why do you think Eric had something to do with it?"

"He served your father his last meal, didn't he?"

"So what?" Shirley shouted. "So fucking what! Big damn deal! Just 'cause he--look here, Ennis, you got Eric dead wrong. Eric is not a killer!"

"You sure about that?"

"What kind of question is that? I tell you what, if you start harassing Eric, I'll go to the mayor and tell him about you and your damn fake polygraph machine! I won't sit by and watch you railroad Eric. He had nothing to gain from Daddy's death. Nothing! You hear me? Nothing!"

"You and him live together. Isn't it reasonable to assume when you obtain your daddy's money he would benefit?"

"Yes, you're right, but you're damn wrong about Eric, Ennis. He has his problems, I can't deny that. He's not a murderer."

"He would, more than likely, also benefit from Ruth Ann."

"Ha! You kidding me? Ruth Ann won't give her own flesh and blood a dime. What makes you think she'll give Eric a slug nickel?"

Sheriff Bledsoe rubbed his moustache with both hands. Shirley noticed his fingers were trembling.

"Shirley, I shouldn't be the one telling you this. Your sister and..." He drifted off.

"What?"

Sheriff Bledsoe shook his head.

"Ennis, you do know everything you see on TV isn't necessarily true. Homemade polygraph machines, rub-away weight loss ointments, gadgets from the Acme Supply Company. You can't set your watch by those things in the real world, Ennis. Well, you can, but if you're an elected official…" She paused and smiled at him. "You see where I'm going with this?"

"Eric and Ruth Ann were having an affair."

Shirley jumped up and backhanded the box. It skidded across the floor and crashed into the wall--Kablam!--sending five boards and bulb shards in every direction.

Sheriff Bledsoe stood up. "Hey, now!"

"A damn lie!" Shirley hissed through clenched teeth. "A damn lie! Take it back! Take it back! Take it back now, fat ass!"

Sheriff Bledsoe backed up a step, the wall at his back. "Shirley," pointing a shaky finger at her, "you need to calm down and sit down. You just damaged government property, a felony offense!"

"I don't give a damn! You take back what you said!" Sheriff Bledsoe looked past her, and Shirley followed his gaze to a holstered gun on a hat rack. "You gotta get through me to get it!"

"Yesterday I caught Eric sneaking behind Ruth Ann's house. He was--"

"Don't mean a damn thing! You take back the mess you said about Eric and my sister!" She grabbed the chair with one hand and lifted it up. "Take it back!"

"Check yourself," raising his hands. "I'm trying to explain to you what--if you hit me with that chair, you're going to jail!"

"I don't give a damn!"

225

"Shirley, you're bucking serious trouble here. You can't threaten a sheriff."

The chair was getting heavy, but Shirley raised it higher. "You still haven't taken back what you said about my sister. It's a blatant lie, and you know it!"

"They...they both admitted it, Shirley."

Shirley shouted, "A damn lie!" whirled like a javelin thrower and hurled the chair. It smashed into the wall, a foot below the ceiling, a foot above Sheriff Bledsoe's head.

He yelped and ran.

A second or two, Shirley stood there, her entire body shaking...then crumbled to the floor. "It's not true!" she sobbed. "It's not true...it's not true...it's not true...it's not true..." She lay there a long time, sobbing.

"I'm sorry, Shirley," Sheriff Bledsoe said.

She had to collect herself somehow; she didn't want to give Fat Ass the satisfaction of seeing her like this. She tried to get up but couldn't get her limbs to cooperate. Her entire body felt numb. She grabbed the edge of the desk with both hands and, with great effort, pulled herself up.

Unsteady on her feet--one wrong move in either direction she would topple--she combed back her hair with one hand and tried to smooth the wrinkles out of her culottes with the other.

"Are we finished here, Sheriff?" she muttered, dimly aware he held a gun.

"Yes, Shirley. I'm sorry. You need me to give you a ride home?"

"No, I don't need a ride." Her voice low and slurred. "I'll see you later, Sheriff Barnes." She staggered toward the door, almost tripping on a board in her path.

An anguished moan escaped her lips, knees buckled but she maintained her balance. After opening the door she stood there a moment, leaning on the doorframe.

"Ruth Ann," and stumbled out onto the sidewalk.

Chapter 23

"Remember what I told you?" Eric asked his son, playing in the front yard with his friend. This was Eric's third time sticking his head outside and asking the boy.

"Yeah, Daddy," Paul said. "I heard you the first time. When I see Momma, come tell you."

"The second you see her," Eric emphasized. "Not a minute later. You got that?"

Paul nodded. Eric looked down the dirt road that led to the highway. Shirley would have to walk down that road, unless someone gave her a ride. No matter how she returned home he needed to see her before she saw him.

Inside he checked the back door to ensure it was unlocked. It was. If drama commenced he couldn't afford precious seconds fumbling with the deadbolt.

He then went into the bedroom and lay on the bed. Just the second he'd relaxed, a car horn blew out front. He jumped up and peeked out the bedroom window. Mr. Joyner across the street stepped out and got into a mini-bus.

Again Eric leaned his head out the front door and looked down the dirt road. He waited for the dust stirred up by the mini-bus to settle. The road was empty. "Don't forget!" he yelled at Paul and closed the door.

Maybe I should move my ass now while the getting ghost is good.

If Sheriff Bledsoe hadn't told Shirley about Ruth Ann and him, he could always come back later.

"Yeah," he said. "Hell yeah!"

If Sheriff Bledsoe *had* told Shirley, he'd already be down the road, well out of harm's way.

Since last night, after Shirley told him she was going in bright and early to take the polygraph test, he hadn't had a moment's rest.

He'd had a vision--he thought it was a vision because he was wide awake--of Shirley choking him unconscious and setting him afire with gasoline.

Immediately after, he got down on his knees and proposed to her. "Marry me, baby!" He then took her into the bedroom and gave her the premium package, which required two bottles of Karo syrup and three rolls of Saran Wrap, and had resulted in a very stiff neck and a numb jaw.

With any other woman the premium package would have been more than enough to forgive him any transgression. With Shirley, however...*the premium package might not mean shit!*

He sat down on the couch and stared at the television. A daytime talk show: a diminutive white woman, though physically restrained by two muscular bodyguards, was beating the hell out of a large, pot-bellied white man.

"Damn this," getting to his feet. "I'm getting the hell outta here!"

As he was starting for the bedroom, to get his overnight bag, Paul stepped inside.

"What?" Eric said.

Paul shrugged and plopped down on the couch.

"Boy, I really need you to stay outside, keep an eye out for your momma."

"My bad, Daddy, I forgot. Momma's coming."

Eric's bowels liquefied. He rushed to the door and looked out. Sure enough, about four blocks away, Shirley was walking down the road.

"Oh, shit! Paul, get on your bike, ride down to your momma, tell her I said I love her, then ride back and tell me what she said."

"Do what?"

"Hurry up! What you waiting on? Go! Shit! Go!" He pushed Paul out onto the front porch. "Hurry up, you wasting time!"

Paul slowpoked into the yard and got onto his bike. "Tell her what?"

"Dammit, boy! Tell her I love her and come back and tell me what she said. Now go! Hurry the hell up!"

Paul rode off.

Shirley was three and a half blocks away now. *Is she pissed?* Gnawing on a knuckle, bouncing on his heels, Eric watched Paul ride past his mother and then turn around and ride alongside her. Paul pointed at him as he conferred with Shirley.

Too stupid to be genetically linked to me, Eric thought as he watched Paul ride back.

Shirley was only three blocks away now, but still he couldn't see her face clearly enough to gauge her temperament.

Paul stopped his bike three houses short and started chatting with a girl. Eric waved frantically to get his attention.

"Get yo ADD-ass over here!" Whistled. Paul finally noticed and took his sweet time riding over. "What she say? What did she say?"

"She said she wanted to ride my bike."

"What? Your momma wanted to ride your bike?"

"Naw, Daddy. Felicia wanted to ride my bike. I told her no. Last time she put it on a flat, didn't fix it."

"Dammit, boy! What did your momma say?"

"Oh, yeah. She said…uh…I forgot what she said."

231

Eric looked down the road and gulped.

Shirley was running at full sprint. Something--*a shoe?*--no, a sandal tumbled behind her to the side of the road like a cup tossed out of a moving vehicle...Shirley didn't break stride, her arms barely swinging but her legs moving at an incredible clip. The other sandal fell away.

He couldn't remember ever seeing Shirley walk fast...and now she was literally running out of her shoes...*Running!*...all two hundred and thirty pounds of her. She looked like a...a bear...a grizzly bear...a well-fed grizzly bear with fat jiggling and bouncing with each step.

How in the world could something so big move so swiftly?...*How?*...She was less than a block away now. Eric saw her facial expression and he completely forgot about bears, grizzlies or otherwise...

Shirley was pissed!

* * * * *

"Telephone," Lester said, gently nudging his wife.

Ruth Ann rolled onto her back and gave him a pointed look. "I don't want to be bothered. Take a message." She grabbed Teddy and rolled onto her stomach and pressed a pillow over her head.

"It's Eric," Lester said. "He said it's an emergency."

Ruth Ann snatched the pillow away. "Lester, what did I just say? Hello! Take a message, I'll call em back."

"He said it's an emergency."

"Take a damn message!"

"She's not here," Lester said into the cordless phone. "I thought she was here, she's not…I don't know when she'll be back. Huh? Yes, I sure will…No, I won't forget…I'll tell her as soon as she comes in…Bye now."

"Thanks, Lester. That man is a pest and a worthless bum. I don't know why Shirley puts up with him. Nothing but trash. Won't work, won't hustle, just thinks someone should take care of him. Pitiful."

"Go back to sleep, Ruthie. I should not have awakened you." The doorbell rang, followed by insistent knocking.

"Lester, I'm definitely not up for any visitors. I don't care who it is. I feel weak."

"Okay, honey, I'll handle it."

Lester was exiting the room when Ruth Ann said, "By the way, what did Eric want?"

"He said Sheriff Bledsoe gave Shirley the blues and she'll probably come here to talk to you about it."

Louder knocks at the door.

In a flash Ruth Ann sat up on the edge of the bed. "He said what? Who gave who what? When?"

A loud noise: someone was kicking the door.

"Wait a minute!" Lester shouted over his shoulder. "Hold on, Ruthie, let me get the door. That's probably Shirley."

He was closing the door when Ruth Ann flew across the room in two steps and grabbed his arm. "No, wait! Don't answer it!"

"Ruthie, you're pulling on me."

"Come on, Lester, let's make love."

"Again? I thought you were feeling weak?"

"I am. Your lovemaking invigorates me. C'mon, Lester!"

Loud taps on the front room window. "Okay, Ruthie. Let me get the door first."

"Don't let em in, Lester!"

"Why not?"

"We didn't let your mother in. Why should we treat my family any differently? Besides, I don't want to be bothered. I just want to lie in bed with my husband."

"Ruthie, honey, both vehicles are in the driveway."

Clangalangalangalangalang!

"What the hell?"

They both knew what it was: a shattered window. Lester jerked free of Ruth Ann and went to look.

Ruth Ann closed the door, hurried to the lone window in the bedroom, raised the windowpane and pushed the aluminum screen to the ground. Then she dropped to her knees, clasped her hands and said a quick prayer before scurrying underneath the bed.

A second later she heard Shirley's voice inside the house: "Where's her funky ass at?"

Lester's voice: "What's wrong with you, Shirley? Why you break my damn window?"

Ruth Ann felt the vibrations of heavy footsteps. The bedroom door swung open and bounced off the wall. Shirley's dusty sandals came into view, the right one missing the rear strap. Her toenails were long and sharp. One kick, Ruth Ann thought, and I'll spend the rest of my days in dialysis. The sandals moved toward the bedroom window.

"Nasty heifer ran!" Shirley said. "Just like Eric."

Lester's steel-toe work boots came into view. "Why you break the window, Shirley? You know how much it's gonna cost--where's Ruth Ann?"

"She heard me coming and jumped her smelly ass out the window and ran."

"What? No, she didn't." The work boots moved toward the window. "She's sick. The doctor told her to stay in bed and rest."

"When she comes back, tell her that her scuzzy ass is mine!"

"What's going on, Shirley?"

Please don't tell him!

"You don't know, do you?" Shirley said. "Bless your heart."

"Know what?"

"You better sit down."

"Shirley, you're making me nervous. What's going on?"

The work boots and sandals came closer to the bed. Lester sat down and the springs squeaked. Ruth Ann noticed a splintered slat a few inches above her head.

Shirley cleared her throat. "I hate to tell you this, Lester, but you should know."

Lester's right work boot started tapping on the hardwood floor.

Shirley must have noticed too because she said, "First off, Lester, don't ding out like you did before. I'm going to kick her rotten ass well enough for the both of us. Ain't no need you hurting yourself or doing something crazy. Okay?"

"Okay," Lester said, voice squeaky.

Ruth Ann's stomach ached, as if she'd been kicked. She wished she'd jumped out the window: hearing Shirley's account would be more painful than being seen running through the neighborhood in her pajamas.

Now both of Lester's work boots were tapping so rapidly the entire bed vibrated.

Shirley said, "I'm not sure you can handle this. Maybe I should get one of your family members to break the news." The sandals started toward the door.

Thank you, Jesus!

The sandals stopped. "I'm going to tell you anyway. Ruth Ann...Ruth Ann..." Shirley hesitated. "Ruth Ann..."

"Killed your father?"

"No. Why you say that?"

"I don't know. I guess I'm thinking the worst."

"Lester, it's worse than anything you can imagine. Shameful, too. Shameful and disgusting."

Lester groaned, and Ruth Ann stared at the work boots working like two synchronized pistons. "I don't want to hear it. If it's gonna hurt my marriage, I don't want to hear a word about it."

"If you don't want to hear it I won't tell it." The sandals were on the move again, almost out the door.

"Tell me!" The sandals came back. "I'll go crazy if you don't tell me."

"Exactly why I'm not sure I should tell you, Lester. If you must ding out, don't go the self-mutilation route again, okay? It's not your fault."

"Tell me, Shirley."

Shirley sighed. "Lester, Ruth Ann is a slut!"

The work boots stopped. "What do you mean?"

"Just what I said. Ruth Ann is a dirty, rotten, lowlife slut!"

"You…you can't mean…She's your sister. She's my wife! She's--"

"A slut!"

"Why--what--who…Who told you that?"

"Sheriff Bledsoe."

"Sheriff Bledsoe called my wife a slut?"

"Not exactly. He told me about Ruth Ann and…and…" A long pause. "And Eric."

"Eric who?"

"My Eric, Lester. My baby's daddy." Another long pause. "The man whom I was engaged to marry."

"Uh-uh, Shirley. You got it wrong, terribly wrong! Ruth Ann can't stand Eric. She hates his guts. Sheriff Bledsoe has it wrong too, and I don't appreciate him calling my wife names."

"It's true, Lester. I didn't wanna believe it at first. I know it hurts. I'm sorry, Lester, it's true."

"Bullshit!" Lester shouted. "Pure bullshit! It ain't true! You keep saying it is, I'm asking you to leave my house!"

"I'll leave," starting for the door once more. "Eric almost broke his neck running out the back door. Ruth Ann just had a heart attack, but she's healthy enough to jump out the window and run when she heard me coming."

"Doesn't mean anything. I know my wife. She wouldn't stoop so low, mess with her sister's man. No, Shirley, she wouldn't debase herself. She wouldn't, she just wouldn't!"

"They both admitted it to Sheriff Bledsoe."

"That's what he says! Who the hell is he, Al Sharpton? He ain't above lying."

"Lester, you believe what you wanna. Tell Ruth Ann I'll eventually catch her and put a foot up her rancid ass. I mean that! So don't forget to tell her."

"Okay, Shirley. I'll make sure I tell her."

Ruth Ann watched the sandals saunter out the door and disappear down the hallway. Seconds later she heard them click-clocking on the sidewalk out front.

Would Lester stand by and watch Shirley make good on her threat? Did Lester cultivate a seed of doubt what Shirley had told him. She hoped he did, prayed he did, but knew deep down he didn't. Somehow she had to plant a seed of doubt in his mind.

How?

How about this: she and Eric confessed to an affair because…because…because Sheriff Bledsoe, for some idiotic reason, thought he, Lester, had something to do with her daddy's murder, and she, his beloved wife, couldn't stomach the thought of Sheriff Bledsoe hassling her husband over something he knew absolutely nothing about.

Yes, she thought, it might work. A little weak--*weak as hell, really*--but it might work.

She started to crawl from underneath the bed. "Aaaauugggh!"

She froze. Someone was screaming, and since she and Lester were the only two in the room and she hadn't uttered a peep…

"Aaaauugggh!"

Her heartbeat drummed inside her ears.

"Noooo!" The work boots stomped the floor, then disappeared above the bed.

A pounding noise...a guttural scream...more pounding. *What's Lester beating?* Tuffs of cotton floated to the floor. A button bounced onto the floor and rolled underneath the closet door.

Teddy!

Her favorite bed partner! *Lester's killing him!*

Teddy landed on the floor, an arm's length away, mutilated, his right arm missing, small legs bent abnormally behind his back, only one of three buttons remaining on his deflated tummy.

Ruth Ann considered grabbing him and pulling him to safety. Then Lester pounced on Teddy like a predator attacking small prey and punched him and punched him and punched him and punched him and punched him...

Ruth Ann winced with each punch. Lester, unsatisfied with the damage he'd inflicted, clamped his teeth on Teddy's one remaining eye and flailed the eviscerated body in every direction...The eye wouldn't give.

Lester started growling, shook his head more violently, and still the eye wouldn't give. He stopped, Teddy dangling under his clenched teeth by a gossamer, and stared into Ruth Ann's face.

She managed a nervous smile and said, "Hello, honey."

Chapter 24

"Is it too tight?" Robert Earl asked Albert. The boa constrictor, eyes bulging, tongue flitting, flipped and flopped like a worm on a hot plate. "Shoots!" Robert Earl said, and removed the dog collar cinched around Albert's neck. "I guess it is too tight."

Immediately, Albert stopped flip-flopping. Maybe this ain't a good idea, Robert Earl thought, noticing a dark crease where the collar had been.

He'd figured Albert had tired of being confined to a box and desired an unfettered view of the great outdoors. So he hooked one end of a ten-foot dog collar to the clothesline, which would have given Albert plenty of wriggle room, and tied the other end to Albert's neck--well, the area just below the snake's head.

The problem was he couldn't adjust the collar to a proper fit. Too loose, Albert slipped free. A wee too snug, Albert gagged and whipped and then played dead, as it was doing now.

"You can stop it now, Albert." The snake didn't budge. Robert Earl nudged Albert with his hand. Nothing. Pushed it, and Albert rolled halfway on his back.

He's never done this before.

Robert Earl picked it up and the snake hung flaccidly in his hands. "Albert?"

Just then Estafay called from the back porch, "Robert! Robert, Shirley wants to talk to you."

Robert Earl dropped Albert to the ground and pretended to study his neighbor's yard. "Tell her I'll call her back."

"She's here."

"I'm coming." He took another look at Albert, a twisted white-and-orange knot on the ground.

Inside the house, Shirley was sitting at the kitchen table. "Robert Earl," she said, "I need to borrow a gun."

"What you need a gun for?"

"I'm gonna bust a cap in Ruth Ann's stanky ass," Shirley said matter-of-factly.

"Are you serious?"

"I sure am. When I get through with Ruth Ann, Eric's next."

"Why? What for?"

242

"It's rather personal. Just go get the gun. I also need to borrow your truck. It shouldn't take long to do what I gotta do."

"You're joking, aren't you?"

Estafay came into the kitchen. "What's the matter, Robert?"

"Family business," Shirley said. "Robert Earl, why don't you go get it so I can go."

"Shirley," Robert Earl said, biting a thumbnail, "I don't know if I should do it. I might get into serious trouble. Sheriff Bledsoe just cut me slack on some stuff. I give you one of my guns, you shoot somebody, my butt in hot water again. Sheriff Bledsoe told me the next time my name popped up in some mess, I'm done."

"Sheriff Bledsoe played a trick on you," Shirley said. "The polygraph machine was a--"

Estafay interrupted her. "Sheriff Bledsoe cut you slack on what, Robert?"

"I can't do it, Shirley," Robert Earl said.

"Cut you slack on what?" Estafay insisted.

Robert Earl shook his head. "Nothing, honey."

"Why not?" Shirley asked. "You don't like Ruth Ann. Remember when she and daddy laughed at you? Wasn't no call for her to do that."

You laughed, too.

"I would like to know," Estafay said, poking him in the chest with two fingers, "what the Sheriff cut you slack on."

243

"Give me a gun, Robert Earl. I won't kill her. I'll just give her a limp. Each step she takes she'll think about what she did to me."

Robert Earl held up both hands. "Timeout! Both of y'all ganging up on me. A tag team--it ain't fair!"

"Give me a gun, Robert Earl, I'm outta here."

"Shirley, I told you I can't do it."

"A rifle, anything that shoots."

"I still would like to know," Estafay shouted, "why Sheriff Bledsoe cut you slack. What did you do? I pray for your sake it wasn't anything nasty."

"That's it!" Robert Earl shouted. "I'm calling Momma." He went to the phone in the living room and called his mother.

Leonard picked up on the third ring. "Harris residence."

"Let me speak to Momma."

"What's the matter, Robert Earl?"

"Put Momma on the phone, will you?" Waiting for his mother to pick up he thought about Albert. *Dead! At an early age. No Albert, no gas station and exotic snake farm.*

"Hello," Ida said.

"Momma, you need to come get Shirley. She's over here begging me for a gun."

"Lord have mercy! Why?"

"She said she's going to bust a cap in Ruth Ann's butt for something or another." He heard a thud on the other end. "Estafay is bothering me, too."

244

Leonard: "Robert Earl, what the hell did you say to Mother? She just fainted!"

"Wake her up." The line went dead. He returned to the kitchen. "Estafay, Shirley, Momma said for y'all to leave me alone and stop pestering me."

"Please, Robert Earl!" Shirley said. "Grow up! What kind of man calls his momma to defend him?"

"A man like me."

"Hmmph. She ain't my momma," Estafay said. "She oughta tend to her own heathens before she tell me anything."

Shirley studied Estafay. "What do you mean?"

"You know what I mean."

"No, I don't. Explain it to me."

Estafay moved closer to Robert Earl. "You know, remove the heathen from thy own house before you try to influence a child of God in her own."

"What?" Shirley said. "I think you hide behind your so-called religion. 'Remove the heathen from thy own house.' Sounds like a sly way of putting my family down. What you think, Robert Earl? Is it an insult, or what?"

Robert Earl shifted from foot to foot, stuck a finger in his ear and dug furiously. "Uh…you know…uh…" casting nervous glances at Estafay. "Kinda, sorta, if you think about it, in a way it does sound like an insult."

245

"You damn right it does!" Shirley said. "My momma didn't raise heathens, Estafay! You picked a bad time to tell me she did. A very bad time!" Shirley stood up, her chair falling to the floor. "I strongly suggest you take the shit back!"

Estafay moved directly behind Robert Earl. "Robert, tell your sister it's time she leave."

Shirley pointed a finger at her. "You tell me! You tell me to leave! You big and bad enough to call my family heathens to my face, you tell me to leave your house!"

"Robert," Estafay whispered, "feel free to step in anytime."

Robert Earl stared at the hulking figure dressed in navy-blue culottes and realized he had a tough decision to make: attempt to protect his wife's honor, get his butt whooped and a trip to the hospital via Emergency Medical Transport; or jump out of the way and let Estafay go for what she know, and then have her berate him for weeks for not intervening on her behalf?

Shirley advanced, fists clenched. Robert Earl, now convinced that weeks of Estafay berating him wouldn't hurt so much, tried to move out of the way...Estafay moved when he moved.

"Estafay," looking at her naked wrist as if a watch was there, "I'm waiting, and I have yet to hear you take back anything. Ten...nine..."

"Robert, do something!" Estafay pleaded. "Say something!"

"Take it back, Estafay," Robert Earl said. "It'll save us a lot of medical expenses."

"…seven…six…"

"Robert, this is my house!"

"…four…"

"I will not be threatened inside my own home!"

"…two…"

Just then Ida and Leonard rushed into the kitchen. "Shirley!" Ida shouted. "What the hell are you doing?"

"I'm fixin' to put a foot up Estafay's ass!"

"Estafay?" Leonard said. "I thought you were upset with Ruth Ann?"

"You need to leave," Robert Earl told Leonard. "Now!"

"He's with me," Ida said.

"Momma, you can stay," Robert Earl said. "No man who chokes me is welcome in my house. He can wait outside."

"Momma," Shirley said, "Estafay called your children heathens to my face. You want a piece of her sanctified ass?"

Robert Earl said, "Two against one ain't fair. Y'all let Estafay call one of her church friends and make it even."

"Boy, be quiet!" Ida said. "Shirley, stop talking foolish. You're a grown woman--act like it!" She frowned at Ida. "As for you, my children might not be a religious bunch, but they're not heathens."

"Mrs. Harris, I didn't mean any disrespect," Estafay said.

"Yes, you did!" Shirley said.

"Robert Earl," Ida said, "can't you control your home? Why are you putting up with this foolishness? Boy, take charge of your home!"

"I tried, Momma. They--"

"No, you didn't!" Shirley said. "You let Estafay talk about your family."

"Be quiet, Shirley," Ida said. "This isn't your house. What's gotten into you? If you don't like what somebody says about you in their house, go home! And what's this mess you needing a gun?"

Robert Earl said, "How the whole thing got started."

"Why you need a gun, Shirley?" Leonard asked.

Shirley stared at the floor, then met her mother's eyes. "Sorry, Momma, I'm popping a cap in Ruth Ann's slimy ass."

"Why?" Ida shouted. "Why? She's your sister."

Tears rolled down Shirley's face. "Momma, she's been fooling with my husband."

Ida moaned, stumbled to a chair and sat down. She closed her eyes and rubbed her temples. "Jesus...Jesus! Help me, Jesus!"

Leonard said, "Shirley, I didn't know you and Eric were married."

"We were going to get married soon."

"Are you sure about this? Have you talked to Ruth Ann?"

"I went to her house and she jumped out the window and ran. I can't catch her on foot. I need something to shorten the distance."

Ida moaned again.

"She's your sister," Leonard said. "Remember?"

Shirley shook her head. "Leonard, did she remember she was my sister when she slept with my baby's daddy? Hell no, she didn't! Ruth Ann doesn't give a damn about nobody but Ruth Ann. As of today she's no longer my sister. She's nothing to me...just another..." She caught herself.

Ida started crying.

"Momma, I'm not gonna kill her. I'll just give her a disability. She broke up my home, Momma."

"Jesus, Jesus!" Ida wailed. "I kilt my husband and now these heathens trying to kill each other. Take me, Jesus! I want to be with my husband!"

"Did you really kill him, Momma?" Robert Earl asked. "If you did you might as well 'fess up to the authorities."

"Shut up, Robert Earl!" Leonard shouted.

"Excuse me," Robert Earl said. "I need my money. If she did it, she did it."

"Shut up!" Leonard and Shirley yelled.

"Jesus!" Ida said. "I'm ready! Take me! Right now, Jesus. I'm ready!"

Leonard massaged Ida's shoulders. "Shirley, you can't shoot your sister. You shouldn't even be thinking of such nonsense. Stop talking about it. You're upsetting Mother."

"I'm sorry, Momma," Shirley said, tears cascading down her face. "I didn't intend for you to find out about any of this."

"Shirley," Robert Earl said, "it would be very hard for you to bust a cap in your sister's butt without Momma finding out about it."

Shirley stopped crying and gave him a cold look. "The first time I've heard you say anything that made sense." She started to leave the kitchen; Robert Earl gave her a wide berth.

Leonard said, "Promise me you're not doing something stupid. Something you'll regret, Shirley."

Shirley stopped in the doorway. "I'm sorry, Leonard."

"Grab her, Robert Earl!" Leonard shouted.

Shirley turned slowly and stared at Robert Earl, who hadn't moved an inch. "Don't be a fool," she whispered.

Robert Earl swallowed and said, "Hadn't planned to be."

Shirley walked out of the kitchen, her footsteps creaking against the hardwood floor in the living room, and then they heard the sound of the front door opening and closing.

"Go catch her, Robert Earl," Leonard said. "Catch her before she does something we'll all regret."

"You go catch her!" Robert Earl said. "I'll watch Momma and you run out there and catch her. She's overweight and out of her mind--someone you give plenty of leaving alone. You heard her. 'Don't be a fool!'" Leonard shook his head. Robert Earl ignored him. "Momma, would you like me to get you something? Something to eat? Drink?"

"Arsenic," Ida said.

Robert Earl looked at Estafay. "Honey, do we have any arsenic?"

Estafay rolled her eyes at him. "I don't know what it is."

"What is it, Momma?" Robert Earl asked. "If we don't have it I'll go get it."

Ida muttered something.

"Say again, Momma, I didn't hear you."

"Poison," Ida said. "Poison!"

Chapter 25

"You're not going to hurt me, are you, Lester?" Ruth Ann said, regretting the question the second she'd asked it. She, while underneath the bed, was at his mercy. No way could she get out quickly enough if he decided to…Her mind raced with possibilities and stopped at the worst-case scenario: Lester setting the bed afire.

Lester scooted to the far wall and sat with his back against it. "Is it true?"

"No! It's a misunderstanding. A major, misinformed misunderstanding."

"All those nights you said you were with your girlfriends, with your folks, you were with him, weren't you?"

"No, Lester. No, no, no! It's not true."

"While I was here alone, waiting for you, worried something might've happened to you." He closed his eyes and bounced his head against the wall.

"Lester, honey, you got it all wrong. It's a major misguided misunderstanding."

"You know what's stupid? I convinced myself I was lucky to have you. I thought you were doing me a favor because of this scar on my face."

"Listen to me, Lester. Sheriff Bledsoe--I mean, we--not we...me...I...I thought..." She forgot what she intended to say. *Damn!*

"Why wouldn't you allow me to touch you months at a time?"

"Wait a minute," starting to crawl out. She could think better on her feet. "Let me get out from under here."

She was halfway out when Lester said, "I really think you should stay under there. I'm afraid what I might do if you come out."

Oh-oh, Ruth Ann thought as she quickly pushed herself back under the bed.

"Today," Lester said, "when we were making love--no, when I was making love to you, your mind wasn't in it. I can't remember the last time your mind was in it. Your body was there, mind wasn't. I wonder if you display the same level of enthusiasm with Eric as you do with me. Probably not. Tell me, do you love him?"

"Lester, please! Don't be ridiculous! You know I couldn't care less about that man!"

"Then it was only about sex. You could have gotten sex from me and saved the motel fare."

"What motel fare, Lester? You're letting your imagination run wild."

"Three months ago I found a motel receipt in the trash."

"Hello! We're investigating trash now?"

"You goddamn right!" Lester shouted. Ruth Ann stiffened. "Don't bitch-play me! It's not working this time! My so-called wife gone hours at a time every other night, won't sleep with me--*me*, her fucking husband!--comes back all tired and wore out--you're damn right, I'm deep in trash!"

The silence that followed seemed more portentous than his outburst.

Loud music from a passing car out front flowed through the window. Al Green's *Love and Happiness*. How ironic, Ruth Ann thought.

Calmer, Lester said, "Wasn't I good to you?"

Ruth Ann didn't respond; yes or no, she knew, would aggravate him.

"Busted my ass night after night pulling overtime at that damn paper mill 'cause you said, 'Lester, I want this. Lester, I want that.' Like that damn Expedition out there--you didn't need it and I can't afford it. All the while you're fucking a fifty-cent nigger can't buy you a nine-nine-cent burger." He shook his head in disgust.

"Lester, I--"

"Shut up!" Lester snapped. "You can save the lies." A long moment he glared at her. Ruth Ann tried to hold his gaze but couldn't. "Tell the truth, it's the burn mark, isn't it?" Ruth Ann shook her head. "You a damn lie!" Lester shouted. "Don't lie to me! You've lied to me enough, don't you think? Is it the goddamn burn mark on my mouth?"

Ruth Ann closed her eyes. No way could she answer that.

"Would you like to know how I got this mark you detest so much?"

No, I don't!

She only wanted to escape from underneath this bed, put on some clothes and seek shelter in another state or country. "If you need to tell it, Lester."

"Yes, I need to tell it!" He bounced his head against the wall again and then spoke in a low voice.

"You had someone call Tina and tell her we were at the motel in Lake Village. No way could she have known where we were. You unlocked the door after I locked it. You made damn sure she caught us and she did. She left me, just like you'd planned...just like you'd schemed. At first I tried to convince myself I'd traded up, replaced my chubby, church-going wife with a hot, sexy eighteen-year-old.

"It dawned on me I'd tossed a good woman away for a girl. Tina can't hold a pole to you in bed, but Tina is a woman, a real woman. She listened, really listened, to what I had to say, and she cared. She really and truly cared about me. Me! When someone loves you, truly loves you, you can feel it, you can feel it in your bones."

He paused, tears dripping. "I realized I'd made a mistake, and I knew I had to get my wife back. I got down on my knees and begged Tina to come back. She wouldn't even consider it. 'A little girl, Lester! A little girl!' was all she'd say to me. I hurt her.

"Then she refused to see me at all, stopped taking my calls, told her family to tell me the marriage was over. When the man served me with the divorce papers, I lost it, just couldn't take it. Somehow I had to win her back, let her know I'd made a stupid mistake.

"My cousin George, he and I got drunk, pissy drunk, two pints of Bacardi One-Fifty-One. I got him to take me over to Tina's sister's house. Nell said Tina wasn't there, told me to go home and sober up. I don't remember bringing the gas can with me, but I had it. Told Nell to tell Tina if she didn't talk to me, I'd drink gas and kill myself.

"I put the nozzle in my mouth and Nell slammed the door. Sloppy drunk, I still had enough sense not to drink gasoline. I spit it out. I don't know who started the bullshit I tried to kill myself drinking acid.

"Nell must've called the police because George and I heard sirens. He helped me back into the car and we took off. I was okay then. Heart still broke, but physically I was okay. Hell, George and I were laughing. He stopped in front of my apartment and asked was I going to be all right. Yeah, I told him and picked up his cigarettes and took one out. A damn cigarette!

"Drunk, I forgot I'd gargled with gasoline minutes before. I put a match to the cigarette and--swoosh!--a big, blue flame! I started running...screaming. I couldn't see, I couldn't hear, couldn't breathe, just felt fire. When I revived I was in the hospital, head all bandaged up, tubes running everywhere."

"I was there by your side," Ruth Ann said. "Remember, Lester? I was there by your side, day and night."

"Six weeks later," Lester said, ignoring her comment, "after the painful surgeries, I realized I was marked for life. Each time I look into a mirror I'm reminded of the fact I betrayed my wife. I deserve this mark."

"I'm sorry, Lester."

"Sorry for what? My scar or the fact it turns you off so much?"

Ruth Ann didn't reply.

"Which one is it?"

"For everything, I guess."

"You guess! I don't guess, I know for a fact I've ruined my life for a self-centered little girl I never should've looked twice at. You don't give a damn about nobody but yourself. I always knew it, tried to pretend it wasn't true."

He leaned forward and picked up Teddy. Ruth Ann watched, horrified, as he squeezed Teddy's neck, all the while staring at her. "Is Eric his father?"

"What? What did you say?"

"You heard me."

"Whose father? What are you talking about?"

"Shane. Is Eric his father?"

"No! How can you say such a thing? Shane is almost eighteen-years-old. You know whatshisface hasn't been here that long."

"Then who is his father?"

"What's the matter with you? You know who his father is."

"No, I don't. Tell me." He squeezed Teddy harder, its head expanding to the pressure.

"You are, Lester! You know you are!"

Teddy's head popped and ejected a plume of cotton. Lester tossed it to the floor. "You think I would allow a man like your father to raise a child of mine? You think I'd let my child run wild, live out in the woods like a damn animal?"

Ruth Ann's expression shifted from shock to anger. In all these years, Lester had never talked to her like this, had never mentioned Shane's name, not once. If he'd doubted Shane's paternity, why hadn't he said so a long time ago?

"No need of looking at me like I'm crazy, Ruth Ann. You know damn well I'm not his father. More shit you threw in my face and expected me to overlook. I did. Now the charade is over."

Lester got to his feet. "Part of this is my fault--I never should've allowed it to go on this long. This time, however, I'm not hurting myself. Not this time, Ruth Ann. Though I can't guarantee I won't hurt you. If I were you I'd be out of here before I come back, which should be in five minutes…or less." He stormed out, slamming the door behind him.

Ruth Ann crawled out from under the bed before the sound of his footsteps faded down the hallway. She snatched a pillowcase off a pillow…*Where my keys?*…She stuffed an assortment of bras, socks and panties into the pillowcase.

Shit! Keys and cell phone on the cabinet in the kitchen. She was headed to her closet when she heard footsteps in the hallway. Without hesitation she rushed to the window, threw the pillowcase to the ground and dove out behind it.

Chapter 26

Sheriff Bledsoe poked his solar plexus with four fingers, hoping to ease the rumbling in his gut. If the commotion held in one spot, he could deal with it. It didn't. It erupted in his gut, spewed poisonous, burning gas into his chest, throat and sinuses.

Before Shirley smashed his polygraph machine, the eruptions were sporadic, three or four times a day at the most. Now his innards were churning out large quantities of toxic material by the hour. At this rate, an EPA inspector would soon knock on his door with a citation.

And the pain! Gut-wrenching pain! Eyes-watering pain! Tongue-biting pain! Doubling-over-in-public pain! Am-I-having-a-heart-attack pain?

But no more. Today he was taking matters in his own hands. Why suffer when relief was right around the corner? Or, in his case, in the adjacent county, Drew County, where he'd made an appointment with Doctor Cobb, the only gastroenterologist in a fifty-mile radius.

After Doctor Cobb's secretary told him that she could squeeze him in as a walk-in at four o'clock, Sheriff Bledsoe ran to his cruiser. Emergency lights flashing, sirens wailing, he sped down Highway 82, eighty-…ninety-…one hundred-miles-per-hour…It was a quarter till four. At one hundred-miles-per-hour he would arrive at the doctor's office with minutes to spare.

Yes indeed, relief was less than twenty miles away. Doctor Cobb, he hoped, would prescribe the purple pill he'd seen advertised on television. He couldn't remember the name, but the commercial, where several people stood next to a bubbling lava pool agonizing they weren't made aware of the pill earlier, replayed in his mind.

Apparently acid indigestion was serious business.

He flew past a hitchhiker walking east, back to town. He looked in the rearview mirror and slowed down…A female in her pajamas carrying a pillowcase.

A nutcase.

Only a nutcase would hitchhike in this heat. Leave her be, the pain in his stomach told him. She'd be nearing town when he got back from his appointment.

"Fiddle faddle!" he cursed, bringing the cruiser to a stop. When he drove back, the hitchhiker was sitting in the shade of a sycamore tree, inspecting her feet. He exited the cruiser and approached her with a hand on his weapon. Closer, he saw blisters on her feet. Her hair and the Bugs Bunny pajamas she had on dripped sweat.

"Excuse me, Ma'am."

Ruth Ann looked up. "Hello, Sheriff. Mighty hot out here, ain't it?"

"Ruth Ann," astonished. "What you doing out here?"

"Sitting in the shade for a spell. Asphalt hot enough to cook an egg."

"Yes, it is." He remembered his talk with Shirley. "Did you and Lester have a fight?"

"No, no, no. I decided to take a walk. To keep up circulation."

"Barefoot? In your jammies?"

"Don't knock it, they keep you cool."

"What's in the pillowcase?"

"Just a few things I'm donating to Goodwill."

He extended a hand. "C'mon. We'll sort this out in the car before one of us have a heatstroke."

Ruth Ann gimped to the cruiser. "I'm glad you stopped. You'd be surprised the number of people slow down, look at you crazy and keep going." She got into the backseat and fanned herself with her hands. "Man, this air feels good!"

"You want me to take you home?"

"No, no, no! Let me cool off a few minutes and I'll be on my way."

"You know I'm not letting you walk the highway. Anywhere else you'd like to go?"

"Now is a good time as any to get your polygraph test over and done with."

Sheriff Bledsoe suppressed a burp. "On hold right now. Problems with the machine. Tell the truth, did you and Lester get into a fight?"

"No, Sheriff. I've told you already we didn't."

"Yeah, yeah, yeah. You were taking a walk to improve circulation, no shoes, the hottest day of the year, and you have a new Expedition parked in the driveway. You keep lying to me we'll go have a little talk with Lester."

"We had an argument. Lester didn't hit me."

"He wouldn't let you get your shoes?"

"I'm sure he would have. I just, you know, I just wanted to leave. Didn't think to get my shoes."

"Legally speaking, you and he are married, what's his is yours and yours is his. If you want to go back and get some of your stuff, you're within your legal rights. I'll go with you, make sure everything is peaceful."

"No thanks, Sheriff. Very nice of you, but I'd rather not."

Sheriff Bledsoe started to speak when a black Dodge Ram stopped directly behind them. "Speak of the devil."

Lester exited the truck, an overstuffed plastic garbage bag in each hand, and approached the cruiser.

Sheriff Bledsoe got out to intercept him. "How you doing, Lester?"

"Here's some more of her shit!" Lester said, throwing the bags to the ground, huffing and puffing as if he'd run a marathon. "Everything else b-b-b-belongs..." He started sniffling like a cat trying to dislodge a fur ball, and then he let loose, crying loudly and miserably. "...b-b-b-b-belongs to me!"

"Hold on now, Lester."

Lester pointed at Ruth Ann, staring at them through the back window, wide-eyed.

"Did you use a rubber?" Lester shouted at her. "Did you use a damn rubber?"

Ruth Ann quickly turned face front in her seat. Lester charged for the car. Sheriff Bledsoe grabbed him by the waist just as he was reaching for the door handle.

"Lester! Lester! Lester!" Sheriff Bledsoe clamped him in a headlock. "Lester, calm down!"

"Okayokayokay, Sheriff!"

"I'm going to let you go. If you try it again I'm going to arrest you. You understand?" He released him. "Are you okay?"

Still crying: "I've been scratching ever since she left. Ask her did they use a rubber. Tell her I want my momma's ring back, too. She ain't worthy of it!"

"Lester, you're working yourself in a frenzy. Calm down."

"She ain't no good, Sheriff! Fucking that sorry, no-good Eric Barnes!" Hyperventilating: "I know she has a damn coochie disease! Ask her did he use a rubber."

"By God, Lester! Calm down! The first thing you need to do is calm down. Take a deep breath and hold it, okay? Do that for me, please."

Lester held his breath for a split second and exhaled nasally.

"Now don't you feel better?" Sheriff Bledsoe said, though Lester continued crying, snot and tears flowing at an even pace. "Whatever she did it's not worth losing control over, is it?"

Lester strained to respond, couldn't, hiccupping and crying.

Sheriff Bledsoe patted his back. "This is going to take time, Lester. Try not to--" Before he could finish, Lester bear hugged him, crying on his shoulder. A wet sensation spread down his back.

"S-s-s-sh-sh-sh-she...d-d-did me...w-r-r-r-rong....S-s-s-s-sh-sh-sheriff!"

My God! My dear God!

If only he'd followed his first mind and kept going. Someone would've stopped and given Ruth Ann a ride into town. This very minute he should have been walking into a drugstore with the prescription for the purple pill in hand. He glanced at his wristwatch. A quarter after four. *Geez!*

"Lester…Lester, why don't you go home and rest up. Later on, after you've relaxed a bit, call someone, a relative, your pastor, one of your friends."

Lester continued crying.

What if, Sheriff Bledsoe thought, a state trooper drove up? *And here I am on the highway letting a man cry on my shoulder.*

A trucker drove by in the opposite lane to avoid coming too close to the vehicles on the shoulder, rubber-necking, a curious look on his face.

Sheriff Bledsoe pried Lester's arms loose. "Go home, Lester. Go home, take a hot bath and relax. In a few days this won't seem the end of the world."

Lester wiped his eyes with the back of his hand. "I'm sorry, Sheriff. Dirty bitch brings out the worst in me."

"No need for name-calling. Just go home and relax, for Pete's sake. All right? If you think about doing something crazy, call me first. Understand?"

Lester nodded and pressed two fingers against his right nostril and blew phlegm to the pavement. "O-okay, Sheriff, I will," extending the same hand he'd used to blow his nose.

Sheriff Bledsoe declined the shake. "Just go home, Lester. Don't forget what I told you."

Lester stared malevolently at the back of Ruth Ann's head, then got into his truck and drove off.

"You think he'll be all right?" Ruth Ann asked the moment Sheriff Bledsoe got into the cruiser.

"I hope so. He's pretty tore up now. Does he have anyone he can commiserate with?"

"His mother and his sister. I doubt if he'll talk to them, though."

Sheriff Bledsoe pulled the stick into drive. "I'll check on him later. Where do you want me to drop you off?"

"My mother's. Sheriff, don't forget my stuff. My pillowcase, too." He pushed the stick back into park and started out to retrieve her belongings. "One other thing, Sheriff?"

"What?"

"You got snot all over the back of your shirt."

He got out, slamming the door behind him, wondering would he dishonor his badge if he kicked her out and made her walk.

Chapter 27

The phone rang and rang. "Pick up the phone," Leonard said into the cell phone. "I know you're there, pick up the phone."

He knew Victor was back in Chicago because he himself had left the answering machine on. The ringing continued. He folded the cell phone.

Already he was desperately missing Victor. What if Victor sought solace in the arms of his ex, Dwight. The mere thought made him sick to his stomach.

If he and Victor didn't get back together, what would he do? Go back to dating? A risky proposition in itself. Liars, players, whiners, haters, baiters, all dressed up in pretty packages, but not one worth the pain and trouble.

Could he roll the dice again and find another Victor? Honest, compassionate, intelligent, handsome, responsible and faithful.

He thought he heard something and went to check on his mother. She lay in bed snoring, the sheet covering her entire body. He could scarcely detect her chest rising and falling.

Mother, he mused, still believed covering up the monsters would overlook you. He closed the bedroom door and stepped into the kitchen.

His mother was another reason why lately he felt so uneasy. He didn't believe, couldn't believe, she was capable of murdering anyone. *Yes, but she keeps confessing to murder!* He wondered if profound grief could convince someone they had murdered a loved one. If Victor was murdered, he could imagine blaming himself, but seriously doubted he would start confessing he'd killed him.

The damn gopher poison in her closet didn't help matters, either. Not one bit.

He made himself a cup of coffee and stepped out onto the front porch. Heat worms wriggled from the street and roofs of neighbor's homes. Patches of dead, sunburned grass spread throughout the front yard. As usual, the neighborhood, comprised mostly of senior citizens, was quiet. A sewage odor wafted from the paper mill, less than five blocks away.

Why am I still here?

His home was in Chicago, where his job was, where the love of his life was. Why had he so casually let Victor walk out of his life?

He took a handkerchief out of his pocket, spread it out on the top step and sat down.

The money! *The reason I'm still here.*

Sheriff Bledsoe had warned him not to leave town--an empty threat; he hadn't murdered his father. He took a sip and said, "The damn money!"

Someone, Shirley most likely, could have looked after his mother had he gone back to Chicago with Victor. In fact, his mother seemed perfectly capable of taking care of herself.

An impulse: get up, pack your stuff and catch the next flight to Chicago. No, he couldn't. Leave now and all the time he'd invested here would have been for naught. And why run to Chicago only needing to return a few weeks later to sign the papers for his share of the money.

There's a such thing as a fax, you know.

No, he would wait. If Victor went back to Dwight, then to hell with him.

A cruiser pulled up in the driveway, and Leonard remembered he was scheduled for a polygraph test.

The back window rolled down and Ruth Ann poked her head out. "Leonard, is Shirley here?"

"No, she isn't."

Sheriff Bledsoe got out and opened the door for Ruth Ann.

"Sheriff Bledsoe," Leonard said, "I'm ready for the polygraph test."

Sheriff Bledsoe ignored him, opened the trunk and retrieved two garbage bags and a pillowcase and tossed them on the driveway, splitting one of the bags. Then, without so much as a good-bye, he got into the cruiser and sped off.

"What's the matter with him?" Leonard asked Ruth Ann. "PJ's in vogue now?"

"Have you seen Shirley today?"

"Saw her earlier. Why?"

Ruth Ann hobbled up to the porch and sat beside him. "Momma in the house?"

"Asleep."

Ruth Ann combed back her hair with both hands. "Whew! It's been one hectic day."

"You've recovered miraculously from your heart attack, haven't you?"

"What are you insinuating?"

"Nothing. Just yesterday you were in the hospital, a heart attack, allegedly. Now you're on your feet…" He took a sip of coffee. "…running from Shirley."

"Who said I was running from Shirley?"

Leonard worked his gaze from her blisters to her eyes. "Shirley."

"What else did Shirley say?"

"Not much." He took another sip. "She mentioned something about you jumping out a window and running when she came to your house."

"Was she angry? I mean, really angry?"

"Well," Leonard said, drawing the word out, "I guess you can say she was angry. A more accurate description, stark-raving pissed off."

"Damn! What time did she come here? What did Momma say? Did she upset Momma?"

"She didn't come here. Mother didn't say much, and yes, Mother was upset."

"Damn! Back up. What you mean she didn't come here?"

"She didn't come here. We were at Robert Earl's house."

Ruth Ann took the cup from him and sipped. "Don't you believe in sugar? Shirley called a family meeting to discuss my business?"

"No, not exactly. *Your business* wasn't the main reason why Mother and I went there." He waited till she put the cup to her mouth. "We rushed over there because Shirley was pressing Robert Earl for a gun."

Ruth Ann spat the coffee out and started coughing. Leonard patted her hard on the back.

"I'm...okay!" Ruth Ann said. "Wh-why did she want a gun?"

"Aw shucks, Ruth Ann. You can't pay Shirley any attention. You know how she carries on when she thinks someone done her wrong. She's liable to say anything, the first thing pops in her head."

"Yeah, yeah, I know. Why she want a gun?"

Leonard took the cup out of her hand, took a quick sip, and handed it back. Ruth Ann took a sip and Leonard said, "To bust a cap in your slimy ass. Her words, not mine."

Ruth Ann started coughing again, but this time Leonard did not pat her back. "You're enjoying this, aren't you?"

"How could you, Ruth Ann? You know Shirley worships the ground Eric walks on." She stared at the sidewalk, speechless. "She worshipped you, too. She's devastated. The two people she loved the most betrayed her. The least you can do is apologize to her."

"And get shot!"

"I don't think she'll shoot you. I really don't. A day or two she'll cool off. She'll still be pissed, but by then she'll have come to her senses. Then you should go to her and apologize. She won't accept it at first, but she needs to hear you say it. You know how she is."

"I most certainly damn do! Remember when Robert Earl shot her favorite doll with a BB gun?" Leonard shook his head. "Maybe you were too young. I remember. She hit him in the mouth with a baseball bat...two weeks later!"

"Is that how Robert Earl lost his teeth?"

"I guess, I'm not sure. All I know, Shirley doesn't cool off, not the way normal people do. She has to hurt someone, spill blood, expose guts, break bones, then she cools off!"

Leonard laughed. "Ruth Ann, she was just a kid then."

"Damn that! I'll apologize later, next millennium!"

"Robert Earl didn't give her a gun."

"She may have gotten one from someone else."

"I doubt it," chuckling.

"Leonard, if she were gunning for you, I doubt you'd be so amused."

"I would not have slept with her man."

Ruth Ann snorted. "Oh, really? How can you be so sure?"

Leonard stared at her, not blinking, his face instantly hot. "Fuck you!"

"I'm sorry, Leonard, I shouldn't have said that. I'm sorry."

Leonard stood up. He didn't want her near him another second. "I guess you'll be staying here," he whispered, tempering his heat.

"If you don't mind?"

"It's not my house." If it were his, she wouldn't be allowed on the lawn. He started for the door.

Ruth Ann got up. "Leonard, wait. I apologize. I don't want you mad at me, too. Sometimes I open my mouth before I think."

"My being gay is the great equalizer, isn't it? Correction, the great dehumanizer. Isn't it? Stab your sister, your only sister, in the back, yet that pales in comparison to my sexual orientation?"

"No. You're reading too much into what I said. I was being flip. I'm sorry."

"I'm going inside. There's soap and hot water in the bathroom. You stink!" He stepped inside, slamming the screen door in her face.

An hour later, his mother still asleep, Ruth Ann rumbling around in her old room, Leonard's face remained hot, had actually heated up several degrees.

He'd tried to cool off and simply couldn't. Of course he'd heard worse, had been called worse. Yet any comment on his sexuality by a family member, especially Ruth Ann, burned him to no end.

He tried to redirect his thoughts to something positive, but *"Oh, really? How can you be so sure?"* kept playing inside his head. He picked up a book, couldn't complete the first paragraph, and tossed it aside.

He heard footsteps padding to the bathroom…running water. *Perhaps she'll slip and fall.*

If she were a man he would have…He picked up the phone and called Robert Earl's number.

"Hel…lo," Robert Earl said, food in his mouth.

"Robert Earl, how do you get in touch with Shirley?"

When Ruth Ann, freshly showered, wearing a T-shirt, blue jeans and a pair of faded pink tennis shoes, stepped into the living room, Leonard had managed two pages of the book.

"A good read?" Ruth Ann asked.

"Nope," not looking up.

275

"Momma still asleep?"

"Yup."

"You want something to eat?"

"Nope."

"You sure?"

"Yup."

"You're still mad at me, aren't you?"

"Nope."

"Yes, you are."

He didn't reply.

"Maybe later you and I could go catch a movie or something. A Madea movie is playing at the Dollar Cinema. I heard it's good. You wanna go?"

"Nope." He could feel her eyes burning holes in the side of his head. She walked into the kitchen and he heard the refrigerator door open and close.

"Leonard, we could ride over to the mall in Greeneville. I'll drive."

"Nope."

She came back into the living room. Leonard shot her a glance and saw she was eating ice cream from the carton. *Germy.* She plopped down beside him on the couch.

"If you don't want to talk to me, Leonard, no problem." She stuck a spoonful of ice cream in her mouth and slurped loudly. To

Leonard the noise had the same effect as a dentist's drill. He rolled his eyes at her and scooted to the far end of the couch.

Ruth Ann slurped again. "Put the book down, Leonard, and let's talk."

He put the book closer to his face.

"*Pleasure*," she said, reading the title. "I read it. Had me wondering if *he* had a yoni. You don't talk to me, I'll keep irritating you."

He snapped the book closed. "What do you want to talk about?"

"Anything. It doesn't matter to me. Your job in Chicago, your friends. Whatever, I'm all ears."

"Let's see…" He pinched his chin as if deep in thought. "What shall we talk about? Oh, I almost forgot. Shirley is on her way here."

"What?"

"Shirley is on her way here."

"You're lying!" She moved the curtains and peered out the window. "I know you're lying!"

"Afraid not."

"The phone didn't ring, not once! Unless it rang when I was in the shower." She turned and gave him the coldest look he'd seen in a long time. "You called her, didn't you?"

Leonard couldn't help it, he smiled.

"Why, Leonard? Why? You wanna see Shirley hurt me?"

"Leonard?" Ida called from the bedroom.

"If you'll excuse me," Leonard said, "I need to check on my mother."

"Go right ahead, I'm on my way out. If it's not a problem, would you bring my stuff inside the house." She opened the front door and then closed it.

"One thing before I go," and reached behind her head and lifted her T-shirt. "See this," pinching the tag. "A label. Hanes, I believe. A label, all it is. No more, no less. Yes, it can rub, annoy, aggravate--but what hurts more than overreacting to it? Leonard, I made a stupid remark and I'm sorry I did. Was it so painful, so debilitating, you want to see me get hurt?"

Leonard didn't answer, a smug smile on his lips.

"A label, Leonard. If it ain't you don't even think about wearing it."

She made her way into the kitchen, and then Leonard heard the back door open and slam shut.

Chapter 28

"My momma and daddy told me not to see you no more," Linda Riley said, opening the door just enough to reveal her head. "My daddy said he's gonna do something to you when he finds out who you are."

Man, she's hard to look at, Eric thought. Cockeyed, the left pupil way over yonder, as though she was trying to see behind her. Above her small, egg-shaped head sat an uneven afro, patches of scalp showing, as if she'd tried to cut her own hair but couldn't quite figure where to start or stop.

Long hairs sprouted from her nose. Her bottom lip puffed out and over, revealing black gums and yellow teeth, rental space between each.

Eric said, "I thought you was a big girl. You always do what your momma and daddy tell you?"

"I am a big girl! Twenty-two December thirteenth," and stuck her thumb into her mouth.

"Open the door if you a big girl," staring at a patch of acne dotting her narrow forehead.

"Mumma staid I crant hab eenie crumprinee!"

"What? Take your thumb out your mouth when you talk."

Linda plucked it out. "Momma said I can't have any company." She returned the thumb to her mouth, sucked on it contentedly, and took it out again. "My momma beat me with a broom when your wife walked me home and told her about us."

"She ain't my wife."

Pointing her wet thumb at him: "The hell you say! Why you run off when she came in?"

Why am I talking to her? She didn't have a lick of sense. What in the hell did he see in her in the first place? *I had to have been drunk, had to have been.*

He turned to leave. "Gotta go. Tell your daddy I said hi."

Walking down the steps, he heard the door close and then open. "Come on!" she said. "Come on 'fore somebody sees you and calls my momma!"

He turned and saw what had attracted him to her. She had the most voluptuous body he'd ever seen outside of a Playboy magazine.

Underneath a hot-pink halter-top were two perfectly shaped, mouth-watering knockers, the tips pointed up without any means of support. The skin on her hourglass midriff was a shade lighter than her facial complexion.

He stared at her belly button, distended, like the beginning of a balloon. Had to be another flaw somewhere, Eric thought before staring at her long legs wrapped tightly in a pair of white Capri pants. No shoes.

Barbie with a gargoyle's head. Man, God sure works in mysterious ways.

"Are you coming in, or what?" she asked.

He bolted up the stairs and into the house. The Riley's living room was furnished with a black three-piece sectional couch and matching loveseat and ottoman, all covered in plastic. On a flat-screen television Chris Hansen stepped out from behind a curtain and startled a man removing liquor and condoms from a paper sack.

Cigar smoke and raspberry air freshener lingered in the air. On the wall behind the couch was a huge velvet picture of a black panther emerging out of tall grass.

"What does your daddy do?" Eric asked. "Work at the zoo?"

"No. He's the assistant warden over at Tucker."

"Really? I wish you'd told me before." He sat down in the loveseat.

"Would it have made a difference?"

Eric smiled at her. "No, it wouldna've. Remember what I told you?"

"Heavy on the slob?"

"Yes, and what else?" She shrugged. "Come here and I'll show you."

She started toward him, stopped suddenly, her eyes going everywhere except in the same direction, and they both listened intently to a car pulling into the driveway. Seconds later a car door slammed.

"Daddy!" she whispered, looking terrified. "Run!"

Eric jumped up, head jerking right to left. "I'm going out the back door!"

"Uh-uh! Malcolm is back there." She pointed toward the couch. "Hide behind there."

"Who is Malcolm?"

"Daddy's pit bull. Hurry!"

The front door opened just as Eric was ducking into the small space where the couch catty-cornered against the wall.

"Hi, Daddy," he heard Linda say. "What you doing home this early?"

"I live here," a man said. "You forgot? I live here, pay the bills here. What's wrong with you?"

"Nothing, Daddy."

"You acting strange. When the last time you talked to the bolus?"

"You told me not to talk to him anymore, Daddy. You want me to fix you something to eat? I'll make you a sandwich and bring it to your room."

Eric didn't hear the man respond. *What the hell is a bolus?*

"Daddy, don't you want to go lie down, get off your feet. I know you're tired."

"You go lie down!" the man said. Eric heard and felt someone sitting on the couch. "I'm fine right here."

The man was close, an arm's length away. Eric started sweating, profusely.

The man started sniffing. "What's that smell?"

"What smell? I don't smell nothing."

"Smells like Brute. Who's been here?"

"Nobody, Daddy. Nobody's been here."

Sweat dripped into Eric's eyes, but he didn't dare move a muscle.

"I'm going to say this one last time," the man said. "You go near that man again, I'll beat the black off you, you hear me? I wish he would come here. I wish he would! It'll be the last place he go."

"I know, Daddy, I know."

"I might as well be a damn garbage man! Work with trash all day, then come home and deal with it." He mumbled expletives. "What you say his name was?"

"I don't know his name."

"You a damn lie! You said his name was Eric. You hop in bed with a man and you don't know his name?"

"I just know him as Eric, Daddy." She sounded on the verge of crying.

"Yeah, I bet." Silence, then vehemently: "Get outta my face! Get outta my damn face! You make me sick!"

I'm dead, Eric thought. *D-E-A-D!* Why the hell did he come here? He should have taken his lumps with Shirley, who would have roughed him up, but not killed him.

Coming here had seemed a good idea, initially. After a night of sleeping inside the Laundromat, he figured he could get a hot shower and a hot meal while the troll's parents were at work. He also figured he could punish a poonanny.

But now in this man's house, crouched behind his couch, all he stood to get was a well-whooped ass.

A cell phone rang.

"Hello," the man said. "I was just thinking about you…Yeah, we still have a deal…No, not yet…No…She claims she doesn't know his full name. When I get it, I'll get his address…Not a problem…I have the money now…Yes, half upfront, half later. Yes…Yes…Yes, most definitely…I don't want to flush the wrong bolus, know what I mean?" The man laughed and said good-bye. "Linda!" he shouted.

A moment later: "Yes, Daddy?"

"Are you sure you told me all you know about whatsmajigga? I drive you around you should remember where his house is."

"I don't think so."

"What's his last name?"

"I'm sorry, Daddy, I don't know."

Eric heard a grunt and what sounded like a shoe striking a wall.

"Get your lying ass outta here!" the man shouted.

He's seriously planning to hurt me.

All the man needed was his last name...*and then what?* Busted kneecaps? A contract killing? Probably the latter, considering a kneecap busting didn't usually require upfront money.

If he survived this he would change: stop chasing women, stop looking at pornography. All those magazines under the mattress would have to go.

Shirley, he vowed, would be the recipient of his first act of atonement. He would beg her forgiveness. No matter if she kicked his ass; he deserved it. The man interrupted his thoughts by throwing an arm on the headrest.

Eric stared at the large, stubby, dark-skinned fingers grasping the remote control. Those were the fingers of a very strong man. *Shit, those fingers could crush a man's windpipe.*

Eric couldn't take his eyes off those fingers, and then, to his horror, the remote control slipped from those large, stubby, dark-skinned, life-threatening fingers and landed on his shoulder. The man cursed and then Eric saw ten large, dark-skinned, stubby, life-threatening, windpipe-crushing fingers grab hold of the headrest.

In seconds, the man's face would appear...*and I'll be dead!*

Chapter 29

Ruth Ann is a slut.

A convoy of log trucks was parked along the street, diesel engines running, several drivers asleep on their steering wheel. Ruth Ann walked along the sidewalk, a chain-link fence to her right, beyond it the SuperWood paper mill. Dirt-gray smoke plumed from two concrete stacks, dispersing an odor of Pine-Sol and manure.

Ruth Ann is a slut.

At a distance inside the plant, a Tigercat track loader grabbed logs on a truck and placed them on a conveyor belt that ran up and disappeared into a large white building. An aluminum chute stretched out the opposite side of the building and spewed a mountain of sawdust.

Ruth Ann is a slut.

The blisters on her feet hurt like hell and the sun, though starting its descent, braised her exposed skin. T-shirt and jeans felt hot and sticky. Sawdust irritated her eyes. Yet the most uncomfortable thing at the moment was those five words Shirley had told Lester.

Ruth Ann is a slut.

She hadn't considered what Shirley had said until she'd started walking, and now couldn't stop thinking about it. Why not whore? Ruth Ann wondered. Whore would have inflicted the same slap to the face, delivered the same blow to the gut.

The other word sounded so mean…so nasty…so…so slutty. *I'm not a slut!*

She slowed her pace, ugly words floating in her head, sapping her energy.

Think of something else! Think of something else!

The paper mill behind her now, she wondered where she was headed. She lifted her T-shirt, exposing her midriff, and wiped the sweat off her face and neck.

A white man driving an old red-and-white truck stopped ahead of her and she waved him off. She wasn't a slut; she didn't just jump in a truck with any-old-body. The truck was the exact model, color and make Lester had owned a long time ago.

Back then, the truck was Lester's and her only vehicle. Whenever she needed to drive it, Lester would sneak out and jot down the mileage. Three miles away from the house she would stop, reach under and up the dash and unplug the odometer. She'd had big-time countrified fun in Lester's old truck...*chasing bucks in a truck*...until the accident.

Which changed everything!

She remembered the night she stepped into the juke joint on the outskirts of Greenville, Mississippi. Marijuana and cigarette smoke hovered in a cloud below the ceiling, an antique jukebox blasted Marvin Gaye's *Sexual Healing*, the sound of men and women laughing and talking louder than the music. Far more men than women. She could feel their eyes on her, prying for insight into her yellow, short, skin-tight leather skirt, desiring her.

She sat in a booth in back and watched. Simply watched, declining three invites to dance. Someone sent a rum and Coke to her table...and then another...and another.

Computer Love played on the jukebox...and she lost it, utterly lost it, hypnotized by Roger Troutman's seductive lyrics and the synchronized beat, and found herself on the dance floor, eyes closed, limbs in-synch with the music, her mind in a faraway place, a sensuous place, absent a facially scarred husband whose idea of a great Friday night was a rented movie and microwave popcorn.

She sensed someone dancing before her and opened her eyes...A tall, light-skinned, freckle-faced man in blue jeans and a green hospital shirt stood before her, nodding his head to the beat. Handsome, with the whitest teeth she'd ever seen. *Computer Love* faded and was followed by *If Loving You Is Wrong.*

He pulled her to him, and she buried her head in his chest. He smelled of Vicks Vapor Rub, though she didn't think it odd. They danced again and again, slow songs, fast songs, rap songs, until they were exhausted.

After two more rum and Cokes, he and she were on the bed of Lester's red-and-white truck parked in back of the juke joint, dogs barking, the December air cool though bearable, under a sea of stars, her yellow skirt bunched up around her waist, her knees against her shoulders, panties hanging on one ankle, with him bouncing on top of her.

Ten weeks later she returned to the juke joint, this time with something more important on her mind than having a good time. She was pregnant. The tall, light-skinned man with freckles needed to help cover prenatal expenses. He wasn't there.

She described him to a group of gray-haired men playing dominoes. Two of them laughed. Yes, they knew him, Drew Tubbs. He'd gone home, they told her. Where's home? Little Rock, the oldest-looking man said. Roger's Hall, the state hospital, he added. He wouldn't be coming back. He'd escaped, and a doctor and the police had come and taken him back.

Drew Tubbs, they told her, had snipped off his own tongue with wire cutters after smoking marijuana and watching Benny Hinn, which partly explained why she couldn't remember what he'd said to get her to the truck.

She threw up on the juke joint floor and needed assistance to Lester's truck; then drove home in a fugue and threw up again after calling the state hospital and looking up schizoaffective disorder in the medical dictionary.

A loud moo startled her into the present; she was walking along the fence to the sale barn, filled with cows and bulls. The stench smelled similar to the paper mill. *Where the hell am I going?* A mile or so she'd be on the outskirts of town. The only stop before here and Hamburg was the park. Aunt Jean lived in Hamburg, but she didn't take kindly to company, family or no.

Lester had known all along Shane wasn't his.

All those years he hadn't said a word. The day she came out of the hospital she took four-day-old Shane to her mother's house and left him.

Every day, for three long weeks, Ida would bring Shane back to her, railing she needed to take care of her own child, and then, before Ida could drive back home, Ruth Ann would take him right back and leave him with her father. Shane got colicky from all the back-and-forth so Ida stopped dropping him off. And not once did Lester utter a peep.

Ruth Ann is a slut.

"No, I'm not!" she said, and looked to see if anyone noticed. No one was around; nothing here except smelly cows and stinky bulls and the long, empty road before her.

How could she have known Drew was a bona fide bozo? Yes, Property of the State Hospital was stenciled on the back of his shirt, but never in a million years would she have guessed his was the real deal. The hospital should have been more specific: The Nut Wearing This Shirt Is An Escaped Fruitcake. *Hello!*

Somehow, someway, she would make it up to Shirley. And Lester. And Shane.

She would...*what?* What could she do? Then she remembered Shane occasionally camped out in the Boy Scout campground. He wasn't at her mother's so more than likely he was there.

Yes, she would go and spend time with her son and let him know she cared about him. The campground wasn't too far away, a country mile at the most. She picked up her pace.

When she made it to the parking lot of Count Pulaski State Park, it was dusk and her eagerness to reunite with her son had waned. The woods looked spooky. Shane could wait, she thought. After all, he'd been waiting for his mother seventeen years--one more day wouldn't hurt.

But where else could she go? Now she wished she'd maintained at least one girlfriend.

No, you can't trust women. Turn your head one minute and your girlfriend's sleeping with your man.

Nowhere else to go, she realized her only option was Shane or the highway.

Soon it would be dark; she needed to make a decision. *What if Shane isn't there?* She'd be in the woods, alone, in the dark, with snakes and bugs and all sorts of creepy critters.

She turned and walked away. A few steps, she imagined herself running on the highway just ahead of a truckload of intoxicated white boys. She turned and walked back. Stopped. Said a prayer. Took a deep breath and started up the trail.

A few feet in she was enveloped in darkness. She slowed to a shuffle, occasionally veering off the trail, bumping into trees and bushes.

Don't let your mind play tricks on you.

No problem she was a woman alone in the woods, searching for a son she'd given up at birth. *No fucking problem!* If only her heart thought the same and stopped thumping loudly in her ears.

What if Shane held a grudge? What if he's on medication and forgot to bring it with him?

Wekeeee! Wekeeeee!

Ruth Ann froze solid. *What the hell was that?* She stood there listening intently, her imagination racing. *To hell with this!* The highway was probably safer, and if a truckload of intoxicated white boys chased her, they wouldn't catch her. No way, not on an open highway. Here anything could sneak up on her.

Wekeeee! Wekeeee!

Don't run! A cricket, all it was. Didn't sound like a cricket, though, a little too loud. *A super cricket. A super cricket in heat.*

Wekeeee! Wekeeee!

From which direction she couldn't tell. She whirled around, took a step, whirled again and bumped into something...something human...She let out a shrill scream.

"It's me," a voice said.

"Shane! Is it you?" Too dark to make him out, only shades of darkness.

"Yeah, it's me."

"It's me, Shane. Your mother."

"I know who you are. What you doing out here?"

A good question. "I-I don't know. I guess I wanted to see you, baby."

"Baby! I'm not your baby. You never wanted to see me before. You and Chester never came to see me when I was living with Pa-pa. Why you want to see me now?"

"Lester," she corrected him. "His name is Lester."

"Lester, Chester, Molester, all the same to me."

"He's your father!"

"Ha! The one time he come to the house to see Pa-pa he wouldn't even look at me. My father lives in Little Rock. He sent me my bow and a picture of him in a Houdini jacket. Somebody lied to you."

"Shane! Don't you dare talk to me like that! I'm your mother. Don't you ever talk to me like that! You hear me? Never!"

He didn't respond, and she wondered if now, at night, in the woods, was the ideal time to teach him manners.

She lowered her voice: "How are you getting along out here?"

He didn't answer and started giggling. She'd never heard him giggle before. It sent a chill down her spine. "What's so funny?"

He stopped giggling. "You want to see where I live? I fixed it up all myself."

"Yes, Shane. Sure, why not," though not particularly desiring to do so, especially if he started giggling again. Men, especially young men meeting their mother in the woods after a seventeen-year absence, shouldn't giggle. She would tell him that. Tomorrow, when the sun came up.

Shane took her hand and started up the trail, a little too fast to her liking. *What's the rush?*

"There's a buncha ways to get up here," Shane said. "The trails are the easiest, but usually I go through the trees. This way you can really get the feel of the surroundings."

"Great. I'll remember my next visit."

The ground leveled and Shane stopped. "Home," he announced. "You can't see em now, there're two cabins up here. Lightning struck a tree and it landed on one of em. I don't live in it, though. C'mon." He led her inside a cabin and released her hand. "Right here," patting on something, "is my bed. I made the frame out of pinewood. The pillow out of rags and quail feathers."

"Nice." She heard him moving across the room.

295

"This here's the couch."

"What you make it out of?"

"Nothing. It was here when I got here."

"Is it what I'm smelling? Sorta stale, isn't it?"

"Naw," and giggled. God, she wished he'd stop that. "It's not the couch, it's me. I haven't had a bath since I been here. Too much trouble."

Too much info. "No big deal."

"You want something to eat?"

"No!"

"I got some turkey, squirrel and possum meat drying out back. Got turtle eggs, too. Think I got a little rabbit meat left over from the other day. You like rabbit meat, don't ya?"

Yes, from the store and refrigerated. "Thanks, I'm not hungry."

"You sure? Won't be no trouble. Rabbit meat and turtle eggs, don't it just make your mouth water?"

Yes, to spit. "No, thank you, Shane, I'm fine. I'd like it if you turn the lights on."

"No lights out here. If I start a fire it'll be too hot. You staying the night? You can take my bed. I'll sleep on the couch."

Ruth Ann couldn't speak. Maybe it was the lack of inflection in his tone, the casual way he'd said it. She didn't know him, had never taken the time to get to know him. Yet here he was in the woods alone, living in a manner unfit for a grown man, roughing it--*and he offered me his bed.*

Her legs went weak, eyes welled up. She sat down on the floor.

"Guess you can have the pillow, too," Shane said.

That broke the dam and she started crying.

Shane said, "You can take the couch."

She couldn't stop crying long enough to tell him that wasn't the problem.

Shane crossed to her. "Don't cry." He knelt beside her and wrapped an arm around her shoulder. "I'm sorry," he said. "I'm sorry. Please don't cry! I apologize what I said about Luther. Stop crying, please!"

She tried to tell him the name was Lester, not Luther, but the words wouldn't form. Her entire body shook, and she was aware she hadn't cried like this since she was in grade school.

Shane patted her back…her head…shoulder. "Don't cry! I'll start a fire out front and it'll shine a little light in here. If you want I'll push the bed onto the porch. Stop crying, please!"

She tried to stop…couldn't.

Shane got up, and she heard him padding across the room and then a ruffling sound. He returned and said, "You can have this…if you stop crying." Something furry brushed her face and she jumped. "It's all right. It's my lucky rabbit foot. You can have it."

Ruth Ann shook her head and pressed both hands firmly over her mouth, successfully stifling the noise but not the ache.

"Thank goodness!" Shane said, utterly relieved.

Chapter 30

Robert Earl banged his head against the kitchen table. Bang! "No!" Bang! "No!" Bang! "No!" Bang!

"Stop it, Robert," Estafay said.

Robert Earl banged his head once more and stared at his wife. "Did you hear what she just said? Daddy left all the money to Ruth Ann. All of it! I quit my job, we're knee-deep in debt. Where you prefer to sleep? A homeless shelter, under a bridge, the library?" He banged his head again and again.

"Stop the nonsense, Robert. Stop it now!" Estafay said, and turned her attention to Shirley, sitting opposite Robert Earl, wearing a gray sweat suit. "Shirley, first let me say I hold no grudge against you. How do we know what you say is true?"

"It's true. I have no reason to lie to you."

Estafay sidled between Shirley and the fridge and stood behind Robert Earl--hands covering his face, shaking his head--and massaged his shoulders.

"Just yesterday," Estafay said, "you were looking for a gun to shoot Ruth Ann. Today you're telling us all the money is going to her. You see why we find this hard to believe?"

"I see," and reached down the front of her sweat suit and retrieved a rolled-up sheet of paper. She straightened it out and slid it across the table toward Robert Earl, who banged his head on it, leaving a sweaty smudge. "Read it, Robert Earl."

"Where did you get this?" Estafay asked as Robert Earl read the paper.

"Does it matter?"

"Dag gummit!" Robert Earl shouted, and crumbled the paper against his forehead.

Shirley said, "Robert Earl, I need it back."

Robert Earl squeezed his temples. "Dag gummit! Dag gummit!"

Estafay bopped him over the head with an open palm. "Get thee behind me, Satan!"

Robert Earl groaned. Religious condemnation was the last thing he wanted to hear now. How sanctimonious would she be when they both were standing in a soup line? Or elbowing each other for space inside a cardboard box?

"There is a way," Shirley said, staring at the plastic fruit bowl in the center of the table, "to change the circumstances. A way we can guarantee our share of the money."

"Beg Ruth Ann?" Robert Earl said.

Shirley shook her head.

"Contest the will?"

"We could. It'll take a long time and the lawyers will slice off a big chunk of the cake once it settles. Not exactly what I had in mind."

"What, then?"

"Ruth Ann is on the run. She's running from me and I think she's running from Lester. She was over to Momma's, didn't stay long. I talked to Leonard and I got the feeling he's pissed off at her, too. She--"

"I'm sorry to hear it, Shirley," Robert Earl interrupted. "Get to how we'll get our share of the money."

Shirley cut him an irritated look and continued, "She doesn't have her vehicle. She's on foot. Doesn't have any friends, least none I know of. So where can she go? My bet, she's out there in the woods with Shane." She stopped and took a sip of water from a jelly glass. "You know where the Boy Scout camp is, don't you, Robert Earl? Going toward Hamburg?"

Robert Earl nodded, eyes saying, "So what?"

Shirley picked up a plastic orange from the bowl and bounced it on the table. "You know, Robert Earl, bad things happen in the woods. Terrible things." She put the orange back. "Horrible things! You know what I mean, Robert Earl?"

"No, I don't."

"Accidents. Fatal accidents! You could fall off a cliff, get bit by a poisonous snake, you could accidentally shoot yourself. Get the picture, Robert Earl?"

"Snakes, even poisonous snakes, seldom bite people. It happens, rarely. If a snake bit you it probably wouldn't kill you. Unless you panic. Shirley, snakes are a lot like dogs, they can sense fear. With a snake, though, you can't tie it up and expect it to stay calm. It will rather die than be shackled."

Estafay said, "Not what she's talking about, Robert. Not what she's talking about at all. She's talking murder."

"Murder!" Robert Earl said.

"I didn't say murder," Shirley said. "Estafay said murder."

"Yes, I did," Estafay said. "Murder. Exactly what you're insinuating, isn't it?"

Shirley didn't respond.

"Is it true?" Robert Earl asked.

"Perchance Ruth Ann befell an accident," Shirley said, "then the money will be split one less person, which increases the amount to each. A fourth of a million is a lot more than a fifth of a million."

Robert Earl mumbled and touched his fingers to his thumb. "Really?"

"Really," Shirley said. "Figure it out on paper."

"You want me to drop you off over there?" Robert Earl said. "Come on, I'll drop you off."

"Robert!" Estafay said. "Robert, I won't have this talk of evildoing in my house. A child of God resides in this house, and I won't let it be blasphemed, or used for devil's work."

"Estafay, honey, why don't you go lie down? You look tired. Go rest up a bit."

"I don't wanna lie down. How can I lie down while devil's work is being planned under my roof?"

Shirley smiled at Robert Earl and said, "Estafay, sit down and shut up or get out!"

Estafay's mouth popped open. She held it agape a beat before saying, "Are you talking to me?"

"Your name Estafay, isn't it?"

Estafay stood there looking shocked, and Robert Earl could feel her eyes searing the top of his head. She muttered something under her breath and then stormed out of the kitchen.

Shirley said, "We also need to inform Leonard."

"You really think we oughta bring the fag into this?"

"Don't call him that!" Shirley snapped. "His name is Leonard, and he needs to know."

"What about Momma?"

"She doesn't need to know. It'll only upset her."

Robert Earl scratched his neck and looked toward the ceiling. "It scares me to even think about this thing. In a way, it feels sorta…you know…wrong! Wouldn't it be a lot easier to beg Ruth Ann for some of the money? We get on her nerves she's bound to give us something to get rid of us. The other way you're talking--I can imagine the nightmares I'll have."

"Robert Earl, you remember Billy Wafer?"

"Yeah. Blind Billy. Why?"

"Remember, Ruth Ann was in junior high and she called herself dating Billy. She walked him to Duncan's store and she left him there. Billy's momma came to the house and told Momma and Daddy how Ruth Ann left Billy at the store and stole his wallet. Ruth Ann swore up and down she didn't take it. Momma beat her ass so long I started crying. I even thought about stopping Momma. Two weeks later I was looking for something under my bed and guess what I found?"

"What?"

"A wallet! A wallet with the initials BW. There were some Braille papers in it and nothing else, not a penny. Now what does that tell you?"

Robert Earl looked confused for a moment, then said, "Ruth Ann was sneaking a guy named Braille into the room?"

Shirley sighed and shook her head. "You ever wonder why during recess you had the playground all to yourself. Why they brought your lunch tray to the classroom?"

Robert Earl smiled. "They liked me. All the teachers said I was special."

"Were they crying when they said it?"

"Like babies. Every day. How you know?"

"Ruth Ann stole money from a blind kid. You think someone like her would give a damn how hard you begged? She couldn't care less."

"You might be right, Shirley." He pounded his fists on the table and several plastic fruit fell out of the bowl. "This is a heckuva fix we're in!" He hit the table again and two red apples and an orange rolled to the floor.

"Do it!" he said. "Just do it! Don't make her suffer no more than you just have to. Whatever you do, don't mention my name under any circumstances. Sheriff Bledsoe specifically warned me not to get into trouble again. He might give you a pass since this is your first time."

They heard Estafay, in the living room, singing *I Still Have Joy* off key. Robert Earl got up and closed the kitchen door.

Shirley said, "Everybody knows Ruth Ann stabbed me in the back. If something, something accidental, were to happen to her, I'd be the prime suspect. When it happens I can't be in the vicinity."

"Don't look at me. I can't do it! No can do! If it was somebody else, somebody I just met on the street, I might be able to do it. Someone I know, someone I was raised up with--I just can't do it!"

A thought occurred to him and his eyes lit up. "Hey, I got an idea! The fag! Excuse me, I mean Leonard. I bet he'll do it. I bet he will."

Shirley gave him a hard, long look. He couldn't figure if she was considering his suggestion or willing herself to cool down.

She stood up and said, "Okay, Robert Earl, I'll talk to Leonard, see what he thinks."

Robert Earl followed her to the door and when Shirley opened it, Estafay was there, stooped over, head level to the keyhole.

Chapter 31

Leonard sat on the hot hood of the Lumina parked in front of the jail. *Where the hell is Sheriff Bledsoe?* He stepped to the window and looked in. Too dark to see inside. He returned to the Lumina. Several people walked by, almost everyone saying hi or nodding hello.

The heat from the hood and the afternoon sun forced him to get up and go stand in the shade of the tattered green awning to the barbershop next door to the jail. Still, sweat poured down his face.

Minutes later, Sheriff Bledsoe drove up in his cruiser. Not noticing Leonard, he got out whistling, a plastic Wal-Mart bag hanging on his wrist.

Leonard stepped toward him and said, "Hey, Sheriff."

Sheriff Bledsoe stopped whistling and frowned. "Yeah," he grunted.

"We need to talk."

Sheriff Bledsoe opened the door. "I figured as much. Come on in." Leonard followed him inside. Sheriff Bledsoe flipped the light switch and said, "You mind I fixed myself a stiff drink?"

"No, go right ahead."

Sheriff Bledsoe sat down and emptied the bag on a desk. Bottles of Maalox, Mylanta, Kaopectate, Pepto Bismo, Milk of Magnesia, and several small boxes of Tagamet HB, Pepsid AC, and Zantac 75 fell out. He retrieved a Styrofoam cup from a trash can and took out two pills from each box.

He looked up at Leonard. "Sit down, this'll only take a minute or two."

Leonard sat down on a swivel chair missing two rollers. Sheriff Bledsoe put the pills into an envelope, folded it and bit it several times. He opened the envelope over the cup and a pinkish-blue powder spilled out. Then he opened the bottles and poured a dollop of each into the cup. After stirring the mixture with a finger, he put the cup to his mouth, grimaced, winked at Leonard and drank it dry.

He wiped his chalky-white moustache clean and said, "Ugh! That hits the spot."

"Sheriff, you really don't have to take all that. There's new medicine will clear up indigestion. Ask your doctor."

Sheriff Bledsoe gave him a look. "Yeah, tell me about it." He tossed the cup into the trash can. "You know, I used to think gas jokes were the funniest thing in the world. All those kid movies where somebody breaks wind or can't make it to the bathroom in time just had me rolling on the floor laughing. The bathroom scene in *Dumb and Dumber* had me grinning three days." He shook his head, clucked his tongue. "That was then, when I didn't know any better. It ain't funny. It ain't funny at all."

Is he drunk on antacids?

"Enough with my problems," Sheriff Bledsoe said. "What do you have on your mind?"

"I…" Leonard searched for words. The business with the antacids made him forget what he intended to say.

"Let me take a guess. You're itching to get back to the windy city, resume your life. Furthermore, you don't like the way I've handled this investigation. You think I don't know what I'm doing. Guess what? You're one hundred percent right. I'm as lost as Newt Gingrich on *Soul Train*. Yes, I made some mistakes, some big mistakes, whoppers. The good news is I'm not giving up. I'm going to nab whoever murdered your father."

"I'm glad to hear your determination, Sheriff. It's not what I wanted to talk with you. I'm concerned about Ruth Ann."

"Ruth Ann?"

"Yes. I think her life is in danger."

"Lester is upset, but I doubt he'll do anything to her."

308

"You know about the rift between Shirley and Ruth Ann?"

"Yes, I know all about it."

"You think maybe Ruth Ann should be under surveillance for her protection?"

"Don't worry about Lester. Last night I stopped by and talked with him. He's not going to do anything stupid."

"Lester isn't who I'm worried about, Sheriff?"

"Who are you worried about?"

Leonard winced. "I really don't think Shirley would intentionally hurt Ruth Ann. Best to be safe than sorry, right?"

"You think Shirley might harm Ruth Ann?"

"No, no, no! I didn't say that. I'm saying, you know, maybe it wouldn't be a bad idea to keep an eye on Ruth Ann, at least for a couple of days or so."

"Look around here," Sheriff Bledsoe said. "This operation here is what big-city folks call low-rent. In Chicago the police can provide twenty-four-hour surveillance. Here in Dawson, population less than five thousand, it can't be done. Tell Ruth Ann to chill out for a few more days, till tempers cool a bit."

"What if tempers don't cool? What if tempers have already boiled over?"

"Something you're not telling me. Take the guesswork out and tell it straight."

"Shirley came over to the house not an hour ago and showed me a copy of Daddy's will."

"Where was Ruth Ann?"

"She's gone. Shirley said she's with her son at the Boy Scout camp."

"Ruth Ann has a son? I didn't know that."

"Yes. His name is Shane."

"By Lester?"

"Yes…I think so. Anyway, Shirley said--"

"Let me see the will."

"I'm sorry, I didn't bring it with me. I should have. There's been so much going on lately I can't think straight."

"I was starting to think the will didn't exist. Where did Shirley get it?"

"I don't know. I read it, couldn't believe it. Daddy willed all his money to Ruth Ann." Leonard shook his head. "The whole kit and caboodle. Every damn dime! I should have known he wouldn't leave me anything. Ruth Ann, she's the stingiest person I know. I'll never forget, I was five-years-old, my first tooth. Woke up the next morning…nothing! No tooth, no money. Not a damn thing! I know she took it."

"I'm a little confused here," Sheriff Bledsoe said. "First you come in here sounding all concerned with Ruth Ann's welfare. Now you sound bitter. Tell me what's really going on?"

Leonard looked down and noticed a red chip of glass near his foot. He looked up and said, "There's a provision in the will you should know about. In the event of Ruth Ann's death, the money will be split among her surviving siblings."

"I'm on board now. You think whoever poisoned your father might go after Ruth Ann?"

Leonard nodded.

"Who else has seen the will?"

"Shirley told me she showed Robert Earl a copy and he crushed it against his head. She didn't mention showing it to anyone else."

"Was Shirley upset she'd been left out of the will?"

"It's hard to say. Shirley's been looking upset ever since I got here."

"I need to see that will. Robert Earl crushed a copy against his head, huh? I can see him doing that. Are you worried Robert Earl might do something to Ruth Ann?"

"Nooooo! Robert Earl is too far left of center, and he's a big chicken. He…"

"He what?"

Leonard didn't respond.

"You know what makes my job difficult? People who think the police are psychic. They think if they provide a piece of the truth, enough to shield themselves or someone else, the police will have enough to solve the puzzle. You're holding back.

"You come in here seeking help, then you give me a couple pieces to a five-hundred-piece puzzle. I ain't that good, what should be obvious to you by now. Come clean and we might be able to wrap this thing up. Then you can go back to Chicago, and I can stop having these acid reflux attacks."

Leonard started to speak and said nothing.

"Suit yourself. If something happens to Ruth Ann, or someone else in your family, and you had a chance to stop it...." He paused for maximum guilt effect. "Maybe your conscience could live with it, I know mine couldn't."

Damn! Leonard thought. Another guilt trip. This one damned convincing, too.

If his mother found out his reticence contributed to the death of one of her children...Too painful to consider.

Yet he couldn't mention the haunted look in Shirley's eyes when she handed him the will. And he certainly couldn't discuss the phone conversation he'd had with Robert Earl.

"You did it?" Robert Earl had asked.

"Did what?"

"You know? The H-I-T?"

"What hit?"

"You know, the hit on the Ruth Ann? Shirley didn't tell you? Oh-oh, I've said too much on the phone."

No way could he mention that crazy exchange. He didn't hate Ruth Ann. He didn't particularly like her, either. Yet he definitely didn't want to see her dead.

"Well?" Sheriff Bledsoe said.

Leonard shrugged. "That's it, Sheriff. I don't know what more to tell you." Sheriff Bledsoe intensified the stare.

Enough, already!

If Sheriff Bledsoe investigated crimes as well as he stared people down, he could have his own crime show on television. Leonard stood up, his knees stiff again. Stress. "I've got to go, Sheriff."

"I'd sure like to see the will. I could drop by and check it out?"

"I got a few errands to run. I'll bring it here later this evening." Stiff knees and guilt complexes and all, he limped across the room and out the door.

Chapter 32

A redheaded woodpecker drilled on a cottonwood tree behind the cabin. The noise awoke Ruth Ann, fuzzy on where she was and how she got here. Above her no ceiling, only rafters festooned with spider webs.

She looked to her left and saw Shane sitting on a bed, sharpening something with a stone. "Good morning," she said, smelling her breath, wishing she'd brought toothpaste. Shane grunted and continued what he was doing.

The cabin was smaller than she'd thought. The floor simply a dirty slab of concrete. A large rock fireplace dominated one side of the room. The walls, hewed logs, were soot-black and oozed resin. No window or back door.

Ruth Ann stared at Shane, shirtless, wearing only black slacks torn and frayed at the cuffs. The same pants he'd worn to the funeral. She couldn't distinguish his face with his head down, intently focused on whatever he was doing.

Uncombed light-brown afro speckled with green bits. Hands and bare feet particularly dirty. Yet he looked very much a man. Tall, lean, muscular, curly hairs sprouting on his chest, he was the twin image of his father.

"Where's the restroom?" she asked him. "I need to freshen up."

Shane stopped his work and looked up at her. "No bathroom. You can go behind a tree. No one will see you."

"Never mind. What are you doing?"

"Sharpening my arrows," resuming his work.

Ruth Ann sat up and noticed the couch she'd slept on was orange. An orange, paisley couch. *It stinks!* She sniffed her T-shirt. *Ugh!* The same odor as the couch. *Orange funk.*

"Shane, is there any water around here?"

"Behind the cabin, not too far down, there's a stream."

Does it have a faucet, hot and cold taps? "Shane, honey, how long do you plan to live out here?"

He looked up and smiled, teeth straight but yellow. "This is my home. You're the one visiting."

"Don't you get lonely here? I mean, don't you think about girls. A handsome-looking young man like yourself, some girl would be glad to get her hooks into you."

Shane shook his head. "Girls laugh at me. Always have. I don't even say nothing and they start laughing. Here I don't get laughed at."

"Sugar, at sometime or other, everyone gets laughed at. It's no big deal. I promise you all the girls won't laugh at you, not with your looks. You'll never know if you stay up here. You have to get out, take chances. You can't hide from life."

Shane stood up, countenance conveying discomfort with the conversation. "I'm going hunting. I thought there was enough meat. It isn't. There's two turtle eggs round back. You can eat em." He started for the door, stopped and stepped to her. "Don't move."

"What?"

"There's a tick on your neck."

Slapping her neck: "What!" She felt something…*A bump?…My God, a tick!*…She screamed. "Get it off me, Shane! Get it off me!"

Shane tilted her head with one hand and pinched her neck with the other. "Here it is," presenting a small brown bug with a white dot on its back.

Ruth Ann almost fainted. "What if it has Rocky Mountain spotted fever? Or West Nile disease? I'm dead!"

"I doubt it. They bite me all the time. The head is still in. You'll know if you start getting sick."

"What! The head is still in?"

"I didn't get it all out, just the body."

"I feel sick already," rubbing her neck. She did feel queasy and her neck felt a little swollen where the tick was imbedded.

"I'm going hunting. Might be a while 'fore I get back."

"Shane, you can't leave! A tick with a dot bit me!"

"We need food," and walked out.

Ruth Ann started to follow him but didn't. If some unknown tick virus was circulating through her body, she'd better conserve her energy. When Shane came back she would have him walk her down the hill. He could stay as long as he liked, but she'd overstayed her welcome.

She couldn't get the tick out of her mind. If she'd been infected with a deadly virus, what would be the first symptom? What if she was too weak to yell for help?

She jumped up and stripped out of her clothes. The tick might have brought a relative or two along with him. She scrutinized her entire body, including the bottom of her feet, and didn't find anything. She put her clothes back on and lay down on the couch.

An hour later: "Peekaboo!" *Shane, back already.* "Ruth Ann, wake up." Not Shane--a woman's voice. She opened her eyes and screamed.

"Howdy," Shirley said, standing over her, pointing a gun in her face.

"Shirley, please! Please, Shirley! Don't shoot me! Don't shoot me! Think about Momma--this'll kill her."

"Shut up! You didn't think about Momma, did you? Didn't think about any of your family, did you? Your husband, your son, my son, me, nobody! Only thought about your-damned-self, as usual."

"Shirley, please! I don't want to die!"

"I'm sure you don't. Didn't you think I'd be a teeny weenie bit upset when I found out about you and Eric? Didn't you think Shirley might ding out and do something drastic?"

"Yes, I did!"

"Anything you have to say before you go?"

"Please, Shirley! Please! Don't do this to me!"

Shirley thumbed the trigger. "That's it? Nothing for Momma? Shane? Lester? What about Eric? Surely you want to leave him a message."

Ruth Ann covered her face with both hands. "Oh God!"

"One last thing before you go. Do you love him?"

"Love who?"

"Lil Wayne, dammit! You know who!"

"Just shoot me and get it over with!"

"Take your hands down and look at me! And answer the damn question! Do you love him?"

Ruth Ann shook her head…and felt the gun on the back of her hand.

"Take your hands down and talk to me or I'll shoot you in your knee."

Ruth Ann dropped her hands and said, "No! No, I do not!"

"Tell me why, Ruth Ann? Why were you fucking him?"

Ruth Ann stared at her knees, opened her mouth and closed it. A lone tear trickled down her face.

"Shirley, I don't know why!" She started crying. "I'm sorry, Shirley. I'm so sorry! I never meant to hurt you. I swear I didn't. It just happened. It shouldn't have happened, but it happened. I swear to God I never intended to hurt you! Never! Go ahead, Shirley, kill me! I don't deserve to live! Kill me!"

"You're so right," backing up a step. "Close your eyes, you'll never know what hit you."

Ruth Ann's eyes bulged. "Wait a minute, Shirley!" She raised her hands, shielding her face. "Just wait a minute! Maybe we could work this out another way. Why don't you just beat me down? Okay? You don't have to shoot me. Just beat me bloody!"

"You do your dirt and when it's time to pay the piper, you squeal like a chicken."

"Bawk-bawk-bawk-bawk!"

"Funny. Doesn't change anything. Have a nice trip. See ya!"

Ruth Ann closed her eyes. *This is it, the end!* Seconds ticked by...no bang.

She opened one eye...Shirley was sitting on the bed, the gun on the floor between them. She rolled onto the floor, grabbed the gun and pointed it at Shirley. "Don't move!"

Shirley rolled her eyes at her. "I knew you would do that. It's a pellet gun, Ruth Ann, and it's not loaded."

"Pellet gun?" She read the word on the barrel. *Mattel*. "Shirley, I-what-why-how come--"

"Sit down and listen to what I have to say."

Ruth Ann shuffled to the couch, staring at the gun. *Pellet gun!*

"Each month Mrs. Avery sends me a two hundred-dollar check. Lord knows I need the money. The twenty years I worked for Mrs. Avery I always did what she told me, never stole anything, never disrespected her--and, believe me, some days she almost drove me crazy.

"When Obama got elected something snapped in Mrs. Avery. I'd be working and she'd come get me, want me to listen to a multi-millionaire got rich sitting on his butt dissing welfare recipients complain about a paltry increase in the minimum wage, ignoring the fact if he'd went deaf before he got rich, he'd be praising Obamacare.

"'Mrs. Avery, I don't have time for this! I got work to do.'

"'Listen, Shirley, you'll learn something.'

"'The man is out of touch, thinks black folks still saying 'right on, right on' and 'jive honky.'

"'Y'all don't say that anymore?'

"'Not since the seventies. Bo Snerdley should update him.'

"'Shirley, you know he's trying to take our future and country away from us.'

"'Is he? He must've relapsed on OxyContin.'

"'Not him! Your president.'

"'How is he trying to do all that?'

"She never answered that one.

"'Shirley, look what he's done to your people.'

"'*My* people, Mrs. Avery? The Harris tribe? What did he do to *my* people?'

"'Nothing! He's done nothing for your people! African American unemployment has skyrocketed a whopping two percent since he's been in office.'

"Now she and I both know if President Obama so much as declared Popsicle Day for African Americans, she and a buncha other like-minded people would take to the streets, pulling their hair out and stomping their feet in one mass hysterical hissy conniption. The back-in-the-day bunch will be in the mix, too, crying it ain't enough and looking for a shitty-assed mule. I know the history, but I feel sorry for anyone who desires to own a mule.

"Last year Mrs. Avery's husband died and she found out her youngest boy had blown all their millions on cocaine and leveraged funds. Now she lives in a ratty duplex on Mallory Street and walks seven miles each day back and forth to work at McDonalds. Poor, just like me and a lotta other folks. Each week faced with tough decisions. Rent or fill the prescription? Food or the light bill? Not enough money to do both. Kid's clothes or the gas bill?

"You either got it or you don't. If you ain't got it, you need to figure a way to get it or learn to live without it. Doesn't matter what you used to have, what you used to do, what you gonna do when you get it again. All anyone cares about is do you have it now. Everywhere you go--bank, hospital, courthouse, wherever--the second someone sees you don't have it now, you might as well sit down because you fixin' to wait a long time. 'You ain't got no money, what's your rush?' The more money involved, the longer the wait.

"I know Mrs. Avery is having a helluva hard time adjusting to now and she can't afford to send me two hundred dollars. She can barely feed herself. She thinks I'm in far worse shape than she. So each check I put in another envelope and mail it back to her with a note. Thank You, Mrs. Avery, But There Are Some Things I Cannot Do. This Is One Of Them.

"Ruth Ann, someone could have a put a gun to my head and I would not have done what you did to me. Never! Hungry, dead broke, living on the street, there are some things you should never do."

"Shirley, you're not going to beat me down?"

"You didn't hear a damn thing I said, did you? Not one word. It doesn't matter. You're no longer my sister. You're bad news. Somebody ask you who I am, tell em you don't know. Tell em I'm an acquaintance, someone you used to know. Don't tell em I'm your sister because you're no longer related to me in any way."

Ruth Ann laid the gun on the couch and stood up. "I do love you, Shirley."

"Don't you dare! You hear me? Don't ever say that shit to me again!"

Ruth Ann swallowed. "You're serious, aren't you?"

"Do I look like I'm bullshitting? I'm not! Sit down and let me finish what I have to say. Where's Shane?"

"Out hunting. Shirley, how long we supposed to act like we're not sisters?"

"Forever! Shut up and listen! I want a life, a real life, not this nightmare I'm currently living. I aim to have it, one way or the other. I also want Eric. He's a dog, a dirty dog, but he's my dog. I picked him and I'm keeping him. I'm not giving him up to you or no one else. We're still getting married. No, before you ask, you're not welcome at the wedding. Don't even send a card. I've thought about this long and hard, and there's no reason to change my plans because my former sister doesn't give a fuck about nobody but herself.

"I want a computer for my son. A car for Mrs. Avery so she can at least drive to work. I want a home of my own. You know how I'm going to get all this? The money Daddy left for us, is how. Once I get it, Eric, Paul and me, we're getting the hell out of Dawson. You feel me, Ruth Ann?"

Ruth Ann nodded.

"Good. Then you'll have no problem helping me out, will you?"

"Uh, what do you want me to do?"

"Help me catch whoever killed Daddy."

Ruth Ann eyed Shirley toe to head, from her well-worn sandals to her extra-large gray sweat suit to her hair, a tangled mess. She forced herself to look in Shirley's steely brown eyes. "How do you propose to do that?"

Shirley smiled at her.

"Why do I have a bad feeling about this? An hour ago a humongous tick with an hourglass on its back bit me. Its head is still in my neck. I may not have long to live."

"My sympathies lay with the tick."

"What exactly do you want me to do?"

"Nothing, really. Stay here for a couple days."

"That's it? I guess I can do that."

"When the killer comes here, I'll nab him or her."

Ruth Ann cleared her throat. "What makes you think the killer will come here?"

Shirley smiled again. "I sent out invitations."

"Invitations? Shirley, honey, don't take this the wrong way. Killers rarely answer invitations. They view those the same as going to the police and confessing."

"I'm not your honey. I told everyone Daddy left all his money to you. My friend Darlene designed a fake will on her computer and I showed it to em as proof."

"So everybody thinks I'm getting all the money?"

"Yes."

"You think whoever killed Daddy will now come looking for me?"

"Amazing! Morally deficient with a degree of intelligence."

"If the killer takes the bait and comes up here to kill me, you're going to nab him with an empty pellet gun?"

"Yes."

"Shirley, why didn't you just get a real gun and shoot me? Same results."

"I couldn't get hold of a real gun. I was lucky to get this one. No one knows it's a pellet gun. It'll work."

"I know! What if the killer comes with a real gun, then what? Huh? What you gonna do? The killer firing real bullets while you're shooting blanks. No, you can't even do that. You don't have any pellets."

"No doubt in my mind you're the scariest-assed woman ever snapped on a bra. Listen, this killer is cunning, organized, methodical. He's not coming in with guns blazing."

"Organized? Methodical? You finally got cable, didn't you? Shirley, I really think we should let Sheriff Bledsoe handle the investigation."

"Sheriff Bledsoe? Ha! He couldn't find smut on the Internet. I'll be too old to enjoy the money by the time he figures out who did it."

"Maybe so, but I don't think it's a good idea. I'll do anything but that. When Shane comes back I'm outta here."

Shirley raised her chin and looked down at Ruth Ann. "You owe me and you are going to pay me! One way or the other."

"Couldn't you take a check?" Beseechingly: "I don't like this, Shirley! I really don't. Somebody could get hurt. Me!"

Chapter 33

Various birds chirped discordantly, hamsters and gerbils rattled exercise wheels, water-purifying machines percolated in aquariums. The entire pet shop, including the assistants, smelled of feces.

Robert Earl, a beatific expression on his face, stood in front of a large aquarium that housed an inert albino boa constrictor, the same color as Albert, orange-and-white. But by comparison, this snake made Albert look like a worm. Robert Earl judged it to be about twelve-feet long and as thick as a man's arm.

He wanted it, desperately. He just knew this snake was much smarter than Albert. This snake could be taught a bunch of tricks. This snake wouldn't belly-up under a little pressure around its neck. People would pay good money to see this snake.

"May I help you?" an assistant asked.

Robert Earl, eyes never leaving the object of his affection, said, "How much does he cost?"

"Three hundred and seventy-five dollars."

Robert Earl looked at the young woman wearing a blue apron with the store's name stitched on the pocket. "That's not much," he said, though he'd almost said, "Are you outta your mind?"

"I'm just looking," he told her.

"If you need anything, give me a nod," the woman said before moving on.

Robert Earl gave the snake another longing look before walking out.

Getting into his truck, he said, "Fuck!" He only had ten dollars and some change. All the snakes he'd owned someone had given him or he'd caught himself; he had no idea a snake could cost so much. Plus he'd driven all the way out here, Greenville, Mississippi. Fifty miles!

The gas hand was almost on E. "Fuck!"

He hadn't tossed the F-bomb since his tour in the Marine Corps. "Fuck!" It felt good to say it. He started the truck and drove off. "Fuck!"

A rusty Ford pickup pulling a lone cow in a cattle trailer slowed him on the narrow two-lane bridge over the Mississippi River.

The Ford slowed to walking speed, and Robert Earl could see the driver looking right to left, admiring the picturesque view of gulls and pigeons gliding below an azure sky and above a collage of painted fields dotted with grazing cows and rusty tin buildings halved by a band of muddy-brown water.

Robert Earl blew the horn. The wind shifted and the stench of cow manure hit him full face. Blew the horn again. The driver, an elderly white man--*who else?*--stuck his hand out the window and waved, as if he were in a parade.

"Fuck!" Robert Earl shouted. "Get out the damn way, you coot!"

The Ford inched along even slower. For the next fifteen minutes it took to cross the half-mile long bridge, Robert Earl cursed and screamed, veins pulsing in his forehead, cow manure assaulting his nostrils, and the old fart up ahead waving and strolling along as if he were lead float in the Rose Parade.

At the foot of the bridge, just past the sign that said Arkansas, The Land of Opportunity, Robert Earl jerked his truck in the opposite lane, an eighteen-wheeler approaching less than a quarter mile away, and drove alongside the Ford. "Get out the damn way, grandpa!"

The eighteen-wheeler less than a block away now, air horn blaring, Robert Earl jerked his truck in front of the Ford, narrowly missing the bumper.

Maybe I should have let that big rig hit me, he thought. *End my misery. Rotten rascal had a million dollars and couldn't leave me a rusty dime*. He should've been able to walk into the pet store and buy four or five snakes.

Instead he had to walk out in shame, the assistant well aware he didn't have enough money to buy a guppy, much less an expensive boa constrictor.

He and Estafay had a little money in a cookie jar, but he couldn't get it, not with the rent due and the light bill two days past the shut-off notice. Estafay would blow a fuse if she had to sit in the dark while he trained his new high-dollar snake in the backyard.

"Fuck!"

An hour later Robert Earl trudged up Maumelle Trail. The time had come for him to take matters in his own hands. He would convince Ruth Ann to give him some of the money; would not take no for an answer.

No sireee!

He patted the back pocket of his overalls. The knife was there. He hoped he wouldn't have to use it, but he wouldn't return to his truck without a guarantee he'd get some of that money.

The sun would be setting soon, and though he knew these woods like the back of his hand, he didn't want to be out here at night. Ruth Ann's boy didn't have good sense; no telling what he might do if there were a full moon.

He walked up to the cabin and knocked on the door. No one answered. He pushed it open and stepped in. Ruth Ann lay asleep on an orange couch.

Nudging her awake, he said, "We need to talk."

Ruth Ann stared at him dreamily, and then jumped to her feet, a hand over her mouth.

"We need to talk, Ruth Ann."

She backed away from him. "Robert Earl!" she shouted, looking about the room. "Hello! Robert Earl is here! He's in the cabin…with me!"

"What's wrong with you? Why you acting crazy? Where's the boy?"

"There's nothing wrong with me, Robert Earl!" Ruth Ann shouted even louder. "What makes you think there could possibly be something wrong with me!"

"Why you hollering?"

"Am I hollering, Robert Earl?" Trembling: "Am I hollering, Robert Earl?"

"Yes, you're hollering, making me nervous." He sat down on the couch. "We need to talk. I need some of that money, and I won't take no for an answer."

"No problem!" She backed up against the wall. "No problem, Robert Earl! Hello!"

"I wish you stop hollering. I ain't deaf. Sit down and talk to me."

"I don't want to sit down! Hello! I'm fine here!"

"I need some of that money. I have a dream. Ain't got a dime to my name. It ain't fair Daddy giving you *all* the money. You know

331

he was wrong. If you don't give me some…" He produced a red pocketknife and flipped open a four-inch blade.

Ruth Ann screamed.

Robert Earl looked at the blade and then up at Ruth Ann, her eyes bucked, tongue wriggling as she screamed. "I don't get some of the money, I'm gonna hurt myself!"

"Freeze, brain trauma!" Shirley shouted, bursting into the cabin with a gun in her hand.

Robert Earl threw his hands up. "What the--Shirley, what are you doing?"

"Drop the knife!"

Robert Earl threw it down. "Shirley, watch where you're pointing that thing."

"You sure took a long time," Ruth Ann said. "I could've been dead."

"I went looking for the lady's restroom. Couldn't find it."

"Shirley, what's going on? Stop pointing that thing at me!"

"So it was you, Robert Earl," Shirley said. "Who would've imagined? I didn't think you had enough sense to jaywalk without getting run over."

"Shirley, what are you talking about?"

"Don't play dumber than usual. You killed Daddy and you were fixin' to kill Ruth Ann. Tie him up, Ruth Ann."

"Tie him up? Tie him up with what?"

"What y'all been smoking up here? I didn't kill Daddy. Tie me up? For what?"

"Shirley," Ruth Ann said, "he didn't threaten to kill me. He said if I didn't give him some of the money he would hurt himself."

Robert Earl said, "I mean it, too. If I don't get some of Daddy's money I'm going to do something bad to myself."

Shirley lowered the gun to her side. "What were you going to do, Robert Earl? Nick yourself?"

"Wouldna gone that far. I was just going to hold the knife to my throat."

"For Pete's sake!" Shirley said.

"How 'bout it, Ruth Ann?" Robert Earl said.

"How about what?"

"The money? I've quit my job. Bills due. Estafay plans to get a lot of cosmetic surgery. Not to mention--"

"She can sure use it," Shirley said.

"--my dream."

"The snake gas station?" Ruth Ann said.

"Combination gas station and exotic snake farm. There's a snake in Greenville I need to buy before somebody else gets it."

"You call that a dream?" Shirley said.

"Yes, I do."

"You need a mule."

"Can a mule do tricks?"

"Did any number of your teachers suddenly disappear, left town without telling a soul?"

"Why you keep asking about my childhood?" To Ruth Ann: "Sis, you're not letting your oldest brother, your only straight brother, lose his dream and get kicked out on the street, are you? I'm begging you. Please! If I had money you wouldn't have to ask--I'd just give it to you."

"Would you, really?"

"Yes. In a heartbeat. Whatever you needed."

"Stop your begging, straight brother," Shirley said. "You'll get your share."

"What? Is that right, Ruth Ann?"

Ruth Ann nodded.

Robert Earl jumped up in the air several times, shaking the entire cabin. "Yes! Yes! Yes! Yes! Thank you, Ruth Ann. Thank you! I told Shirley you were reasonable. I knew you were better off alive than dead."

"What?" Ruth Ann said.

"Nothing. You're my favorite sister." He hugged her. "You know I wouldn't let nobody kill you."

Shirley laughed. "Robert Earl, Ruth Ann has nothing to do with you getting your share of the money."

"Huh?" quickly releasing Ruth Ann.

"Shirley set a trap. She faked the will. Daddy didn't leave all the money to me."

Robert Earl stared at them both. "Which lie you want me to believe?"

"I faked the will," Shirley said, "to draw Daddy's killer up here. Once I catch whoever did it, we'll all get our share of the money."

"I see," he said. "A trick…to catch the killer. You sure had me fooled."

"Keep taking the bee pollen, Robert Earl. It's finally starting to kick in."

Robert Earl stared at the door. "If the killer comes here, he's going to kill Ruth Ann." He swallowed. "And whoever else is here. I need to get my butt out of here. Now! What if there's gunplay?" Shirley held up the gun. "I might not know long division, Shirley, but that sure looks like a pellet gun to me."

"I told you, Shirley!" Ruth Ann said.

"Robert Earl," Shirley said, "why don't you stay here and help us catch the killer? If the gun doesn't work, you can hold the killer at bay with your knife."

"Do I look stupid?" Shirley nodded. "Shirley, you've been watching too much television. I'm going home. Y'all know my number. Call me and let me know how it worked out." He started for the door.

"Ruth Ann!" a voice cried from outside.

Robert Earl froze. "Ruth Ann, someone is looking for you."

Chapter 34

"Linda!" the man called.

"Yes, Daddy."

"I dropped the remote. Come get it."

Eric exhaled in relief when Linda leaned over the couch and retrieved the remote control. Thank God the man was lazy. Eric's legs were numb. He'd ducked behind the couch in an uncomfortable position: knees bent; butt resting on his ankles; hands flat on the floor; head scrunched down to keep from showing above the headrest. And he now needed to pee.

A few minutes later a foul odor drifted behind the couch. *Hog maw?* Sure smelled like it.

Eric heard snoring. *The man sleeping!* Eric raised his head to take a peek.

If he could have seen himself, he would have viewed a sweaty forehead slowly rising above the headrest, followed by bucked eyes flitting in every direction, and finally a mouth, opened wide, the bottom lip quivering. The smell much stronger now, he locked onto the source...feet...

...funky feet!

Eric stared at the man's washboard stomach and massive chest. Though asleep, the man's muscles were taut, twitching. Eric chanced a look into the man's face: brown-skinned, square chin, broad nose and an inch-long scar below the right eye.

The man's mouth fell open, and Eric gulped.

Silver teeth! Upper and lowers, all silver.

Why would someone have all their teeth silver?

To bite the shit outta somebody and never let go.

A moment Eric thought to huddle behind the couch and remain there till eternity. No, uh-uh, he had to get out. *How?*

The man stopped snoring, raised his legs to a bent position, coughed and continued snoring.

Eric resumed breathing. *Jesus, pull me out of this one I'll join church. Visit old folks at the nursing home. Donate money to those pitiful-looking puppies on TV.*

Jesus, just get me out of here!

337

He waited for a miracle; none came. Only one option available: he had to clear the couch without waking the man. He waited a few minutes more before standing up and carefully hoisting his right leg over the man to the front of the couch. *Damn!* Should have gone with the left first, he thought, more strength in the right.

Dammit! He inhaled, held it and hopped off his left foot…A perfect maneuver…He was clearing the couch, the man…and then his right foot landed on something other than the floor.

A damn shoe!

His ankle twisted and he fell backward. *Oh shit!* He landed on his back on the couch, legs akimbo, his groin only a few inches from the man's feet.

Again the man stopped snoring, and Eric watched the man's chest stop rising and falling as well. *Is he dead?* The snoring restarted and the man crossed his right leg over the left and rested his feet squarely in Eric's crotch. Rivulets of sweat dripped down Eric's face and the stench of the man's feet almost made him hurl.

A monk, he promised. If Jesus got him out of this, he would become a monk. *Promise! On my dead momma's grave!* The man rubbed his nose and dug his feet deeper into Eric's crotch, pressing his genitals in a most painful manner.

Certain he would lose his most vital organ, Eric grabbed a throw pillow, lifted the man legs, extricated himself gently but quickly and lowered the man's feet onto the pillow. He tiptoed to the door, eased the chain free and quietly unlocked the deadbolt.

Free at last, thank God almighty, free at last!

He opened the door. If the man awoke now, no chance could he catch him. Not in a million years.

Eric stuck out his tongue at him and whispered, "You better lay off the steroids, mercury mouth. They'll give you titties, shrink your stones." When he turned to leave, a woman appeared in the doorway.

"Who the hell are you?" she said. Eric tried to push past her, but couldn't get around her wide body. "Who the hell are you?"

Eric tried again to push past her, and she knocked him back with her substantial stomach.

"Walter!" the woman screamed. "Walter!"

Eric saw the man getting up from the couch. No time for bullshit now! He faked toward the woman's right, then broke through on her left. On the porch, gearing up for top speed, he felt hands grab his wrist, pulling him.

"Walter! Walter! Walter!" She held on tight. Eric jerked hard; the woman's grip loosened. He jerked again, pulling free momentarily…The woman caught hold of the sleeve to his favorite shirt, a gold silk Sean Jean that Shirley had bought him for Father's Day. The shirt slid down his shoulder…She was pulling it right off his back.

"Walter!"

Eric pulled the woman into the front yard. "Lemme go, lady! Lemme go!" He grabbed her wrist to prevent her pulling his shirt off. "Let...me...go!"

The woman fell on her butt, using her weight for leverage, almost pulling him down with her. "Walter! Walter! Walter!"

Where the hell Walter?

Eric dragged the woman halfway across the yard, almost to the sidewalk. He heard a ripping sound and saw his shirt tearing at the shoulder seam. He made a fist with his free hand and waved it in her face.

"Let go! Or I'll knock the shit out of you!" She didn't. He reared back...and saw Walter running out of the house, looking distressed, a shotgun in his hands. He stopped a few feet short and aimed the shotgun at Eric's head.

"Stand clear, Colleen!" Walter yelled. "I got him!"

Immediately the woman let go and rolled away. Eric stood there, paralytic, apoplectic, his only thought on two black holes. When something came out of those holes, his life would be officially over.

Kabooom! The noise was deafening.

"Run!" a voice yelled. "Run!" *Am I in heaven?* "Run!" He opened his eyes...Linda was on the man's back, covering his eyes with her hands. "Run, Forest, run!"

Who the fuck is Forest?

"Run, fool!"

So he did, faster than he'd ever run in his life. He continued running, through the neighborhood, into the woods, along the highway, through more woods, down a dirt road, and finally up four steps and into a mobile home.

Inside he fell to his knees, huffing and puffing, vaguely aware Darlene, sitting on the couch, and Paul and one of his friends, lying on the floor in front of the television, were staring at him.

"Who's he?" Paul's friend asked.

"My daddy."

Eric fell face first to the floor.

"Is he al'ight?"

"Daddy, you al'ight?"

Eric raised his head from the floor and sputtered, "Where's...your...momma?" Then he vomited and dropped his head into the mess.

"He's al'ight," Paul said. "He's al'ight."

Chapter 35

Leonard watched people get on the Greyhound bus. All he had to do was get out of the car and get on that bus. To hell where it was going, just get on it and go, leave all his headaches and worries behind in this chickenshit town.

Dawson, Arkansas, wasn't big enough for Greyhound to station a hub; only a small sign of a greyhound hanging on a stanchion outside of Quik-Print.

The car, Leonard thought. *I can't leave it here and get on the bus. I'll have to return it to the rental company in El Dorado.* The bus departed. He sat in the car for a few more minutes before driving away.

Ida's car was gone when he arrived at the house. He assumed she'd gone to the store. He called Robert Earl's number. No one answered. Then he called Shirley's friend's number and no one answered there. The house was dead silent and there was a smell he couldn't quite place.

During the drive back, he decided the best thing to do was call a family meeting. Bring everyone together and have them lay their grievances on the table. He would set the tone by apologizing to Ruth Ann and Robert Earl, and, he hoped, Shirley and Ruth Ann would do likewise.

No blood spilled, no bones broken, no fratricide; and then everything would return to normal: dismal and depressing, though normal.

Sooner than the dust settled, he would get the hell out of Bucktussle and return to Chicago. Once there he would seek Victor and tell him he still love him, tell him the lure of money had gone to his head, made him talk foolish.

Leonard got up and headed toward the kitchen. He stopped, one foot on the diamond-white linoleum in the kitchen, the other on the red tile in the living room.

A scream rose to his throat…The kitchen was devastated, as if a typhoon had hit it. The refrigerator door was wide open, all its contents--eggs, milk, butter, Arm and Hammer baking soda, soda pops, ice cubes, orange juice, water jugs, pork chops, lettuce, chicken, and half a watermelon--scattered in a heap in front of it.

343

His mother's microwave hung by the cord in front of a cabinet. The dinette table was flipped on its side and two of the four matching chairs were missing. His mother's china set in a million pieces near the back door.

All the cabinet doors were open, the shelves bare. Broken bottles, dented canned goods and crushed boxes littered the floor.

Leonard saw a busted Heinz vinegar bottle and realized it was what he smelled in the living room. On the stove was a burnt piece of paper. Leonard, thinking the worst--*an aborted suicide note*-- stepped closer, noodles crunching under his shoes. Though the paper was burned to ash, he could still make out the heading.

Again he almost screamed.

He ran from room to room calling his mother. "Mother!...Mother!...Mother!" Running to the bathroom he remembered his mother's car wasn't in the driveway.

Mother had seen the will he'd absentmindedly left on the kitchen table and she'd gone berserk. Feeling faint, Leonard sat on the floor inside the bathroom. *Mother poisoned Daddy!*

The realization made his head hurt. "No!" he shouted. "Lord, no!" *Yes, she did. You know she did.*

The gopher poison in the closet, her repeated confessions, the wrecked kitchen, all pointed to one person.

Mother!

"Ruth Ann!" and jumped to his feet. He would have to warn her.

He sped down the highway, dangerously passing other vehicles, so focused on preventing another family tragedy he didn't realize the Lumina clocked eighty-miles-per-hour. His mind raced faster than that.

Ruth Ann could be a bitch at times, a greedy, selfish bitch. Still she didn't deserve to die. His mother--*God, she's an old woman!* Her husband just died. *She killed him!* Could you really blame her? Daddy wasn't exactly a loving husband. His shit-talking, someone was bound to knock him off sooner or later. Mother, she just hurried things along. A mercy killing, all it was. *A mercy killing.* Any judge with common sense would understand that.

She'll probably have to do some jail time.

He envisioned his mother in a cell, hunkered on the floor under a bunk, while a hirsute dyke shouted salacious obscenities at her. He stomped the accelerator to the floor; the speedometer maxed out at a hundred and twenty.

Find Ruth Ann, take her to a motel out of town, and then find his mother, bring her home and put her to bed. *Then what?* Figure it out when you get there, he thought as he slowed down on the curved road leading into the park.

Seconds later he slammed on the brakes, almost slid into a tree, jumped out and ran up the trail, not noticing Robert Earl's rusty Datsun parked nearby.

Nearing the cabin, he shouted, "Ruth Ann?" No answer. He started yelling for Shane when Ruth Ann appeared in the doorway.

345

"Ruth Ann, thank God I found you!" She said nothing, only stared at him, looking frightened. "What's the matter? Have you seen Mother?"

"No, I haven't seen her."

"Good. Get your shoes, I'm taking you away from here. Go on, get your shoes. You're coming with me. I'm taking you someplace no one will find you. Hurry up!"

"You need to do something, Shirley!" said someone inside the cabin. The voice sounded like an adult trying to imitate a child.

Shirley appeared in the doorway, pointed a gun at him and shouted, "Freeze, sugar britches!"

"What are you doing?" Leonard said.

"Get those hands up where I can see them!"

"Shirley, what--" She cocked the trigger. His hands shot up. "Why are you pointing a gun at me?"

Shirley stepped out onto the porch. "Hey, you behind the door, get out here and tie this young man up."

"I don't think so!"

"Who is that?" Leonard asked. "Robert Earl?"

"No, it *isn't*!"

Ruth Ann stepped out and stared at him over Shirley's shoulder. "Why, Leonard? Why did you do it?"

"Why did I do what? Ruth Ann, what the hell is going on?"

Ruth Ann gave him a nasty look. "You killed Daddy."

"What! Shirley, talk to me, please! What the hell is going on here?"

"Where were you planning to take Ruth Ann?" Shirley asked.

"To a psychiatrist. Next to a mall where she can get out of that dirty T-shirt. I'm here to save her life. For my troubles I'm rewarded with you sticking a gun in my face."

"What did you mean telling Ruth Ann someplace no one will find you?"

"Good question," from inside the cabin.

"Shirley," Leonard started softly, then shouted, "will you please stop pointing that goddamn gun at me!"

Shirley lowered the gun. "He didn't do it. He's not the one."

"How do you know?" Ruth Ann asked.

"Excellent question!"

"His eyes," Shirley said.

Ruth Ann stared into his eyes, looking to see what Shirley had seen that she'd missed.

"Has this entire family gone crazy?" Leonard said. "Ruth Ann, would you please stop looking at me like that!" She looked away. "Thank you!"

"What you come up here for?" Shirley said.

"I didn't come here to have a damn gun pointed at me, for damn sure!"

"Sorry 'bout that."

"Shirley, that makes me feel so much better. I came here to get Ruth Ann. I think Mother might be looking to do her harm."

Ruth Ann groaned.

Shirley said, "Why you think Momma would harm Ruth Ann?"

Leonard told them about the gopher poison in the closet, the upheaval in the kitchen and the burnt will on the stove.

"Momma!" Ruth Ann said, shaking her head. "It's hard to believe!"

"It's hard to believe," Shirley said, "because it isn't true. Momma didn't do it. I know my momma, she didn't do it."

"Lord knows I would like to believe Mother wouldn't hurt anyone. I hate to say it, everything points to her."

"I agree with Leonard," Ruth Ann said. "There's no other family member left."

"What about Robert Earl?" Leonard said.

"What about him?" from inside the cabin.

"Who is it in there, Shirley?"

"Your big brother. He's scared."

"No, I'm not!"

Leonard stepped into the cabin. Robert Earl was kneeling behind the door. "What are you doing?"

"What it look like?"

"Looks like you're hiding." Ruth Ann and Shirley stepped inside. "Where's Shane?" he asked Ruth Ann.

"He went to get some food."

"Taco Bell, I hope. So you and Shirley buried the hatchet?"

Ruth Ann glanced nervously at Shirley.

Shirley said, "Ruth Ann and I haven't buried anything. We never will. She's not my sister, never will be, never has been. Right now we're working together."

He looked at Ruth Ann, her eyes closed, holding back tears. "At least y'all not shooting at each other. Shirley, what were you implying when you said freeze, sugar britches?"

"It's a pellet gun," Shirley said.

"Wasn't the question," Robert Earl said.

Shirley sat down on the bed. "Look, Leonard, the will is a fake. I forged it to lure Daddy's killer up here. When we catch the killer you can collect your share of the money and go back to Chicago."

"A pellet gun! What you intend to do with a pellet gun, sting somebody?"

"I asked the same thing," Ruth Ann said.

"It had you convinced, didn't it?" Shirley said.

"Yes, it did," Leonard said. "I don't know anything about guns. Really, Shirley, I think we should get out of here. Someone might get hurt or killed. I understand what you're trying to do, but it's much too dangerous. We'll let the police handle this. They have real guns."

"You got my vote," Robert Earl said.

Leonard started for the door. "Everyone ready?"

"Ruth Ann and I are staying," Shirley said.

Robert Earl stood up. "Good luck," he said to Shirley. "Let's go, little brother."

"Robert Earl, we can't leave two women alone in the woods."

"Why not?"

"What about you, Ruth Ann?" Leonard said. "I know you're not agreeing to this silliness." Ruth Ann cast an uneasy look at Shirley. "What will it be, Ruth Ann? Stay here and get hurt? Or walk down the hill with me like a woman with good sense?"

"She's staying," Shirley said.

"Are you, Ruth Ann?"

A long moment they all waited for Ruth Ann to respond. Robert Earl broke the silence: "I'm ready when you are, little brother."

"Shirley," Ruth Ann said, "I'd like to go with them. Maybe I'll come back after a change of clothes. I want to go with them. Please, Shirley!"

Shirley sat there silently, staring at the floor. Then she snapped: "Go! Dammit, go! I'll handle this my-damn-self!"

"You're going, too, Shirley," Leonard said.

Shirley rolled her head on her neck. "You and what Seal Team making me go, Leonard?"

"Robert Earl," Leonard said, "you take her on the left, I'll take her on the right. On the count of three...one...two--"

"I'll beat the shit outta both of you if y'all come near me!"

Robert Earl said, "I don't have a major problem with her staying."

"Chicken!" Leonard said. "Ruth Ann, help me out here!"

"Bawk-bawk-bawk-bawk!"

"Shirley, please!" Leonard said. "It's going dark out there. Listen to reason. We can't leave you here. We love you. How could we live with ourselves knowing we left you here to fend for yourself and something bad happened to you? Stop acting childish and let's go!"

"I said I was staying. Don't ask me again! If you're going, go! Leave me the hell alone!"

Leonard started toward her and said, "One of us is taking an ass-whooping. You or--" Before he could finish, Shirley sprung off the bed with a quickness. She rammed him and backed him against the wall, her forearm pressing his chest so hard he feared a rib might crack.

"Understand...one...damn thing..." Shirley said. With each pause she gave his chest a push. "Don't...ever...threaten me..." He could smell Vienna Sausage on her breath. "...again...because...I will..." He couldn't breathe and wondered how long before he passed out. "...take you up on it! Do...you...hear...me?" He tried to nod yes, but could only blink. "Do...you...hear--"

A gunshot rang out from outside, close.

"What was that?" Ruth Ann asked.

"Gunfire," Shirley said, and released Leonard. He slid to the floor holding his chest.

"A pellet gun?" Ruth Ann said.

"I don't think so," Robert Earl said. "It sounded like a thirty-eight."

"Robert Earl," Leonard wheezed, clutching his chest as if he'd been shot, "would you grant me one small favor?" Robert Earl didn't answer. "The next time I threaten Shirley, no matter how slight, would you..." He paused and coughed into his hand. "Would you be so kind as to kill me? Would you do that for me, Robert Earl?"

Robert Earl didn't respond.

The next thirty minutes or so they waited in silence. The room slowly faded into darkness.

Robert Earl said, "I can't deal with this. It's possible it was a hunter, or someone shooting a can. I'm getting out of here. I can't take it! Anybody wanna go with me?"

"Hello," Ruth Ann said. "I'm with you. You go first and don't run off and leave me."

"What? It was my idea. I'm not going first!"

"Okay, Robert Earl. Whatever. Don't run off and leave me."

"You better keep up, I'll be moving pretty fast."

"Robert Earl, if you're leading the way, shouldn't you go out the door first? It's dark out there--you go first and I'll hold onto your belt."

"I'm not wearing a belt. I have on overalls."

"Well, I'll hold onto it."

There was a silence.

Robert Earl said, "You're complicating this thing, Ruth Ann. You go out the door first--I'll be right behind you. *Then* you can hold onto my overalls and follow me. It's that simple."

"It makes more sense, Robert Earl, if we started out the door in the same position we're going down the hill. It doesn't make any sense at all for us to get out there in the dark and start fumbling around for each other, now does it?"

Silence again.

"I got a better idea," Robert Earl said. "We'll back out, you going first. Once we get outside we take off."

"Robert Earl, that's crazy. We might trip."

"I won't trip."

"What if *I* trip?"

"You get left."

"No, Robert Earl. I got a better idea. We'll--"

"Get out!" Shirley shouted. "Get the hell out! Two overgrown chickens! Y'all be here in the morning debating who should go first! Both of you go at the same damn time!"

Leonard heard the door open. The same picture inside showed outside. A pure black screen.

"Where are you, Ruth Ann?" Robert Earl said. "You ready?"

"I'm right here behind you and I'm ready."

"Naw! You trying to be slick. Shirley said at the same time."

"Okayokay. Let my hand go! You don't have to hold my hand."

"I can hold your hand if you holding my overalls."

"Why?"

"Because!"

Shirley said, "Y'all damn lucky I don't have a real gun."

Just then a voice outside called, "Ruth Ann?"

"I changed my mind," Robert Earl said, and closed the door.

Chapter 36

"GERD, what we call it," Doctor Cobb said over the phone. "Otherwise known as gastroesophageal reflux disease. Basically, it's the recurrent regurgitation of food and acid from the stomach into the esophagus."

"Yeah," Sheriff Bledsoe said. "It hurts like the dickens, too. Doc, I need something for this. I'm dying over here. Pain in my stomach, back, chest, neck, throat."

"Mr. Bledsoe, if you're in pain I strongly suggest you go to the hospital. Laymen often mistake angina for GERD."

"Doc, I just got back from the hospital. They determined I wasn't having a heart attack and sent me on my way, still hurting.

No prescription, no have-a-good-day. Nothing! Look, Doc, all I need is the purple pill, the one on the commercial."

"Nexium esomeprazole, one of several proton inhibitors."

"Yeah, exactly, on the tip of my tongue. If you could write me a prescription, I think it'll do the trick."

"Over-the-counter products, Mr. Bledsoe, are also effective reducing acid production in the stomach. Tagamet HB, Zantac 75, Pepsid AC. If one of those doesn't work come see me Monday morning. Good-bye, Mr. Bledsoe."

"Wait, wait, wait! Doc, I tried all those. In fact I mixed up a batch of stuff this morning--didn't work. I know it's Sunday and I shouldn't have called your house. I'm in pain here!"

"All right, Mr. Bledsoe, I'll give you a prescription. I shouldn't do this without first examining you. If it doesn't alleviate your discomfort come see me in the morning."

"Doc, I can't thank you enough. How do I get to your house? I'm on my way."

"Hold your horses, Mr. Bledsoe. I'll call Tim Hudson at the Wal-Mart pharmacy. He'll fix you up. You may need to hurry, he closes at seven."

Sheriff Bledsoe thanked him ten times, hung up the phone and looked at his watch. A quarter till seven. He didn't need to hurry; Wal-Mart was a five-minute drive away. He got into the cruiser and just as he was reaching to turn off the dual band radio, it called his name.

"Ennis? You there, Ennis? Pick up."

He stared at the radio as if it were a bomb. He wasn't aware his eyes filled with tears.

"Ennis? Pick up if you're there."

He grabbed the mike, put it to his mouth, put it down and picked it up again. "Ennis, here," he said, voice cracking.

The city of Dawson couldn't afford its own dispatcher, so Tracy Walls, the dispatcher in Ashley County, provided the service for a nominal fee. She rarely radioed Sheriff Bledsoe except in emergencies.

From his stomach came a loud rumbling noise, similar to stampeding cattle. Excruciating pain would soon follow. He leaned to his right and massaged his chest, a futile attempt to head off the oncoming agony.

"Ennis, a man just called, said there's a family disturbance next door. Shots fired. A shotgun, he said. Ten-Fifteen Dixie Drive. You want me to call the state police for backup?"

After the pain subsided a bit, he sat up and stared out the window, up at the sky, wondering if he had somehow been cursed. Maybe his misery was for the time he posted his ex-wife's boyfriend's car as a stolen vehicle.

"No," he said into the mike. "Ten-four, I'm on it. I'll let you know if I need backup."

On average there were two or three shootings a year in Dawson. Just his luck, a few minutes from the purple pill, which he was certain would end his misery, a dang shooting occurred. It was enough to make a man swear.

Ten minutes later he knocked on a door and a man appeared in a side window and said, "Next door."

He crossed the yard to where Walter and Colleen Riley were standing on the porch. "How you doing, Walter?" Neighbors were looking on.

"Not good," Walter said.

"What's going on? I heard someone out here shooting."

"I was."

"What for?" looking for a weapon.

"A pervert broke into our home," Colleen said. She wore a blue uniform, a Hillard Catfish Farm patch on the right arm. "We almost got him."

"How you know he was a pervert?"

She and Walter exchanged looks. "We know," she said.

"Why don't we go into the house and discuss this," and saw the shotgun propped behind a plastic lawn chair on the porch. "Bring it in with you, Walter."

"We can't get in, Sheriff," Colleen said.

"Why not? He's not inside, is he?"

"No," Walter said. "Our daughter pushed something against the door and locked us out."

"Why she do that?"

"I don't know. She needs her ass whooped, for one thing."

Sheriff Bledsoe knocked on the door. "How old is she?"

"Twenty-one."

"What's her name?"

"Linda."

"Linda, this is Sheriff Bledsoe. Open the door, sweetheart." He waited. "Linda, if you don't open the door, I'll have to break it down. You don't want me to break your parent's door, do you?"

He heard something scrape across the floor and then the door opened. One look at her and another herd stampeded inside his stomach.

"I'ma beat your ass!" Walter said to Linda. "When I start working on your ass I'm beating you for old and new. Mostly new!"

"Hold the threats, Walter," Sheriff Bledsoe said. "C'mon, let's go inside and figure out what's going on here."

"Ain't no threat," Walter said, staring at his daughter.

Inside, after Walter put the shotgun behind the door, Sheriff Bledsoe requested everyone take a seat. Colleen and Walter sat on the couch while Linda remained standing.

Sheriff Bledsoe said, "Did someone break into your house?"

"Yes," Colleen and Walter said.

"No, he didn't!" Linda said. "I let him in. He didn't break in. I let him in. We didn't do nothing."

"Dammit!" Walter shouted. "Go to your room!"

"Wait a minute, Walter," Sheriff Bledsoe said. "Let her talk." To Linda: "Who did you let in?"

She looked at her father and stuck her thumb into her mouth. "Erbic."

"Who?"

She took her thumb out. "Eric."

"What's his last name?"

"I don't know his last name."

"Tall, lanky, bushy eyebrows?"

Linda returned her thumb to her mouth, rubbed her nose with the index finger and nodded.

"Eric Barnes?" Sheriff Bledsoe said.

Walter said, "He'll have to change his name to dead meat when I get through with him."

"Why did you let him in?" Sheriff Bledsoe asked.

She shrugged.

"What did he do when he was here?"

Linda, one eye staring at her father and the other at Sheriff Bledsoe, garbled, "We dint doo nuffin!"

"She's not helping you, Sheriff Bledsoe," Colleen said. "Can she be excused?"

"I guess so," avoiding looking at her. *What the hell was Eric thinking?* "I may need to talk to her again."

"What you waiting on?" Walter shouted at his daughter. Linda ran out of the room and seconds later Sheriff Bledsoe heard a door slam. He thought to tell Walter to lighten up on the girl, but didn't think it would help matters.

Walter said, "I've been trying to get his name for a while. I'm glad you told me."

"Walter, you may already be looking at a weapon discharge violation, so hold the vigilante talk. This is what I'm paid to do, so let me handle it, okay?"

"Hell, Sheriff," Walter said. "You saw her. You can tell she's Super Glued on silly. Can't even talk without sucking on her damn thumb. It ain't right! A rusty butt man! In my house! You know it ain't right, Sheriff. What if she were your daughter?"

"She said nothing happened."

"Maybe nothing happened today," Colleen said. "We know for a fact he's been fooling around with her."

Walter said, "Hell yes, Sheriff. It ain't right! Ain't none of it right! Here I am sleeping on the couch and I hear Colleen screaming, and this fool ran out and started attacking her. Scared me so bad I didn't know what to do first, beat him with my bare hands or shoot him?"

Colleen said, "He didn't attack me. I grabbed him."

Walter pointed to the shotgun behind the door. "I had him--sight alignment, sight picture, right between the eyes. Damned Linda jumped on my back." Shaking his head: "I had him!"

"Walter, you're lucky," Sheriff Bledsoe said. "If you'd shot him, you'd be on your way to jail now."

"Linda's the one who's lucky," Walter said. "She's damn lucky that woman didn't hurt her."

"What woman?"

"His wife, or girlfriend," Colleen said. "She's a big woman. Last year she caught Linda and that man inside her house and she walked Linda home. Told me to keep an eye on my daughter 'cause the next time, she said, Linda wouldn't be able to crawl back. She told me this to my face, about my own daughter. Anyone else I would've raised hell, but she had this look in her eye--it scared me. She was serious than diabetes."

"Shirley Harris," Sheriff Bledsoe said, rubbing his chest. "I'm surprised you don't know her."

"No, I don't know her. Is she any kin to Larry Harris?"

"Yes, he's her father."

"Oh," Colleen said. "Explains why she's keeping house with a pervert."

"What do you mean?"

"Larry worked at Hillard Catfish Farm. We used to call him Loony Larry. He was mad all the time, always telling the supervisor what he would or wouldn't do. I'm surprised he kept his job as long as he did. Somebody told me he ate spoiled pig feet, got sick and died."

"You think someone at his job was angry enough to do something to him?"

"Sheriff," Walter said, "what's this got to do with the situation here? We want to know what you're doing about Eric Barnes."

Colleen said, "Everybody who worked there, including myself, wanted to do something to him one time or another. He had a bad habit of name-calling. You ask him to stop, he'd keep at it, say it more often. He really got to tripping right before he retired. For years he'd been telling everybody how much money he'd invested in the company's stock plan. A million plus, the way he told it. Come to find out he never signed up for the stock plan. He thought it was automatic. All those years and he--"

"What!" Sheriff Bledsoe shouted. "You mean he never had a million dollars? Are you sure?"

"Yes, I'm sure. Everybody--everybody at Hillard knows about it. Ask anyone there, they'll tell you."

Sheriff Bledsoe stared at her.

"Sad news," Walter said. "Sheriff, are you gonna arrest this scumbag? If you don't do something to him, I will." Sheriff Bledsoe kept staring at Colleen, his mind obviously elsewhere.

"Sheriff? Sheriff?"

Sheriff Bledsoe rubbed his chest and squeezed his stomach. "What?"

"Are you listening to me?" Walter said.

"I hear you. I hear you loud and clear," and got up and walked out the door without saying another word.

Chapter 37

"Reap what you sow. Reap what you sow."

Eric talked to himself as he walked to Count Pulaski State Park. "Reap what you sow." His mother had told him that a thousand times. *Man, was she right!* He'd sowed bullshit and he'd definitely reaped bullshit. *Big time!*

Now a worldly lifestyle was behind him, in his past. He'd seen the light. He'd had an out-of-body experience. No, he'd experienced something grander than a floating sensation. He'd experienced a...*What did the white folks call it?*

He walked farther and then it struck him: an epiphany! *Yes! An epiphany!* He'd stared into the grim reaper's eyes, two black holes, and--Kabooom!--*an epiphany!*

Now he had to find Shirley, beg her forgiveness and, if she was willing, marry her. The right thing to do, the epiphany had told him, shortly after the shotgun blast had stopped ringing in his ears. "Marry Shirley!" Loud and clear.

Of course, he realized, Shirley might still be pissed. No matter. Once he told her about his epiphany--though not the part what led up to it--she would just have to forgive him.

He loved her. She was the only woman he needed, the only person who had stuck by him in good times and bad. Why hadn't he realized this a long time ago? Amazing how an epiphany can clear the fog shrouding true love.

The sun was a reddish-orange sliver above the horizon when he came up to Robert Earl's Datsun and a gray Lumina. Three trails, less than a half block apart, led into the woods.

Which one?

Pick the wrong one and he might be lost in the woods a long time. Was he pushing his luck? Eventually Shirley would come home. Wouldn't it be more romantic if he begged her forgiveness and hand in marriage in a public place? *Yes. A lot safer, too.*

Darlene had said Shirley planned to camp in the woods a couple of days, which didn't make sense because Shirley wasn't the outdoor type.

He had to make a choice. Go up or go home? "I'm a man," he said to bolster his confidence. "A man who just experienced an epiphany." Then he started up Hot Springs Trail.

The canopy of branches above the trail extinguished the light. Total darkness. A tad cooler. He tried to remember what he'd learned in his brief stint in the Cub Scouts some twenty-three-years ago. *Be ready, was it? Don't go if you don't have to, more than likely.*

Mosquitoes attacked his hands, neck and face. One contented itself with simply buzzing around his ear.

He kept walking, hands held out in front to avoid walking into a tree. Suddenly he stopped, certain he'd heard something...something moving, something heavy.

Two nights ago Shirley told him about a raccoon she'd seen in the backyard rummaging through trash. A raccoon, she'd explained, didn't come out in daylight and bare its teeth unless it was rabid. A raccoon can easily rip open an aluminum can with its claws. In an attack, a raccoon goes straight for the eyes.

Why the hell did she tell me all that?

She could have simply said, "I think the raccoon in the backyard has rabies," and left it there. No, she had to provide an encyclopedia of information on raccoon behavior.

He slapped at the mosquito buzzing around his ear. His right leg started shaking. A long time he stood there thinking about that damned rabid raccoon.

I'm spooking my own ass, and took a step forward. The noise sounded again. He stopped...*What the hell is it?*

Squinting, he looked right to left and saw nothing but darkness. A mosquito bit him on the exposed flesh where his silk shirt had been torn.

Another noise, like claws sharpened against a rock, sounded directly behind him. He whirled around and the noise stopped.

Something's out here with me.

He could feel it watching him, waiting for him to move again so it could match his footsteps…and then it would jump on his back and sink its rabid fangs into his neck and scratch his eyes out with its aluminum-can-ripping claws.

Scricccccccccck!

"Damn this!" and took flight. Just as he was approaching cruising speed, his left foot touched down on a loose rock and he went sliding down the trail, face first.

"Eric," a woman said, "don't run. It's me."

He lay perfectly still on the ground. *Me who?*

"Eric?" The voice came closer: "Eric, I can't see you. Where are you?"

He placed the voice. "Here…here I am!"

A dark figure approached and knelt beside him. "Eric, are you all right?"

"I'm all right." He rubbed his knee. "I slipped. Mrs. Harris, what you doing out here?" She smelled of vinegar.

She took a while to respond. "The same thing you're doing."

"Body-surfing down rocks?"

She laughed, a pretentious chuckle. "Take my hand, I'll help you up."

He couldn't see it. "Here," she said. "Right in front of you."

He yelped, snatching his hand back. "Shit!" Something she was holding, something sharp. Flexing his hand he felt a thick liquid...*Liquid?*..."You cut my damn hand!"

"I'm sorry."

"Sorry, my ass! I'm bleeding like a stuck pig! What you got in your hand?"

"A knife."

"A knife? What you need with a...?"

He experienced the same bone-chilling fear as when the rabid raccoon started tracking him.

"Give me your belt," she said, casual tone, as if she were asking him to pass the salt and pepper.

He started to say, "I don't need a tourniquet," but was struck with another epiphany, this one telling him to run and to run fast. Squeezing his wrist, stanching the blood flow, he tried to get up.

"Don't!" she said. "You move I'll cut your throat."

A bullfrog croaked. Farther away an owl hooted. Death calls, Eric thought. He could take her. He would have to take her. She'd flipped her lid, blew it a mile high. One kick, he thought, one kick to her head.

"Give me your belt," she repeated.

"I don't have a belt. Don't worry, I'll wrap the sleeve of my shirt around it…if you let me get up."

"Then give me your socks."

Her head was right there; he couldn't quite see it, but from where her voice came it was definitely within kicking range.

One good kick…"My socks are dirty. I'll use my sleeve. It's already torn. Let me up and I'll do it myself."

"You got the wrong idea. Give me your socks. I'm not asking you, I'm telling you."

"You want the socks, you can have the damn socks." He bent forward and fumbled with the string on his tennis shoe.

"Hurry up, please."

"Damn! I'm working with one hand here. Maybe if I could get a little help." The smell of vinegar grew stronger, and he kicked out as hard as he could. By the feel of it, he'd planted one to her stomach. He sprang to his feet and hurried to the figure on the ground gasping for air.

"Who got the wrong idea now?" Two more kicks. "Here are my socks! Shoes, too!" Another kick, this one with the ball of his foot, and she yelled in pain. "Cut me, will ya!" She started crawling away. "You running now, ain't ya?"

He let her get away a bit before starting after her. No need to hurry, he now had the upper hand.

Later he would kick himself for not running away. He most certainly could have.

She was hurt, sucking air, retreating. One more kick; he just had to deliver one more kick to let her know he wasn't someone to be played with.

His right leg reared back, posed to punt her ass at least ten yards, he heard an explosion and saw a bluish-white flame shoot straight up. He didn't need an epiphany to tell him what it was.

Heifer has a gun!

She got to her feet, wheezing and coughing.

"You still want my socks? You can have em!"

"Get…heh heh heh…on…heh heh heh…the…heh heh heh…ground!"

Eric sat down where he stood. "Is this regarding the ten I owe you? I swear I'll pay you when I get it. I don't have it now. I didn't forget I owe you." She didn't respond. "Why you doing this to me? We're almost family, you know, sort of. I've always considered you as family. Really!"

"The socks, please!"

Eric took off his shoes and socks and threw the socks at her.

"The pants and underwear, please!"

"What? What for? Why? Hell no! I'm not out here naked. You crazy!"

"Give them to me or die with them on!" Her tone finally shifted, enraged and impatient.

He wriggled out of his Levis and Fruit of the Loom and tossed them to her. Should he scream? *Beg? Cry? Shit? And what the hell she wants with my underwear?*

"Lie on your stomach," she ordered, "and spread your arms out!"

What? He could already feel pinecones prickling his buttocks. "You cut me! I'm bleeding! Why you doing this to me? Why? I never did anything to you!"

"Shut up! Do what I tell you and you might live."

Might, he thought, as he lay face down on the ground and spread his arms. *Might?*

She stepped near. "Don't be a fool!" A shoe poked his kidney. "One hand at a time, put your hands behind your back." He felt something hard and cold at his neck. "Do you understand?"

Covering his head with both hands: "Uh-huh."

"Not your head! On your back!" He moved his hands to his back and felt a knee weighting his fingers. "Don't you dare move!"

With his socks or underwear, he couldn't tell which, she wrapped his wrists together. Just then, to make matters worse, he felt something crawling in his pubic. She tied his feet together with his pants, he figured, by the thickness of the material.

Semi-naked, hand lacerated, hog-tied with his own clothes, his favorite silk shirt almost torn to shreds, a nutty witch with a gun and her knee on his fingers and a poisonous bug hatching poisonous baby bugs in his privacy, Eric started crying, hysterically.

371

"Sss…ssumthin…ssummthing…crawling…in…my…prrrr…pri vacy!"

She grabbed his hair and jerked his head back. "Serves you right!" Gave his head another jerk and hissed, "You filthy whore!"

Her hand, guided by sharp fingernails, dug underneath his waist, working toward his pubic.

"There it is," she said, and instead of pulling whatever it was off, she pressed it against his skin with a fingernail.

Eric gritted his teeth to stifle a scream.

"It's dead," and grabbed his penis and squeezed extremely hard. "You're not the big man you think you are, are you?"

She released him and stood up. "Get on your feet!"

Eric closed his eyes and tried to remember a prayer. Would he be blessed with two epiphanies in one day? *One more, Lord, please!*

"You heard me, on your feet!" She grabbed his arm and helped him up. "Move!"

It took all of twenty minutes for him to shuffle the short distance to the top of the hill. Ahead, not twenty feet away, he saw the moonlit outline of two cabins, the one on the left caved in, something on it, a tree maybe.

She pushed him down to his knees. "Call her."

No, he wouldn't do it! She would have to kill him. He'd hurt Shirley enough, more than enough, and he wouldn't call her out for this psychotic witch to hurt her. No way! Uh-uh! He had some dignity.

Eric shook his head. "No, I'm not doing it! You might as well kill me 'cause I ain't doing it. She's the mother of my child."

"Is that a fact?" He heard the gun cock and felt it against his temple. "Listen to me, whore, and listen good. You call Ruth Ann out here"--jabbed him twice with the gun--"or you die!"

Ruth Ann?

He didn't owe Ruth Ann a damn thing. "Ruth Ann!" he shouted. "Ruth Ann! Ruth Ann, could you come out here for a minute!"

Chapter 38

The front door was open. *Strange.* "Sheriff Bledsoe," he announced. "Anybody home?"

Hand on his weapon he stepped in. Something's wrong here, he could feel it. People in Dawson often left their doors unlocked, but they didn't leave them wide open.

"Hello! Sheriff Bledsoe coming in!"

The living room looked in order. Into the hallway: "Sheriff Bledsoe! Anybody home?" Looked into all four bedrooms and the bathroom. No one home and nothing out of place.

Heading for the front door he caught a whiff of vinegar. Had someone left a pot boiling? *Pig feet?* He walked into the kitchen and his stomach lurched.

The kitchen looked as if a tornado had hit it. Everything in the cabinets and the fridge was on the floor. The kitchen table flipped over. This wasn't an act of God; this was an act of man, an enraged man...*or woman.*

He slapped his forehead with the palm of his hand. *Ida!* She lied to her children about her husband having a will. One of them must have confronted her with the truth and she went cuckoo, stark-raving mad. *Fiddle faddle!*

He slapped his forehead again. He had her, had her in the palm of his hand. She'd confessed and pleaded to be locked up. And what did he do? *Nothing!* Nothing except run her out of his office.

Already he could hear the mayor's reprimand: "So, Ennis, Mrs. Harris was at the jail voluntarily, her own volition, no coercion or assistance from anyone, pleading, begging to be locked up, because as she claimed vociferously, repeatedly, emphatically, she'd killed her husband. Tell me again, Sheriff Ennis Bledsoe, you did what?"

From his stomach came a strident percolation...and then it erupted, spewing hot acid into his chest, throat, mouth, sinuses...Bent over, hands on his knees, he swayed side to side. After a long moment, the pain ebbing very little, he stood upright.

Whew! The worst one yet. Do that in public and I'll lose half the independent voters.

Pain or no, he had to find Ida, before she hurt someone else, if she hadn't already. One hand on his back, he walked out to the

375

cruiser. Picked up the mike, put it down. No, he wouldn't issue a BOLO for Ida. He had to find her himself.

Lester was home, but he hadn't seen Ida or Ruth Ann. No one answered the door at Robert Earl's house. The young woman at Shirley's home said Shirley was gone, claimed she didn't know when Shirley would be coming back and couldn't recall the last time she'd seen her. Obviously lying. Why? He didn't have a clue.

Wal-Mart, Fred's, Piggly Wiggly, the library, he went inside each and traversed every aisle. No sign of Ida or any of her children.

Waiting for the lone light on Main Street to turn green, he wondered where next to check. A drunk staggered down the steps of the old post office building and stepped into the middle of the street.

The light turned green and the drunk fell in front of the cruiser. *I don't need this now!* Two hands appeared above the hood…then an unkempt gray afro…bloodshot eyes…a small nose under a thin, wet moustache…and a big toothy grin.

Sheriff Bledsoe was shocked. Reverend Stanley Walker slapped the hood with both hands and slurred, "Watch where the hell you're going, Sheriff!"

* * * * *

"Who is it?" Ruth Ann asked.

"I don't know," Leonard said.

"Ruth Ann! Ruth Ann," the voice called, "could you come out here for a minute?"

"Eric!" Ruth Ann and Shirley said in unison.

Robert Earl said, "Ruth Ann, you oughta go out there and see what he want."

"No!" Leonard said. "He might have a gun."

"He's not the one," Shirley said. "Robert Earl, holler back and tell him Ruth Ann is not here."

"Are you crazy! And let him know I'm in here. You holler and tell him. He's your man."

"He didn't call me," Shirley said. "He called Ruth Ann."

Ruth Ann was thankful for the darkness: she could imagine the look Shirley was shooting her way.

"Ruth Ann!" Eric shouted. "I know you're in there! Come out and talk to me!"

"What do you want?" Ruth Ann shouted back, praying he wouldn't say something stupid.

"I-I-I...broke my...head. I broke my leg."

"Somebody's threatening him," Shirley said. "That's not Eric talking."

"Shirley," Leonard said, "how do you know--"

A brick fell to the floor.

"Oh no!" Ruth Ann cried. "He's coming through the fireplace!"

"Robert Earl?" Shirley said. "Robert Earl?"

"What?" Robert Earl said, his voice sounded as if he were outside.

"Where are you?"

"Shirley, if you don't mind, would you stop calling my name!"

"He's in the chimney."

"The chimney?" Leonard said. "How did he get in--Robert Earl, what are you doing in the chimney?"

"Take a guess. And stop calling my name!"

"He's hiding again," Shirley said.

"Figures," Leonard said. "I hope no one pours liquid fire down the chimney."

"Wh-why would anyone do that, Leonard?" Robert Earl asked. "Why? Answer me--why?"

"Robert Earl," Shirley said, "get your scary ass out of there before you get stuck!"

"Ruth Ann!" Eric shouted. "Help me, Ruth Ann!"

Shirley moaned. "Lord, what if he's really hurt. I've gotta go out there!"

"Wait a minute, Shirley," Leonard said. "Please! I said please. Ruth Ann, tell him you have a gun."

"I have a gun!" Ruth Ann shouted. "I know how to use it, too!"

Three gunshots answered back and they all hit the floor. "Bad idea," Ruth Ann said.

"I didn't tell you to say all that!"

"Everybody all right?" Shirley asked.

378

"I'm fine," Leonard said.

"Me, too," Ruth Ann said.

"Robert Earl?" Shirley said. No answer. Louder: "Robert Earl!"

"What is it now?"

"Are you all right?"

"Yes, yes, yes! I'm all right. Will y'all please stop calling my name! I'll let you know when I'm not all right."

"What are we going to do?" Leonard asked.

Shirley said, "Only one door in and one door out. We could rush them. They can't see any better than we can."

"Them? They?" Leonard said. "The only person I've heard out there is Eric. Shirley, don't get upset. Eric intends to kill Ruth Ann, and he might kill us too if we get in his way."

"You're wrong, Leonard. Eric doesn't own a gun. Someone has him at gunpoint. He's almost as scary as Robert Earl. You couldn't pay him to come into the woods at night."

"Maybe, maybe not," Leonard said. "We should put something against the door. The couch will do. Robert Earl, get out of there and help me push the couch against the door."

"Get Shirley or Ruth Ann to help you. Hey, wouldn't it be awfully hard to haul liquid fire up a roof and pour it down a chimney?"

"With a cauldron it would be relatively easy."

"A cauldron? What's a cauldron?"

"It's made to haul liquid fire."

379

"Really? I've never seen one at Wal-Mart."

"You can't buy it at Wal-Mart. Ace Hardware the only place has it."

"You're not juking me, are you, Leonard?"

"You'll know when your scalp melts off your head."

"It'll be too late then. Wouldn't you smell it, the liquid fire? You'd smell it at a distance, wouldn't you?"

"ISN is odorless."

"ISN?"

"Industrial strength napalm. And it sticks to your skin."

"Where you get that at?"

Leonard hesitated. "AutoZone."

Shirley said, "Leonard, stop teasing the idiot and push the couch against the door."

Just then they heard footsteps on the porch…a soft tap on the door.

"Oh shit!" Ruth Ann whispered.

The door creaked opened.

Chapter 39

"I'm not drunk!" Reverend Walker said, pushing Sheriff Bledsoe's hand away. He was wearing a ruffled double-breasted charcoal-colored suit, matching pants and a pair of black Stacy Adams. A red tie, absent shirt, was knotted tightly against his wrinkled neck. He reeked of cheap wine and week-old BO.

"Reverend, please, get in the car. Look, everybody's staring at you. Don't make me use the cuffs, Reverend."

Misery lights illuminating his face, Reverend Walker stared at the small crowd staring at him. Humiliation worked on his face, rheumy brown eyes going to the ground and back up to the crowd.

Mustering dignity, he stood erect, pulled on the hem of his coat and said, "All right, Sheriff." Unassisted, he staggered to the back of the cruiser and got in. The crowd cheered.

Sheriff Bledsoe got behind the wheel wondering what the crowd was expecting. *A beat-down?* "You still live on Highway Eighty-Two, don't you?"

"Take me to jail!"

"To jail?" and looked in the rearview mirror at the bottom of a pint of Wild Irish Rose. "Hey, you can't drink liquor in here!" He switched off the misery lights and drove away, hoping no one saw the reverend upturn the bottle.

"I can't? I didn't see a sign."

He drove past the jail. "Reverend Walker, I'm taking you home. I *should* take you to jail, bringing a wine bottle with you. You know better." He made a right on Highway 82. "Reverend, my mother goes to your church. What she's gonna think when she hears about this? What's your congregation gonna think?"

Reverend Walker laughed. "You don't go to church, do you? Maybe your mother hasn't heard the news. Reverend Walker tried to bury a dog."

Fifteen or twenty minutes to Reverend Walker's house, Sheriff Bledsoe thought. Another ten minutes to get the reverend inside and give his condolences to Mrs. Walker. Plus fifteen or twenty minutes back to Dawson. Almost an hour lost, shot to crap, time when he should've been looking for Ida.

"Reverend Jones and three of the deacons," Reverend Walker continued, "suggested I take a few Sundays off. As if I work for them. Ha! I was preaching when Reverend Jones was loading his

Huggies. Built that church with my own hands. My own hands, hear me!"

To emphasize the point, he clawed the metal divider and shook it. Sheriff Bledsoe looked into the rearview mirror and gave him a frown.

"My church, dammit! Mine! They can't take it away from me!" After a fit of hiccups: "Can they, Sheriff? Can they kick me out my own church?"

Sheriff Bledsoe, wondering if he should visit Ida's house again after dropping off the reverend, shook his head. "I don't think so." He looked into the rearview mirror and again saw the bottom of the bottle. "You'll be home soon, why don't you wait to finish that?"

"Take me to jail, Sheriff. My wife's mad at me. 'Better to live in the wilderness, than with a contentious and angry woman.' Proverbs, chapter twenty-one...I forgot which verse." He made a gargling noise, which Sheriff Bledsoe feared was the precursor to an expensive interior detail.

"The elder Sisters called her the other day and said they were going to join another church if I preached again. Guess what she told them? 'I don't blame you. I wasn't married to him I would, too.' I just had to get a drink. Haven't had a drink in forty-five years. Glad I did, too. Wonder where I parked my car?"

Sunlight flickered through the trees as Sheriff Bledsoe sped down the highway at seventy-miles-per. A large purple splatter suddenly appeared on the windshield. He turned the wipers on and pushed the fluid button. Purple goo smeared across the windshield. It would be dark soon. Reverend Walker's house was less than five minutes away.

"Lord almighty, how was I to know!" Reverend Walker said. "The average person digs a hole in the backyard, drops the mutt into it, says a few words and fills the hole. I'd known she was serious, I'd never gone along with it. God knows I wouldn't have.

"They dressed it up, rolled it in and by God I intended to bury it. I don't go back on my word, Sheriff. Nobody'll tell you Reverend Stanley Lucious Walker ain't a man of his word. It would've worked if not for the boy...Somebody should lay hands on that boy...just beat the living shit out of him!

"He ran, Sheriff. Ran! Up one side of the church and down the other, with a big, goofy nut chasing him. I was shocked more than anyone. Hell, I was mortified. A dead dog in a three-piece suit flying in the air, landing in my lap. A beast grabbed the microphone and put me in a headlock. You ask me, I'm the one who deserves an apology."

Sheriff Bledsoe pulled into the driveway of a three-story antebellum. The front yard adorned with ceramics: two lions guarded the front walk; a donkey pulled a red wagon carrying a small man wearing an oversized sombrero; a large elephant sprouted water from its trunk into a small pond. Near the porch a white jockey offered a ring.

"Here ya go, Reverend, home sweet home."

"No, Sheriff, take me to jail. I've been gone three days--she'll kill me if she sees me like this. One night is all I'm asking."

"I'm sorry, Reverend." He got out and opened the rear door. Reverend Walker crossed his arms and stared at his lap. "Come on, Reverend. A good night sleep and tomorrow everything won't look so bad."

"It'll be worse tomorrow. Monday. My wife doesn't work Mondays. I don't know the whereabouts of my car and I'll be stuck here with her. You know what I'll be thinking when she rants and raves how big a fool I am?"

Sheriff Bledsoe gently took hold of his shoulder. "Come on, Reverend. Tell me as we go inside."

"Three words, Sheriff. Kenny Damned G!"

"Who? The dog?"

"A dead dog," shaking his head. "I lost everything because of a damn stanky dead dog."

Sheriff Bledsoe released his shoulder. "All this time you've been rambling about Larry Harris' dog?"

Reverend Walker gave him a look asking, "Where the hell have you been?"

Sheriff Bledsoe looked at the house. A gold ornamental light fixture glowed above the door and only one of the second-story rooms cast a light. No one had stuck their head out to see what was going on.

"Reverend, you sure you wanna sleep at the jail tonight?"

"I sure do."

Getting behind the wheel: "Well, tonight you're my guest. You can sleep in as long as you like. I won't bother you. I probably won't even be there. Only one thing I'm requesting. I need you to tell me again about the beast and the flying dog. This time I need all the details."

"I'd be glad to oblige. My mind, however, is a little fuzzy now. You think we could stop and pick up another bottle? I'll buy. A little something to knock the cobwebs off my memory."

Sheriff Bledsoe backed out of the driveway. "I had a feeling you would say that."

* * * * *

"Say it like you mean it!" she told Eric. "You're playing games. I don't have time for games," jerking his head back, popping something in his neck. "Say it like you mean it!"

"Ruth Ann," he shouted with all the passion he could muster. "Help me!"

"I have a gun," Ruth Ann shouted back. "I know how to use it, too!"

She stepped in front of Eric and fired three shots over the cabin. On the third shot, Eric stood up and started hopping as fast as he could...fell down, somehow got up, and continued hopping.

The bondage around his legs loosened a bit and he ran...hopped...ran...hopped...ran...

"Get back here!" she said, and he worried a bullet in the back. He kept going...tried to run only, tripped and stumbled head over end down an incline. At the bottom he couldn't get back to his feet.

How did I do it the first time?

Footsteps...leaves crunching. He froze. Crunch crunch crunch crunch...coming closer and closer...and closer. And then--*another epiphany!*--the crunching kept going, right past him, farther away.

He tried again to get to his feet...couldn't. He would have to wait, and hopefully soon the police would come. So he lay there on his side, arms numb, right hand throbbing, face scratched and smarting, heart racing, and waited...

...and waited, for what seemed like hours. He heard leaves crunching. *She's coming back!* He held his breath. Once again she passed right by him, the crunching continuing up the incline.

Damn this! He had to move. After kicking the restraint off one leg, he leaned on his right shoulder and painfully scraped his face along the ground toward his knees, and sat up, his bottom resting on his ankles.

He pushed up, swung one leg in front, staggered up on it and stood up. *Thank you, Jesus!* The crunching noise started again…from down the hill, coming toward him. *How?* It had to be someone else.

"Help! Help me! Help me!"

A figure ran to him and clutched his throat.

"Were you expecting someone else?" she said. "A savior? Huh?" He started choking; she released him. "Do you want to die?"

Eric caught his breath before saying, "No!"

"Then get back up there and get Ruth Ann to come out."

"I tried! I tried the best I could. Maybe you should go in there and get her yourself."

"Maybe I should shoot you and let you die out here. What you think about those apples, whore?"

"I think I can get her to come out this time."

"You've got five minutes to convince her to come out. If you don't, I'll shoot you instead."

"Why you doing this to me? Why? I never did anything to you. I know I owe you ten dollars--can't pay it till I get it."

She pushed him. "Move!"

"Tell the truth, wasn't I always nice to you? I treated you with respect."

She whacked the back of his head and he fell to the ground.

"Ohhhhh! You bust my head! Is it bleeding?" She hadn't really hit him that hard. He was playing for sympathy.

"Get up!"

"Ohhhhh! My head! I can't see! Hannity! Hannity, is it you? Ohhhhh!" Maybe the nut role might work. "Hannity, you've gone stale, bro--same shit every day!" He was in the middle of another "Ohhhh!" when steel kissed his tonsils.

"Get up and shut up!"

Immediately all pain ceased, and she didn't have to worry about him saying anything. How could he with four inches of gun barrel shoved into his mouth.

"Keep jerking me," she said, "I'll shoot in your mouth. You don't want me to ejaculate prematurely, do you?"

"I sheer daunt!"

She yanked the gun out. He spat to rid the bloody-metallic taste.

She led him near the same spot as before.

"Five minutes, whore! You call her and tell her to get her butt out here."

Chapter 40

Ruth Ann closed her eyes and braced herself. Death had entered the cabin, with her name on its lips. "Ruth Ann?" the intruder repeated.

"Grab him!" Leonard shouted.

Ruth Ann heard footsteps shuffling across the floor…poundings, someone saying oomph…more poundings, grunting and groaning.

"I got him," Shirley said. "Ow! Hold up! Leonard, is that you?"

"Yes, it's me."

"Stop hitting him. I got him in a headlock. Check his pockets for a weapon. Hurry up!"

Ruth Ann opened her eyes and tried to distinguish the milieu, but it was too dark. "You got him, Shirley?"

"I sure do, and it ain't Eric."

"Something's missing!" Leonard said. "It's not a he!"

A rustle came from the fireplace. "Robert Earl?" Shirley said.

"What?"

"Glad you could join us. It's over now."

"It's not a he," Leonard said. "It's a woman!"

"I heard you the first time, Leonard. You checked her for a weapon, didn't you?"

"Yes, she's clean."

"Anybody got a lighter…a match?"

"No, I don't have one."

"I don't, either," Ruth Ann said.

"I have a penlight," Robert Earl said. "No matches or a lighter."

"Robert Earl, if it's not too much trouble, would you turn it on, please!"

A small ray of light appeared, pointed directly in Robert Earl's face, grinning sheepishly, without a single tooth in his mouth.

"Leonard," Shirley said, "would you please take the light from the toothless wonder and shine it over here so we can see who we got!"

"Oh!" and played the light toward Shirley.

"Oh my God!" Leonard shouted.

"Jesus!" Ruth Ann exclaimed.

Shirley screamed.

"Momma," Robert Earl said. "Y'all killed her!"

"Let her go!" Leonard shouted at Shirley. She did, and Ida crumpled to the floor. Everyone except Robert Earl knelt down beside her.

"Momma," Shirley said, patting Ida's face. "Momma, wake up! Momma, wake up!" The light moved away. "Robert Earl, keep the fucking light over here!"

"Sorry."

"Mother, please wake up!"

Ida blinked open her eyes, the right halfway, a black crescent forming underneath. Her expression bewildered and frightened, she tried to make out her surroundings.

"She's all right!" Leonard said. "She's going to be all right!"

"Momma, say something," Ruth Ann said.

Ida scanned her children's faces. In a slurred whisper: "Was there a specific reason why y'all kicked my ass?"

"Wasn't me," Robert Earl said.

"Momma, I'm so sorry!" Shirley said. "Momma, we thought you were someone else."

"Mother, it was a mistake. We didn't know it was you."

Ida pushed Shirley's hand away from her face. "Sorry, hell! You punched me in the eye, put me in a chokehold! Who was it feeling underneath my damn clothes?"

"Ask Leonard," Robert Earl said.

"Robert Earl," Shirley said, "why don't you go hide again? I'll let you know if someone shows up with napalm. Go on!" Robert Earl didn't move. Shirley returned her attention to Ida. "We're sorry, Momma. Lord knows we are. We thought you were someone looking for Ruth Ann."

"I was looking for Ruth Ann," Ida said. "Damn! Didn't you hear me calling her name when I came in?"

"Oh-oh," Robert Earl said.

"Momma," Ruth Ann said, "why you come up here looking for me?"

Ida sighed and stared at Ruth Ann, and then at Shirley and Leonard. "Robert Earl, son, would you stop shining the light in my face?"

"No can do, Momma. We have to hand you over to the sheriff."

"She didn't do it, moron!" Shirley said.

"The only person left is your boyfriend."

"He didn't do it, either!"

"Seems to me we're running out of suspects."

Ida stared directly into the light. "When he stops shining the light in my face, I'll tell you why I come up here."

Shirley snatched the penlight out of his hand. "Go ahead, Momma."

"I found a will on the table," Ida said. "I snapped. I didn't know if someone was messing with my mind, trying to drive me crazy, or setting a trap for Ruth Ann. I tore up the kitchen."

"We know, Momma," Shirley said. "The will is a fake. I should have told you. I didn't want you to worry."

"Lord forgive me," Ida said. "I might as well say it. There ain't no will, never was one. I lied about there being one. You can hate me if you want, but there it is."

"Shirley, Leonard," Robert Earl said, "I think y'all hurt Momma when y'all beat her up. She's talking out of her head."

"Momma," Shirley said, "what are you saying? I don't understand."

"Your daddy never saved any money. He thought he was in his company's stock-sharing plan--he wasn't. They never told him he had to sign the papers. When he learned the truth, he did sign up, but then he was too close to retirement to save any real money."

"Why?" Leonard said. "Why did you tell Robert Earl he had a will?"

"Because...because I missed my kids. Your daddy did, too. We had Shane, but still we missed our kids. Y'all were too busy to stop by for a few minutes. You'd say you were coming and never show up. We'd wait, not wanting to go anywhere in fear of missing you coming by. Hours later, nothing! Not even a phone call to tell us you couldn't make it. I'd cook a big meal, and a few days later I'd have to throw it out. Larry and I could only eat so much.

"We were lonely. I didn't think it too much to ask your children to stop by every now and again and sit a spell. So I said what I said. Next thing you know the phone ringing off the hook day and night, family started coming over not knowing when to leave. I was going to tell everybody the truth at the barbecue…" She let out a soft cry. "…and someone murdered your father."

Something knocked on the far wall. Shirley pointed the light at the noise. Robert Earl was banging his head.

He stopped and glared at Ida. "Bingo wasn't an option, Momma? You know how much debt I'm in because of you?"

"Shut up, Robert Earl!" Leonard said.

"Make me! I'm in worse shape now than when I started. No job, no credit! Nothing from nothing leaves a headache! I saw a snake I needed to buy, couldn't afford it. All 'cause Momma and Daddy didn't think Viagra."

"Robert Earl," Shirley said, "you keep disrespecting Momma, I'll pop the tumor in your big head!"

"You might as well do what you gotta do. I'm already tore up from the floor up."

"I'm sorry, son," Ida said. "I shouldna lied to you. Lord knows I didn't think it would come to all this. Just knew one of y'all would figure it out. Nobody thought the obvious. The man woke up in the middle of night to steal a rotten tooth to avoid forking over a quarter--and now he's willing out money, and he ain't sick!"

"It was Daddy who did that?" Leonard asked.

"Yes, he did. I thought once y'all figured it out, we would laugh about it and y'all would start dropping by once in a while."

"Did Daddy know anything about this?" Ruth Ann asked.

"No. He was curious why all a sudden everyone started calling and coming by. He wouldn't admit it to nobody, even me, but he was glad y'all…" She broke, sobbing loudly. "He was a stingy, foul-mouthed cuss …but I loved him!"

Robert Earl said, "Give me a break!"

"It's all right, Mother," Leonard said. "Everything is going to be all right."

"I think about him every minute," Ida sobbed. "Every second! I never intended to kill him!"

"Mother, you didn't kill him. You couldn't have known."

"Depends on who you asking," Robert Earl said. "She hasn't said anything about the gopher poison in her closet."

"Shirley," Leonard said, "what's stopping you from kicking his ass? You didn't hesitate tossing me across the room. Kick his ass and make him shut up! He's not helping the situation here at all."

"What's he talking about?" Ida said. "Gopher poison?"

"Mother, I found a box of poison in your closet."

"Your father bought it for Shirley and she never got it. Shirley, you remember you told your daddy you were having problems with raccoons near your house?"

"Yes, you're right, Momma."

"Ruth Ann!" Eric called from outside. "Please come help me! Please, Ruth Ann!"

"Robert Earl," Shirley said, "are you still feeling suicidal?"

"Nope. Not at the moment."

"Who is that?" Ida said.

"Eric," Leonard said.

"Why don't he come inside?"

"He wants Ruth Ann, Mother."

"What in heaven for? And where's Shane?"

"Ruth Ann!" a woman shouted. "Ruth Ann, I know you hear me!"

"Who is she?" Leonard asked.

"Estafay!" Shirley said. "Estafay! I knew it was her!"

"Ruth Ann, you've got thirty seconds to get out here, or I'll blow your boyfriend's testicles off. I mean it, too! I sure will. You better get out here. Now!"

"If you do," Shirley shouted, "I swear to God, Estafay, I'll kill you!"

"Who are you?" Estafay shouted.

"It's me. Shirley. Estafay, let Eric go!"

"Come out and get him, fatso!"

"I'm going to kill that heifer! Momma, I swear to God, I'm going to kill that crazy heifer!"

"Robert Earl?" Ida said. No answer. "Robert Earl?"

"What?" Robert Earl said, his voice far off again.

"Is he outside?" Ida asked.

Shirley pointed the light at Robert Earl's dusty hiking boots inside the chimney.

"How did he--What's he doing in there?" Ida asked.

397

"He's hiding, Mother."

"Robert Earl," Ida said, "get outta there! Your wife is out there--you hear her! Go out there and talk some sense into her so everybody can go home. Get out of there, Robert Earl, and start acting like a man."

"Estafay killed Daddy, Momma," Shirley said.

"How you figure that, Shirley?" Robert Earl said.

"Ruth Ann," Shirley said, "you remember the day before the barbecue? You told Estafay she didn't have to buy all the meat herself. You tried to give her some money and she wouldn't take it. The meat she brought to the house was separated in Tupperware bowls. One for chicken, another for ribs, one for hot dogs and one for neck bones."

"Yes," Ruth Ann said. "You're right."

Robert Earl said, "Why y'all trying to pin it on Estafay? She's a sanctified woman. A little high strung, yes. She's still a good, sanctified woman. Shirley, you gave everybody else the benefit of doubt--give Estafay one, too."

"You might be right, Robert Earl. I doubt it. There's only one way to find out. You go out there and talk to her. Maybe she's teed off because not one of us contributed to her church building fund. Who knows? You go out there and find out what her problem is."

"Ruth Ann," Estafay called, "you're down to five seconds!"

"Robert Earl, what are you going to do?" Leonard said.

"All right, already, I'm going. Somebody help me out of here."

Leonard moved to assist him--and then a shot rang out.

"Wait a minute," Robert Earl said.

Chapter 41

Eric, on his knees, Estafay's fingernails pinching his neck, whispered what little he remembered of The Lord's Prayer.

Estafay said, "I don't think Shirley cares if you live or die, whore."

"Shirley is nothing to play with. I wouldn't hurt me if I were you. Shirley will beat the shit out of you, then beat you again for messing yourself. I were you I'd leave now."

"If she's so tough why hasn't she brought her fat butt out here? She cares the same what happens to you as Ruth Ann. Diddlysquat!"

"Can you blame her? You got a gun. Put it down and she'll come out. I know she will."

Estafay squeezed his neck harder and he felt a warm trickle slide down his chest. "Do you feel me as stupid?"

"No, I don't," he grunted. *Insane, not stupid!* "Let me go and I'll forget all about this. Swear to God! I don't know nothing! Nothing!"

"Ruth Ann," Estafay shouted, "you're down to five seconds."

"In prison, Mrs. Harris, them women lift weights all day and love to wrestle. Two or three of em hold you down and make you eat something real ugly and smelly. Let me go--no wrestling for you."

"How would you know?"

"Believe me, I know. The smell worse than sardines. It'll leave a bad taste in your mouth Listerine can't touch. You need to think about the long-term consequences of what you're doing."

"Here's something for you to think about."

Kapooow!

The gunshot echoed through the woods. Eric's left foot jerked and he felt a strange sensation...a burning pain...*She's standing on my toes*...The pain increased...and increased...His foot felt on fire...*She's burning my foot!*...

The heat flamed up his leg, burned in his groin, sizzled in his stomach, heated his chest and burst inside his head...*My God!...She shot me!*...He dropped to the ground on his side.

"You shot me! You shot me! You shot me!"

"Scream!"

"You shot me!"

"I said scream!" Estafay stepped on his injured foot and hopped up and down on it.

"Aaauugggggghhhh!"

"Louder!"

"Aaaaauugggggggghhhhhhh!"

* * * * *

The door opened and slammed shut…opened and slammed shut. "No, Shirley!" Ida said. "We're not letting you go out there!"

"She's killing him!" Shirley cried. "Momma, she's killing him! Please, Momma, let me out!"

The door opened and slammed shut, opened and slammed shut, opened and slammed shut…

"Help us, Ruth Ann!" Leonard said, breathing hard. "We can't hold it!"

Ruth Ann didn't budge, paralyzed by fear and guilt. *All this is my fault.*

Shirley screamed…and the door opened and slammed shut again.

"Ruth Ann, would you please help us!"

She didn't move. She'd caused Shirley this anguish; to get in her way now would be dangerous. Shirley loved Eric, more than she herself could ever love any man.

Shirley was more than willing to risk getting shot for Eric. Ruth Ann couldn't think of anyone for whom she would risk her life.

Except...*Shirley!*

"Ruth Ann, you better get out here!" Estafay shouted. "He's going fast."

Again Shirley screamed and this time the door opened and took longer to slam shut.

"I'm going out there," Ruth Ann said.

"Ruth Ann, please," Leonard said. "We're doing all we can to keep Shirley in, you know we're not letting you go out there. She has a gun!"

"Estafay!" Ida shouted. "Estafay, this is Ida. Listen to me. There's no money, no money at all. It was a lie. Do you hear me? A lie. I made it all up. Stop this foolishness!"

No response from Estafay. Eric screamed again.

"Let him go, Estafay!" Shirley cried. "Please! Please, Estafay! I'm begging you! Oh God, please, Estafay! I'll give you all I have...just let him go! Please! I'm begging..."

Her voice gave way to loud, gut-wrenching sobs and she collapsed onto the floor.

"Robert Earl!" Ida said. "Robert Earl, you take your butt out there and talk to your wife! You hear me! Go out there and talk to your wife!"

"Momma, I don't think it's a good idea," Robert Earl said. "She sounds awfully upset. What if she shoots me?"

"Get out there!" Ida shouted.

* * * * *

Just as Eric started slipping into unconsciousness, Estafay stepped off his foot. The heat reduced a few degrees, yet still burned like hell. He looked up at the stars, blinking in a strange pattern, one section sparkling and then other sections following suit.

I'm losing it! I'm going to die out here!

A footstep sounded on the porch. "Hey, honey. It's me! Robert Earl. Don't shoot!"

"Robert Earl, help me! She shot me!" Estafay kicked his foot. "Ohhhhhh!"

"Shut up!" To Robert Earl: "What you doing out here? I thought you went to Greenville to look at a snake."

"I went there and saw a good one. Didn't have enough money to buy it. Honey, you didn't bring my Smith and Wesson out here, did you?"

404

"No, I didn't. It's the Colt, the rusty one."

Crazy bitch shot me and he's worried which gun she used!

Robert Earl stepped closer. "You didn't neuter Eric, did you?"

"No. Such a small target I never would've hit it."

"What?"

"My aim was low."

"Honey, what's this about?"

"Are you still with me, Robert?"

"What are you talking about? You know I am. You're my wife."

Eric's heart sank.

"Good," Estafay said. "I knew you would be. Who else is inside?"

"Shirley, Ruth Ann, Momma and Leonard."

"Leonard? What's he doing in there? Not a problem. Robert, we need to burn the cabin down."

"I'll go tell Momma them to come out and we'll burn it down. All this time you just wanted to burn the cabin down. I told Shirley there was a simple explanation for this."

"Robert, we need to burn it down with them inside it."

"Do what? What did you say?"

Eric salvaged a sliver of hope.

"Robert, we can't let them go. They'll go straight to the police and we'll go to jail for a long time." Pause. "And we won't get a dime of the money."

"Estafay, there's no money. Momma told a bald-faced lie to get us visiting her and Daddy."

"If she'll lie about one thing, she'll lie about everything! Go set the cabin afire and I'll take care of him."

A long silence. A cricket fiddled near the porch. A mosquito stung Eric just below the right eye; he didn't feel it.

"Fuck!" Robert Earl said. "Estafay, honey, this ain't right! I can't do it!"

"Why the potty mouth?"

"Sorry, honey. They're my people. I'm related to every one of em. I can't burn em up. Imagine the nightmares I'd have."

"I'll do it! Like I have to do everything else. Can you shoot him, or is it asking too much?"

Robert Earl sighed. "He's not related to me. If he dies Shirley will be highly PO'ed. You should've heard her in there a while ago. We'll have to live the rest of our life watching out for her. We might have to leave the country."

Eric heard Estafay breathing hard through her nose.

"Plus," Robert Earl continued, "Sheriff Bledsoe gave me a heckuva pass on something I did a long time ago, before I met you. He told me the next time I got into any trouble would be the last time. I burn somebody I'll be looking at the electric chair. Besides, Estafay, it just ain't right! Did God tell you to do this?"

"Was it right your family treated me the way they did? They didn't know me, didn't know me from Eve. When decent people meet someone the first time they just say hello, or they don't say anything at all. Your daddy called me a name to my face, Robert. Ruth Ann fell on her knees laughing. Were they right to treat me the way they did?"

"No, they weren't right. I hate it happened just as much as you do."

"Enough talk, let's get this over with so I can go home and cook supper."

"Estafay, I...I can't do it!"

"Go home then!" Estafay shouted at him. "Go home! I'll handle this myself. Take the roast out the freezer when you get there."

Wekeee! Wekeeee!

Eric looked and thought he saw something move near the side of the cabin.

"What was that?" Robert Earl said.

"A bat," Estafay said. "Go home. I got work to do."

"Aw shucks, Estafay. Why don't we both go home together and forget about this?"

"Robert, I'm going to explain it to you one last time. I shot this whore here. Everyone in there knows I shot him. They'll tell the police and we--you and I!--will go to jail."

"Eric," Robert Earl said, "you wouldn't sic the police on Estafay, would you?"

They're both crazy! "Of course not!"

"He's lying," Estafay said.

"Eric, you promise?"

"Cross my heart, on my momma's honor!"

"See, Estafay, he's not going to the police."

"Go home!" Estafay said. Kapoooow!

"Ohhhhh!" Eric shouted, and then realized she hadn't shot him again. He looked toward Robert Earl's shadowy form…gone. He heard footsteps fading in the distance.

Crazy bastard flying home. When he gets there, he'll take the roast out the freezer and sit his big, stupid ass down without thinking once to call the police.

"Alone again, you and I," Estafay said. "The time has come for us to go our separate ways. Anything you'd like to say before you go to hell?"

"If you kill me I'll come back and haunt you! I swear I will!"

Estafay laughed. The gun barrel bumped the back of his head. "Guess I'll see you when you get back."

Eric closed his eyes, faintly aware he'd released his bowels.

Chapter 42

Gas, Sheriff Bledsoe thought, soured my memory. He forgot
Leonard had told him Ruth Ann was at the Boy Scout camp.

Otherwise he could've avoided taking the good reverend to the
liquor store, contributing to the purchase of a gallon of Wild Irish
Rose, driving to the jail and then back to the liquor store because the
good reverend suddenly decided Wild Irish Rose with Ginseng was
what he really wanted.

The cruiser headlights rolled across a gray Lumina, a yellow
Datsun truck and a blue Camry. *Ida's car!* He killed the engine and
looked around. Totally dark outside of the area spotted by the
headlights.

Reaching for his hat, he heard gunfire. He grabbed the mike. "Tracy, come in!" Static. "Tracy, come in!" No response. "Tracy, come in!"

He turned off the headlights and all went black. "Tracy, come in!" No time to wait, he felt under the passenger seat for the flashlight, found it, and got out.

In Iraq, the first time, he wouldn't sit next to a guy who wouldn't cuff his cigarette; and now he'd be running in the woods like a neon target.

He waved the beam left to right. A handcrafted plaque marked Maumelle Trail indicated a break in the trees. It looked a good entrance as any, so he started in at full sprint, flashlight in one hand, trusty .357 Magnum in the other.

Not twenty feet up the trail, Sheriff Bledsoe heard something coming toward him. "Police! Halt!" It sounded like a horse, hooves clopping incredibly fast.

A blur appeared in the light and before he could blink, whatever it was ran smack into him, sending him airborne, knocking the flashlight and the .357 magnum out of his hands. He landed on his back on a thorn bush.

"Sheriff!" he shouted, getting to his feet. "Freeze, right where you are!"

Gurgling and groaning. "Ohhh, my head!"

"Don't move!" Sheriff Bledsoe warned. "I've got a gun!" *Somewhere around here.*

410

"You busted my head!"

"Robert Earl?"

"You broke my nose, too!"

He spotted the flashlight, still shining, picked it up and pointed it at the noise. Robert Earl lay flat on his back, hands over his face.

"Robert Earl, you all right?"

"Uh-uh!"

Where's the gun? He played the light in every direction and didn't see it. He dropped to all fours and inspected the ground. It had to be somewhere close.

"Robert Earl, who's shooting up there?" No response. Thorns scratching his hand, he probed the base of the bush. Nothing.

"Robert Earl, you busted your nose, is all. Who's up there shooting?"

Robert Earl hawked and spat. "*You* busted my nose!" His voice a nasal twang. "I didn't bust it myself. Hey! Listen to me! Oh no, like a homo!"

Sheriff Bledsoe tossed up clods of dirt. "What's going on up there?"

"What you looking for?"

"Nothing!"

"You looking for something. What did you lose?"

"Don't worry about me, Robert Earl." *Where in the world is my gun?* "Stop evading the question. What's going on up there?"

"I don't know."

He stopped searching and pointed the light at Robert Earl sitting up, pinching his nose, head tilted back, overalls blood splattered.

"Robert Earl, what's going on up there? Don't lie to me!"

Robert Earl shook his head and shrugged.

"Don't BS me! I heard a gunshot and you come running like a scalded hog. Don't tell me you don't…" A thought occurred to him. "Stand up, Robert Earl!" he demanded, standing up himself. "Interlock your fingers behind your head. Do it now! Slowly."

Robert Earl stood up, left hand behind his head, right hand pinching his nose.

"Both hands behind your head! Do it!"

"Sheriff, if I let go my nose will start bleeding again."

"Do it!"

Clean, save for a bunch of junk in his pockets. Time wasted; someone could be up there hurt--and he couldn't find his blasted gun.

He resumed searching for it. "One more time, Robert Earl, and if you lie to me again I'm charging you with what you did to that Chinese girl. Who's shooting up there? Your mother?"

"She was Okinawan, not Chinese." He hawked and spat again. Then, in a stream: "I told Estafay to come home with me and she wouldn't listen--I couldn't burn nobody up 'cause they my family and burnt bodies stink worse than burnt cats and I didn't want the nightmares and she said Eric would tell even though he promised he wouldn't and she shot in the air and told me to go home and--"

"Hey, hey, hey! Slow down. Estafay shot in the air?"

"Yes."

"Where's your mother?"

"In the cabin."

"Does your mother have a gun, too?"

"They laughed at her."

"Laughed at who?"

"Estafay…and me."

What the hell? "Anybody up there hurt?"

"Eric. Estafay…Estafay sort of shot him."

"What?" He lay flat on his stomach and fanned his arms and legs. The gun was nowhere to be found. It seemed it had sprouted legs and walked away.

"Robert Earl," stirring up clouds of dust, "how did she sort of shot him?"

"I guess she sort of aimed and pulled the trigger."

What? He fanned faster.

Robert Earl sighed. "She's gonna set the cabin on fire with Momma them in it."

"What! Momma them? Who are them?"

"Momma, Shirley, Ruth Ann, Leonard."

The entire family! He quit the search and stood up. "Listen closely, Robert Earl. Go to my patrol car, get Tracy on the radio and tell her to send everything she's got to this location. Police, fire department, EMT's, everything she's got."

413

"You deputizing me, aren't you?"

"Yeah, yeah. Go!"

Robert Earl headed down the trail pinching his nose.

He had a bad feeling Robert Earl would somehow muck up the simple task, but didn't have any other choice except to send him. And he didn't have any other choice but to go up the hill without his weapon.

The flashlight showing the way, he ran up the trail. Twenty feet later his lungs betrayed him and he started walking as fast he could.

What I'm going to do without my gun?

He didn't have a clue.

Chapter 43

"He's sure taking a long time," Ruth Ann said. "I bet him and Estafay out there arguing. He lets her run all over him."

Leonard said, "I hope she doesn't persuade Robert Earl to join her."

Ida said, "He wouldn't turn against his family. He ain't the stupidest person in the world."

"Mother, I'm sorry. He thinks he can train a snake to jump through a hoop. He *is* the stupidest."

Ida started to respond when a gunshot rang out. "Oh my Lord!"

"Eric!" Shirley said, her voice hoarse. "She shot him again!"

"I'm going out there, Leonard," Ruth Ann said. "She came here looking for me. No reason for anyone else to get hurt."

"Ruth Ann, we can't let you go out there."

"You don't have a choice. I'm going out there."

"I'm going with you," Shirley said.

"No, Shirley," Ruth Ann said. "If Eric is injured, you'll need to be there for him and your son. Let me do this myself. I owe you, remember?"

Leonard said, "Remember what you told me? A label--if it don't fit don't think about wearing it. You're donning the hero jacket because you feel guilty. Getting yourself killed won't change anything. You'll just be dead."

"I love you, Shirley," Ruth Ann said, ignoring Leonard. "Whatever happens remember I love you. I've always have and I always will. What I did was inexcusable, but I never intended to hurt you."

She crossed to the door and opened it. "It's high time I started acting like a big sister," and stepped out and closed the door behind her.

"Estafay!" She heard trepidation in her voice and shouted louder, "Estafay, I'm here!" This is it, she thought. *The end of my life!*

"Well, well, well," Estafay said, "if it ain't the delectable Mrs. Ruth Ann. I'm glad you could finally join us. Eric was on his way out."

Ruth Ann squinted, unable to distinguish Estafay, some twenty feet or so away. "Hello, Estafay. Where's Eric?"

"He's right here. Say something, Eric."

Ruth Ann heard a thud and Eric said, "Ohhhhh!"

Estafay said, "You'll have to excuse him. His foot has been troubling him lately."

"Is he all right?"

"Not at all."

"Where's Robert Earl?"

"I sent him home. You didn't think he would go against his wife, did you?"

"Estafay, I don't know what to think."

"You should think about gnashing teeth and eternal suffering. You've heard of Hell, haven't you?"

Ruth Ann couldn't see a gun, but sensed Estafay was pointing one at her. "Yes, believe it or not, I have. Before you shoot me, would you please tell me why? Why, Estafay?"

"Why I shot your boyfriend? Or why I dispatched the heathen you called Daddy?"

"None of this makes sense. You killed my daddy, his dog. You even tried to frame me. Daddy never did anything to…" She remembered her father calling Estafay an orangutan. "All these years you held a grudge. You could've slapped Daddy's face. You could've egged his truck. You could've told him what he said hurt your feelings, deeply offended you. You didn't have to kill him!"

"'Behold, all who are incensed against you shall be put to shame and confounded; those who strive against you shall be as nothing and shall perish.'"

"Do you know what literal misinterpretation means?"

"Do you?"

"It means you glossed over the essence, love and compassion, and locked onto a verse more suitable to your psychosis."

"Beware the false prophets."

"Beware nuts with unresolved resentments. How did Eric *incense* you?"

"He's a whore! A vile, disgusting whore!"

"Who the hell do you think you are? Reading the Bible grants you the authority to judge who's evil? Please! You are a murderer, a cold-blooded murderer! God cannot be happy with you justifying murder in His name."

"What do you know of God?" Estafay sneered. "A sullied, lifelong whore talking to me about God! Blasphemy! What do you think an unrepentant whore, a whore who ruts with her sister's man, is worth in the eyes of God?"

That stung, and knocked her against the ropes.

"Yeah…oh yeah…well…well, I might be a whore, but I've never killed anybody!" Weak, though it was the best she could do after absorbing an uppercut. She tried again: "I'll bet you this, when we get to Hell, your seat will be a helluva lot hotter than mine." Even weaker.

"Not hardly, harlot. I know grace, redemption, salvation, the rapture. You worship the flesh, I worship the word of God. There's no comparison between you and me."

"You're so right. Something has raptured inside your head. You have truly lost your bug-eyed mind!"

"No, no, no!" Eric said. "Don't agitate her! She'll shoot you!"

Ruth Ann said, "I don't give a damn! If she's going to shoot me, then let her shoot. It won't change a damn thing! I'll be dead and she'll still be ugly and out of her crazy fucking bug-eyed mind!"

"Watch your mouth, Ruth Ann!" Startled, she looked to her right. Ida stood beside her.

Another voice, to her left, Shirley's: "You intend to kill us all, Estafay? What you'll have to do if you shoot Ruth Ann. You might get one or two of us, I doubt you'll get all of us. It's a family thang now, Estafay. We're in it together. And if you shoot me, you better make damn sure I drop!"

Estafay laughed.

"Mrs. Harris," Leonard said, standing behind Ruth Ann, "right now you're looking at short jail time. Continue with this and you'll be looking at life in prison, possibly the death penalty. It'll be hard on you, Estafay. Prison is no place for a woman of your virtue."

"Smite by a Sodomite," Estafay said, stepping closer. Gradually, Ruth Ann was able to make out her doughy form. She stopped a few feet short, the gun held out in front. "A sexual deviant appealing to my ego."

"He's not a sexual deviant," Ruth Ann said. "He's my brother!"

Estafay chuckled. "He can't be both? Shirley, I've never held anything against you. You soiled yourself taking a whore in your bosom."

"I love Eric. Something you wouldn't understand, Estafay."

"I wasn't talking about him."

"I love Ruth Ann, too," Shirley said. "And I don't appreciate you calling her that."

"What do you call a woman who'll lay with her sister's man? Skank? Slut? Skeezer? Dog bitch?"

Ruth Ann's face got hot. "Shut up!"

Estafay laughed and stepped to Ruth Ann. "Did I say something touched a nerve, something befitting, something true? Skank? Slut? Dog--"

"Stop this nonsense, Estafay!" Ida said. "Enough is enough! Stop it now!"

"Drop it!" a voice boomed out of the darkness.

A flashlight outlined Estafay in a black scarf, black shirt, black pants and black tennis shoes.

Sheriff Bledsoe shouted, "Sheriff! Drop the gun, Estafay! Drop it right now!"

"Thank you, Jesus!" Eric cried. "Thank you, thank you, thank you! Thank you, Jesus!"

Estafay didn't drop the gun; she kept it pointed at Ruth Ann.

"Drop the gun, Estafay! Drop it! I said drop it right now!"

Estafay shook her head. "No, Sheriff. Ruth Ann and I are checking out together. Same departure time, different destination."

"Aw hell!" Sheriff Bledsoe said.

"Shoot her, Sheriff!" Eric yelled. "Shoot her! What you waiting on?"

Estafay grinned at her. "When you get there, look through the flames and see who's burning with you. It won't be me," and cocked the pistol with the palm of her left hand.

Ruth Ann closed her eyes.

Thulink!

Thulink? A misfire? She opened her eyes...A stick...*No!*...An arrow was wrapped around Estafay's head...*A prop?...Where did she get it from?*

Ida screamed.

Estafay looked surprised, eyes and mouth agape, blood filling in both.

Sweet Jesus, it ain't a prop! The real deal! Someone shot Estafay with an arrow!

The gun slipped from Estafay's fingers. Her eyes rolled to the back of her head, arms went limp...torso started jerking as if she were belly dancing.

Ida screamed again.

Estafay leaned forward...and collapsed into Ruth Ann's arms.

"Who's there?" Sheriff Bledsoe said, shining the light at the side of the cabin. "Who's there?"

"What happened? What happened?" Ruth Ann shouted, holding Estafay up by her armpits. "What happened? What happened?"

"Let her go!" Shirley said. "Ruth Ann, let her go!"

"What happened?"

"Dammit, I said let her go!"

"What happ--" Claaap! Something slammed into the left side of her face, almost knocking her down…Estafay hit the dirt. She thought she'd been whacked with a two-by-four.

Shirley shook her. "Snap out of it!" Ruth Ann ran her tongue across the roof of her mouth, worried she'd lost the ability to taste. "Are you okay?"

She rubbed her face. Numb. "Shirley, was that absolutely necessary?"

Shirley answered by taking her hand and leading her to where Eric lay on the ground. Shirley knelt beside him and removed the underwear wrapped around his wrists and used it as a tourniquet on his leg.

"Is it over, Shirley?" Ruth Ann said. "Is it really over?"

"It's over. Try not to think about it just yet."

Sheriff Bledsoe came over and played the light on Eric. "Is he all right?"

"He's lost a lot of blood," Shirley said. "We need to get him to a hospital. He's going to be all right."

"Did anyone see who shot the arrow?"

Ruth Ann started to speak but Shirley cut her off. "No. No, we didn't. We saw the same thing you saw, Sheriff, which was nothing. Right, Ruth Ann?"

"I'm not sure what I saw."

"I saw it, Sheriff," Eric piped in. "An angel, swear to God! An angel! I saw it with my own eyes." He grimaced in pain as he propped up on an elbow and pointed at the cabin. "Standing over there, right side the cabin, I saw it. I was right here looking dead at it."

Shirley patted his head. "He's delirious. He's lost a lot of blood."

"I'm not delirious! I saw it! A black angel! I couldn't believe it myself. A black angel right before my eyes! I prayed to God, Shirley, and He sent us an angel. It's an epiphany--no, no! It's a miracle! A miracle!"

Shirley wiped his face with the hem of her sweat shirt. "Eric, baby, relax. If you say you saw an angel I believe you. Now you know if God sends you an angel, He expects you to walk true the rest of your life. No tipping, slipping, tripping, sliding--walk straight and true, you know what I'm saying?"

Eric nodded. "I know what you saying, Shirley. I know exactly what you saying."

"What did this angel look like?" Sheriff Bledsoe asked.

"It was black. I guess God sends black angels to black folks and white angels to white folks."

"Yeah, yeah. What was he wearing?"

"It was naked. Naked than a jaybird. How I knew it was an angel. It had a bow and arrow, too."

Sheriff Bledsoe grunted. "Angels, black or white, don't shoot people with arrows."

"Let it go, Sheriff," Shirley said. "It's over, let it go."

Sheriff Bledsoe ignored her and turned his attention to Ruth Ann. "Where's your son? I was told your son was up here. Where is he?"

She started to speak and again Shirley cut her off. "Ruth Ann, go check on Momma and Leonard. Go see how they're doing. Turn around and walk straight ahead. Go on now. Go check on em."

Leaving, Ruth Ann heard Shirley say, "Ennis Bledsoe, why you digging up bones when you should be helping me get my future husband to a hospital? No one asked why you come up here without a gun, did they? The mayor hasn't asked about the polygraph machine you rigged up, has he? Some bones are best left in the ground. You don't dig up mine, I won't dig up yours. You dig what I'm saying, Sheriff Ennis Lee Bledsoe?"

"I think I do," Sheriff Bledsoe said dryly.

Ida and Leonard stood in front of the damaged cabin, Ida crying on his shoulder.

"How's Momma doing?" Ruth Ann asked.

"She'll be all right in a bit," Leonard said. "How's Eric?"

"Shirley said he's going to be all right."

"Good. I'm taking Mother down the hill. Tonight we're staying at the Holiday Inn in Greensville. Tell Shirley to come by tomorrow before we leave town. You come by, too."

"We? Where are you going?"

"Mother and I are going to Chicago to stay. Are you ready to go, Mother?" Ida nodded. They started toward the trail, Leonard pointing the penlight in front of them.

Ruth Ann thought to go hug her mother before they left, but she didn't. She watched them disappear into the darkness.

Wekeeee! Wekeeee!

The sound came from behind the cabin.

"Shane! Shane! Shane!"

"Ruth Ann," Shirley called, "we need your help to carry Eric down."

"Shane!" Ruth Ann crossed to the side of the cabin. "Shane!" Shirley came up behind her. "Shane, come back! Come back, Shane!"

Shirley put a hand on Ruth Ann's shoulder. "C'mon. He's all right. He knows his way around out here."

"Are you sure? He's out there all by himself, after all has happened. I know I couldn't handle it. Are you sure, Shirley?"

"Trust me." In a quavering voice she added, "Would your little sister lie to you?"

Ruth Ann knew she was supposed to say, "No, she wouldn't," but her throat constricted and she couldn't get the words out. She swallowed, closed her eyes, inhaled deeply, cleared her throat and again tried to push the words out. Nothing.

So she wrapped her arms around her little sister's broad shoulders and hugged her tightly, and through her sobs she finally blurted, "I love you, Shirley!"

Epilogue

Eric slowly made his way up the aisle on crutches, dressed in a diamond-white double-breasted Giorgio Brutini suit and a black Bentley shoe on his right foot. The left pant was folded up below the knee and held in place by a safety pin.

He took his place in front of Reverend Jones, the pastor of Greater Paradise Church. Robert Earl, in a brown three-piece corduroy suit, the seat stitched with pink thread, stood to his left, looking uncomfortable. A petite young woman walked up front and started singing *Let's Get Married*.

The young woman put all she had into the song, eyes closed, shaking her head, arching her back on high notes, raising her hand to God, yet, Ruth Ann thought, she sounded like a wounded walrus.

Shane, wearing blue dress slacks, white shirt, blue tie and white tennis shoes, walked Shirley up the aisle.

Shirley looked absolutely stunning. A pearl tiara was inserted into a light-brown bun cascading wavy curls down her back. Light mascara, a touch of orange on her cheeks, a brush of candy-apple on her smiling lips. Rhinestone necklace. Navy blue satin gauntlets. In a navy blue satin, strapless gown with a beaded split front, she moved with the grace of a princess.

Ruth Ann stood up and took her picture.

"I can't believe it!" said someone behind her.

Ruth Ann sat down and turned. "Believe what?" she asked, not sure which of the three women sitting behind her had made the remark.

The middle one, a young woman wearing a teal-green column dress, her head draped in patently ridiculous long braid extensions, said, "I can't believe she's marrying him."

Ruth Ann couldn't help herself. "Oh, and why can't you?"

"He's a dog," the young woman whispered.

Ruth Ann turned her attention to the ceremony, and the woman touched her on the shoulder of her black lace-trimmed blouse.

"I know this for a fact. A one-legged dog now, but he's still a dog." Ruth Ann brushed the area where the woman had touched her. "He slept with her sister!"

"Which sister?" Ruth Ann whispered.

"Which sister! She only has one sister."

"What does she look like?"

The woman started coughing: "Woof woof woof!"

It took a second for Ruth Ann to realize she wasn't coughing.

"Woof woof woof!"

A damn dog!

Reverend Jones read Shirley and Eric the wedding vows, but Ruth Ann wasn't listening, unnerved and pissed that the woman had slyly called her a dog.

She checked the impulse to whirl around and backslap the woman. *Claaap! Teach the little tart to keep her mouth shut at social functions.* Instead she turned, smiling, looked the woman straight in the eye.

"Hello. My name is Ruth Ann, Shirley's sister. Your name?"

The tart's mouth dropped, eyes going left to right, searching for an escape if things got ugly. "D-D-Darlene. Darlene Pryor."

Ruth Ann turned face front and attempted to focus on the proceedings.

"Anyone here who have reasons that these two not be joined in holy matrimony?" Reverend Jones asked the congregation of fifty or so people.

Shirley looked over her shoulder directly at Ruth Ann, who smiled at her. Shirley smiled back.

"Speak now or forever hold your peace," Reverend Jones said.

Ruth Ann again turned and smiled at Darlene. "Little girl, this is your opportunity to raise your hand, state your disapproval."

429

Darlene didn't respond. "When you go home to yo momma, ask her if she knows someone literate to instruct you the rules of public etiquette."

"You may kiss the bride," Reverend Jones said, and Eric kissed Shirley, bending her backward.

"Ohhhh!" a collective sigh from the congregation.

Eric's crutches fell to the floor and the kiss continued…and continued…and continued…and then Eric lost his balance and they both fell to the floor.

"Oh-oh!" someone said.

Shirley helped Eric to his feet, handed him his crutches and said, "Ain't he something!"

The congregation laughed.

Eric said, "Give God the glory."

Ruth Ann tossed a handful of rice in the air as Eric and Shirley came down the aisle. Shirley never looked happier. Halfway she remembered to toss the bouquet, and Darlene practically dove over two pews to catch it.

Won't help one bit! Skinny tricks like her need more than a bouquet to land a husband. Without a father brandishing a shotgun or a lucky lotto number, she's a spinster for life.

A few hours later, Ruth Ann sat on the steps of her mother's porch. She didn't attend the wedding reception held at the Rialto theater downtown. Didn't feel up to it. She felt homesick and lonely.

She wondered what Lester was doing and resisted the urge to call him. What could she say?

Lester, I miss you, I miss my bed, my car, my life, and I'm sick and tired of staying at my mother's house. May I please come home?

Sounded good and was very true, but Lester...*What's going on with him?* He hadn't once come by to check on her after the tragedy at the park.

Shirley invited him to her wedding and he neglected to attend. *Does he have another woman?* She shook her head. *No way!* She hadn't been gone long. *Three months isn't long at all.*

A truck stopped in front of the house and Robert Earl and Shane, still wearing their wedding clothes, got out and walked up to the porch.

"How was the reception?"

"We left early," Robert Earl said. "I don't like to eat with a man got one leg. Spoils my appetite."

"Momma," Shane said, "I'm going to work for Uncle Earl."

Ruth Ann hadn't got used to him calling her Momma. "Do what?"

"Work at my station," Robert Earl said.

"What station?"

"The one I'm building."

She looked from Robert Earl to Shane, who appeared excited by the proposition. "Robert Earl, Shane is seeing a therapist. I don't think it's a good idea filling his head with fantasies."

Robert Earl smiled at her with his new dentures, as if she were senile. "She who has no confidence in her big brother is not welcome at Robert Earl and Shane's Gas Station and Exotic Snake Farm."

"Momma, you hear that? I'm a business partner. Ain't that right, Uncle Earl?"

"Yes, indeed. Both our names will be in bright lights. I'll be the CEO, the chief everyone obeys. Shane will be in charge of pumping gas, wiping windshields, keeping the place clean. The technical stuff."

"Momma, can you believe it? I'll be pumping gas."

Ruth Ann sighed, disturbed that Robert Earl was falsely encouraging Shane. "Robert Earl, how you propose to do all this?"

"How you think? With money, of course." He pulled out his wallet, attached to a silver chain, and took out a piece of paper. "Look at this."

Ruth Ann reached for the paper and Robert Earl snatched it away.

"You look with your eyes, not your hands!" He unfolded the paper and waved it in front of her face.

She glimpsed the amount on a check. "Seventy-five thousand dollars!"

"Hush! Don't tell the whole dang neighborhood. And close your mouth before a bug flies in it."

"You mean they paid you? The insurance company paid after all what happened? I'm shocked."

"You? You should've seen me when I first got the check."

"Robert Earl, can I borrow a couple hundred?"

His face tightened up. "I don't know."

"What you mean you don't know? You said--"

"I know what I said! Dang! Don't start begging--make people hate you!"

"What's the name of the insurance company?"

"Non-yo business! Next door to YU Tripping."

"Robert Earl, I can't believe you won't let me borrow at least fifty dollars!"

"Give it a day or two, it'll sink in. A month ago I called Leonard and told him about the policy I found in Estafay's stuff and he hooked me up with his buddy, Victor. Don't tell nobody..."

He paused and patted Shane on the shoulder. "Go get your uncle a glass of Kool-Aid. Wash your hands and put some ice in it." Shane ran inside the house. "Don't tell nobody I told you, Ruth Ann. Leonard and Victor are planning to get married next year. Yours truly won't be there."

Shane came out of the house empty-handed. "No Kool-Aid. Some orange juice. You want that?"

"No, don't worry about it. Victor works for an insurance company. He told me not to worry, let him handle everything. Last week I got this check."

"You're sharing it with Shane?"

"No, I'm not. I am making him my business partner. I owe him that much. He does have a way with animals and such."

Ruth Ann squeezed Shane's shoulder. "Are you sure this is what you want to do?"

"You bet, Momma!"

Robert Earl said, "We're going to my house to teach Albert Number Two some new tricks. You wanna come watch?"

"Albert Number Two, is he a snake?"

"Yup."

"Hope you don't mind me asking. What tricks can a snake possibly do?"

"Wag its tail, heel, stay put, stay still, play dead, roll over with a little help. A buncha stuff. C'mon, let's go."

"No, y'all go 'head."

Robert Earl and Shane returned to the truck and were halfway down the block when she yelled, "Robert Earl!"

The brake lights brightened. Ruth Ann closed the front door and crossed the grass to the street.

Robert Earl backed up and stopped. "What?"

"Can you drop me off? I'm going home."

"Yeah. Scoot over, Shane."

"No, I'll ride in back." She climbed into the truck bed and sat on the hump over the wheel.

A change was in the air. The wind blowing her hair felt good on her face. In a few weeks it would be even cooler and sunset would occur earlier. Dirt in the bed swirled up and caught in her eyes and mouth. In the sky two streaks of jet exhaust overlapped. A cross, Ruth Ann thought. *A good sign.*

Robert Earl stopped the truck and she hesitated before getting out. "Thanks, Robert Earl. Shane, you be careful. I love you." Shane nodded.

Robert Earl tapped the horn before driving away.

She checked the mailbox at the end of the driveway. Empty. Her Expedition was parked outside of the garage, which meant Lester had driven it. Dusty. He could have at least washed it.

At the front door she wondered whether to knock, ring the doorbell, or simply barge in. Hand trembling, she knocked softly on the screen door. No one answered. She took a deep breath and stepped in.

Lester sat in the brown La-Z-Boy by the window, his lower face hidden behind a newspaper. *He saw and heard me coming and he just sat there.* He was dressed in...*What the hell is he wearing?*...Brown baggy short pants, a black-and-gold starter jersey and leather sandals. She'd never seen Lester wear sandals in her life.

She wondered if she'd walked into the wrong house. "Lester?"

The man before her had waves in his short-cropped hair, a hairstyle sported by young men.

"Lester?"

A glance at the life-sized portrait of her and Lester on the far wall confirmed she was in the right house. *Who the hell is this man sitting in Lester's chair?* She wished he would remove the paper from his face.

The man spoke, "How are you doing, Ruth Ann?"

The voice definitely belonged to Lester. She cleared her throat and said, "I'm fine. How are you?"

Looking at her over the top of the paper: "I'm fine. I heard what happened. I'm sorry."

Why doesn't he put the damn paper away? Nothing can be that damn interesting. "It was a terrible ordeal, Lester, just terrible. I don't think I'll ever get over it. I'm traumatized."

"You'll get over it. You're a strong woman, Ruth Ann. A very strong woman."

What the hell does that mean? "You don't mind me coming over, do you?"

"No, not at all. I'm headed out in a few minutes."

"To work?" He shook his head. "Where?"

"Not important."

Not important? Since when? A thought struck her and she inhaled deeply, trying to detect the slightest scent of perfume.

Some woman has been here! In my house!

She could feel it, though didn't see anything revealing. *Some woman has been here!*

"Lester, may I use the bathroom? I was riding in the back of Robert Earl's truck and--"

"You know where it is."

On her way there she pushed the bedroom door open. The bed was unmade, but nothing else was out of place.

Inside the bathroom she immediately checked the hamper and medicine cabinet. Nothing to indicate another woman's presence.

Some woman has been here!

"Find everything you were looking for?" Lester asked upon her return.

"What do you mean by that?"

"Nothing. I moved a few things around while you were gone."

"Such as?" Ruth Ann snapped.

"Nothing major. A few whatnots. By the way, what brings you by?"

Ruth Ann couldn't decide which irritated her more: the question, or the annoyed manner in which he'd said it. Not to mention his insistence on hiding behind the damn paper. She sat down on the couch.

"Nothing, really. Shirley got married today. A nice wedding. Very nice. I was just sitting round the house, you know," addressing the floor, and she noticed in her periphery the newspaper on the end table. "I was thinking…" She looked at him…gasped and put her hand to her mouth. She saw it, or rather she didn't see it.

My God!

The scar wasn't there!

"What happened to your face, Lester?" She realized it was a stupid question as soon as she said it.

Lester laughed. "I had it removed. A friend told me about this doctor in Jackson, Mississippi. He's from Europe somewhere, and he specializes in removing scars and tattoos with a laser."

"May I touch it?" Another stupid question. Lester didn't respond.

Silence. Uncomfortable silence. Awkward silence.

"It's not half as hot as it was last week," she said, for lack of anything else to say.

Lester nodded.

"Lester, you really look good. Really, you do. I don't mean to stare--you really look good. Momma moved to Chicago with Leonard. They couldn't make the wedding. Leonard and his partner took her on a cruise to the Bahamas. You really look good, I'm not lying. The insurance company paid Robert Earl and he plans to open the gas station he's been harping about. He's taking Shane in as partner. Uh...I can't get over how good you look. Lester, may I come home?"

Lester stood up and she saw the frown on his unmarked face. The doctor had done a remarkably good job, not even a hint of a scar.

"Lester, I want to come home. Please! I'm not the selfish woman I was. I've grown up. I didn't realize what I had--what *we* had--until I lost it. Lester, let me come home. Please! Don't make me beg."

"Okay," Lester said. She stood up and moved to hug him. Lester stopped her short with an outstretched hand. "You can come back. I won't be here."

"What? What are you saying?"

"Apparently you haven't gotten the papers yet. I filed for divorce, Ruth Ann."

Struck dizzy, she fought the need to sit down. "No, Lester! Divorce is not the answer. Not after twenty years of marriage. Are you willing to throw everything away? All we've worked hard to get? Because of a little..." She saw the brick wall and applied the brakes.

"A little what? A little affair?"

"I was wrong! I admit it. I was wrong! But I don't think we should throw away all we worked so hard to get. Not without a fight! Don't we owe ourselves another try? Let's give it one more try, Lester. One more! This time I'll do the heavy lifting. Promise! I won't let you down. Promise!"

Lester took a long time to respond. "Sorry, Ruth Ann, it's over. You can have the house and everything else except my truck."

"You'll continue paying for everything, won't you?" The sharp arch of one eye and the twitching of the other indicated a definitive no. "I can't pay for it!"

"Guess you'll have to get a job."

"A job! In this economy? No one will hire me at my age, no track record whatsoever! I won't let you do this to me, Lester. I'll contest the divorce."

"Ruth Ann, please! You're still young, attractive; you'll find someone else to take care of you in no time."

"An insult, Lester. A damn insult! I don't want someone else, I want you. Nobody else. Nobody but you! *You*, Lester! My husband." She crossed to him and took his hands in hers. "I love you, Lester."

"That's nice," Lester said.

She looked him straight in the eye and squeezed his hands. "Baby, honey, sugar, stop this crazy talk. Give me one more chance." She tiptoed and kissed his lips. Lester didn't respond. "One chance to show you how much I love you." She kissed him again, searching for his tongue. He didn't allow her entrance. "Let me right this wrong, Lester."

He freed his hands and gently pushed her back. "I've met someone else." He massaged his temples. "We're thinking about getting married."

Another dizzy spell descended on her. "Are you kidding me? Tell me you're kidding me." He shook his head. "You gotta be kidding me! I haven't been gone three months. You're telling me you met someone within three months and now you're talking marriage. You know how crazy you sound? Who? Who is she?"

"I don't think you know her."

440

"She from here? Dawson? I hope you thought enough of me not to mess with somebody I know. What's her name?"

"Darlene Pryor."

Ruth Ann frowned, trying to place the name. She didn't know her, yet the name rang a bell. "You're right, I don't know her. Where does she live?"

"She lives next door to Shirley. She was at the wedding."

The room started spinning faster and faster. She staggered to the couch and collapsed onto it. "What did she wear to the wedding?"

"A green dress."

Ruth Ann swooned and thought she would be sick. "Long braids?" Lester nodded, and Ruth Ann shook her head. "It's not real, Lester. I bet you a million dollars her hair isn't real!"

"Yeah, well, I got to go. I'll come by tomorrow and get my things."

Ruth Ann sat up to wage a last-ditch effort.

"Lester...honey...she'll break your heart. Fake women wear fake hair. You'll never be able to trust her. She's a child, Lester, looking for a sugar daddy to take care of her."

Lester started for the door. Ruth Ann sprang to her feet, crossed the room in three steps and grabbed his arm just as he was opening the screen door.

"You're pulling on me again, Ruth Ann."

She released him. "Lester, don't I deserve one last chance?"

A red-white-and-blue van rode by in the street, a loud speaker announcing, "Ice cream! Snow cones! Bomb pops!"

Lester watched it disappear around the corner before turning to her. "If you answer one question honestly, I'll…I will consider one more try."

"What, honey, what? Do I love you? Yes, I do. I most certainly do!"

"No, that's not what I want to ask you." He looked her straight in the eye, and she forced herself not to blink. "Was Eric the first?"

She looked away. *The million dollar question.* "The first what?"

"You know."

She met his eyes briefly. "Yes," she whispered.

"Then who's Shane's father? He's not mine and he's not Eric's. Who?"

A cough itched her throat. "Two questions, Lester," showing him two fingers. "Two! You said one."

"Who is Shane's father?"

She met his eyes, and though hers were blinking rapidly, she held his gaze. "You," she mumbled. "You're his father, Lester."

Lester stared at her for a minute, his expression as blank as a sheet of paper. He gave her a quick peck on her forehead, walked out the door, got into his truck and drove away without once looking back.

18425670R00265

Made in the USA
Middletown, DE
06 March 2015